POL

Tom Grace was born, raised, and still lives in Michigan. He studied architecture at the University of Michigan, where he developed his strict eye for detail. In just over twenty years of practice, Tom has worked on projects ranging from modest home renovations to major urban designs for Chicago and London. His superior knowledge of technology has found its way into his writing and has earned him tremendous acclaim as a result.

Tom credits his second career as a writer in equal parts to a voracious appetite for books, an over-active imagination, and a compulsive desire to set challenging long-term goals for himself.

Tom Grace lives with his wife, five children and a yellow Labrador. His interests are architecture and current affairs; he also enjoys scuba diving, martial arts and running marathons. To find out more about Tom go to www.tomgrace.net.

TOM

Polar Quest

AVON

This novel is entirely a work of fiction.
The names, characters and incidents portrayed in it are
the work of the author's imagination. Any resemblance to
actual persons, living or dead, events or localities is
entirely coincidental.

AVON
A division of HarperCollins*Publishers*
77–85 Fulham Palace Road,
London W6 8JB

www.harpercollins.co.uk

A Paperback Edition 2010
1

First published in the U.S.A as *Twisted Web* by Pocket Books,
New York, NY, 2003

Copyright © 2003 The Kilkenny Group, LLC

Tom Grace asserts the moral right to
be identified as the author of this work

A catalogue record for this book is
available from the British Library

ISBN-13: 978-1-84756-124-4

Set in Minion by Palimpsest Book Production Limited,
Grangemouth, Stirlingshire

Printed and bound in Great Britain by
Clays Ltd, St Ives plc

Mixed Sources
Product group from well-managed
forests and other controlled sources
www.fsc.org Cert no. SW-COC-001806
© 1996 Forest Stewardship Council

FSC is a non-profit international organisation established
to promote the responsible management of the world's forests.
Products carrying the FSC label are independently certified
to assure consumers that they come from forests that are managed
to meet the social, economic and ecological needs
of present and future generations.

Find out more about HarperCollins and the environment at
www.harpercollins.co.uk/green

To Robert Hopps,
who shared with me a daughter
and a lifetime of interesting stories

To Craig Hopps,
who lived a full life in far too brief a time

Acknowledgements

In the course of writing this story, I received generous assistance from a number of people. In particular, I wish to thank:

Dr Vladmir Papitashvili for an insider's view of research at both poles and life at Vostok Station.

World-class ice boater Ron Sherry, who taught me much about winter's fastest sport.

The men and women of the 109th Airlift Wing of the New York Air National Guard, who flew me around Greenland in LC-130s and put me down on top of the glacier, and Major Bob Bullock for his help in understanding the logistics of servicing research stations on both poles.

The fine staff at Kangerlussuaq International Science Support (KISS) for providing me with a base of operations in Greenland.

The Honorable Daniel P. Ryan, Michigan 3rd Circuit Court, for his guidance on matters of criminal justice.

Forensic scientist Leslie Nixon of Michigan State Police Crime Lab for an education in the handling of DNA evidence.

Professor Buford Price of the University of California, Berkeley for explaining the AMANDA project and opening the door for me onto the world of polar research projects.

Hana Odeh, a research scientist at the University of Michigan, for her help with laboratory procedures.

Paul Cousins of Cousins' Heritage Inn for his gourmet advice.

Geppetto's Workshop for some insight to the Enth platform which provides real-time access to data, anywhere, over the Internet.

Dr David Gorski for his advice on medical issues and a tour through New Jersey's Research Row.

My thanks also to:

Rob McMahon, who saw me through the crafting of most of this story.

Mitchell Ivers, whose editorial guidance aided me in the final stages of this book.

Louise Burke, Seale Ballenger, Lisa Keim, Louise Braverman, Barry Porter, Steve Fallert, Staci Shands, and the fine people at Pocket Books for their support.

Esther Margolis for your generous gifts of time and insight. I will be forever grateful for all that you have done.

And – My wife, Kathy, who dreams the dreams with me.

1

JANUARY 22

Tucson, Arizona

The *Ice Queen* – a sexy Nordic blonde with pouty lips and ice blue eyes – gazed down at Kuhn. Her lusty smile and the mink bikini that barely contained her physical charms were warm reminders of his past. Like a Vargas pinup girl, she sat atop a globe that displayed her frozen domain: Antarctica.

Kuhn ran his hand over the aircraft's smooth aluminum skin, paying his respects. The patches on Kuhn's weathered aviator jacket matched those on the aircraft: US NAVY VXE-6 SQUADRON. Beneath the side cockpit window, just above the rendered image of the *Ice Queen*, stenciled letters read:

CDR GREGORY KUHN

COMMANDING OFFICER

For almost a quarter century, Kuhn had piloted XD-10, the *Ice Queen*. She was a Lockheed LC-130R, a variant of the venerable C-130 Hercules transport equipped with skis mounted to her fuselage so she could land on ice.

As ungainly as she looked, the Hercules could actually fly and was designed to do one thing: lift heavy loads. Except for the cockpit, the fuselage of the *Ice Queen* was a cavern of empty space big enough to accommodate several large trucks. Ninety-eight feet in length, she sat low to the ground, like a cylindrical railroad car with a ramp in her tapered tail that folded down like a drawbridge. Her wings spanned 132 feet, and the *Ice Queen* used every inch of her lifting surface and every ounce of power from the four Allison T56 prop engines to propel her into the sky.

The *Ice Queen* and her sisters once formed the backbone of the VXE-6 Squadron. Since the mid-fifties, the squadron had fulfilled the mission objectives of the ongoing Operation Deep Freeze, providing logistical support to research stations in the Antarctic. It was a tough job that earned the unit the unofficial nickname Ice Pirates. VXE-6 had owned the skies over the frozen southern continent until the end of the 1999 season, when the squadron returned to its home base at Point Mugu Naval Air Station and was disestablished.

Like many veterans of VXE-6, Kuhn felt anger and a sense of loss when the squadron was phased out, its planes mothballed and its mission reassigned to a National Guard air wing. He'd flown over Antarctica for twenty-four years and had fallen in love with the icy untamed wilderness.

In the years since, the *Ice Queen* sat tightly wrapped in a plastic cocoon in the high desert air of Arizona.

She was one of the hundreds of military and commercial aircraft that sat row upon row in the Boneyard, as the Aircraft Storage and Reclamation Facility was known.

'The old bitch looks pretty good, eh, Greg?'

Kuhn turned as Len Holland walked up.

'Is that any way to talk about a lady?' Kuhn asked.

Holland shook Kuhn's hand, then looked over at the *Ice Queen*. 'Hard to believe our planes have been sitting in the desert all these years.'

'No different than the day we left them here.' Kuhn nodded down the flight line at another LC-130R. '*Polar Pete* came out of hibernation just fine, too. Where's the rest of the guys?'

'Right behind me.'

Ten men emerged from the flight operations building, all sporting aviator jackets similar to Kuhn's. Each plane flew with a crew of six men – a pilot, a copilot, a navigator, a flight engineer, and two cargo handlers. Escorting the flight crews was a man in a button-down shirt with a bolo tie and a clipboard.

'Commander Kuhn,' the escort said warmly. 'I'm Jim Evers, the manager here at ASRF.' Evers pronounced the facility acronym *ay-surf*. 'Both XD-10 and XD-11 have been checked out, and all systems are flight ready.'

Kuhn pulled a thick envelope from his breast pocket and handed it to Evers. 'Here's our flight plan for this short hop to Waco.'

Evers pocketed the envelope. 'Your planes are fueled, so once you finish your preflight you can get out of here.'

'Thanks.' As Evers walked away, Kuhn turned to the

3

two flight crews. 'You guys know the drill. Let's get these old birds in the air.'

The *Ice Queen* and *Polar Pete* flew a low route across southern Texas, carefully avoiding civilian air-traffic control radar as they bypassed Waco and headed into the Gulf of Mexico. The flight crossed over the Yucatan peninsula, then turned south toward Honduras.

'I'm picking up the beacon,' the navigator announced. 'Bearing two-one-five.'

Kuhn glanced out his window at the rain forest below, the thick foliage barely a hundred feet beneath the aircraft.

'About friggin' time,' Kuhn said impatiently. He had wanted to land before sunset, but an unexpected head wind had increased their flight time.

Kuhn deftly turned the *Ice Queen* until his heading matched the one his navigator had given him. Five minutes later, he saw a gaping hole in the jungle canopy. The runway looked to be in good condition and certainly long and wide enough to handle a Hercules. Along one side of the runway, he saw a cluster of large tents, a few heavy trucks, a helicopter, and a tall pole with a windsock fluttering in the breeze.

'X-Ray Delta One Zero to X-Ray Delta One One, over.'

'One One, over,' Holland replied.

'I'm going to circle around and land. You follow me in.'

'Lead the way, One Zero. X-Ray Delta One One out.'

Kuhn piloted the *Ice Queen* in a smooth arc that aimed the nose of his plane down the length of the runway. Descending, he skimmed over the treetops and then dropped into the clearing. Sunbaked earth exploded into clouds of dust when the wheels touched down, the gray plume trailing the *Ice Queen* down the length of the runway. Holland waited until the dust cloud settled before making his approach.

'Just like riding a bike,' Holland said as he brought his plane down perfectly.

Once on the ground, Holland taxied *Polar Pete* behind a jeep with a sign that read FOLLOW ME and was led to a space beside the *Ice Queen*. A man with orange-tipped wands guided the plane into position and, once there, signaled Holland to cut his engines.

As Kuhn, Holland, and their crews stepped out of the planes into the steamy heat of the Honduran jungle, five brown-skinned men trotted out from the tents. Each grabbed a length of steel pipe from a large pile and began assembling scaffolding around the aircraft.

'Commander Kuhn.'

Kuhn turned as a tall, lanky man dressed in military-style khakis walked toward him. The man had thick black hair and a full beard that gave him the look of a left-wing revolutionary.

'Sumner Duroc?' Kuhn asked.

'Yes, it is a pleasure to finally meet you,' Duroc said perfunctorily in Gallic-tinged English.

'You cut this strip?' Kuhn asked.

'No, the Nicaraguan Contras cleared this area to receive supplies from you Americans. We merely restored it. Did you encounter any problems?'

'None,' Kuhn replied. 'Everything went according to plan and both aircraft are flying perfectly.'

'Good. For the next few days I expect you and your men to work with my staff in preparing for our mission.'

'My men'll be ready, but right now we're in need of a bite to eat and some down time.'

'Tents have been assigned to you and your crew.' Duroc made a motion with his hand, and a swarthy man dressed in khaki ran over. 'Commander, this is my executive officer, Leon Albret. Leon, show the commander and his men their quarters, then take them to the mess tent and see that they are fed.'

'Yes, sir.'

After finishing his dinner, Kuhn stepped out of the mess tent and walked back over to the planes. Both were now enmeshed in a framework of vertical poles, crossbars, and wooden planks. A diesel generator purred nearby, powering work lights attached to the scaffolding. At several points, tall poles rose out of the scaffolding to support a broad sheet of camouflage fabric that completely covered both planes. The fabric not only hid the aircraft from view, but during coming days it would also prevent the sun from heating the aluminum skin on the planes like a skillet.

Duroc stood alongside the *Ice Queen*, watching as the workmen began the tedious process of carefully stripping off the aircraft's paint scheme and markings.

'Your men got this rigging up pretty quick,' Kuhn said as he walked up to Duroc.

'That's what they were paid to do.'

'Do they know what they're doin' to my plane? I'd hate to have one of them break somethin'.'

'Like you, they were hired because of their skills,' Duroc replied. 'These are not the first planes they've rechristened.'

'It's gotta make you sick to see her like that,' Holland remarked, 'all done up like she's air force – a guard unit at that.'

Kuhn nodded as he studied the new paint scheme that decorated his beloved *Ice Queen*. In two days, the Hondurans had stripped her down to bare metal, removing the red-black scheme and her sexy namesake. Now she bore air force markings and her wingtips and tail were painted orange. Stenciled letters identified the *Ice Queen* and *Polar Pete* as *Skier-98* and *Skier-99* – aircraft currently assigned to the National Guard unit that took over the Antarctica mission from the navy.

'Make you sick enough to turn down Duroc's money?' Kuhn asked.

'Hell, no. I just don't like flying false colors.'

'It don't matter what she's wearing on the outside,' Kuhn said, 'underneath, she's still the *Ice Queen*.'

'Looks like shit, don't it?' Holland said. 'Got no personality whatsoever.'

'Maybe,' Kuhn replied, 'but for the first time in the history of VXE-6, we're going to really live up to our nickname.'

Duroc, Albret, and the rest of the two flight crews emerged from the camp and walked over to where Kuhn stood with Holland.

'Commander, are your aircraft ready to fly?' Duroc asked.

'Yes, sir,' Kuhn replied. 'The tanks are all topped off and it doesn't look like your paint crew did any damage.'

'Good.' Duroc nodded to Albret, who handed packets to Kuhn and Holland. 'Here are the flight plan and the latest weather reports.'

Kuhn opened the manila envelope and glanced over the southbound route. From Honduras, the planes would fly along the Pacific coast of South America, landing at remote airstrips to rest and refuel. In the final leg, they were to cross over southern Chile into Argentina.

'I will meet you in Rio Gallegos,' Duroc said. 'There, we will load the men and equipment required for the mission. Any questions?'

'Not a one,' Kuhn replied, holding out his hand. 'I guess we'll see you in Argentina.'

Duroc stood near the helicopter and watched the two LC-130s depart. The cargo planes circled the jungle airstrip once, then veered south toward the Pacific coast. Finding these unique planes and the crews to fly them was one of the more formidable challenges of this project, and he was pleased with his success. So far, everything was proceeding as planned, but Duroc knew that there was still much to be accomplished and many places where things could go disastrously wrong.

'The workmen are in the mess tent, as you ordered,' Albret announced. 'They are eager for their wages.'

'Understandably so.'

Duroc unlocked the cargo compartment of the Bell 427 and pulled out a Halliburton briefcase.

'Put the rest of our gear on board while I take care of the men,' Duroc ordered.

Albret nodded and jogged away as Duroc walked over to the largest tent in the compound. Inside, he found the five Hondurans laughing and enjoying the cold beer Duroc had provided. All eyes turned to him as he entered the tent.

'Gentlemen,' Duroc said, easily slipping into Spanish, 'I wish to thank you for your excellent work over these past few days. As we agreed, here is five hundred thousand dollars in U.S. currency.' Duroc set the briefcase down atop the table where the men were seated and opened it so the contents faced the men. Inside, the case was filled with neat bundles of U.S. twenty-dollar bills. 'It has been a pleasure doing business with you.'

Duroc shook a few hands and the rest of the Hondurans raised their bottles in his honor. One of the men picked up a battered guitar and began strumming – they were rich and it was time to celebrate. Duroc smiled and left what promised to be a wild day of drinking.

By the time Duroc returned to the helicopter, Albret had their gear loaded and the rotors turning. Duroc slipped on a pair of dark aviator sunglasses and climbed into the copilot's seat. Albret ran through the rest of his checklist, powered up the twin turbine engines, and lifted off.

As the helicopter rose above the treetops and began to move away from the runway, Duroc keyed a command into the onboard computer that instructed it to transmit a series of pulses at a specific frequency. Less than two seconds later, a thin layer of plastic explosive lining the interior of the briefcase exploded.

The five men barely felt the searing heat from the blast

or the shards of fragmented metal from the briefcase. Everything within fifty feet of the bomb disappeared in a fireball that incinerated the encampment. The explosion left a crater twenty feet across and ten feet deep.

Duroc's helicopter sped over the rain forest toward Tegucigalpa, where he and Albret would board a private jet for Argentina.

2

LV Research Station, Antarctica

Collins stood beneath a clear blue sky bathed in the whitest light he had ever known, a light blinding with brilliant intensity. The hard-packed crystals of ice that covered the glacial plateau glowed in dazzling imitation of the sun. Were it not for the yellow-lens goggles protecting his eyes, he would have been snow-blind as soon as he stepped outside the station. From his vantage point, less than seven hundred miles from the South Pole, the sun traced another unbroken ellipse in the sky. Endless day.

Click.

Ansel Adams could've worked some real magic down here, Collins mused as he adjusted the exposure setting on his camera.

Today, the wind, temperature, and sky conspired to produce one of nature's rarest and most dazzling sights: parhelic circles. Sunlight, refracted through tiny airborne ice crystals, created the illusion of luminous halos, arcs,

11

and flaring parabolas in the sky. Collins counted twenty distinct formations dancing around the sun.

Click.

Like a surrealist painting, distance was an illusion in the interior of the southernmost continent. It was generally accepted that the otherworldliness of this place was due in equal parts to extremes in temperature, altitude, and lifelessness. Over fifty years of record keeping by Russian crews manning the Vostok Research Station – Collins's closest neighbors some forty miles to the south – bracketed the local temperature range as between -40 degrees and -128 degrees Fahrenheit.

Satisfied that he'd captured at least one decent image from this spot, Collins moved his camera around to the opposite side of the station. LV Research Station had been home to Collins and his wife, Nedra, since November and had been entirely prefabricated in the U.S. as a mock-up of the habitat for NASA's manned-mission to Mars. At the center of the station stood a short domed tower. Four cylindrical modules – each the size of a railroad tanker car – stood mounted on thick legs and radiated out from the tower in a cruciform configuration. The modules provided space for research, crew quarters, power and environmental systems, and storage.

Beneath LV Station, the sheet of glacial ice that blanketed nearly all of Antarctica rose to a height of 11,500 feet above sea level. Thanks to the katabatic winds – dense sheets of frigid air that flowed down from the nearby ice domes – the rarified air that Collins breathed was even thinner than that of other sites of equal elevation around the world. These winds siphoned low-oxygen air from the upper atmosphere to fill the void left behind as they flowed down toward the coast. When they had first arrived here, it took Collins and his wife several days to acclimate themselves, and both still had to be wary of overexertion.

Collins could attest to the extremes in temperature and altitude, but assumption that this place was totally lifeless was something that he and many other scientists around the world were challenging. Until the latter part of the twentieth century, energy in the form of sunlight was assumed to be essential to the formation of life, but then life was found in the darkest depths of the oceans. When communities of organisms were discovered not merely living but thriving in the superheated mineral-saturated waters of geysers and hydrothermal vents, environments lethal to most other forms of life on earth, scientists were forced to rethink their assumptions about the conditions that might give rise to life. Being more tenacious than anyone had previously considered, life seems to need only three things to start: heat, minerals, and liquid water.

Walking past a row of thirty-inch in diameter metal spheres that contained liquid hydrogen for the station's fuel cells, Collins approached the reason that NASA and a group of partner companies had financed this project. Fifty feet from the station stood a cobalt blue tetrahedron that was as out of place atop the glacial ice of Antarctica as Arthur C. Clarke's monolith on the moon: the Ice Pick probe.

Collins shortened the legs on his tripod, lowering the camera to capture both the hard lines of the probe's first stage and the luminous parhelic circles. Satisfied with the composition, he adjusted the exposure setting and snapped another picture.

'Hey, Philip, how's the show?' Nedra asked, her voice clear over his headset.

'Amazing. You should come out and see it.'

'I snuck a peek out the window. Just wanted to let you know we're ready for another dip in the lake.'

Far beneath LV Station, sandwiched between a glacier and the rocky surface of Antarctica, lay one of the largest lakes on Earth – a body of liquid water that could have easily been seen from space were it not concealed by the ice. When British and Russian scientists confirmed the existence of Lake Vostok in 1996, they theorized that heat rising from the earth's interior through rifts in the crust kept the water from freezing. Seismic activity in the area increased the likelihood of hydrothermal vents in Lake Vostok, meaning that the lake had the water, heat, and minerals necessary to support life. What form that life would take, in a place isolated from the rest of the world for the last 20 million years, was the subject of great speculation.

In 1610, Galileo pointed his telescope at Jupiter and discovered four moons orbiting the giant planet. This discovery came at a time when the whole of Western civilization believed that the earth was the center of the universe. News of Lake Vostok's discovery and the possibility of life in its hidden waters coincided with the arrival at Jupiter of a spacecraft bearing the great astronomer's name. During a fly-by of one of the moons discovered by Galileo – an ice-covered rock named Europa – the

14

spacecraft transmitted a series of images as astounding to the scientists at NASA's Jet Propulsion Laboratory as the discovery of the moon itself was to Galileo four hundred years earlier.

Europa was named after the mythical Phoenician princess that Zeus carried off and ravaged. Detailed images from the spacecraft revealed a pattern of fractures on the frozen moon's surface similar to ice flows in the Arctic Ocean – evidence that beneath Europa's frozen shell lay an immense body of liquid water larger than all Earth's oceans. Dark regions mottling the moon's surface revealed ongoing volcanic and seismic activity, likely the result of Jupiter's intense gravity wracking Europa's molten core. With heat, minerals, and liquid water, scientists now saw Europa as the most promising place in our solar system to search for extraterrestrial life.

The complexity of a mission to Europa was unlike anything NASA engineers had encountered since the days of Apollo. Forays to other worlds had thus far only scratched the surface of those celestial bodies. Once on Europa, NASA planned to bore through at least six miles of ice in order to explore a mysterious ocean. A submersible robotic vehicle designed to plumb those hidden waters would not only have to survive a journey in the vacuum of space, but also be able to withstand a crushing pressure that, at a minimum, would equal the deepest place beneath Earth's oceans.

NASA's Europa team, led by Collins and his wife, sought out the best minds in robotics, biologic testing, artificial intelligence, and deep-sea remote vehicles to help tackle the technical problems posed by the mission.

The Europa Lander not only had to perform numerous complex tasks in an extreme environment but, due to the distances involved, it also had to be capable of making decisions on its own.

Early on, Collins's team seized on the idea of exploring Lake Vostok as a full-dress rehearsal for the mission to Europa. Exhaustive testing of various subsystems finally led to the construction of a prototype. Ice Pick incorporated all but three of the main systems to be used by the Europa Lander. The deep-space communications unit was deleted from Ice Pick, since the probe's first stage wouldn't be more than fifty feet from the people controlling it. While it would have been nice to have the genetic analysis module on board, the scientists at UGene were still tweaking it, and any samples retrieved from the lake would be analyzed in their laboratory afterward. The probe's nuclear power supply – a radioisotopic thermoelectric generator – was not included, because an international treaty expressly forbade the importation of nuclear material into Antarctica.

The wind shifted and the parhelic circles slowly faded away. Satisfied that he'd captured what he could, Collins picked up his camera and headed back to the station. He followed the thick orange umbilical line that provided power and communications to Ice Pick.

After a quick look around the station, Collins re-entered the tower air lock and closed the door. He wasted no time stripping down to his jeans and turtleneck – the station's interior was over a hundred degrees warmer than outside. Static sparks crackled as he peeled the

16

woolen balaclava from his head; his black hair and beard were matted down by the protective head covering.

'Water?' Nedra asked as Collins clambered up the spiral stair to the station's main level, scratching his chin.

'Oh, yeah. My mouth is drier than a camel's ass.'

'That's not the image I want in mind the next time you kiss me.'

Nedra filled a tall plastic glass and handed it to him. Keeping hydrated was critical in a place totally devoid of humidity, where the average annual precipitation was less than the Sahara Desert. Collins sat down beside his wife at the long workstation. Nedra's monitor displayed the same information she hoped to receive one day, several years from now, from a spacecraft on the surface of Europa.

'Status?' Collins asked.

'The sample capsules from the last mission are stowed and a new set of empties are on board the hydrobot. Batteries are at one-hundred percent charge.'

'Then let's see if we get lucky today.'

Clinging by actuated crampons to the underside of the glacial ice sheet in the slushy upper boundary of Lake Vostok, the second stage of the Ice Pick probe waited for its next command. It had taken five days in late November for the three-foot in diameter sphere to melt its way straight down through over two miles of glacier. The cryobot liquefied the ice beneath it with the heating panels on its lower hemisphere, and, as it sank, the displaced water refroze above it to prevent contaminants from the surface from entering the hidden lake. A filament of superconducting wire imbedded in a carbon nanotube sleeve emerged from the top of the sphere like

17

a strand of webbing from a spinneret, and ran straight up along the path of the cryobot's descent from beneath the first stage on the surface.

At Nedra's command, the circular heating plate at the lower pole of the cryobot receded about a quarter-inch into the sphere, then slid away to expose an iris diaphragm.

'Equalizing tube pressure,' Nedra announced.

A series of pressure-relief valves slowly opened to allow a flow of water from the lake to gradually enter the cylindrical chamber behind the diaphragm. Once the air inside the chamber had been evacuated and the water pressure inside made equal with that of the surrounding lake, the valves closed.

'The tube is flooded and equalized,' Nedra noted.

Collins switched on the monitor in front of him and gripped the joystick controls. 'Launch the fish.'

The rings of the iris diaphragm rotated to create an eight-inch aperture at the base of the cylindrical chamber. A blast of compressed air shot the two-foot-long, torpedo-shaped hydrobot through the slush into the dark water below.

Once the hydrobot was safely away, three telescoping masts extended out from the bottom of the cryobot. A pre-programmed series of transmissions verified that communications between Ice Pick's second and third stage had been established.

'Hydrobot is in the water,' Nedra said. 'She's all yours.'

The graphical display of gauges and bar graphs on Collins's monitor became colorfully active as the stream of real-time data began flowing in from the hydrobot.

'All systems are up and running,' Collins announced. 'I'm switching on lights and camera and powering up the propulsion system.'

Halogen lights in the bow of the hydrobot illuminated the crystal-clear water as it slipped downward toward the distant lake bottom. The hydrobot's descent slowed, then halted as the screw propeller in its tail dug into the frigid water, spinning in reverse to counteract gravity. A trio of maneuvering thrusters clustered around the hydrobot's center of mass pivoted in response to Collins's command and slowly rotated it like a baton.

'Signal strength is good. The hydrobot's responding to guidance commands,' Collins said, the image on his screen spinning wildly.

'Do you have to do that every time we launch?' Nedra asked, clinching her eyes shut as she rubbed her temples. 'You know it makes me dizzy.'

Collins brought the hydrobot to a level stop. 'Plotting course to the next search area.'

The bow of the hydrobot dipped down and Collins piloted the submersible in a gentle sloping descent toward the bottom. Other than a few gently drifting particles, the water in the upper reaches of Lake Vostok was crystal clear – there was no wind, currents, or tide to stir things up. Through the first three hundred feet of its journey downward, the hydrobot recorded only minor temperature fluctuations in frigid water.

'I think I see something,' Collins announced as the hydrobot entered the search area. The clear water characteristic of the upper lake was giving way to a gray-black haze. 'Visibility is dropping.'

19

Nedra looked over her husband's shoulder. 'Where's the bottom?'

'Fathometer reads about seventy-five feet of water beneath the fish. This is deeper than the surrounding area. May be a rift in the bottom. The haze looks a lot heavier than before. I think we found a smoker.' Collins slowed the hydrobot's descent as it reached the haze. 'Temperature is rising, pushing into the fifties.'

'Let's hold here and take another water sample.'

A clear rigid pipette extended out from the bow of the hydrobot into the water, the submersible's camera relaying the action to the station above. Inside the hydrobot, a pump drew some water into a sterile sample capsule. After the capsule was filled and sealed, the sampling system purged its lines and withdrew the pipette.

'Damn, I wish we had that lab kit on board. It'd be nice to know if we found anything alive down there.'

'You'll just have to wait. We'll know within a couple of weeks after we get home.'

When the sampling was complete, Collins resumed the descent. Sixteen feet down, the water in front of the camera cleared considerably. The hydrobot's lights grazed the underside of the thick silty cloud suspended over the lake bottom. Particles glinted as they fell through the powerful beam of white light.

'I'm going to maintain about thirty feet off the bottom while we take a look around,' Collins said. 'Water temp is now in the mid-seventies.'

'It looks like we're inside a snow globe.'

'Only that's volcanic ash, not white glitter.'

Collins moved the hydrobot forward slowly as they

20

scanned the image of the silty bottom for any sign that life existed inside this remote, alien realm.

'Water temp is moving up,' Collins said. 'There just has to be a vent close by.'

'If you do find one, just make sure you don't get too close or you'll fry the electronics,' Nedra cautioned.

'I know what I'm doing,' Collins snapped.

He brought the hydrobot to a stop and began turning it in a slow horizontal sweep to the right. Forty-three degrees right of his previous heading, he spotted a plume of particles billowing out of a lumpy black mass of rock that jutted up from the lake bottom like a broken fang. The ash gray landscape surrounding the smoker was mottled with patches of white.

'Is that what I think it is?' Nedra asked.

Collins swallowed hard, his throat suddenly feeling very tight and dry. He pushed the hydrobot forward, gliding cautiously toward the nearest field of iridescent white. As he closed the distance, details began to emerge from the indistinct mass – long, thin strands of filaments. Collins brought the hydrobot to a stop just a foot above the edge of the spaghetti-like mass. The gentle turning of the hydrobot's maneuvering thrusters disturbed the water, rippling through the filaments like a breeze through a wheat field. Small, transparent creatures similar to jellyfish darted out of the hydrobot's light.

'I don't think you need that lab kit now,' Nedra said.

Collins's eyes were transfixed on the digital image. 'Send a message to the Jet Propulsion Lab: *Lake Vostok is alive.*'

3

JANUARY 25

Ann Arbor, Michigan

'Is the coffee in there any good?' Nolan Kilkenny asked as he approached the main conference room.

Loretta Quinn, executive assistant to the chairman of the Michigan Applied Research Consortium, looked up from the letter she was preparing and gave Kilkenny an annoyed look. 'Does this look like the counter at Starbucks?'

'No, but you'd be making a killing if it was. Maybe I should talk to the boss about leasing them some space, might be a good way to generate some extra revenue.'

'Don't you dare, Nolan. Knowing your father, he'd probably think it was a marvelous idea and I'd end up with a cappuccino maker next to the fax machine. There's a fresh pot of coffee on the table, and – ' Quinn glanced down at her notes, 'your satellite window opens at four-forty-five, and you only have about ten minutes of air-time.'

'Thanks, Loretta.'

Inside the conference room, Kilkenny set his files and

a legal pad on the granite table and poured coffee into one of the dark blue mugs that bore the consortium's logo. Outside the snow was steadily falling on the wooded grounds surrounding the building.

One of the files he brought with him contained the current financial projections for the biotech firm UGene. The Michigan Applied Research Consortium, known as MARC, had provided UGene with several million dollars of venture capital in exchange for a significant piece of the company. That investment paid its first dividends when Kilkenny orchestrated UGene's initial public offering on Wall Street, a feat which turned him into a paper millionaire.

It still amazed Kilkenny how much his life had changed. Three years earlier, he was a lieutenant in the U.S. Navy, commanding a squad of SEALs and existing on a military paycheck. Now he was crunching numbers and helping promising young companies develop their potential – and getting rich in the process.

'It's called snow,' a basso profundo announced from the doorway, cutting through Kilkenny's drifting thoughts.

'I'm familiar with it, Oz,' Kilkenny replied without looking. 'I grew up here.'

'Then you have my condolences.'

At six-foot-six and 220 pounds, Oswald Eames had the physical presence to justify a voice that broadcast in the Barry White-James Earl Jones spectrum. Kilkenny turned his chair around as Eames entered the conference room, followed by his partner, Lloyd Sutton.

'Thanks for coming, gentlemen,' Kilkenny said. 'Have a seat.'

Sutton shot a nervous glance at Eames as he shed his overcoat. 'What's this all about, Nolan? The fourth-quarter numbers?'

'Partly, though the numbers are fine,' Killkenny said reassuringly. 'I've got the preliminaries from our accountants and there are no surprises.'

Kilkenny handed out copies of the financial statements and quickly ran through the highlights: Bottom line, UGene was generating a modest profit – which was no small feat for a newcomer in the notoriously capital-intensive world of biotechnology. What kept UGene from burning through its IPO cash horde like one of the many over-hyped dot-coms was the total focus of Eames and Sutton on 'bioinformatics' – the company's main product line, biological information. UGene specialized in parsing the genomes encoded in lengthy strands of DNA, identifying genes and proteins, and determining how they function inside living organisms.

'Any updates on the most recent batch of patent applications?' Kilkenny asked.

'It's the Wild West all over again.' Eames's reply masked little of his frustration. Like the work of early cartographers in the American West, what the scientists from the Human Genome Project and Celera produced was little more than the first decent map of a previously uncharted territory. The real work came in exploring this vast frontier, and biotech companies were staking claims – in the form of patents – over potentially valuable sections of genetic real estate.

The genetic gold rush was on, complete with prospectors in lab coats and outlaw claim-jumpers in dark suits armed with lawsuits and patent applications instead of six-shooters. 'Most of our work is clear and uncontested,' Eames continued, 'but there are a few sequences we're going to have to fight for.'

'That's why I prefer my side of the business,' Sutton offered. 'The patents on my work are based on inventions and processes – they're totally unambiguous. Gene patents are a claim of ownership over a naturally occurring molecule.'

'Are you saying we shouldn't try to patent what Oz and his lab team finds?' Kilkenny asked.

'Not at all. As long as it's legal to do so, we have to file patents on our work, if for no other reason than to prevent some company from shutting us out of a potentially profitable line of research.'

'Lloyd and I have had this conversation before,' Eames explained to Kilkenny, 'usually after a couple beers when we're both feeling philosophical.'

'Sounds like the old debate between discovery and invention. You can't patent the fire, but you can patent the matches.'

'Exactly, Nolan,' Sutton agreed.

'Since you brought up your side of the business, Lloyd, how's work coming on that package for NASA?'

'Slow, but we're getting there. The biggest problem we've run into is vibration. Our equipment has to withstand a launch and a jarring impact on Europa.'

'Take a lickin' and keep on tickin',' Eames summarized.

'I sent out a unit this week to NASA for testing. We should know something in a few months.'

'Good,' Kilkenny said. 'Where are we on building depth?'

'We've sampled just over twelve hundred individuals from a variety of ethnic backgrounds,' Eames replied, 'including multiple family members, so we're making progress on building a database of genetic norms and variations. I'm just starting to get DNA in from zoos around the country, as well as material from the agriculture firms you cut deals with, but we're about where we expected to be with the flora and fauna side of our database.'

'What about the *Jurassic Park* stuff?' Kilkenny asked.

Sutton rolled his eyes. He hated Kilkenny's nickname for the extinct and endangered species portion of the database. 'We have the first few samples, with more expected to trickle in over the next few months. Sorry to say, but there's not a T-rex in the lot.'

'Make lousy house pets, anyway,' Eames added. 'Better off sticking with your dogs.'

Kilkenny checked his watch. 'Gentlemen, thanks for the update. Now I have a little surprise for you.'

A high-definition video monitor on the wall of the conference room displayed a bright blue test screen. A moment later, square bits of a still image appeared like scattered pieces of a puzzle trying to assemble itself. The image blinked once and filled the screen as the satellite connection between MARC and the LV Research Station was established.

'Hello from scenic Lake Vostok,' Nedra said with a smile, Collins seated at her side. 'How are things back in the world?'

'Cold, and we're getting a bit of snow right now,' Kilkenny replied.

'You poor boys,' Nedra said. 'It's a lovely morning here. The sun is shining, just like it does all day, every day, and it's a balmy minus forty-four.'

'You want to trade?' Collins asked.

'No way,' Eames replied. 'Michigan is more than cold enough for me. I don't know how you two can stand it down there.'

'Actually, it's very cozy,' Nedra said. 'I've even managed to get a pretty good tan.'

Nedra turned in her chair and rolled the waist of her sweatpants down just enough to reveal a tan line on her hip. Collins laughed at the embarrassed looks on the faces of the three men in Ann Arbor.

'You've been sunbathing at the South Pole?' Kilkenny asked.

'They've been down there too long, Nolan,' Eames said. 'NASA better pull them out ASAP.'

'When there's no wind, the sun's strong enough to keep you warm,' Nedra explained. 'It's like spring skiing at Tahoe.'

'Enough of this chit-chat,' Eames said. 'What are you bringing home for us?'

'It better be more than a T-shirt,' Sutton added.

'Oh, it will be,' Collins promised, 'considering what you've invested in this project.'

Nedra looked directly at Eames and Sutton. 'The life flourishing in Lake Vostok is far beyond anything we anticipated. We've got some great samples for you guys to work on. Did IPL send you any of the pictures?'

'Yeah, just got 'em,' Kilkenny replied. He slid a file across the table to Eames and Sutton.

'Jesus, that's beautiful,' Eames said as he spread the glossy prints on the table.

'Cousteau would've been proud,' Kilkenny agreed.

'We loaded the last samples yesterday and the cryobot is on its way back to the surface,' Collins said. 'As the pictures show, there's some pretty bizarre stuff down there, and we've only just started exploring this lake. I hope we can count on UGene's continued support of this project.'

'Once we get these first samples analyzed, I'm sure there won't be any trouble funding a more comprehensive investigation of Lake Vostok,' Kilkenny predicted. 'Since NASA's announcement in December, I've taken calls from several drug companies offering millions for a peek at your samples.'

'Lloyd and I have increased the scan rate on our sequencers,' Eames said. 'Depending on the size of the genome, it shouldn't take more than a few weeks to decode whatever you're bringing back.'

'And we're working on some more improvements to make the process even faster,' Sutton added.

'I'd be even happier if you'd make your equipment smaller and lighter,' Nedra said. 'As you already know, space on the Europa Lander will be at a premium.'

'We'll do what we can,' Sutton promised.

'While you two are busy raising the cryobot and getting packed for the trip home, I'll be working my way south to pick you up,' Kilkenny announced.

'What? You're coming here?' Collins asked, incredulous.

'Yeah. Something came up and the NSF agreed to let me have a seat on one of their planes. If everything stays on schedule, I'll be knocking on your front door in couple of weeks.'

The image on the wall monitor began to degrade.

'Looks like our time is up,' Kilkenny announced. 'See you soon.'

Collins and his wife waved, then the image disintegrated and the screen turned solid blue. Kilkenny switched the monitor off. 'It's not every day you chat with someone at the South Pole.'

'These photographs are amazing,' Sutton said. 'I don't think I've ever seen anything quite like this.'

'Twenty million years of total isolation will do that to an ecosystem,' Kilkenny said. 'The Galapagos Islands were never cut off like Lake Vostok.'

Eames looked up from the photos. 'All this good news calls for a celebration. Everyone up for dinner?'

'I'm in,' Kilkenny replied.

'I've got plans,' Sutton said apologetically, 'but let me make a quick call. I'm sure I've got time for a drink.'

They ended up at Connor O'Neill's, a Main Street restaurant modeled after the pubs of rural Ireland. In the front corner, a live band filled the place with a rollicking ballad that incited several patrons to holler and clap along with them.

'Evening, Oz,' a waitress called out as they entered, her accent authentic Dublin. 'I see you brought some friends with ya tonight. If you like, there's an open table by the fire.'

'Thanks, Hannah.'

'You come here a lot?' Kilkenny asked.

'I'm a regular,' Eames replied. 'Didn't I ever tell you I was Black Irish?'

Kilkenny considered for a moment if Eames was serious. While it was obvious that most of Eames's lineage was African, Kilkenny had to concede the possibility that, somewhere in the scientist's ancestry, there might be a Spanish sailor who washed up on the Irish coast after the English navy destroyed the famed Armada. 'I guess that would make us cousins.'

Eames turned and smiled at him. 'Glad you finally noticed the family resemblance.'

On the way back, they ordered three pints of amber ale from the bar and settled in at a table by the fireplace.

'To Lake Vostok,' Kilkenny offered, his pint of beer raised.

Eames and Sutton seconded the toast and drained an inch from their glasses.

'May I join you?' a woman asked.

Kilkenny looked up as a woman approached the table. She looked to be in her early forties, with shoulder-length blond hair and the wardrobe of a working professional. To Kilkenny's surprise, Sutton rose and kissed the woman on the cheek.

'Nolan, this is Faye Olson,' he said proudly.

Kilkenny stood and shook Olson's hand. 'A pleasure.'

'For me as well. Lloyd speaks very highly of you.'

Olson then turned to Eames, who remained seated. 'Hi, Oz.'

'Hello, Faye,' Eames replied politely.

Olson shed her overcoat and sat at the table as Sutton flagged down a waitress for a glass of white wine. 'So, what are you celebrating?'

'Just some exciting new things for these two guys to work on,' Kilkenny replied.

'I know how good that feels. I just brought in a big historic restoration project for my firm.'

'You got Gordon Hall?' Sutton asked.

Olson nodded with a smile.

'Congratulations,' Kilkenny said. 'I live out that way. Given the history surrounding that old place, it deserves to be restored. What are your plans?'

'Judge Dexter built the main house in the 1840s, so that's our key date. We'll make some concessions for mechanical and electrical systems, things that can be hidden in the walls,' Olson explained, 'but the rooms and the details will be as authentic as we can make them. Right now, the house is cut up into four apartments, so all that stuff has to go, as well as a couple of houses that were built on the property during the fifties.'

'What about the acreage?'

Olson smiled. 'All seventy acres are included in the National Historic designation, so no developer is getting his hands on it. This was, after all, a stop on the Underground Railroad.'

'So that view will remain unchanged?'

'It'll actually be improved. When we're done, it'll be a pristine example of a Greek Revival mansion set on a rolling meadow.'

'Sounds like an interesting project,' Kilkenny said, picturing in his mind Olson's architectural vision.

'It is,' Olson agreed. 'Lloyd, do you have the tickets?'

Sutton patted his breast pocket. 'Right here.'

'What are you seeing?' Kilkenny asked.

'Natalie Merchant is playing at Hill Auditorium tonight – Faye's a big fan. We're sitting in the main floor center.'

'Good seats,' Kilkenny said. 'I saw her a few years ago. She puts on a very good show.'

Olson glanced at her watch. 'I hate to steal Lloyd away from you, but we have dinner reservations next door and the show starts at eight.'

'Have a good time,' Kilkenny replied.

'Thanks,' Olson said. 'Good to see you again, Oz.'

'You, too,' Eames replied.

As Sutton and Olson departed, the waitress returned and they ordered dinner and another round of beer.

'I had no idea Lloyd was dating anyone,' Kilkenny said. 'I thought he just worked all the time.'

'I think he learned from me that all work and no play makes Jack a lonely man.'

'How'd you teach him that?'

Eames took another sip of his beer. 'Faye is my ex-wife.'

'Oh?'

'It's not as bad as it sounds. My divorce was final last year and they just started dating a few weeks ago. The three of us have known each other for a lot of years. I met Faye when we were undergrads at UCLA. Shook both our families up when we started getting serious, but they got over the black-white thing by the time we got married. We spent the summer after our wedding backpacking across Europe. Those were good times.'

'If you don't mind my asking, what went wrong?'

'It started with grad school. Faye stayed at UCLA and I went to Stanford. Long-distance relationships suck.'

'Yeah, they do,' Kilkenny agreed.

'I hooked up with Lloyd at Stanford and we started laying the groundwork for UGene,' Eames continued. 'After Faye finished up her master's, she moved up to be with me and took a job with a big architecture firm in San Francisco. We shortened the distance, but we still weren't spending enough time together. It was mostly my fault. I fell in love with my work, and a man can only have one true love at a time. By the time I earned my Ph.D., Faye was ready to divorce me. I managed to talk her into giving me a second chance.'

'How'd you pull that off?' Kilkenny asked. 'I'm interested in second chances myself.'

'It was the promise of a fresh start. After Lloyd and I finished up at Stanford, we both signed on with the Life Sciences Initiative here at Michigan. Faye hired on with a preservation firm in town and we bought our first house. Things were pretty good for about three months, then I disappeared into my work again. By the time Lloyd and I officially formed UGene, my marriage was dead.'

'Is it weird that your partner is dating your ex-wife?'

Eames sipped his beer and thought for a moment. 'When you put it like that it sounds like something off a daytime talk show. Look, Lloyd and Faye are both entitled to happiness, and if they can find it together, then who am I to stand in their way?'

'Very noble. Have you gotten over her yet?'

'What kind of question is that?' Eames asked defensively.

'It's just that I recently screwed up a relationship so badly that the woman I thought I'd be going home to is

33

training to leave the planet, and our future is one very big question mark.' Kilkenny raised his hands up. 'So, if I've crossed the line, tell me.'

'If you're asking whether or not I'm carrying a torch for Faye, I guess the answer is no. Our divorce wasn't ugly and I still care for her, but I think I've accepted the fact that we will never be together again.' Eames sipped on his beer. 'So what's *your* sad story?'

'When my hitch with the navy was almost up, a friend of mine here at the U asked if I'd give her a hand with a project she was working on – an optical computer processor.'

'Sounds like something Lloyd would like.'

'It is. Kelsey, my friend, and I have known each other since we were kids. She was quite literally the girl next door.'

'Your old high school sweetheart?'

'No, back then our families were so close that it would've been like dating my sister. After high school, I went to the Naval Academy and was pretty much gone for about twelve years, but we kept in touch. We were just good friends up until a couple of years ago when some crazy things happened that forced us to peel back a few layers. Marriage seemed like the next logical step.'

'There's your mistake, mixing love and logic. Oil and water, my friend, oil and water.'

Kilkenny nodded. 'Our problems started after the craziness was gone and things got back to normal. I know Kelsey loves me . . . and we both take the idea of marriage seriously.'

'So who got cold feet?' Eames asked.

'She did, but it wasn't cold feet as much as a better offer.'

'Another guy?'

'No, a lifelong dream. Kelsey has wanted to be an astronaut since we were kids. She's been in the corps for a few years, and last August, she got the call. I was excited as anyone for her, until we got the bad news.'

'What?'

'NASA needed her to go to Houston ASAP to begin mission training with the rest of the crew. They'd work right up to launch, then she'd spend the next five months on the space station. That kind of schedule wasn't going to leave a whole lot of time to plan a wedding, at least not the kind she had in mind.'

'Why didn't you two just elope?'

Kilkenny smiled grimly. 'That's what I suggested. Not a Vegas quickie at the Elvis chapel, but a small private ceremony. No dice.'

'Most women have pretty strong feelings about their wedding day.'

'So I discovered. I also learned that, according to the etiquette books, a wedding is the bride's party and the groom is just one of the invited guests. Long story short, I misread all the signs and started a fight in which I said some truly boneheaded things to her. During the few days when she wasn't speaking to me, she gave some serious thought to our situation and decided it would be best for both of us if we postponed our engagement until after she returned from space. After all, seventeen months is a long time to be apart.'

'Define postponed.'

'My current status is single and unattached. Kelsey and I parted with no conditions and no promises regarding the future.'

'*Que sera sera.*'

'Yep. Doris Day is singing the sound track to my love life.'

'I hear you, Nolan, and if I can offer you one bit of advice, as a man whose last romantic bridge is so badly burned that there's nothing left but ash and some tiny bits of charcoal, it's this: Get off your ass and do something about it. Wishing won't fix nothing between you and Kelsey, and neither will hiding from it. I wished and hid my way right out of a marriage.'

'Any suggestions?'

Eames took a draw on his beer. 'She's following a dream right now, that's good. Make damn sure she knows you support her all the way and that you'll be waiting for her when she returns from the heavens.'

After dinner, Eames returned to his office at UGene and spent the next several hours reviewing experimental data. His radio was tuned to a campus station that was playing a Natalie Merchant retrospective in connection with the concert. Eames recalled taking Faye to see the sultry vocalist back when she fronted for 10,000 Maniacs.

Eames left his office well after midnight. As he drove toward his home, he gave into an impulse and changed direction. He entered a modest neighborhood of well-kept homes and turned onto a street called Pineview. On their first visit to Ann Arbor, Faye had fallen in love with a cute ranch house that they eventually moved into.

Passing his former home, Eames saw that it was dark and Lloyd Sutton's car was parked in the driveway.

4

JANUARY 30

LV Research Station, Antarctica

Nedra pulled the disk from her computer, labeled it, and placed it in a plastic jewel case. She had burned through a stack of CD-RWs this afternoon, downloading the final record of what she and her husband had accomplished during their time at LV Research Station. She switched off her workstation and set the box of disks into a small storage crate for the journey back to the U.S.

Years of planning, design, and testing had led them to this place, and now their work was done. She and her husband had proved it was possible to explore a world hidden beneath miles of ice, and they were now one step closer to hunting for life on Europa.

'Are you finished yet?' Collins called out from the galley.

Nedra closed the latch on the crate. 'We are now offici-ally packed and ready to go home.'

'Great, now I can open this.'

Nedra heard a loud pop.

'Is that what I think it is?'

'Depends. Do you think it's champagne?'

'Didn't we already drink the one bottle you smuggled in back in December?'

Collins appeared in the doorway of the research wing with two coffee mugs filled with Great Western. 'Yes, but then I found this while I was rummaging around in the wine cellar. Of course, we can't just let it go to waste.'

Nedra and Collins tapped mugs and sipped the effervescent liquid.

'Mmmm,' Nedra purred.

'And for our final meal here at LV, I've prepared some peanut butter and jelly sandwiches.'

Nedra forced a smile. 'Sounds delicious.'

'I know,' Collins said with a sigh, 'but when we get to New Zealand, I'm taking you out for a great meal at the finest restaurant in Christchurch.'

'I'd settle for a long hot bath, room service, and a week of passion in a five-star suite.'

'I'll see what I can – ' Collins paused. 'Do you hear that?'

A low distant rumble started to resonate through the station: the mechanical throb of engines.

'Yeah,' Nedra replied. 'It sounds like the plane.'

'They're early. Something must've changed the schedule.'

'The last weather report I saw looked fine, but I won't complain if they get us home sooner.'

'Your sandwich is in the kitchen. I'm going to go out and meet our ride.'

Collins climbed down to the lower level, donned his gear, and stepped through the air lock. Outside, the wind blew down steadily from the glacial highlands, and the drone of the plane's engines thundered all around the station.

A cloud of powdery snow and ice crystals flared from the broad skis beneath the LC-130, billowing behind the plane like the dust trail behind a car on a dirt road. The plane grew larger as it approached, sliding down the icy runway, and finally came to a stop just short of the station. The pilot taxied the aircraft closer, then turned so that the tail ramp faced the station door.

The plane's engines slowed, but kept running – it was too cold to risk shutting them off. As Collins walked over to the plane, the side door dropped to become a stair and a man dressed in a white hooded snowsuit quickly descended from the plane.

'Kilkenny?' Collins asked expectantly, but he was unable to discern the man's identity.

Duroc reached out, grasped Collins's offered hand, and yanked him forward with a violent jerk. Collins stumbled, tripping as he tried to regain his balance. Duroc pivoted at the waist and struck him in the temple with the palm of his hand, dislodging the goggles from the engineer's face. Collins dropped to his knees as Duroc twisted his arm behind his back.

'Cooperate, and you and your wife will live,' Duroc said, pressing the barrel of a Glock 9mm pistol against Collins's cheek. 'Do you understand, Mr Collins?'

Collins nodded groggily, still dizzy from the blow. As he lifted his head, Collins saw five more men emerge from the plane, each dressed in white camouflage suits and cradling submachine guns.

'Secure the station,' Duroc ordered.

The soldiers approached cautiously, even though they didn't expect any resistance. Their intelligence reports indicated that only Collins and his wife occupied LV Station and that neither was armed.

'Nedra!' Collins shouted as the soldiers swept into the air lock.

Duroc struck Collins on the side of the head with his pistol and the engineer collapsed to the ice, unconscious.

Four soldiers thundered up the spiral stair to the main level, then broke into two-man teams to check the hall-ways while the fifth man covered the stairs from the air lock.

'Philip?' Nedra called out from the kitchen.

She had just refilled her mug with champagne when a soldier swung around the edge of the doorway, his machine gun held shoulder high, the barrel and the man's eyes locked on her face.

'Hands on your head! Now!' the soldier shouted.

Nedra slowly set the bottle on the counter and placed her hands behind her head.

'1 have the woman,' the soldier called out, the thin wire of a lip mike curled around his cheek to the corner of his mouth.

Duroc glanced down at Collins's prone body as he listened through his earpiece to the reports of his men inside the station. He checked his watch; less than thirty seconds had passed since he'd stepped out of the plane and the station was his.

'Fouquet, Cochin,' Duroc said into the tiny microphone nestled at the corner of his mouth.

'*Oui*, Commander,' both men replied.

'Come outside and collect the other prisoner. Secure both in their sleeping quarters for interrogation.'

Overhead, the second LC-130 circled LV Station and began its descent. Duroc smiled, pleased with how well the mission was proceeding. If everything continued to develop according to his plan, no one would ever know they had been here.

5

Skier-98

'Ten-minute warning,' the pilot announced, his voice clear over the speakers imbedded in Kilkenny's helmet.

'Roger,' Kilkenny replied.

The cargo hold of the LC-130 reverberated with a low steady drone. On her wings, four massive Allison engines beat the frigid air with the combined pulling power of fifteen thousand horses in a synchronized effort to keep the sixty-ton plane aloft. Designated *Skier-98* by the New York Air National Guard's 109th Airlift Wing, she was one of a handful of specialized heavy-lift aircraft servicing some of the coldest and most remote places on Earth. From October to March, *Skier-98* plied her trade between New Zealand and Antarctica.

The hold of the Hercules was empty save for Kilkenny and the two crewmen who now stood on either side of the personnel door. All three men were breathing from portable oxygen systems, the air in the depressurized hold far too thin and cold at this altitude to sustain them.

Kilkenny's presence on board was the direct result of some Pentagon muscle-flexing by the man in charge of the navy's special warfare group and Kilkenny's former commanding officer, Rear Admiral Jack Dawson. When Dawson learned of Kilkenny's involvement with NASA's project at Lake Vostok, the admiral used his considerable influence to quietly add an equipment test for the navy to the project task list.

Kilkenny stripped off the *NSF*-issue parka and stood in the center of the empty hold to stretch his muscles. The matte gray suit that covered his body like a second skin felt thin and light. Other than his face, which was concealed by a helmet, not a square inch of Kilkenny was exposed, and vulnerable points on his body were protected with molded panels of Kevlar.

The suit – called SEALskin by the company working with the navy to develop it – incorporated the latest in combat electronics, chemical and biological warfare protection, and exceptional thermal control. Under laboratory conditions, the suit had performed well, but Kilkenny's old C.O. wanted to see just how well it would fare in more realistic settings. Antarctica, in Dawson's mind, was the perfect place to see if SEALskin could keep a man warm.

The two crewmen in the hold with Kilkenny stared at him with puzzled disbelief. He didn't blame them a bit, because he was about to attempt a HAHO (High-Altitude High-Opening) jump out the side of their plane at 35,000 feet and parachute onto the glacial ice below.

* * *

'I have contact with an inbound aircraft,' the radar operator announced.

Sumner Duroc glanced down at the image on the radarscope. 'Range?'

'Eighty kilometers.'

'Keep tracking.'

What intrigued Kilkenny about this jump, and the reason he agreed to do it, was the location; Antarctica was the only continent he had *never* parachuted onto. Only a few people had ever attempted a jump over the southernmost continent, and three of the most recent to do so became so disoriented with altitude sickness that they never opened their chutes and plummeted to their deaths at the South Pole.

'Sixty-five kilometers and closing,' the radar operator called out.

'Are all systems ready?' Duroc asked.

'All systems are green and ready to go.'

'Good. Bring them in a little closer.'

'Five minutes,' the pilot called out.

'Roger,' Kilkenny answered. 'Switch homing beacon on.'

The voice-activated computer strapped to his chest began transmitting a signal that would allow the plane to locate him in the event of an emergency.

'We are receiving a strong signal,' the copilot said. 'Everything looks A-okay for the jump.'

Kilkenny ran through a final inspection of his rip cords

and chute containers. He patted his thigh and found his combat knife strapped right where he wanted it – insurance in case the main chute failed and he needed to do a quick cut away before deploying the reserve.

'Gauges on,' Kilkenny commanded.

A bar strip of information appeared to float in front of him; the face shield of his helmet served double duty as a heads-up display. Kilkenny studied the compact image that displayed his heading, altitude, airspeed, longitude, and latitude – all gleaned from the constellation of Global Positioning Satellites orbiting the planet.

'Fifty-five kilometers and closing,' the radar operator said to Duroc.

'Two minutes,' the pilot called out. 'Sergeant Boehmer, open the door.'

'Door opening,' Boehmer replied.

A blast of frigid air roared into the cargo bay and the low rumbling of the Hercules changed in pitch as the pilot slowed the aircraft down to 135 knots. Kilkenny grabbed hold of the steel anchor line cables and stepped up to the side door.

'Excuse me, sir,' Boehmer shouted over the wind, 'but why are you doing this?'

Behind the tinted visor, Kilkenny smiled. 'Do you know what NAVY stands for, Sergeant?'

'Beg your pardon, sir?'

'Never Again Volunteer Yourself.'

The red caution light blinked off and the jump light flashed green.

'Those are words to live by,' Kilkenny shouted. 'See you on the ground.'

Kilkenny leapt into the turbulent slipstream behind the plane and felt an immediate jolt of acceleration as gravity pulled him downward. With arms and legs outstretched, he sailed through a 6,000-foot free fall. The altimeter on his heads-up display quickly counted off his descent. Beneath the altimeter, a digital readout clocked his rate of fall approaching 140 miles per hour.

His heart pounded in his chest. Adrenaline flooded his bloodstream as his body reacted instinctively to the unnatural sensation of falling. Kilkenny felt the dull sting of air-borne ice particles impacting against his body through the SEALskin, but thankfully the navy's new miracle suit was performing as advertised.

'Range to aircraft is twenty-five kilometers.'

'Lock on target,' Duroc ordered. He then scanned the light blue sky for the aircraft he could not see but knew was there.

At 29,000 feet, Kilkenny pulled his main rip cord. Looking over his right shoulder, he watched the rectangular parabolic wing unfurl and catch the air. The heads-up display showed his altitude at 27,250 feet and his airspeed nearly zero. The deafening roar of wind that accompanied his free fall was gone, and Kilkenny's ears rang in the silence.

'Display flight path to target.'

In response to Kilkenny's voice command, the computer calculated the straight-line distance from his

46

current position to the known coordinates of LV Station and projected a bright yellow line on the display that graphically showed the most direct flight path. The imaginary line, which was updated several times a second, appeared to run from the center of Kilkenny's chest to a point several miles in the distance.

He reached up, grasped the control toggles for the right and left risers, and pulled to release the brakes. The ram-air chute surged forward in full flight mode, rapidly picking up speed. The design of the canopy allowed Kilkenny to control his flight with great precision. Given the right wind conditions, he could stay aloft for hours. Below, an undulating sheet of white spread out in each direction toward the horizon.

'Target lock is established.'

'Fire,' Duroc ordered.

A new line appeared in front of Kilkenny. This one was white and arcing upward from LV Station.

'What the hell?' Kilkenny blurted out, recognizing the launch of a surface-to-air missile.

'COM on,' he commanded. 'Ice Jump One to Skier-Nine-Eight. Take evasive action! You have a missile inbound. Repeat, you have a missile inbound! Do you copy? Over.'

Static and feedback filled his ears. Faintly, buried beneath the electronic noise, he heard the pilot of *Skier-98*.

'Say again, Ice Jump One. We're not – '

The missile homed in on the heat radiating from the Allison engines. It approached at supersonic speed, easily running down the lumbering Hercules. As the missile struck the number three engine, its high-explosive war-head detonated with concussive fury. Hot metal fragments shredded *Skier-98*'s aluminum skin and ignited the wing tanks.

6

'COM off,' Kilkenny commanded angrily, the range on his communications gear too short to reach anyone but the people who'd fired the missile. The static that filled his ears immediately vanished.

A black smudge marked the spot in the sky where *Skier-98* had exploded, and smoky trails followed the descent of the burning wreckage to the ground – ominous stains on an otherwise perfect expanse of blue. Tilting his head toward the ground caused the bright yellow line of his flight path to reappear on the heads-up display.

He checked his altimeter. It read 26,750 feet. Kilkenny calculated his distance to the ice sheet below to be little more than 15,000 feet, just under three miles. With a lift-to-drag ratio of five-to-one, Kilkenny knew he might squeeze roughly fifteen miles of travel out of his ram-air parachute before gravity finally brought him down. As far as he could see, there was nothing but an endless expanse of ice.

'I'll be damned if I'm going to die here,' Kilkenny vowed. 'Clear flight path display.'

The bright yellow line vanished.

'Display map.'

The outline of Antarctica appeared on the heads-up display.

'Zoom in thirty-mile radius of current position. Display all stations.'

The image on the heads-up display raced toward Kilkenny – a greatly accelerated version of his present descent – and stopped at the specified magnification. Two labeled dots appeared on the display, one to either side of the X that marked his position.

Not going there, Kilkenny thought, looking at the dot labeled LV on the right.

He shifted his gaze to the other side of the display; beside the second dot he saw the letters *VOS: Vostok Research Station*.

Kilkenny knew little about the Russian research station, other than that it was dilapidated and ran on a shoestring budget. He considered the possibility that the Russians might be responsible for shooting down *Skier-98*, but couldn't think of a reason compelling enough for them to risk starting World War Three in Antarctica.

Even with the SEALskin suit to keep him warm, Kilkenny had no food or water and the nearest U.S. outpost was several hundred miles away. Eliminating a suicide march across Antarctica, Kilkenny's list of survival options shrank to one.

'Clear map,' Kilkenny commanded. 'Reset destination point to Vostok Station.'

The computer calculated a new flight path and projected it on the heads-up display.

'Twenty-five miles to Vostok,' Kilkenny read off the

display. 'I should be able to fly fifteen of it, but the last ten are going to be on foot.'

Kilkenny banked his chute sharply into a welcome tailwind. In the bright polar daylight, he raced over the nearly flat surface of stark white ice, quickly accelerating past forty miles per hour. The only sound he heard was the wind whistling around his body.

He quickly fell into a familiar pattern: checking his chute, the horizon, and his altimeter. Five hundred feet above the ice, Kilkenny pulled down on the right control toggle and gradually turned his canopy into the wind. As his speed dropped off, Kilkenny pulled down evenly on both toggles and studied the ground below. The ice was now rushing up toward him. His altimeter rapidly counted down his descent, quickly passing through two hundred feet.

At one hundred feet, Kilkenny momentarily eased up on the toggles. The chute surged forward and his rate of fall slowed. An instinct borne from experience took over, and, at precisely the right moment, he pulled the control toggles down as far as they would go, and gently touched down on the icy plain that covered Lake Vostok.

Quickly, before the wind grabbed it, he unbuckled his harness and deflated the ram-air chute. He stripped off his air tank and patted the knife sheath strapped to his right thigh.

In every direction, the landscape looked the same, and the sun's peculiar path in the sky rendered it useless for navigation. Kilkenny turned around until the bright yellow line reappeared on his heads-up display, pointing the way toward Vostok Station.

He ran slowly at first, getting a feel for the terrain. The snow that covered the glacier was hard and fine like sand, and the wind sculpted it into rippling frozen waves. Kilkenny's vision gradually narrowed, focusing only on the next thirty yards ahead and the holographic line that guided him.

Kilkenny pressed on at a deliberate pace, following his guideline and watching the distance readout count down the miles to Vostok Station. At 0.35 miles to go, Kilkenny was gradually able to discern man-made features in the Antarctic landscape. The GPS readout read at 78.5 degrees south latitude, 106.8 degrees east longitude.

The first structures that came into view were the antennas – a field of six to the left of the compound and a single taller one on the right. Closer to Vostok, Kilkenny came upon a small ridge in the snow that extended away in a straight line – a plowed runway.

'Clear display,' Kilkenny commanded.

Kilkenny glanced down the length of the smooth icy surface and saw some small drifts beginning to form. The few man-made ruts he saw in the runway looked like they had been there awhile, but he couldn't tell just how long. He followed the runway until he reached the base of the tall antenna, then followed the plowed pathway into the station compound. Mounds of broken ice lay piled around the edges of the station, remnants of the *Sisyphean* effort by the Russians to keep their buildings from becoming entombed.

Ahead, a tower jutted upward from the one-story building that hunkered around its base. The tower groaned as the wind pressed against the rust-brown steel panels that enclosed its steel frame. Kilkenny remembered the drilling tower from the photographs he'd seen of Vostok Station while being briefed on the Ice Pick project – the Russians had used it to pull almost two miles of core samples from the glacier. Edging his way along the metal-paneled wall of the tower building, Kilkenny reached a small window beside the door. The interior of the building was dark and appeared uninhabited.

He moved up to the corner of the building and carefully studied the remainder of the station compound – a collection of rectangular structures hunkered down against the ice, their shape more a result of quick modular assembly rather than any aesthetic design. The once brightly colored building panels looked faded, aged by six months of extreme sun each year and abrasion from wind-borne particles of ice. Vostok Station was over forty years old and looked even older.

In the distance, Kilkenny saw the striped dome atop a small square building: a radar shack. He worked his way around the perimeter of Vostok Station, carefully moving from building to building to stay out of sight. When he reached the radar shack, he unsheathed his combat knife and tested the door handle. It turned easily.

Kilkenny stepped through the doorway into a large room illuminated by sunlight pouring through a small window. There was no one inside. He glanced at a few printouts spread across a worktable and found telemetry tracking data for high-altitude weather balloons. The dates on the printouts were several years old. Kilkenny stepped back outside and closed the door.

A steady stream of smoke flowed from the metal flue

pipe that penetrated the roof of the building closest to the weather station. Thick black cables ran from the front of the building out onto poles and eventually to the other buildings.

Power house, Kilkenny concluded.

He carefully approached the power house, keeping an eye on the two large buildings set near it. He crept in the shadows alongside the building wall until his face was near the edge of a small window near the main door. Inside, he saw a man towel off his body and begin dressing.

A moment later, the door opened and a bundled figure walked stiffly outside. A white cloud issued from his face, a mix of steamy breath and burnt tobacco. Kilkenny reached out and grabbed hold of the man's collar, and threw him down onto the ice. The man's cigarette struck the ground with a hiss.

Kilkenny pinned the man with a knee to his chest. Dazed and frightened, the man looked up and saw his own face reflected in Kilkenny's helmet.

'*Vy govarite poangltyski?*' Kilkenny demanded, his voice dry and raspy.

'Yes,' the man replied.

'Great, because that's about all the Russian I know. How many people are here?'

'Nine, including myself. We are winter crew.'

'Any military?'

'*Nyet*, civilian all.'

Kilkenny saw a bewildered fear in the man's eyes – the Russian had no idea why he was flat on his back with a knife held to his throat. Kilkenny patted the man down and found no weapons.

'What's your name?' Kilkenny asked. in a more diplomatic tone.

'Yasha.'

'What is your job here?'

'I am crew leader.'

'Okay, Yasha, I'm going to let you up. If you shout or make any sudden movements, I will kill you,' Kilkenny said matter-of-factly. 'Understand?'

The Russian nodded. Kilkenny eased off and pulled him to his feet. They stood in silence for a moment, Yasha taking his first good look at his attacker.

'Where are the others?' Kilkenny asked.

'In the living quarters,' Yasha replied, pointing to one of the larger buildings.

'Let's get inside and round up your people.'

Yasha led him through an air lock and into the building. Once inside, the lanky Russian stripped off his bulky gloves and coat.

Yasha motioned to the left. 'This way.'

The building had the look and feel of a rundown industrial warehouse overrun by urban squatters. Every available bit of space held a steel drum or crate or a piece of equipment, and the recycled air reeked of machine oil and cigarettes. In the galley four men sat at a long table eating and watching a video on an old television.

'Yasha, tell them to stay where they are and put their hands on the table,' Kilkenny commanded. 'Then get the rest of your crew in here.'

The four men seated at the table turned at the sound of an unfamiliar voice. Yasha translated the orders and the men complied. None took their eyes off Kilkenny.

Yasha then walked through a door on the opposite side of the room, shouted, and returned a moment later with four more men. Once the entire crew was seated, Kilkenny sheathed his combat knife.

Standing at the head of the table, Kilkenny removed his helmet and peeled off his balaclava. His thick red hair lay matted against his head and his freckled skin was flushed. He then took a pitcher of water from the table and took a long drink.

'Who speaks English?' Kilkenny asked, his throat less hoarse.

Several of the men turned to Yasha for a translation.

'Only Mati, our radio operator, and I speak English,' Yasha replied. 'The rest speak only Russian.'

'Then you two will have to translate for the others. My name is Nolan Kilkenny. Which one is Mati?'

'I am,' said a man with bushy black hair and spectacles.

'Have there been any transmissions from LV Station in the past few hours?'

'Just one. I overheard a report to McMurdo that the transport plane arrived.'

'It didn't,' Kilkenny said bitterly.

'What?' Mati asked.

'The transport that was to have picked up the crew at LV Station was destroyed not far from here by a surface-to-air missile.'

'Not possible!' Yasha shook his head. 'International treaty bans all military weapons in Antarctica. Bringing missiles here would be insane.'

'Apparently, someone doesn't give a shit about the treaty,' Kilkenny replied.

As soon as Mati translated what Kilkenny had said, the men at the table panicked and excitedly shouted questions at Yasha.

'Hey!' Kilkenny yelled, his voice booming over the others.

The Russians quieted, looking warily at Kilkenny.

'What's the problem?' Kilkenny asked.

'You are,' Yasha replied. 'You are an American soldier. When Mati tells them American plane was shot down, they think that maybe your country blames Russia and you've come to kill us.'

'First, the missile was fired from LV Station and, from what I've seen of this place, you had nothing to do with it. Second, I'm here because this was the nearest shelter I could find. And third, I once was a soldier, but I'm a civilian now, and I won't kill anyone – unless I have to.'

'What you tell us makes no sense,' Mati said. 'How do you know that the plane was shot down? McMurdo believes it landed at LV Station. I heard Collins make the report.'

'When a transport from McMurdo comes here, who reports its arrival?' Kilkenny asked.

'The pilot, but the aircraft that landed at LV had radio problems. That's why Collins radioed in.'

'I'm betting someone had a gun to his head while he was doing it.'

'But how do you know the plane was shot down?' Mati insisted.

'Because I saw it. I was on the plane up until a few minutes before the missile was launched.'

'What do you mean you were on the plane? How did you get off?' Yasha asked.

'Parachute. I was testing some new equipment, but that's not important right now. The six other people on my plane were killed and someone has seized control of LV Station.'

'*Bozha moi*,' Yasha said, shocked. 'These people, do you think they will come here?'

Kilkenny shrugged. 'I don't know. I have no idea who they are or what they're after.'

Mati looked skeptically at Kilkenny. 'So you flew in from McMurdo and just before your plane is to land at LV, you jumped out of it, yes?'

'That's right.'

'Then how did you get here? LV is over sixty kilometers away.'

'When I jumped I was only twenty-five miles, about forty klicks, from here,' Kilkenny explained. 'It was a high-altitude jump – I flew most of the way and covered the rest on foot with GPS. Finding my way across the ice wasn't a problem.'

'What you're saying sounds crazy,' Yasha said. 'How do we know you're telling us the truth?'

'You don't,' Kilkenny fired back angrily. 'But try to come up with a better explanation for how I got here.'

Kilkenny locked eyes with the station leader. He was tired, hungry, and irritable – a combination that left him dangerously close to punching the doubting man in the face.

'If what you've said is true,' Yasha said more diplomatically, 'shouldn't we contact McMurdo?'

'No. If Mati overheard a radio message from Collins reporting that the plane landed safely – '

'That is what I heard,' Mati interjected.

'Then,' Kilkenny continued, 'whoever did this is trying to maintain a fiction that nothing has happened. We have to assume that they're monitoring communications, so if you contact McMurdo to report the downing of *Skier-98*, they'll know their cover's been blown. And that might piss them off enough to bring them here.'

'How did they get a missile to LV?' Mati asked. 'Could they have smuggled something like that through McMurdo?'

'McMurdo is not the only way into Antarctica,' Yasha said.

'The weapon they used wasn't one of those small, shoulder-fired units,' Kilkenny said. 'My plane was shot down about twenty-five kilometers away from LV. To hit a target at that range requires some very serious hardware.'

'Mati and I were at LV two days ago for a farewell meal with Philip and Nedra,' Yasha said. 'No one else was there and we saw nothing unusual. They must have flown this missile launcher in – a traverse from the coast would take too long. But why would anyone do this? LV has no strategic value, no precious metals or natural resources. It's a scientific research station.'

'It does have one thing of value – the Ice Pick probe. It's jam-packed with exotic technology, and right now it's all crated up and ready for the trip back to the States. This is the perfect time to steal it.'

'But why did they shoot down your plane?' Mati asked. 'Why not just come in, take the probe, and leave?'

Kilkenny considered the question for a moment. 'Because they don't want anyone to know the probe was stolen. That message you overheard was to make McMurdo think my plane arrived safely. McMurdo will probably get another message about the time we're scheduled to take off, and that's the last anyone will hear of *Skier-98*. When the plane doesn't arrive, they'll assume it crashed somewhere on the way back.'

'And the weather is getting too cold to search for survivors,' Yasha added. 'We battle all winter long to keep our buildings from being swallowed by the ice. By next October, they won't be able to find any trace of your plane's wreckage.'

Kilkenny envisioned the debris field left by *Skier-98* on the polar plateau slowly disappearing into the ice. Had Kilkenny been aboard when the missile hit, the search teams wouldn't know where to start to look.

'What about Nedra and Philip?' Mati asked. 'What will happen to them?'

'My guess is they'll be killed as soon as the people who took LV Station are ready to leave.'

'Those are good people,' Mati said to Yasha. 'We must tell McMurdo what has happened.'

'You can't,' Kilkenny said sternly. 'If you do, you'll erase any usefulness Philip and Nedra may still have to their captors. And even if you could contact McMurdo quietly, there's no time to bring in anyone to deal with this. My plane was scheduled to take off from LV in less than six hours.'

'This is madness!' Mati said angrily.

'Yasha, you said that you and Mati were at LV Station

two days ago. How did you get there, snowmobiles?' Kilkenny asked.

'No, those are too difficult to keep running here. Mati and I sail iceboats. We race them back in Russia. Here, we just practice. Why?'

'There's a chance we can get Philip and Nedra out of this alive, but I've got to get to LV Station fast.'

7

Yasha led the way toward one of the support buildings, followed by Kilkenny and Mati. When he grasped the lever handle and pulled, a brittle veneer of ice shattered as he opened the door.

'Inside, please,' Yasha said urgently.

The wind slammed the door behind them, knocking Yasha back. He flipped the switches by the door and a dozen fluorescent tubes flickered on. The building housed a large machine shop used to service the station's equipment.

Yasha studied Kilkenny for a moment. 'How much do you weigh? About eighty kilos?'

Kilkenny did the math in his head. 'About that. Why?'

'The masts and planks on our iceboats are designed to bend under our weight. You and Mati are about same weight and build. You should use his boat.'

'It will bring you luck,' Mati said. 'It's good Estonian boat. Everybody knows best iceboaters come from Estonia.'

Near a large overhead door, Kilkenny saw a pair of thirty-foot-long iceboats. The sleek, carbon-fiber hulls – fully enclosed with clear Plexiglas bubble canopies – looked more like F-18s than watercraft. From the stern of the iceboats, a broad plank sprang like an outrigger, ten feet to each side, at the ends of which were fixed runners. A third runner mounted on a pivot stood beneath the tapered nose of each iceboat, providing a means to steer the agile racers.

'They are beautiful, no?' Yasha said proudly as they approached the iceboats.

'Very,' Kilkenny replied. 'I was expecting a DN boat.'

Yasha shook his head. 'No, it's too cold here for open cockpit. These are Skeeter Class.'

'You know about iceboats?' Mati asked with some surprise.

'A little. I helped my grandfather build a few DN boats when I was a kid, but I sailed on water.' Kilkenny ran his hand over the hull's glossy white surface. 'How fast?'

Mati grinned. 'On smooth ice with a good wind, two-hundred-and-fifty kilometres per hour. Here, we sail on mix of rough ice and snow, so we have to use hybrid blade/ski runners. It's not as fast as back home.'

'Show me what I need to know.'

Mati slid the canopy forward along its tracks. Then he stripped off his parks and lay down on his back inside the cockpit of his dark blue iceboat. Mati's body filled most of the long narrow cockpit, his shoulders almost touching the sides. 'You steer with your feet to turn the front runner at the end of the springboard.'

'Push left to go right?' Kilkenny asked.

'Yes.' Mati grabbed the joystick mounted near his right hand. 'Instead of lines, this operates electric winches for adjusting sail and stays. Push forward to let out sail and slow boat down; pull back to trim sail and increase speed. Pushing right will loosen the stays. This will allow mast and plank to bend more – good for acceleration. Pull joystick to left to tighten the stays – it will help point closer to wind. Doing this may also cause you to hike boat up on two runners, so be careful.'

'Hiking boat is fun,' Yasha added, 'but you run risk of capsizing. Not good thing to do on ice.'

'Joystick is spring-loaded,' Mati continued, 'so once you make adjustment, you can let go and the sail will stay where you set it. The art of iceboating is tuning mast and sail to match the conditions. Here, on left side, is small steering wheel. You use it to steer the boat when you run alongside, pushing boat to get it moving. You can also use wheel as a backup, if the foot-pedal steering fails.'

'If it handles anything like my Windrunner, I should be fine.'

'Our boats are equipped with small electric heater and GPS unit.' Mati tapped a small, flat-display panel mounted beneath the front edge of the cockpit opening. 'Yasha and I have made trip to LV several times over summer; route is programmed into the GPS.'

'You will encounter cracks in the ice – don't try to run parallel or you risk dropping runner into crack and wrecking boat,' Yasha advised. 'Just sail over them, perpendicular to the crack.'

'How do I stop?' Kilkenny asked.

'Pull on this,' Mati replied, pointing to a black T-shaped plastic handle mounted to the upper hull above his right leg. 'Pull and hold. The brake drops from under-side of boat and drags across the ice. When you let go, the brake will spring back up.'

Yasha crouched by the front runner. Near the tip of the combination blade/ski, Kilkenny saw a square metal hoop pin connected to the top of the runner. 'Once you stop, point the boat into wind and set this brake in place.' Yasha flipped the metal hope over the front of the runner. 'It will keep boat from blowing away.'

Kilkenny and Yasha assisted Mati in preparing the ice-boat for a sail. Mati fine-tuned the seat to accom-modate Kilkenny's six-foot frame. Ten minutes later, they opened the overhead door on the leeward side of the building and carried Mati's iceboat out into the Antarctic night. They then installed the thirty-foot fiberglass mast and unfurled the Dacron sails. When the boat was rigged, Yasha and Mati gave it a quick visual inspection.

'You're ready to go,' Mati said.

'Great. Mati, you're my backup. Keep monitoring the radio for transmissions from LV. If you hear anything that sounds like a routine departure, that means I failed. Notify McMurdo immediately about what really happened.'

'I understand. Good luck.'

'Thanks for your help.'

Kilkenny climbed into the iceboat and pulled the bubble canopy over his head, then signaled that he was ready to go. Mati and Yasha began pushing the iceboat forward, the wind blowing a steady twenty knots from Kilkenny's right. Beyond the protection of the building, Kilkenny's sail fluttered as it filled with air. Once the sail caught hold of the wind, the Russians let go. Kilkenny quickly pulled away from Vostok Station, the bow aimed at the first way point.

As Kilkenny became more comfortable handling the iceboat, he trimmed the sail to pick up speed. The composite runners attacked the rough surface, alternating between gliding over and slicing through the granular particles of snow and ice. He was amazed at how quickly the sleek craft accelerated, and the zigzag pattern of his tacks kept him on course while using the wind to his advantage. Then, ahead, he caught sight of a small white cyclone forming on the ice.

'Oh, shit!' Kilkenny cursed.

The snow devil raced toward him, its turbulent winds snapping his sail wildly. The iceboat shuddered violently as the snow devil struck it broadside just behind the canopy. The collision broke the grip of the rear runners on the ice and threw the craft into a broach. Kilkenny's shoulder slammed into the hull as the craft lurched into a spin. White rooster tails sprang from each of the runners as their honed edges scraped sideways across the ice.

Kilkenny's shoulder ached and his breathing came in hungry gulps. He braced himself inside the cockpit and pushed hard on the foot pedals, trying to steer in the direction of the spin. The iceboat spun past 270 degrees before the snow devil released it and the runners finally caught hold of the ice again. Weakened by its encounter with the iceboat, the snow devil rapidly lost coherence and dissipated.

After regaining control, Kilkenny eased the sail, pointed the bow directly into the wind, and pulled on the brake. The iceboat quickly came to a stop. Kilkenny lay in the cockpit staring up at the blue sky for a moment, letting the adrenaline rush subside, then pulled himself out of the cockpit to check the boat for any sign of damage from the broach.

Kilkenny knelt down to check the long flat plank beneath the iceboat's stern and, thankfully, found no cracks. He then cleared the coating of shaved ice that covered each of the runners and found them undamaged.

Kilkenny released the parking brake, grabbed hold of the left side of the cockpit, and pushed the iceboat forward. As it moved, he turned it back toward his destination. The sail fluttered, and Kilkenny continued pushing until he felt the wind take hold. He then leapt into the cockpit, braced his feet on the steering pedals, and pulled the canopy closed. After tightening the stays a little, Kilkenny steered into the next tack.

When he reached the outermost of the windward way-points, Kilkenny turned toward LV Station. The wind now blew in his direction of travel and he jibed the iceboat to take the best advantage of it.

The ice that covered Lake Vostok was remarkably flat and covered with rows of ice particles lined up like wind-driven ripples on a glassy lake. Tired and lulled by the drone of blades carving the ice and by the monotonous view, Kilkenny struggled to keep his eyes open.

As he fought to remain awake, one of ripples rose up sharply out of the ice forming a jagged ridge inside of the starboard runner. The brittle ice grated loudly against the carbon-fiber plank, threatening to tear into it like a chain saw. Kilkenny hiked the iceboat onto the port side, pulling it up forty degrees from level.

'C'mon, baby,' Kilkenny urged.

The mast leaned toward the horizon under the load, with the lines straining to keep the sail attached to the iceboat as Kilkenny carved a shallow arc away from the ridge: Ahead, the pressure ridge abruptly turned across Kilkenny's path and he struck it squarely. The iceboat sailed ninety feet through the air, righting itself before slamming down on the ice. Kilkenny's helmet smacked loudly against the canopy.

He blinked to clear the stars from his vision, then checked the GPS and corrected his course.

The drowsiness he'd felt a moment ago was gone.

8

Kilkenny slowed the iceboat as he turned into the final leg of his journey. He sailed with the sun directly behind him, the white hull and blinding sunlight serving as camouflage. Ahead, LV Station stood out from the icy plain. Beyond what was considered the front of the station, Kilkenny saw two large planes with streams of exhaust trailing from their engines.

One hundred yards from the station, he eased back on the sail, turned into the wind, and pulled back on the brake cable. Beneath the hull, a quarter-circle wedge of stainless steel pivoted out like a pelvic fin and dug into the ice. The iceboat quickly scraped to a halt.

Kilkenny opened the canopy and eased his body out of the cockpit. The throb of engines filled the frigid air. The temperature display on Kilkenny's helmet read -48 degrees Fahrenheit. He crouched behind the bow of the iceboat, set the brake, and took a careful look at the station.

Two men on patrol walked around to the back side of the station. Both were dressed in thick white fatigues and cradled a submachine gun. Kilkenny waited for one of the men to spot the white iceboat parked in the distance, but the glare made it almost impossible for either to pick it out from the landscape. The sentries continued their circuit and disappeared around the opposite side of the station.

He unsheathed his k-bar knife and silently crept forward, keeping the station between him and the planes. Each step was a deliberate movement designed to avoid the barking sound made by a careless footstep on dry, tightly packed snow.

Kilkenny reached the end of the windowless storage module and waited. No alarm sounded. No footsteps rushed in his direction. He had crossed the open field undetected.

He carefully rounded the end of the storage module and slipped into the next triangular quadrant of the cruciform station. The low angle of the sun cast a long shadow off the storage module, darkening the area in front of him. Staying in the shadow, he moved up to the next module, crouching beside its thick steel supports. Peering from beneath the elevated module, Kilkenny saw two LC-130s with markings identifying them as *Skier-98* and *Skier-99* of the New York Air National Guard's 109th Airlift Wing.

That one sure as hell is false-flagged, Kilkenny thought, knowing all that remained of the real *Skier-98* was a wide-strewn field of charred debris.

Several men busied themselves loading crates into the hold of *Skier-98*. The tail door of the other plane was already closed. Two men with side arms stood between the aircraft. Kilkenny studied the placement of men and equipment around LV Station, looking for anything he could use to his advantage.

The sentries walked around the far side of the aircraft and turned back toward the station. Both men held a hand in front of his eyes as they faced the low sun. Kilkenny braced himself against the station module and waited.

As they passed his hiding place, Kilkenny attacked. From behind, he grabbed the closest of the two, hooking his right arm over the sentry's shoulder. The man expelled a lungful of air as Kilkenny's arm clamped down and jammed the man's submachine gun into his abdomen. Kilkenny coiled at the waist like a spring, then unwound with a swift turn and drove the k-bar through layers of protective clothing into the soldier's back. The black stainless-steel blade severed the man's aorta and plunged into his heart.

'*Que?*' the other sentry blurted out, his attention drawn by the sudden movements to his left.

As he drove his knife into the back of the one sentry, Kilkenny shifted his weight onto his left foot and snapped a side kick with his right into the throat of the other. The heel of Kilkenny's boot flattened the man's windpipe. He staggered back, his eyes bulging behind yellow-lens goggles as he vainly gasped for air. Acting more on reflex than thought, he squeezed the trigger of his Heckler-Koch MP-5. Kilkenny held the dying sentry up as a shield and several rounds struck the man's body. One grazed across Kilkenny's upper arm and steam slowly rose from the wound as the groove filled with warm blood.

Rushing forward, Kilkenny rammed the choking sentry with his bullet-riddled partner. The man fell onto his back and Kilkenny landed on top of him. He thrust his knife into the side of the sentry's neck, the blade disappearing up to the hilt. The man looked up only to see his own horrified expression reflected in Kilkenny's face shield. As Kilkenny withdrew his knife, a great rush of blood followed it out, staining the white hood of the man's parka and the ice beneath him.

The men loading cargo and servicing the planes dove for cover when they heard the short burst of submachine gunfire. Those armed readied their weapons, scanned the area for threats, and awaited orders. Duroc crouched beside one of the planes with his pistol drawn, searching vainly for some sign of trouble.

'Albret,' Duroc barked out to his executive officer. 'What the hell is going on?'

'All units report!' Albret shouted angrily into his lip mike.

One after another, Duroc's soldiers responded with their status.

'Sir, only the perimeter team has failed to report in,' Albret said. 'The rest of the men are in position and weapons are secure.'

'Idiots! They probably slipped on the ice. Finish loading the plane while I see what the problem is.' Duroc motioned to a pair of soldiers. 'You two, come with me.'

Kilkenny rolled the one sentry off the other, grabbed an MP-5, then searched the bodies for additional ammunition. His arm stung, the blood congealing into an icy scab. For the first time he felt the bone-chilling cold of Antarctica.

After finding two more clips for the MP-5, he stuffed the two bodies, one atop the other, beneath the curved aluminum belly of the elevated module. He then dropped onto his stomach, using the bodies as protective cover. Between the station and the planes, Kilkenny saw men racing about in response to hastily issued orders.

French, Kilkenny thought, *or maybe Spanish. Impossible to tell with those engines running.*

The commander stepped away from one of the planes, yelled something at two soldiers, then all three began moving toward his position. With no clear shot at the commander, Kilkenny tracked the closest of the three with the barrel of his MP-5. At twenty feet, Kilkenny fired a three-round burst that pulverized the man's face.

Duroc saw the muzzle flash in the dark space beneath the station module. The soldier to his left suddenly jerked around, his head thrown back, his face exploding. Blood and torn bits of flesh and bone splattered against Duroc's face, covering his goggles and balaclava. The remaining soldier opened fire on Kilkenny's position.

Duroc could feel blood seeping through the fabric that covered his face, and his goggles were smeared with the rapidly freezing fluid. He flipped back his hood and stripped everything off his head. The frigid air stung his exposed skin.

A fusillade of bullets bore down on Kilkenny's position as the second soldier fired his weapon on full automatic. The two bodies stacked in front of him absorbed several rounds; the rest either punched holes in the module's aluminum skin or chiseled into the ice.

From beneath the module, Kilkenny had a protected

field of fire to the front and side, but was vulnerable to a wide sweep around the rear. The instant the soldier emptied his weapon, Kilkenny popped up, found his target, and fired. The man spun and dropped to the ice.

'*Merde!*' Albret cursed. 'You two, cover the commander. The rest of you, get this plane closed up and ready to leave.'

Search, aquire, fire. The words played in Kilkenny's mind like a mantra. Once he was sure the second soldier wasn't going to get back up, he sought out another target. The commander was lying on his stomach, facing Kilkenny with a pistol. The man had stripped off all the protective gear from his head, and Kilkenny got a clear look at his face. As he lined up the MP-5's site, the commander fired. Kilkenny saw the muzzle flash at the same instant as the bullet struck his helmet an inch above his left eye.

The impact snapped Kilkenny's head back so fast his neck hurt. He dropped behind his barricade, gripping the MP-5 tightly, waiting for his vision to clear.

The two soldiers sent by Albret were more selective with their fire, squeezing off rounds individually to keep Kilkenny pinned down. Duroc and one of the soldiers grabbed hold of the two bodies and dragged them back toward the aircraft while the other man covered their withdrawal.

'Albret, I hit him,' Duroc said. 'Head shot, but he's wearing a helmet. I don't know if it got through.'

Three shots flew out from beneath the module and struck the fuselage of the plane nearby.

'There's your answer,' Albret said.

'Where did this sniper come from?' Duroc demanded.

'Unknown. Except for the transport, the radar has been clear since we arrived. The rest of the perimeter is secure, no sign of any additional threats.'

'He's not one of our men. How did he get here? How did he know?'

'We won't learn that unless we capture him, sir, but we have a more important problem – the aircraft. They are in the open and, as you can see, very difficult to protect from weapons fire. Both are ready to go, and I think we should get them airborne before either is damaged too greatly.'

Duroc considered his executive officer's suggestion. 'See to it. Position the men to protect the first plane. We will depart on the second.'

'I think it would be wise for you to be on board the first plane.' Albret could see the rebuke forming on his superior's lips. 'Hear me out, sir: Our primary objective is to acquire the probe. As commander, you should see that task through to delivery, as if nothing has changed. The men and I will kill this bastard and follow you out on the second plane.'

'Pragmatic as ever, eh, old friend?'

'I just want to make sure I get paid. We came here to do a job. Swallow your goddamned pride, Sumner. The men and I can handle this.'

'I know you can.' Duroc extended his hand to Albret. '*Bonne chance, mon ami.* I'll see you in Rio Gallegos.'

The unmistakable roar of the LC-130s powering up for takeoff flooded the area around the station, drowning out all other sounds with their rhythmic thunder.

Damn, Kilkenny cursed. *They're bugging out.*

Kilkenny squeezed off a few more shots, then pulled out from under the module. As he ran back through the shadows toward the iceboat, the first of the LC-130s began to taxi. Its four engines strained as they pulled the lumbering plane forward, the wide pontoon skis mounted to the fuselage plowing more than gliding across the rough ice runway.

The plane began to pick up speed just as Kilkenny reached his iceboat, struggling to gain lift from a frigid crosswind. As it reached the end of the runway, Kilkenny saw a sudden flash as eight JATO engines ignited. The tail-mounted, solid-fuel rockets provided the powerful burst of thrust the aircraft needed to lift a full load at this altitude. The LC-130 pulled free of the ground and sailed upward.

With two soldiers firing random single shots into Kilkenny's barricade, Albret and another soldier ran around the opposite side of the station. At the base of the tower, they dropped on their stomachs and crawled under the storage module into the sniper's quadrant. From the shadows Albret scanned the entire length of space beneath the next module but only saw the two stacked bodies.

'Hold your fire,' Albret ordered into his lip mike. 'The sniper's gone, but be careful. Pull the bodies of our men out and load them on the plane.'

Albret and the soldier pulled themselves out from under the module and swept the area, looking for a target. The smooth, rounded shape of the elevated modules offered nothing for a man to scale. Looking further, Albret saw nothing moving in the icy wasteland. Where the sun hung low in the sky, the horizon was consumed by the glare.

Kilkenny popped the parking brake, grabbed hold of the cockpit rim, and pushed hard. He turned the iceboat toward the runway, the wind blowing almost perpendicular to his line of travel. As the sail caught hold of the wind and the boat accelerated, Kilkenny leapt into the open cockpit and laid the boat off to a reach, tacking with the crosswind. He sat upright in the open cockpit, steering by hand with the small wheel, bracing the MP-5 against the hull with his leg. The white iceboat leapt forward as Kilkenny sheeted the sail, trying to harness as much wind-driven energy as the agile craft could bear.

Tacking, Kilkenny caught the second plane as it started down the runway. The wind flowed over the open cockpit like a river at a cataract and hammered down on him with a roiling fury. The iceboat was moving well over a hundred miles per hour and its acceleration showed no sign of topping out. As Kilkenny loosened the stays, the mast flexed under the wind load and the plank bowed. The iceboat hunched down toward the ice, lowering its center of gravity as its speed increased.

Lighter and more aerodynamic than the LC-130, the iceboat raced down the runway toward the plane like a cheetah on the Serengeti. As the distance closed, the turbulent zone of prop wash flowing past the wings and tail struck Kilkenny's sail like a stormy head wind and cut into his forward momentum. He tacked to starboard, pointing the bow at the tip of the plane's right wing, then raised the MP-5 and fired. Bullets sparked as they struck metal, burrowing into the engines and control surfaces of the wing.

Both the plane and the iceboat quickly raced down toward the end of the runway, the distance between them widening as Kilkenny followed his starboard tack. Eight bright flares erupted near the tail of the plane as the JATO engines ignited. Skipping at first, the LC-130's nose pulled up, followed by the rest of the huge plane as it lifted off the ground.

Kilkenny turned the iceboat into a wide circle and watched as the LC-130 struggled to gain altitude despite the JATO boost. A flicker of light appeared on the right wing, followed by a sudden flash as bright yellow flames roared out of the inboard engine. The wounded plane slowly banked to the right, smoke billowing from the burning nacelle.

The angle of the bank increased until the left wing pointed vertically upward. Then the LC-130 rolled over, exposing its underside to the sky like a breaching whale before falling headlong back into the sea. Barely a thousand feet in the air, the inverted plane lost all upward momentum, surrendered to gravity, and dove straight into the ground, the JATO rockets speeding its plunge.

The fuselage collapsed on impact, bursting into chunks of twisted metal, the plane's ninety-eight-foot length crumpling down to nothing. A river of aviation fuel poured onto the ice from the ruptured wing tanks. The JATO pods ripped free from the disintegrating airframe and, with several seconds of solid fuel left to burn, roared into the ice then spun wildly about like holiday fire-works. White-hot propellant from the JATO rockets ignited the spilled fuel. Smoke and steam billowed from the wreckage and, eerily, the field of raging flames slowly began to sink as fire battled melting ice.

9

Turning away from the flaming wreckage, Kilkenny sailed back to LV Station and noticed the cluster of spherical tanks that held the station's hydrogen fuel supply. His eyes were drawn to an irregularly shaped mass attached to the shaded side of the tanks.

Kilkenny parked the iceboat off the runway near the station and ran over to the tank farm. It became clear that the mass he'd detected in the shadows was two bodies, with hands bound behind their backs, lying face-down on the ice. Both shot in the back of the head. He rolled the bodies over, even though he already knew who they were.

Kilkenny quickly searched the station for something to wrap the bodies with and a place to store them until they could be taken home. In the crew quarters he found a pair of blankets that had been folded and packed away.

After stowing the bodies in the storage module, Kilkenny stepped into the galley looking for something to drink. He found a plastic glass in the wall cabinet, filled it with water, and slowly drained it. He emptied several more before his thirst was satisfied.

He pulled off his gloves and carefully inspected his right arm. The molded Kevlar panel that covered much of his skin showed evidence of two direct impacts – rounds that likely would have shattered the bone if not for the body armor. Along the edge of the panel, Kilkenny saw the ripped fabric of the bodysuit and the grazing wound. Blood seeped from beneath the thawing scab and Kilkenny felt a stinging sensation.

Still hurts, he thought, *so I guess I didn't get frostbite.*

Kilkenny located the first-aid kit and laid out the items he needed on the galley counter. He ran a finger down the seam in the middle of his chest, opening the Velcro fastener, then gingerly began to strip off the upper half of his SEALskin suit. Imbedded in the frozen scab were threads from the frayed edge of fabric around his wound. When he reached the right sleeve, he pulled down quickly, peeling the scab off with the shirt.

'Son of a – ' Kilkenny growled, his arm throbbing.

Blood swelled into the freshly opened wound. Kilkenny leaned over the sink, flushed it with warm water, then wrapped a sterile dressing tightly around it. He flexed his arm and the dressing stretched without unraveling.

With his injury treated for the moment, he put his shirt back on and went into the operations module. None of the remaining equipment appeared damaged. The station looked ready for a normal end-of-season shut-down. Kilkenny accessed the station computer, made a satellite connection with his computer back at MARC in Ann Arbor, and retrieved the phone number for Jackson Barnett, the Director of Central Intelligence.

* * *

Kilkenny had first met Barnett shortly after he left the navy and returned to Ann Arbor. While working on his doctoral thesis, Kilkenny discovered a hacker stealing information through the MARC computer network. In his pursuit of the hacker, Kilkenny uncovered a ring of industrial spies and located a stolen CIA intelligence-gathering device code-named *Spyder*. Their paths crossed a second time when a wealthy Russian oligarch attempted to steal a promising new energy technology from a physicist working with MARC.

'Nolan, how are things in Ann Arbor?' Barnett drawled, his voice carrying more than a hint of South Carolina.

'I wouldn't know. I'm calling from Antarctica,' Kilkenny replied. 'There's been an incident here that you need to know about.'

'I see. Hold on a minute,' Barnett replied. He punched a few buttons on his phone that put Kilkenny on the speaker and started a recorder. He then picked up a pen and flipped to a blank page on his legal pad. 'Go ahead, Nolan.'

Kilkenny briefly described the work being done at LV Station, then launched into an uninterrupted narrative of events starting with his flight from McMurdo and leading up to the present. Barnett jotted down questions as Kilkenny spoke, key elements he wanted to explore further.

'How long since the plane left?' Barnett asked.

'Less than an hour. The LC-130s aren't fast, so they are still somewhere over Antarctica.'

'You say the New York Air National Guard runs most of the air traffic down there?'

82

'I believe that's the case.'

Barnett wrote the guard unit's information on a slip of paper and walked over to his office door.

'Sally,' Barnett said to his executive assistant. 'Call the Pentagon and see who we can talk to at this unit. This is an emergency situation. I need the top brass right now.'

Sally Kirsch nodded and took the note with one hand as she punched the speed dial with the other.

'Nolan, what about containment? Who knows any of what you've told me?'

'Just the Russian crew at Vostok Station.'

'Any chance they had a hand in this?'

'I doubt it. If they did, I'd be dead right now.'

'Jackson,' Sally interrupted, 'I have General Mark Jolley of the New York Air National Guard on the line.'

'Thanks, Sally. Patch him through.' Barnett waited until he heard a snap of static on the speakerphone. 'General, can you hear me all right?'

'Loud and clear,' Jolley replied. 'I just got a call from the Chairman of the Joint Chiefs ordering me to get in touch with you ASAP. What can I do for you?'

'I appreciate your responsiveness, General. I have you on three-way with Nolan Kilkenny, who is in the middle of Antarctica. Nolan, tell the general about your flight.'

Kilkenny repeated the story of the downing of *Skier-98*.

'My God. Why the hell would some son-of-a-bitch do this?' Jolley asked. 'We're talking an act of war here.'

'Possibly, but we don't know the reason behind the attack,' Barnett explained.

'General,' Kilkenny said, 'the people who shot down

your plane are in the air over Antarctica and I'm sure they're not headed for McMurdo. Any idea where they could go?'

'McMurdo is the main jump point in and out of Antarctica, particularly for something like an LC-130. To skip McMurdo, you need someplace else to refuel.'

'Airborne tankers?' Barnett asked.

'Possibly, but they've got to have fuel, too. Best bet is a string of fuel caches stationed on the way in and out. We've done that before, and a good Herc crew can land just about anywhere.'

'What about radar coverage down here?' Kilkenny asked. 'Is there any way to get a fix on this plane?'

'Antarctica ain't exactly O'Hare International,' Jolley replied. 'Most of the continent isn't covered at all. Once a flight is out of range from Mac Center, we keep tabs on it through regular radio checks. What about a spy satellite?'

'I thought of that as well. We do have a few in polar orbit, but tracking a plane in flight is almost impossible unless we have a good idea where to look. If we're very lucky, we might catch them on the ground refueling, but we wouldn't know it until several hours later.'

'By which time they'd be gone,' Kilkenny added. 'General, in their shoes, where would you go?'

'In an LC-130, you've got four choices: Australia, New Zealand, South America, or South Africa.'

'I'll alert our people in those locations to keep an eye out for this plane,' Barnett said.

'It's hard to mistake it for anything else,' Jolley said. 'Kilkenny, can you locate where my plane went down?'

'I don't have an exact fix, but I can narrow the search area, General. We also need a crash investigation team here at LV to deal with the wreck at the end of the runway. There might be something in it that'll tell us more about who we're dealing with.'

'Timing is going to be tight, but I'll make it happen,' Jolley promised. 'We're running up against the minus 54°C rule.'

'What's that?' Barnett asked.

'All work outside stops when the temperature drops below minus fifty-four degrees Celsius. It's too dangerous for people to be outside in that kind of weather,' Jolley explained. 'Anything else?'

'I'm a little low on provisions right now and the rest of my gear is in storage at McMurdo,' Kilkenny said. 'Also, I need another ride home.'

'We have to keep a lid on this for the moment, General.'

'One of my planes was shot down,' Jolley said incredulously. 'How are we going to keep that quiet?'

'By publicly treating the downing as an accident. LV Station is remote enough that CNN isn't going to send a crew down there to take a look. We release a story that the plane went down on takeoff – a mechanical problem. Give your crash team the real story, so they know what to look for, but to everyone else this was just an accident.'

'What about your guy at LV? How do we explain him?' Jolley asked.

'I'm not here,' Kilkenny replied. 'Never was.'

'I'll see to it they correct any typos on the paperwork at McMurdo,' Jolley said, catching on.

'I have one last question, General,' Kilkenny said. 'You mentioned that a good Herc crew could land almost anywhere. Where would you get a good Herc crew?'

'Lots of guys can fly the Herc, but mine are the only ones trained to land on the ice. The navy had this mission before us, so they probably have a few people with time in the LCs.'

'That's all we have for now, General,' Barnett said. 'I appreciate your help.'

'Thanks, General,' Kilkenny added.

'Just keep me in the loop,' Jolley said before hanging up.

'"*I'm not here. Never was,*"' Barnett parroted. 'Nolan, we'll make a spook out of you yet.'

'Not if I can help it.'

'Now that we've addressed logistics, let's take a look at motive. What is there to gain from this attack?'

'The probe – it's packed with all the latest in artificial intelligence, robotics, and deep-sea exploration technology. I'd peg the R&D price tag just shy of a billion dollars.'

'Did your researchers find anything in the lake?' Barnett asked.

'Yes, they found life in Lake Vostok. All the samples are stored inside the probe. Beyond its unique habitat, the commercial value of this material is completely unknown. The DNA may ultimately prove to be very similar to other more common species on the planet.'

'What about geologic surveying?'

'We did some sampling of the water and the silt on the bottom to determine mineral content. The crust is pretty thin there, so there's some interesting stuff spewing out of the cracks.'

'That may be the motive, Nolan. Several nations have competing territorial claims in Antarctica. Not much has been done with regard to these claims, but if valuable mineral rights were at stake, the situation could become quite different. If someone thought the United States was using a scientific research station as a cover to search for natural resources – say a new oil field – they might see preventing us from making such a discovery as in their national interest.'

'Which leads us back to an act of war.'

'Exactly.'

10

Rio Gallegos, Argentina

Greg Kuhn flew through the bottom of an overcast sky and lined his plane up with the runway. This was his third night landing in eighteen hours – the first two being nothing more than pit stops at fuel caches secretly placed along his egress route from Lake Vostok.

Kuhn and his crew had put in almost thirty-six hours of airtime in something less than three days on this mission, far more than navy regulations or the FAA would ever permit. Then again, neither the navy nor the overnight express carrier he flew for in recent years would ever consider paying him what Duroc offered.

A strong wind blew down from the Andes to the west, buffeting against Kuhn's plane. Instinctively, he corrected his speed and pitch. The wheels lightly touched down on the old tarmac runway and Kuhn taxied toward a collection of buildings. In the darkness, he saw a signalman waving him in with a pair of illuminated orange wands. Once in position, Kuhn was given the signal to cut power.

A short distance from the plane, Kuhn saw a black Hummer, a military personnel transport, an aviation fuel truck, a forklift, and a semi truck with a cargo container mounted on its trailer.

'Well done, gentlemen,' Kuhn said to his flight crew, relaxing for the first time in days. He then switched on the plane's intercom. 'Loadmaster, make ready to off-load our cargo.'

'Aye aye, sir,' a voice crackled back through the speaker.

As soon as the loadmaster opened the passenger door, Sumner Duroc stepped out of the plane carrying a Halliburton case and walked toward the jeeps. A uniformed man with a thick black mustache stood waiting beside the Hummer, his hands thrust deep into the pockets of his long leather coat.

'General, is everything ready?' Duroc asked.

'*Si*, the arrangements are as you specified. Once my men have loaded your cargo into the container, it will be taken down to the docks and placed on board the freighter.' The general handed Duroc an envelope. 'Here is the inspection paperwork and the container manifest for your security equipment.'

The ramp door in the tail of the LC-130 groaned as it slowly lowered to the ground. The general motioned with his hand, and his men moved toward the plane to assist the loadmaster and his mate with the cargo.

'Where is the other plane?' the general asked.

'It didn't make the return flight.'

Duroc and the general watched as the soldiers quickly

moved the crates from the plane onto the truck. Kuhn and his copilot inspected their plane as the fuel truck refilled the tanks for the final leg of their journey. As soon as the last of the cargo had been removed, Kuhn handed a clipboard to his copilot and walked over to Duroc.

'We lay over here until daylight, right?' Kuhn asked.

'That is correct,' Duroc replied.

'Good, because me and the crew could use a little sack time. I'd hate to have come all this way just to auger in over some cattle ranch because I nodded off at the wheel. I also believe it's time to transfer the rest of our money.'

'You are correct, Commander.'

Duroc set the Halliburton case on the hood of the Hummer and opened it – a laptop computer and a satellite phone were securely nestled in the case's padded interior. He booted up the computer and quickly established a secure connection with a bank in Switzerland. He keyed in an alphanumeric account number, then pulled what appeared to be the video camera viewfinder from the case and held it up to his right eye. The device, which was wired directly into the back of the laptop, scanned the unique pattern of the blood vessels in his retina and passed the data on to the computer in Zurich. The bank's computer compared the scan to the data in its secure files and verified Duroc's identity.

'Per our agreement, I am now transferring the balance of the six million dollars into your account. Of course, now you only have to divide it six ways.'

'I hadn't thought about that,' Kuhn admitted, realizing that the loss of the second LC-130 had caused his pay to double. 'My men knew the risks involved, as did yours.'

Duroc nodded, briefly thinking about his trusted friend Leon Albret. He keyed in a few more commands, shut the computer down, and closed the case.

'Commander Kuhn, this is where we part company. Fuel has been cached for you at runways along your route back to the United States. At your final stop, a ground crew will also restore your plane's original markings.'

'I'm sure the old girl will appreciate that. She never flew in anything but navy colors before this.'

'Make contact with our man at ASRF before you start the last leg of your flight. Good luck.'

Kuhn grasped Duroc's hand firmly. 'You too.'

After six hours of sleep, Kuhn roused his crew and ran through his preflight checklist. His old plane had flown well despite the years she lay in storage, and his crew had performed as if no time had passed since they left the navy.

Once airborne Kuhn laid in a straight-line course that roughly paralleled the Argentine coast. Kuhn estimated approximately six hours of flying time to reach Buenos Aires, given the current weather and wind conditions. The skies were mottled with large billowy clouds and foamy whitecaps broke the blue-green surface of the Golfo San Jorge below.

Lieutenant Aurelio Rodriguez flew his French-built Mirage III at forty-five thousand feet across the assigned patrol area – a rectangular stretch of space that ran along the Argentine coast from Bahia Blanca in the north to the Golfo San

Jorge in the south. His regular patrol of this area was part of the government's response to the increasing flow of illegal drugs through Argentina to Europe and the United States.

Rodriguez rarely encountered anything during his patrols, but during the mission briefing, his commanding officer told him to look sharp today. According to a well-placed informer, a large shipment of drugs was scheduled to fly out of southern Patagonia aboard a plane disguised to look like one of the United States military transports used to service research stations in Antarctica.

A blip appeared on the Mirage's radar, an aircraft almost due south of his position, flying at twenty-six thousand feet on a north-north-east heading. The plane was not broadcasting a commercial identification, which immediately made Rodriguez suspicious. He maintained his altitude and began mentally plotting a course that would allow him to get behind the unidentified aircraft.

Rodriguez maintained a five-mile separation as the two aircraft passed by each other, then brought his Mirage around and into a parallel course. The delta-winged fighter easily closed the distance on the slower plane, which Rodriguez visually identified as a variant of the Lockheed C-130. He brought the Mirage into position, just behind and off to the right of the plane. The markings indicated that the aircraft belonged to the United States Air Force. Rodriguez pulled alongside the transport and switched his radio to send.

'Argentine Air Force Alfa Zulu Three Zero,' Rodriguez announced over the radio, 'United States Air Force Sierra Kilo Nine Eight, over.'

'I copy, Alfa Zulu Three Zero, over.'

'Sierra Kilo Nine Eight, what is your purpose and destination? Over.'

'Emergency transport of injured personnel from San Martin research station to Buenos Aires, over.'

'Sierra Kilo Nine Eight, maintain speed and heading. Alfa Zulu Three Zero, out.'

'What do you suppose that was all about?' Kuhn's copilot asked, staring out the window at the needle-nosed Mirage fighter.

'He's just checking us out. Right now he's contacting his base for confirmation of our story. That's where the general comes in. He'll tell them we're legit and this guy will fly off and find something else to do.'

'Negative, repeat negative, Alfa Zulu Three Zero. United States Air Force Sierra Kilo Nine Eight is *not* on emergency transport mission and is *not* authorized to land in Buenos Aires. Aircraft is illegal drug transport. You are authorized to fire on Sierra Kilo Nine Eight. Do you copy? Over.'

'I copy. Alfa Zulu Three Zero out.'

The Mirage rolled ninety degrees, then peeled off to the right, away from the LC-130.

'I guess you were right, Greg,' the copilot said. 'Our shadow just took a hike.'

'Money buys you friends in high places,' Kuhn said confidently.

Rodriguez flew the Mirage in a tight flat arc behind the LC-130, throttling up the SNECMA Altar 93-C turbojet engine after running it at near-stall to keep pace with the lumbering transport. The Mirage responded with a thundering burst of acceleration. As he circled around the transport, he switched his avionics from navigation to attack mode and selected the Mirage's two DEFA 30mm cannons. Rodriguez leveled out of his turn and aimed the attack fighter at the center of the LC-130.

An audible tone buzzed in Rodriguez's helmet – his weapon's system had locked onto the aircraft. Cruising at five-hundred knots, the Mirage closed quickly and Rodriguez squeezed the trigger.

Two streams of shells erupted from the Mirage, white tracer lines marking the trajectory of fire. The LC-130's left wing disintegrated, the wing tanks exploding as the white-hot rounds tore through the thin aluminum skin. Rodriguez continued firing as he banked the Mirage, strafing the side and tail of the aircraft as he pulled away from his kill. A trail of black smoke marked the *Ice Queen's* fiery descent. The shattered hulk crashed into the Atlantic and disappeared.

11

Lake Vostok, Antarctica

For the second time in a day, the air around LV Station filled with the roar of engines. Less than ten hours after talking with Barnett and Jolley, a Twin Otter arrived from McMurdo. This time, an LC-130 circled the station, checking the condition of the runway. A scorched crater in the ice marked the spot where a similar plane had recently crashed.

'Will you look at that?' the pilot said to his cockpit crew as they passed over the wreckage.

The pilot lined up the Hercules and set it down on the ice. As he taxied back toward the station, a pair of helicopters landed nearby.

Kilkenny stepped out of the station to greet the new arrivals. A thickset man emerged from the passenger door of the Hercules and quickly walked toward him.

'You must be Kilkenny?' the man asked.

'I am,' Kilkenny said, extending his hand.

'Major Don Saunders,' the officer replied with a grip that was firm even through the gloves. 'Other than get my crew down here ASAP and check in with you, my orders are a little light on detail. I assume this has something to do with that wreck at the end of this skating rink of a runway? Mind filling me in on what's going on?'

'Sure thing, Major. If you care to step inside, I can lay everything out for you.'

'Wonderful,' Saunders said, delighted. 'So, what's the story? That plane out there crash on takeoff?'

'Something like that,' Kilkenny replied. 'This isn't going to be your standard crash investigation.'

'Oh, how's that?'

'First, this entire operation is classified.'

'That's one thing that *was* made clear to me before I left.'

'Second, your team is going to be working on two separate crash sites. You saw one at the end of the runway. The other is about thirty miles from here. The cause of both is already known.'

'How can you possibly know what caused these two planes to crash?' Saunders asked dubiously.

'I never said they crashed. The first was destroyed by a surface-to-air missile.'

'An SAM, here?'

'Yeah, and it wasn't a Stinger, either. Something with a lot more range and a bigger bang.'

'What happened to the one at the end of the runway?'

'I attempted to force the pilot to abort his takeoff by shooting out one of its engines. It didn't work out.

Both of the planes you'll be working on bore Air Force markings and the number 33498 on the tail. The one at the end of the runway was a fake.'

'If you don't mind my asking, what the hell happened here?'

'In a nutshell, a military force flew here in a pair of planes similar to the one you just came in on. They seized this station, killed the two people who were working here, and stole their research. Then they shot my plane down, about thirty seconds after I jumped out of it. I caught up with them just as they were getting ready to leave. You've seen what's left of one of their planes. The other escaped.'

Saunders thought for a moment, then nodded his head. 'So what are my objectives?'

'In the case of the aircraft brought down by the SAM try to locate the wreckage and retrieve any remains of the crew. Those men deserve to be brought home.'

'Absolutely. What about the other one?'

'Different matter,' Kilkenny replied. 'You are to recover what you can of the aircraft. We need to know everything about that plane and its cargo. In that wreckage is evidence we'll need to nail the bastards responsible for this attack.'

'I'll do what I can. Do you know where the other plane is?'

'I can get you close.' Kilkenny brought up a map of the area on a high-resolution monitor. '*Skier-98* was hit about here.'

'Got any idea about altitude and speed?'

'When I jumped, she was at thirty-five thousand feet

and had slowed to one-hundred-thirty-five knots. She was a little over four miles above the top of the glacier, flying on this vector toward the station, into a slight head wind.'

Saunders ran through the math in his head, estimating the dispersal pattern and the rate of fall of the debris. He rapped one of his thick knuckles against the monitor. 'If I swagged this right, what's left of your plane ought to be right around there.'

'Swagged?' Kilkenny asked.

Saunders fished a note card from his breast pocket and scrawled down the coordinates.

'*Silly Wild Ass Guess*,' Saunders said with a grin. 'It's a technical term.'

12

Jim Evers parked his Honda Civic in the visitors lot of the Saguaro National Park. After strapping on his helmet and a Camelback backpack, he removed his Cannondale mountain bike from the trunk rack. He left ASRF early every Friday, weather permitting, to get in a few hours on the trails before dark. This was the best time to ride because he almost always had the park to himself.

As Evers mounted his bike and rode onto the trail, Sumner Duroc stepped out of the passenger side of a GM pickup and, with the driver, unloaded two mountain bikes from the back. Duroc then carefully fastened a Styrofoam cooler to the rack above his rear wheel. The two men then followed Evers out into the Arizona desert.

Two hours into his ride, Evers felt the water he'd consumed straining his bladder. He was several miles from the nearest rest room and each jarring bump on the rocky trail only increased his desire for relief. He pulled off the trail and looked around. The only people in sight were two men a couple hundred yards behind him.

They'll understand a call of nature, Evers reasoned. He set his bike down and stepped around a clump of brush.

As he relieved himself, Evers heard the bikers approaching up the rough trail. He expected them to pass, but then heard their tires skid to a halt.

'I'm okay,' Evers called out. 'Just takin' a leak.'

'Very good, Mr Evers,' Duroc answered. 'It would be unfortunate if you'd been injured.'

Evers pulled up his shorts. 'Excuse me? Do I know you?'

'We've recently done business together, a matter involving a pair of aircraft.'

'Duroc?' Evers asked nervously as he approached the two men. Both had dismounted and were standing beside their bikes. 'What are you doing here?'

'I am here to see you. We ran into some difficulties and I wondered if you had mentioned our arrangement to anyone.'

'God, no,' Evers replied. 'I'm not stupid.'

'No one ever said you were. Still . . .'

On Duroc's cue, the driver punched Evers in the abdomen. Evers folded at the waist, knees buckling. The driver then grabbed Evers and locked him in a full nelson.

'Do you know what you are to me, Mr Evers?' Duroc asked.

'I kept my end of the deal,' Evers replied, struggling for air.

'You are a risk.'

Duroc removed the cooler from his bike and held it in front of Evers. Several holes had been drilled through the top of the cooler and Evers heard an angry rattle from within.

'Life is full of risks. We encounter them every day.'

Duroc walked off the trail to the place where Evers had urinated. He carefully set the cooler down, then kicked it over. The Styrofoam lid popped off and a Western Diamondback rattlesnake darted out. It coiled up beneath the brush, tail buzzing as it took in the new environment.

The driver pushed Evers off the trail to where Duroc stood, several feet away from the snake.

'I swear I didn't tell anyone!' Evers protested, struggling vainly against the driver's hold on him.

Duroc nodded. The driver shoved Evers toward the brush. Evers tripped and slid on his hands and knees. The rattlesnake, sensing a threat, shook its tail furiously. Evers recoiled, pulling back onto his knees. The driver then kicked him from behind. The blow ruptured the water bag inside the Camelback and thrust Evers into the brush. Instinctively, Evers held up his arms to shield his face. The rattlesnake shot out and struck him in the upper right arm. Evers screamed, his arm on fire with pain and venom. Then the snake let go and raced away into the desert.

'You've got to help me,' Evers pleaded, his fear giving way to shock. He gripped his arm tightly above the wound; it was already growing numb.

'The two aircraft you provided me have been lost,' Duroc explained as he retrieved the cooler, 'and their absence will be difficult to hide. Questions will be asked, and unfortunately you, my friend, know things that could prove most damaging to me. *Adieu.*'

The driver grabbed Evers by the helmet and tilted his head, then swung his fist like a hammer into the side of his neck. The blow briefly flattened Evers's jugular vein, knocking the blood pressure in his brain out of balance. Evers blacked out and fell to the ground.

13

New York City

'I see we've run out of time,' the seminar moderator announced to the displeasure of the many attendees waiting with questions. 'That concludes this afternoon's session. I'd like to thank our presenters, Leslie Siwik of the Michigan State Police and Oswald Eames and Lloyd Sutton of UGene, for their insights on forensic DNA analysis and genetic information processing. Thank you all for attending.'

The audience that filled the 250-seat conference room offered Eames, Sutton, and Siwik an enthusiastic round of applause. For the next few minutes, the three presenters graciously accepted compliments offered by several attendees shuffling past the head table.

Their presentation at this year's Genetic Technology Conference evolved out of a contract UGene had signed with the Michigan State Police to help cut through their backlog of DNA samples. Siwik, who ran the Northville

Laboratory's Biology/DNA Unit for the State Police, served as UGene's point of contact for the project.

'I think that went well,' Sutton said as he gathered his notes.

'Well? You think our presentation went well?' Eames asked, surprised by his partner's mild reaction. 'We were outstanding.'

Siwik stared out into the half-empty room with a broad smile on her face. 'That was amazing, Oz. I mean totally incredible.'

'Uh-oh, Lloyd. I think she likes it.'

Eames nodded. 'How are we going to put this young lady back in the lab now that she's had a taste of the big time?'

Siwik turned to her copresenters. 'This was nothing like defending my thesis.'

'Of course not,' Eames replied. 'These people are your peers. They wanted to hear what you had to say.'

'You guys are the best. I learned so much from you both, I wonder why I'm up here with you. Thank you for sharing the spotlight with me.'

'Share?' Eames asked. 'You were only up there with us because you're a cute young blonde. Do you think anyone would have paid good money to come here just to listen to me and Lloyd?'

'Hell, no,' Siwik replied, laughing.

'Face it, Leslie, you're just set decoration,' Sutton added. 'We needed you to get 'em through the door and keep 'em in their seats.'

Siwik beamed. This was one of the biggest moments of her career. She had just presented an important paper at a prestigious biotech conference and it was an un-qualified success. Eames had encouraged her to expand her professional horizons and mentored Siwik through the process of preparing an academic paper on their work. After the conference, their paper would be published in a scientific journal for the worldwide audience.

'So, I'm just a science bimbo?' Siwik asked.

'No,' Eames replied seriously. 'Bimbo implies you're not smart, which is far from the truth. The term you're looking for is science *vixen*.'

'You really should have your own calendar,' Sutton said. 'Each month in a different, revealing lab coat.'

'I can see the centerfold now – me wearing nothing but my Nobel Prize medal.' Siwik struck a pose, pursing her lips seductively.

Eames and Sutton laughed, causing Siwik to quickly lose her composure and join them.

'Oz, seriously, thanks for making me do this,' Siwik said.

'My pleasure.'

Siwik checked her watch. 'I'm going to go call my husband. He'll be so proud of me.'

'He damn well better be or I'll knock some sense into him. You tell Ed I said so.'

Siwik laughed, grabbed her briefcase, and walked out of the room, still basking in the glow of her moment. As she left, a man dressed in an expensive suit walked up the aisle toward them.

'Good evening, gentlemen. I have a car waiting outside, if you'll just follow me.'

'A car, why?' Eames asked.

'You have a dinner engagement this evening with my employer, Charles Lafitte,' the man replied, only to receive a baffled look from Eames. 'It was scheduled last week, sir.'

'Lloyd, do you know what this guy is talking about?' Eames asked, his surprise turning to suspicion.

Sutton nodded sheepishly. 'I accepted Lafitte's invitation for both of us.'

'Why? You know what he wants and you know how I feel about selling the company.'

'Yeah, I know. And I'm sorry to sandbag you like this, but UGene's a public company now, and, like it or not, we have a fiduciary responsibility to our shareholders to listen if someone wants to make an offer. Vielogic's a big player with very deep pockets, and I'm interested to hear what Lafitte has to say.'

'Your call.' Eames turned to the well-dressed messenger. 'On my own behalf, I accept Mr Lafitte's gracious invitation.'

'Excellent. This way, gentlemen.'

Eames and Sutton were led out onto the sidewalk in front of the convention center and found a driver standing beside a dark blue Mercedes Guard S500 waiting for them. Eventually they arrived at Central Park West and were let off in front of an imposing stone building that faced the park.

A uniformed doorman greeted them and, after passing a cursory check-in with building security inside the lobby, they boarded a finely crafted elevator that was a product of a different age. They exited at the top floor into a wood-paneled foyer with a marble-tiled floor and a crystal chandelier. An oversized mahogany door swung open in front of them invitingly.

'Good evening, gentlemen,' the butler said. 'May I take your coats?'

'Certainly,' Sutton replied.

'Monsieur Lafitte is waiting for you in the salon,' the butler said as they handed him their coats. 'This way, please.'

He led them down a short hallway and into a palatial two-story cube of space capped by a shallow dome in which a trompe l'oeil of Michelangelo's *Creation of Man* floated in the heavens.

'Stunning, *n'est ce pas?*' an accented baritone voice inquired.

'Very much so,' Eames replied, turning his gaze toward his host.

Charles Lafitte stood near one of the arched windows that ran along the east wall overlooking Central Park, a silhouette against the lights of the city.

'This painting has always been a favorite of mine. I am especially intrigued by the point where the fingers of God and man touch – the passing of the spark of life. Perhaps that is the real reason I became involved with biotechnology, to discover the secrets of that spark.'

Lafitte stepped out from the shadows, a man of medium height and build whose most distinguishing feature was a lean, angular face crowned by a pristine, hairless head. According to legend, both Lafitte's shaven pate and his career in biotechnology were the result of a teenage battle with leukemia. For thirty-eight years,

Lafitte chose to remain bald as a personal reminder of the frailty of the human body.

'I try to let this room speak for itself,' Lafitte explained as he walked toward them, hands clasped behind his back. 'Somehow, I feel the effect would be diminished if I were to stand in the middle when someone sees it for the first time.'

'I'm no architect,' Sutton admitted, 'but I must say that it certainly is impressive.'

'*Merci.* So, we finally meet. I am pleased that you accepted my invitation.'

'Thank you for offering it,' Eames replied as he shook Lafitte's hand. 'I've heard that your dinners are legendary.'

'I do enjoy a fine meal and stimulating conversation.'

A petite woman in a simple black dress walked through the archway in the far wall of the salon, her Manolo Blahnik houndstooth mules tapping lightly against the wood floor with each graceful step. She wore a silver necklace with matching earrings, and a mane of short auburn hair covered her head with wavy ringlets.

'Completing our table this evening,' Lafitte said, 'is my colleague, Dr Dominique Martineau.'

'Good evening,' Martineau said. 'It's a pleasure to meet you both. Dr Eames, I have followed your work with great interest.'

'And I yours,' Eames said politely.

'Has Charles regaled you with his explanation for the painting on the ceiling yet?'

'He has,' Sutton replied.

'Dominique.' Lafitte's voice carried a mild reproach.

'Oh, hush,' Martineau retorted with a dismissive wave

of her hand. 'You've had your fun, now leave me mine. Do you gentlemen believe in the spark that endows life?'

'I'll admit to believing that something happens when you put the right chemicals together,' Sutton answered, 'but I wouldn't go so far as to say it's proof of a divine creator.'

'And you, Dr Eames?'

'Unlike my partner, I do still cling to the idea that there's more to life than the right recipe.'

'And as you make your discoveries, do you feel as if you are peeking over the shoulder of the creator?'

Sutton shot a glance at Eames, whose face broke with an embarrassed smile.

'The thought has crossed my mind once or twice,' Eames admitted.

Martineau smiled. 'I told you, Charles, he is a kindred spirit. There are times in my lab when I feel just a little of what it might be like to be God.'

The butler returned with a silver tray bearing four champagne flutes filled with a golden, effervescent liquid. After Lafitte and his guests had taken a glass, the butler announced that dinner was ready to be served.

'This way,' Lafitte said with a sweeping gesture of his arm.

As with the salon, Lafitte's architects and interior designers crafted an elegant dining space with rich woods, finely detailed moldings, multilayered wall finishes, and a tasteful selection of traditional art and furnishings. The lighting was subdued and accented by candles, and classical music flowed softly from concealed speakers.

Eames guessed that Lafitte could easily accommodate twenty guests for dinner in the space.

After they were seated, Lafitte's staff brought out the first course – a pheasant consommé with quenelles. At a leisurely pace, they were presented with a succession of culinary experiences: Dover sole with citrus buerre blanc served with a glass of Pierre Frick gewürztraminer, sautéed foie gras with champagne grapes and pan sauce, and passion fruit sorbet.

Eames sipped on his white wine, savoring the skillful mixture of taste, aroma, and presentation. 'Whatever you are paying your chef is worth it.'

'There are only a few chefs in all of New York who could match what we've been served tonight,' Martineau boasted.

'I will pass along your kind words,' Lafitte replied, 'but now that we have cleansed our palates, it is time for the entrée.'

The dishes from the third course were removed and the butler reappeared with a 1980 Haut-Brion. Lafitte took a sip of the Bordeaux, carefully judged its taste, and pronounced it acceptable. A moment later, the staff presented the main course: baby lamb chops with persil-lide and rosemary sauce accompanied by a hearts of palm salad served with aged sherry vinaigrette.

'Are you familiar with Grenache?' Lafitte asked as he reached for his wineglass.

'The grape?' Eames asked.

'Yes, a most versatile fruit of the vine.'

Sutton swirled his glass and inhaled the aroma. 'Is that what we're drinking?'

Lafitte shook his head. 'The château that produced this

particular vintage cultivates three red grapes and two white, but none are Grenache. In the vineyards of Bordeaux, Grenache would be out of place, but elsewhere it is quite welcome. After the Spanish white Airén, Grenache is the most widely planted wine grape in the world.'

'What makes it so popular?' Eames asked.

'Adaptability. The Grenache grape grows quite well in hot, dry regions, and its vine wood is very sturdy. That is why you find it in places where less hardy vines would wither and die.'

'Sounds almost like a weed,' Sutton opined.

'It is most tenacious, and amazingly productive. Carefully pruned, a vineyard of Grenache can yield three to four tons of dark, exquisitely flavorful grapes per acre.' Lafitte spoke almost wistfully, recalling a delicious vintage of Châteauneuf-du-Pape. 'Unfortunately, that same vineyard in less thoughtful hands can more than double that harvest, producing a pale, generic swill best served from a cardboard box. Its use in mass-produced wines has tainted the image of Grenache in the minds of many wine drinkers around the world, scaring some off from some exceptional vintages.'

'I've heard there's more to wine than just grapes,' Eames said.

'Quite true. Master vintners are artists who craft taste and smell into a memorable experience. But even an artist can be limited by the materials he has to work with. Grenache adapts beautifully to its environment, and the flavors found in an Australian vineyard will be different from grapes grown in Spain, Africa, or California.'

'An evolutionary survivor,' Sutton offered.

Lafitte nodded. 'Hence my admiration for this humble grape. Any vine can grow in a perfect environment, but Grenache thrives in harsh places.'

'There is much to be learned from organisms that possess that particular trait,' Martineau added.

Eames thought about the foothold of life held in the dark waters of Lake Vostok as he washed down a last bite of lamb. 'I couldn't agree more.'

'And now, for the final course,' Lafitte announced.

The dishes and glasses quickly disappeared and, once again, the butler presented his final wine selection for the evening – a Château D'Yquem Sauternes. After receiving Lafitte's approval, he filled the remaining glasses with the sweet wine.

The diners were then presented with an individual Baked Alaska for dessert. Each studied the artfully constructed layers of chocolate cake, ice cream, and meringue, appreciating the chef's skill while simultaneously deciding where to start. They consumed the final course with a minimum of conversation, enjoying both the dessert and its fine complement in the wine.

'Everything was simply incredible,' Sutton said, 'but I do hope that was the final course.'

'All that remains is an after-dinner drink.'

'Gentlemen, this has been a most enjoyable evening,' Martineau said, getting up from her seat, 'but that was my cue to make a gracious exit. Good evening.'

The three men stood as Martineau left the dining room. Lafitte then led them into the library. The butler appeared with three glasses of cognac and Lafitte opened an ancient wooden humidor.

'Cigar, gentlemen?'

'Sure,' Eames said.

Sutton nodded.

Lafitte selected three hand-rolled Dominicans. 'I think you will find these quite enjoyable.'

Lafitte clipped the ends of his cigar, then handed the nipper to Eames. The ritual continued with the lighting of the cigars and the silent savoring of the first smoky taste.

'So, what did you want to talk about?' Eames asked.

'Acquisition, of course. I am very much interested in your company.'

'The five percent you already own of our company tells us that,' Sutton said.

'And you have given me a good return on my investment, but my interest goes beyond money. I believe your research will prove invaluable to other divisions of Vielogic.'

'Why not just license our technology?' Eames asked.

'Owning your technology will give me a competitive advantage, a license will not.'

'I prefer to remain independent,' Eames replied.

'Where do you stand, Lloyd?' Lafitte asked.

'I'm more willing than Oz to entertain an offer if I think it's in the company's best interest, but our independence means a lot to me as well.'

'Could you put a price on it?'

'Yes,' Eames replied, 'but it would be more than money. We'd need to maintain control of the direction of our research and ownership of the patents on our work.'

'I am certain we could come to an arrangement.'

'There's also the matter of ethics.'

'Ethics?' Lafitte asked.

'Oz, I don't think this is the time for – '

'Yes, ethics,' Eames answered, cutting Sutton off. 'Vielogic conducts fetal tissue research, does it not?'

'Yes, in fact Dr Martineau is one of the world's leading authorities in this field. It is very important work. Lives will be saved because of our research.'

'Perhaps, but lives are currently being lost because of it, too.'

'What are you talking about?'

'Paying reproductive health clinics to provide your labs with a steady supply of aborted fetuses. Creating human embryos in the lab for the purpose of harvesting stem cells.'

Lafitte nodded. 'For the moment, it is the only way to maintain a large-enough stock of cells for our research.'

'It may be a source of cells to you,' Eames said contemptuously, 'but I was raised to believe that life begins at conception. So far, I haven't seen anything in my research to change that view.'

Insulted, Lafitte stepped up to Eames. 'Are you accusing me of murder?'

'I guess I am,' Eames replied.

Sutton studied Eames and Lafitte carefully. They stood just a foot apart, Lafitte looking small in comparison. He understood his partner's position, but questioning their host's morality struck Sutton as rude. In Lafitte's place, he would have been tempted to take a swing at Eames, despite their difference in size.

'Gentlemen, we've all had a bit to drink,' Sutton said

diplomatically. 'I suggest we call it a night before something more regrettable occurs.'

Lafitte held his ground, staring angrily at Eames.

'Oz, we're leaving now.'

The butler suddenly appeared at the doorway. Still looking down at the French billionaire, Eames gave a curt nod and backed away.

14

After Eames and Sutton departed, Lafitte whipped off his tie and stormed back to the master suite. He was furious. He entered the bedroom and found Martineau curled up on a chaise in the corner of the bedroom, reading.

'Things finished up rather quickly,' Martineau commented.

'The bastard insulted me in my own home.'

'Eames?'

Lafitte nodded. 'He called your research immoral. He accused me of killing babies!'

'Charles, you already knew how squeamish Eames was about certain avenues of research.'

'Yes, but I didn't call him an idealistic idiot.'

'At least not to his face.'

Martineau pressed up against Lafitte's back, her hands encircling his waist to unfasten his belt and trousers. 'Other than this little incident, I thought tonight was a success. How did Eames and Sutton respond when you told them of your interest in acquiring UGene?'

'Sutton was willing to hear me out, but Eames – there will be no dealing with him.'

'Which is what you expected, is it not?' Martineau's hands were working the buttons on his shirt.

'True, but I always hope for a surprise.'

'If it's a surprise you want . . .'

Martineau took Lafitte's hand and placed it on her thigh, his fingers touching the bare skin of her leg below the hem of her dress. She pressed her hand firmly over his, then guided his hand slowly upward. Eyes closed, Lafitte's excitement grew as his hand progressed across the smooth warm surface. Thigh gave way to hip, then round to abdomen, each transition an uninterrupted exploration of flesh. She drew his hand around the region she knew he most wanted to touch, playfully bringing him closer but savoring the anticipation. Martineau breathed hotly on his neck then slid his hand down from her navel.

'I've been waiting all night to finally get you alone,' Martineau explained.

'Had I known, dinner would have ended much sooner.'

'Had you known, you would have made passionate love to me on the table in front of your guests.' Martineau smiled devilishly. 'Not that I wouldn't mind being served between courses – a feast of love, so to speak.'

Martineau turned Lafitte around to face her, then backed him into the bed. His loosened trousers slid down to his knees. She pushed him back onto the mattress and unzipped the back of her dress. It slipped off her shoulders and flowed down the contours of her body like a black waterfall. She then pulled his boxers down and straddled his supine body.

Martineau and Lafitte made love for nearly an hour, pacing themselves by alternating between tender caresses and vigorous passion. Though in his early fifties, Lafitte enjoyed testing his limits with the sexually demanding Martineau, and both preferred the physical challenge of marathons to short sprints.

'Enough,' Lafitte said with a labored sigh, pulling away from Martineau and collapsing onto the bed.

Martineau rolled onto her side and draped her arm across his chest. Lafitte's heart hammered as he gulped air like a drowning man.

'Are you all right?' she asked.

'Fine, just tired. And you?'

'I am flushed like a virgin.'

Lafitte ran his hand along the curve of her back. Her skin felt smooth and hot. 'I spoke with my physician today.'

'And did he tell you what a fine specimen you are?'

'For a man my age, but the effects of time are beginning to show.'

'Anything of concern?'

'A few bits of chemistry are a little off, but mostly I'm afflicted with gradual erosion. I am getting old, Dominique, and I don't want the physical decay that comes with longevity.'

'I know, Charles, and I'm just as concerned as you are – possibly more so. Aging is far less kind to women.'

'You are showing no ill effects thus far.'

'*Merci*, but a woman can detect the subtle changes and I am no longer twenty-five. We're getting closer to understanding how to reset the cellular clock, but this work takes time.'

'How much time? Years? Decades? I cannot wait that long. Eames and Sutton have the means to accelerate your research. I will have UGene.'

15

Ann Arbor, Michigan

Lloyd Sutton pulled his car into the driveway of Faye Olson's home.

'Thanks for dinner, Lloyd,' Olson said.

'My pleasure. I've been wanting to try out that new Cajun place.'

'I know it's getting late, but would you like to come in? I can put on some coffee or get you something to drink.'

'That sounds great. If I went home now, I'd probably end up messing around with some new algorithms. Given the choice, I'd rather stay up late talking to you.'

Olson smiled as Sutton walked around the car and opened her door. At her front porch, Sutton reached into her purse to retrieve her keys, but they weren't there.

'That's odd,' she said with a laugh. 'I would have sworn I put them in here. Have you and Oz found that early Alzheimer's gene yet?'

120

'No. Maybe,' Sutton said blankly. 'I don't remember.'

'Lloyd, you are so bad.'

Olson pulled a spare key from its hiding place in the carriage light and opened the door. Sutton followed her inside. The living room was cozy, filled with books and pictures of family and friends. A few included Sutton with Eames and Olson from their Stanford days.

'What can I get you?' Olson asked.

'How about a bowl of popcorn and a beer?'

'You never change. Here, let me take your coat. You know where the fridge is. There are some Coronas on the bottom shelf. Get one for me, too.'

Sutton stepped through a rounded archway into the narrow kitchen. In the corner, he saw the same round table he'd shared many meals at with Eames and Olson when they were still married. The door to the basement stairs and the backyard stood ajar. The landing was dark.

'Lloyd,' Olson called out from the bedroom. 'I hope you don't mind if I change into some sweats, but I've had about all of those parity hose I can take in one day.'

Sutton laughed warmly. 'Go right ahead. It's not like we're trying to impress each other.'

As Sutton grabbed two bottles of beer and closed the refrigerator door, he heard a footfall behind him. Before he could turn, a muscular arm reached around and clamped down hard on his chest. The bottles slipped from his hand and shattered on the linoleum floor. Sutton turned his head, but was unable to catch sight of his attacker. Then he felt a knife slice through his neck back to the bone.

'What was that?' Olson called out from the bedroom. 'Did you drop something?'

A gurgle of air bubbled up from the wound. The killer dropped Sutton's body on the kitchen floor and blood pooled around his feet. He retrieved a partially filled black plastic garbage bag from the stair landing and moved into the living room, leaving a trail of bloody footprints behind.

The killer stood at the bedroom door and peered through the narrow opening. Olson's skirt and blouse lay on the back of a chair, and she was seated on the side of the bed removing the hose from her legs. He pressed his hand against the face of the door and pushed it open. The door squeaked loudly.

'Lloyd!' Olson said, shocked and embarrassed, 'I'm half-naked here.'

As Olson turned to grab the robe off her bed, she saw that it was not Sutton who had entered her bedroom.

16

Ann Arbor, Michigan

'Nine-one-one. What is your emergency?' Irene Yale asked as the call came in.

'He stabbed me,' a woman's voice replied hoarsely.

'Who stabbed you, ma'am?' Yale asked.

The address where the call had originated appeared on Yale's screen.

'My ex-husband, Oz, stabbed me. I'm bleeding, bleeding all over,' the woman sobbed. 'God, it hurts.'

Yale highlighted the address on her screen and ordered police and paramedic units to be dispatched to the house on the city's north side.

'Is your ex-husband still there with you?'

'I don't know, I don't think so,' the woman said, her words broken by erratic gasps.

'I want you to stay on the line until the police arrive. Do you understand me?'

No reply.

'Ma'am? Ma'am, are you still there?' Yale asked urgently.

'What's the story, Vera?' Detective J. R. Fink asked Officer Vera Andrews as he stepped out of his unmarked car.

'The house belongs to a woman named Faye Olson. Shortly after midnight, nine-one-one received a call from a woman reporting that she'd been stabbed. I arrived on the scene and searched the house.' Andrews's voice cracked slightly. 'I found two bodies inside – a man in the kitchen and a woman in the bedroom. The man had his throat slit. The woman was nude and had been stabbed repeatedly – the phone was on the floor by her bedside. The paramedics arrived a couple of minutes after I did, but there was nothing for them to do. I secured the house and called you guys.'

'Good work, Vera,' Fink said. 'I'm going inside. Let me know when the evidence techs show up.'

'Will do.'

As Fink walked toward Olson's house, he pulled on a pair of latex gloves and steeled himself for the crime scene. He stepped through the doorway and knelt near a bloody shoe print on the living room carpet by the kitchen archway.

'The killer is a *big* guy,' Fink said to himself.

Fink estimated the killer's shoe size to be at least a thirteen. He saw several other partial prints on the carpet, bloody remnants of the killer's movements through the house.

Moving into the kitchen, he saw the first body just as the killer left it. A white male in his early to mid-forties lay in a prone position on the floor, his head tilted back like a Pez dispenser. Sprays of blood marked the walls, describing the arc of the attack that left the man dead. The glass remains of two beer bottles lay on the floor around and probably beneath the victim, their pale yellow contents pooled with blood. The two broken bottlenecks still had their caps – they were never even opened.

Fink moved slowly around the kitchen, trying to absorb as much of the fresh crime scene as he could. He knew that his best chance for catching the killer would come in the early hours of his investigation.

Inside the bedroom, the nude body of a petite white female – approximately the same age as the other victim – lay supine on the bed. Several deep stab wounds marred her chest and abdomen and, like the man in the kitchen, her throat was sliced down to the bone.

A blouse and skirt were draped neatly over the back of a chair, probably placed their by the victim before she was attacked. Long shallow slits on her chest and thighs indicated that her undergarments had been cut from her body and thrown with haste onto the floor.

On the dresser, Fink found a purse. He carefully opened it and began looking through its contents. In the main compartment, he found a thick leather wallet containing cash and several credit cards.

Robbery doesn't appear to be the motive, Fink noted.

Mixed in with the credit cards, he found a Michigan driver's license issued to a Faye Olson of Ann Arbor. Fink studied the smiling face in the license photo, then looked again at the face of the victim – a match.

Surveying the rest of the house, Fink found a man's

blazer in the hall closet. He carefully probed the jacket and found what he was looking for. Fink extracted a thin bill-fold from an interior pocket and opened it. It still contained a significant amount of cash, credit cards, and a Michigan drivers license issued to Lloyd Sutton.

In the living room, Fink found several framed photographs on the walls and sitting atop end tables. A few of the pictures showed the two victims together with a large, African-American male.

'All right, people,' Fink announced to the assembled evidence technicians. 'I want this house run through a sieve. If there is anything in there that we can use to identify whoever did this, I want it found.'

The techs gathered their equipment and followed Fink into the house.

'Get a full series of both victims in situ. Do the woman first,' Fink commanded the photographer.

The photographer moved into the bedroom and began firing away with his camera. He took pictures of Olson from several different angles, amassing as complete a description of the crime scene as possible. He finished the roll with several close-up shots of the wounds on Olson's body.

In the living room, Fink oversaw the technicians at work. He felt the excitement of the hunt amid the whirl of activity around him.

'I'm done with the bodies,' the photographer announced as he left the kitchen.

'Great,' Fink replied. He then leaned out the front door. 'Beverly, we're ready for you in here.'

A woman with a curly mass of strawberry blond hair flowing out from a knit cap led a pair of young men with gurneys into the bungalow. Atop each gurney was a black rubber body bag.

'What a mess,' Washtenaw County Medical Examiner Beverly Porter declared as she surveyed the crime scene. 'Do we have an ID on the victims?'

'Yeah,' Fink replied. 'The woman is Faye Olson, the male is Lloyd Sutton.'

Porter filled out the toe tags for the bodies and handed them to her assistants. 'I'll get to work on these today. The rape kit will be on its way to the State Police crime lab later this afternoon.'

'Thanks, Beverly,' Fink replied. 'I appreciate it.'

17

Ann Arbor, Michigan

'*My ex-husband, Oz, stabbed me. I'm bleeding, bleeding all over. God, it hurts.*'

Fink rewound the 911 tape and listened to it again. In her last breaths, Faye Olson had put a name to her killer. As soon as he learned the victim had made the call to 911, he requested that a tape be made and run out to him at the crime scene.

The entire conversation was just a few seconds long, but it gave Fink a direction to follow. He popped the tape out of the dash, locked it in the glove box of his car, and walked back into Olson's house. It was almost dawn and the evidence technicians were still at work dusting for prints and taking samples.

'Anybody see anything like a personal phone book or a wedding album?' he asked.

'There's a phone book in the kitchen, in the drawer closest to the phone,' one of the techs replied. 'I saw a box in the small bedroom closet that had photo albums in it. What you're looking for might be in there.'

'Thanks.'

Fink stepped in the smaller of the two bedrooms and found the box. There were five thick albums inside. He thumbed through the first one and found pictures of Olson with the large man he'd seen in the picture in the living room. Both were younger in these pictures, mid-twenties at most.

In the third album, he found pictures of an outdoor wedding ceremony – the tall man had been Olson's husband. There was also a laminated copy of the engraved invitation for the wedding of Faye Elizabeth Olson and Oswald Raymond Eames.

Fink went to the kitchen and pulled Olson's phone book from the drawer. He flipped the book open to E and found what he was looking for at the top of the list. Eames lived in a condominium complex on Ann Arbor's south side. Fink copied down Eames's work and home information into a small notebook.

'Good morning, Detective,' the judge said as Fink entered his home. 'What can I do for you?'

'I need a search warrant, sir.'

'Can I get you a cup of coffee? My wife just put on a pot.'

'No, sir. I'm fine.'

The judge led Fink to his study and sat down behind an oak desk. Volumes of legal tomes lined the shelves around the room.

'Your Honor, there's been a double homicide at a home

in Ann Arbor – a man and a woman. There's evidence that the woman was raped as well. We have a suspect and I'd like a warrant to collect a blood sample.'

'Probable cause?'

Fink nodded. 'The suspect was ID'ed by one of the victims on a nine-one-one call.'

'Good enough.'

Fink pulled the warrant he'd drafted out of his pocket and handed it to the judge. The judge looked the document over, found everything in order, and signed it.

An Ann Arbor Police patrol car followed Fink's Chevrolet as he turned off Ellsworth into one of the bland industrial-research parks that proliferated near the municipal airport. The two cars pulled up in front of the sign that read UGENE.

'May I help you?' the receptionist asked politely as Fink and two uniformed officers stepped into the lobby.

'Yes, we're here to see Oswald Eames,' Fink replied.

'Can I ask what this is regarding?'

'It's police business.'

'He's off his phone. I can show you back to his office.'

The receptionist buzzed them through and led Fink and the patrolmen back to Eames's office. Fink immediately recognized Eames from the photographs in Olson's home. Eames stood from behind his desk and towered over Fink and the two uniformed officers.

'What can I do for you, gentlemen?' Eames asked genially.

'Oswald Eames,' Fink began, 'you have the right to remain silent.'

'Excuse me?' Eames asked in disbelief. 'Am I being arrested?'

'Yes, you are,' Fink replied.

Fink continued with the recitation of Eames's Miranda rights, his eyes locked on the scientist's face. Eames stared right back at him with bewildered anger.

'Do you understand these rights as I have explained them to you?' Fink asked.

Eames stood silent. For a brief instant, he had the feeling of being outside himself, observing the unreal scene. 'I understand my rights, Detective. What I don't understand is why.'

'You're under arrest for murder.'

'You have got to be kidding! I'm no murderer.'

'There's evidence that says otherwise.'

'Your evidence is fucked. Who am I accused of killing?'

'Faye Olson and Lloyd Sutton.'

Eames looked at Fink as if he hadn't understood. 'What? Faye and Lloyd are dead? But I just saw Lloyd yesterday. They're both dead? God, Jesus, no!'

Weeping, he sagged as if a heavy weight suddenly bore down on his shoulders, his legs too weak to support the load. He placed his hands on the desktop, bracing himself, then dropped into his chair. Between sobs, Eames moaned 'Jesus, no,' over and over.

To Fink and the two officers, Eames seemed oblivious of them, retreating into a sorrow that was either genuine or well presented for their benefit. Regardless of the nature of his grief, Fink directed the officers to cuff Eames's wrists and remove him to the squad car.

18

FEBRUARY 15, 1:45 PM

Ypsilanti, Michigan

'I want Sutton in the locker and Olson on the table,' Beverly Porter told her assistants upon their return to the Washtenaw County Medical Examiner's Office.

The gurneys carrying the bodies were wheeled away, and Porter entered the women's locker room and changed into surgical scrubs. She then pulled two evidence collection kits out of the supply closet and returned to the examination room. Olson's body lay on the stainless-steel table awaiting her. Porter slipped a new cassette into the recorder and switched the machine on.

'The victim is a Caucasian female in her early forties with shoulder-length blond hair and blue eyes.' Porter then measured Olson's height and weight. 'There are no distinguishing marks on the body. Bruising on and around the face indicates that the victim was struck repeatedly. Bruising and abrasions around the wrists indicate the victim was restrained during the attack.'

Porter then described in great detail each of the stab wounds inflicted on Olson's chest and abdomen. The final count numbered seventeen. Each of the wounds was deep, the result of a strong downward thrust from a right-handed attacker poised over the victim while she lay on her back.

'The depth of the wounds indicates the attacker possessed great physical strength,' she commented with professional detachment.

Porter opened the rape kit and laid out the tools she would use to collect forensic evidence from the victim's body. First, she took a sterile swab and carefully wiped the interior of Olson's mouth, collecting cells from both the victim and possibly her attacker. Porter smeared the tip of the swab against a glass slide, then placed the swab in a labeled, double-sealed envelope. The process was repeated with swabs of Olson's anus and vagina.

'The vaginal walls show significant bruising and tearing, indicating a forced entry,' Porter noted.

She unwrapped a plastic comb and carefully ran it through the tuft of blond hair around Olson's loins, collecting the loose hair in an envelope labeled *Pubic Hair Combings*. Mixed in with the blond hairs were several tightly curled strands of black. Porter sealed the envelope and placed it in the box.

Using a pair of plastic tweezers from the kit, Porter plucked several pubic hairs from Olson's body, which she placed in an envelope marked *Pubic Hair, Pulled*. She then repeated the procedure on the victim's head, plucking several strands of Olson's blond hair that she placed in an envelope marked *Head Hair, Pulled*. Porter then scraped Olson's fingernails and drew blood samples.

Porter carefully checked the body for any additional foreign matter, then repackaged and sealed the rape kit. She set a second rape kit on a wheeled metal tray table and rolled it over to the morgue. There, she pulled open the drawer that held Lloyd Sutton's body. Porter drew the white sheet that covered the body down past his groin and pulled several pubic and head hairs with the plastic tweezers from the kit. After drawing blood, she re-covered Sutton's body and slid the drawer closed.

After filling out the paperwork on the second kit, Porter picked up the phone and dialed an internal number.

'Hi, it's Beverly,' she said to one of her assistants. 'I finished the evidence kits on that double homicide. They're ready to go over to Northville.'

19

LV Station, Antarctica

'I think we got all we're going to get, Major,' Kilkenny said into Twin Otter's radio. 'Any other remains are either scattered outside our search grid or were buried by snow during that last squall.'

'All right, Kilkenny,' Saunders replied. 'Pack it in and head back.'

'Roger that. Out.'

Bright orange flags dotted the ice in front of Kilkenny, markers that described an imaginary grid laid over *Skier-98's* debris field. Square by square, Kilkenny and the crewmen assigned to him searched for the remains of the crew. It was a gruesome task made only a bit more tolerable by the sub-zero temperatures. It was simply too cold for decomposition to begin. What they found instead were the broken pieces of six men, scorched and frozen.

Two body bags in the hold of the small plane contained

135

all they could find in the twelve days since they located the wreck, five of which had been lost to weather.

The crash site at the end of the runway looked like a tent city with fabric windbreaks scattered over sections of the wreck as protection against the bone-chilling gusts. Behind the windbreaks, men armed with hammers, chisels, and heat guns worked at the ice. Pumps with insulated hoses drew off the fresh melt and quickly ejected it away from the site before it froze again. Saunders and his crew were fighting an uphill battle against a rock-hard mass of crystal-clear ice.

'The crew remains are on their way back to McMurdo,' Kilkenny announced after locating Saunders in a hole behind one of the windbreaks. 'How's it going here?'

'Sucks,' Saunders replied bitterly. 'This fuckin' wreckage is fused in the ice. With this cold it might as well be concrete.'

'Do we know anything more about this plane?'

Saunders spat on ice. 'Based on some of what we pulled out so far, I think it's a genuine LC-130. Unfortunately, we haven't located the plate.'

'The plate?'

'Yeah. Most planes are fitted with a unique identification plate by the manufacturer – it's like thc VIN plate on a car. You can change the tail number on a plane same as a license plate, but the ID number on the manufacturer's plate is forever. If we find it, we'll know exactly where this bird came from.'

'Major!' a man called out from one of the tents. 'We got something you should see.'

Kilkenny followed Saunders behind another wind-break.

Like archaeologists at a dig, the soldiers had marked off the site with orange string to form a grid. They were systematically excavating each square in their effort to recover the remains of the shattered aircraft. Each object they found in the ice was photographed in place, then removed and tagged for further analysis.

'Watch your step,' the soldier advised. 'It's a bit slick where we've been using the heat guns.'

A corner of a large mass of blackened and deformed metal protruded from a melted hole. Kilkenny saw a cast metal wheel and a section of caterpillar track.

'This sure isn't part of the plane, sir,' the soldier offered. 'What do you make of it?'

'The station wasn't equipped with any vehicles, Major, not even a snowmobile,' Kilkenny said.

'Based on what we know happened here, I'd say it's the SAM launcher.' Saunders looked closely at the tracks. 'Definitely not U.S. hardware, probably Russian or Chinese.'

'Major, how much of the aircraft's hold would the launcher have taken up?' Kilkenny asked.

'Most of it,' Saunders replied.

'Then that answers one of the big questions – the raiders got away with what they came for.' Kilkenny stared down at the ice surrounding the exposed corner of the launcher, then picked a hammer and struck it. The blow reverberated inside the launcher. 'Doesn't sound like much water got inside and I think I see a hatch under the ice. I want to take a look inside – maybe this thing has an ID plate, too.'

'You heard the man,' Saunders said. 'Let's move some ice.'

Kilkenny worked alongside the crewmen, tearing away at the ice. It took almost an hour to carve out a passage large enough for a man to reach the metal hatch. Kilkenny rapped on it with the hammer and still got a hollow return. He heated the edges of the hatch to melt the thin ice hidden in the crack, then sprayed the joints, hinges, and crank with a penetrating lubricant. The metal protested as he turned the crank and, slowly, the dogs holding the hatch closed released.

Kilkenny wriggled through the narrow opening and deliberately lowered himself inside the launcher. The floor of the vehicle tilted at an extreme angle and, in the lowest corner, he saw ice.

'Hand me a light and the camera,' Kilkenny called out.

The crewman reached through the opening with the equipment. Kilkenny switched the flashlight on and twisted the end for a wide beam. The launcher was like all the armored vehicles he'd ever been in – cramped and utilitarian. Slowly sweeping the interior with the light, Kilkenny carefully worked his way down toward the engine compartment in the rear. There, he located a thin steel ID plate fastened to the framing. The plate contained several numbers and the labels were in Cyrillic. Kilkenny snapped a few pictures, then climbed out.

'I want the pictures of that plate on a disk as soon as possible so I can get 'em to Langley. Maybe they can tell us where this thing came from.'

Kilkenny checked the message board in the operations module and found an urgent message from his father. He quickly calculated the seventeen-hour time difference and decided to take the chance on waking his father. The phone rang twice before Sean Kilkenny answered.

'Hey, Dad, it's Nolan. I got your message.'

'Oswald Eames was arrested this morning.' Sean's voice sounded numb and flat. 'He may have murdered his ex-wife and Lloyd Sutton.'

'Why do the police think Eames did it?'

'I don't know the specifics. He's being arraigned on Monday, but the media's playing this like an O.L. sequel. There's already been a protest because both victims were white and Eames is black. When are you getting back?'

'We're not scheduled to pull out until next week,' Nolan replied. 'Damn it! I could've caught a ride to McMurdo this morning, if I'd known. The flight schedules here are already screwed up because of the crash, but if I can swing something I'll try to leave sooner.'

'Do what you can, because as long as Eames is in jail, you're the acting CEO of UGene.'

20

'All rise,' the bailiff announced. 'The Fourteenth District Court of Washtenaw County is now in session. The Honorable Paulette Davis presiding.'

Davis ascended the platform, surveyed her courtroom, then struck the gavel and sat down.

'First case,' Davis said.

'The People versus Oswald Eames for the purpose of arraignment,' the clerk announced.

The clerk handed a thin file to Davis. From a secured corridor, Oswald Eames was led into the courtroom by two deputies. The prisoner, wearing an ill-fitting orange jumpsuit, towered over both of the officers. Eames was brought over to the table reserved for the defense counsel, where Tiv Balogh stood waiting for him.

'Good morning, Mr Balogh,' Eames said as the officers removed his handcuffs.

Balogh was a lightly built man who stood a full foot

shorter than his client. His head was completely free of hair except for a pair of dark gray eyebrows and a bushy mustache.

'Good morning, Oz,' Balogh replied. 'Let's see if we can't get you out of here today.'

'Very well,' Davis called out from the bench. 'In the matter of the People versus Oswald Eames. This is an arraignment hearing. Appearances for the record.'

A fortyish man about Balogh's height stood at the opposing counsel's table. 'Kurt McPherson for the prosecution, Your Honor.'

'Tiv Balogh for the defense, Your Honor. I have advised my client of his constitutional rights. We waive the formal reading of the information and my client stands mute to all charges.'

'I am entering a not guilty plea to all charges on behalf of the defendant,' Davis said as she scrawled a notation in the file. 'The defense may proceed with discovery. Now for the matter of bail. Mr McPherson?'

'Your Honor, due to the brutal nature of the crimes and our belief that the defendant is a flight risk, we request that no bail be granted.'

'Your Honor,' Balogh countered, 'while I agree with opposing counsel as to the nature of the crimes, my client has not yet been found guilty of them nor any other crime. My client is a respected scientist and he has no prior criminal history of any kind.'

Davis thought for a moment. 'The constitution permits me to hold a defendant in jail without bond for certain offenses, murder being one of them. The defendant is remanded to the Washtenaw County Sheriff.'

'Your Honor – '

'I have made my decision regarding bail,' Davis said, cutting him off. 'Moving on now to the matter of the preliminary examination. Mr Balogh?'

'Your Honor, I request that a preliminary examination be scheduled at the court's earliest convenience.'

'Very well.' Davis glanced down at the district court's calendar. 'The preliminary examination is set for the twenty-seventh of February at one o'clock.'

21

Langley, Virginia

Jackson Barnett looked over the report on the ID plate Kilkenny had found inside the SAM launcher. The U.S. designation for the weapon was the SA-17, though NATO referred to it more colorfully as a *Grizzly*.

Barnett's phone emitted an electronic purr and he picked up the handset. 'Yeah, Sally.'

'I have Igor Fydorov on the line.'

'Put him through.'

'Director Barnett, I understand you wish to speak with me.'

'Yes. There's a delicate matter we need to discuss regarding Russian military hardware being sold on the open market.'

'My country sells some of our weapons abroad, as does yours,' Fydorov replied matter-of-factly. 'For us, it is a good source of hard currency.'

'Yes, but I wasn't aware that your country was selling

its top lines. The specific weapon I'm referring to is a mobile surface-to-air missile system, what you call *Ural*. It was used to destroy one of our military aircraft. This unprovoked attack took place over peaceful, international airspace – something most civilized nations view as an act of war.'

'When did this happen?' Fydorov asked. Barnett had his undivided attention.

'A few weeks ago.'

Fydorov tried to recall any news about U.S. aircraft that crossed his desk recently. 'Antarctica?'

Like playing poker, Barnett carefully considered how much of his hand he would show. 'Yes.'

'I can assure you, my country had nothing to do with that.'

'I'm glad to hear it.'

'This weapon could have come from China or Belarus. We have been helping both countries upgrade their air defenses.'

'I'm afraid not. You see, we've recovered the launcher and it's definitely one of yours. If, as you say, Russia had nothing to do with this attack, then I'm sure you won't mind helping us determine how this weapon got into the hands of those who did.'

22

Livonia, Michigan

Leslie Siwik and her husband returned home from Jackson Hole a little stiff but otherwise pleased with their annual week on the Western slopes. She switched on the kitchen television and, as she started to unload her suitcase in the laundry room, heard a news anchor announce the arraignment of scientist-entrepreneur Oswald Eames for the murder of his partner and ex-wife.

Siwik rushed back to the kitchen as the newscast moved on to a three-car accident on the Lodge Freeway. Flipping through the other local channels, she caught the story again, this time with Eames standing before the judge wearing an orange prison jumpsuit at his arraignment. Stunned, Siwik then grabbed her phone and hit the speed dial.

'Please be there, please be there,' she pleaded like a mantra.

'Forensic biology unit,' a voice answered after the sixth ring.

145

'Art, thank God you haven't gone home,' Siwik blurted out. 'It's Leslie. I need you to do me a favor.'

'I was just on my way out, but sure, what?'

'Check the fridge in the Evidence Processing Area. I'm looking for anything that's come in from that double homicide in Ann Arbor.'

'The UGene thing?'

'Yes. They've arrested Oswald Eames for it.'

'No way! Not Oz,' Art said, disbelieving. 'Hold on, I'll take a look.'

The line went silent and Siwik waited nervously for an answer. A moment later, she heard a click and Art was back.

'Yeah, it looks like we got a couple kits and a blood draw.'

'Thanks, Art,' Siwik said, relieved. 'Leave the lights on, I'm coming in.'

'Should we even be handling this evidence? I mean, we both know Oz. Isn't this some kind of conflict of interest?'

'Not the way I see it. The crime happened in our part of the state, that's why the evidence came to us. And every other state lab has the same problem we have regarding personal knowledge of the suspect; without UGene we'd never have cut through our backlog. We could send the evidence to the feds, but it could be months before we get an answer, all the while leaving Oz in limbo.'

'But won't the prosecutor try to nail you for personal bias?'

'If I do my job right and keep the chain of evidence

intact, no one will be able to refute my findings. This is DNA, Art, I either make a match or I don't. The markers don't lie.'

Siwik returned to the lab that night and went to work on the materials from the Olson-Sutton murders with a single-minded attention to precise laboratory procedure. Her aim was nothing less than a perfect analysis of the forensic evidence.

As with any jigsaw puzzle, Siwik began by sorting out the pieces. The blood drawn from the two victims and Eames provided proof of identity, while the two evidence collection kits contained proof of the crime. She knew the crime in question on the lab bench before her was not murder but rape, and, as the two acts in this case were inextricably linked, proof of one was enough to imply guilt in the other.

From the rape kit, Siwik tested the swabs for the presence of acid phosphatase, an enzyme found in high concentration in seminal fluid. She detected no color change in the swabs from Olson's mouth and anus, but the vaginal swabs turned a pinkish purple color. She then applied the 'Christmas Tree' stain to the slides made from the vaginal swabs by the medical examiner.

Under the microscope, the epithelial cells swabbed from Olson's vagina appeared like green fried eggs with bright red yolks. Intermixed with the cells were a tangle of sperm with bright green tails. The sperm cells' red ovoid heads fluoresced under the light of the microscope, making it easy for Siwik to count the sperm cells present on the slide. The sperm count was good, providing more than enough DNA to identify the man responsible for leaving it behind inside Olson's body.

She also compared the pubic hairs collected from Olson's body with those pulled from Olson and Sutton. Most of the combed hairs belonged to the victim, but the remainder were similar enough for Siwik to conclude they came from one person, and that person was not Lloyd Sutton.

Through a process known as differential extraction, Siwik wrung the vaginal and sperm cells from one of the cotton swabs, then carefully separated the cells of the killer from those of his victim. She ruptured these cells with a lysing agent, causing them to disgorge their load of DNA, then ran both samples through a series of spin and rinse cycles. Each iteration refined and purified her samples of the precious coiled strands of genetic material.

After the last cycle, Siwik gently swirled a test tube freshly filled with *Tris-EDTA*. At the base of the tube, a small white pellet dissolved into the clear solution, and suspended in the preserving medium were the genetic blueprints of a man. As she stared into the tube, she prayed the microscopic strands would exonerate Oswald Eames.

She processed the blood samples in much the same manner as the cells harvested from the evidence collection kit. The case had yielded five distinct samples of DNA, four from known sources and one belonging to a murderer. Siwik's interest lay not in the six billion base pairs of the human genome, but rather in thirteen much smaller tracts of short tandem repeats known in forensic circles as the FBI's *CODIS Core STR Loci*.

Using a PCR machine, she amplified her samples, chemically replicating those selected tracts of DNA over and over until she had millions of tiny copies. Siwik loaded these into a 310 Genetic Analyzer and programmed the machine for an overnight run. In the darkness of the lab, the analyzer stretched out the tiny stands of DNA and meticulously read the STRs like supermarket bar codes with a ten milliwatt argon-ion laser.

On the morning of the fifth day of her investigation, Siwik returned to the lab and went straight to the genetic analyzer's ink-jet color printer. There she found several pages neatly piled in the output tray.

Siwik first checked the report for her experimental controls, samples of test DNA that provide known results, and was relieved to find that she hadn't screwed anything up and that the PCR machine had functioned properly. She then compared the chart for Olson's blood with that of the cells recovered from the swab. It was a perfect match, proving that both samples had come from Olson. The result wasn't unexpected, but it provided an additional check on her work.

In comparing Olson's blood with her assailant's semen, Siwik found no correlation for the core loci or the gender identifier, which meant that she'd successfully isolated the killer's DNA from that of his victim and the sample of unknown origin bore a clean genetic fingerprint.

Setting Olson's charts aside, Siwik compared Sutton's profile to that of the murderer. Both men registered X and Y chromosomes, but the length of the STRs indicated two different sets of parents. None of the thirteen core loci matched, proving that Sutton did not have sex with Olson prior to their murders.

'Now for you, Oz,' Siwik whispered hopefully.

Siwik laid the charts from Eames's blood sample on the counter next to those of the killer. She compared the first loci and her heart sank when she saw the match.

'Easy, girl,' she admonished herself. 'That's only one point. You've got twelve more to go.'

Point by point, she compared the two genetic profiles, and with each match found herself praying that the next would show something wildly different, something that would prove Oswald Eames's innocence. After nine points, Siwik began to feel a sickening inevitability. She knew the odds, and with each match the probability that both samples had come from the same man grew exponentially.

Tears welled up in her eyes as she moved her fingers to the last of the thirteen loci. As with all the others, they were identical. Siwik felt horrified and betrayed. The graphs illustrated the inescapable conclusion that Oswald Eames – a man she knew and liked, a brilliant scientist whom she viewed as both colleague and mentor – was guilty.

23

Langley, Virginia

Roxanne Tao stepped off the elevator onto the seventh floor of the CIA's original headquarters building. Dressed in a conservative gray suit, her long black hair drawn back with an ornamental clasp, Tao looked more like a vendor making a sales call on an important client than one of the agency's deep-cover agents.

'I have an appointment with DCI Barnett,' Tao announced curtly at the desk of Jackson Barnett's executive assistant.

Sally Kirsch looked up from her computer screen and glanced at the photo ID clipped to Tao's lapel. 'Please have a seat, Ms Tao. The director will be with you in a moment.'

Tao glanced at Kirsch's multiline phone to see if the Director of Central Intelligence was talking with someone. All the lights were dark. She turned away and sat in the reception area to await her audience.

During her career as an agent, she had spent most of her time in the field gathering intelligence. She had trained at the Farm, as did everyone who worked in the field, and had certainly visited the portion of the Langley campus that housed the Directorate of Operations, but this was her first trip to the hallowed seventh floor.

Tao was more annoyed than anxious over her summons to the DCI's office. She viewed much of what happened in the agency outside operations as bureaucracy – a necessary evil, but one to be avoided whenever possible.

'The director will see you now,' Kirsch said after the clock in the lower right corner of her computer screen reached 2:30 P.M.

Kirsch stood, opened the door she guarded, and lead Tao into the office. Barnett stood at his desk looking over a stack of files.

'These are ready to go back, Sally,' Barnett said, handing the files to Kirsch. 'Ms Tao, I'm so pleased to finally meet you.'

Tao shook Barnett's hand. 'And I you, Mr Barnett.'

'Let's sit over here,' Barnett said, indicating a pair of leather chairs arranged around a coffee table. 'Can we get you anything?'

'No, thank you, I'm fine. Why did you want to see me?'

'Straight to business, very well. You are here because the Deputy Director of Operations, a man for whom I have the utmost respect, has informed me of your demand for reassignment back in the field.'

'Yes, and the DDO has refused my request,' Tao said bitterly. 'He feels my talents are better utilized at the Farm training new agents.'

'He's right. I prefer to have people with real-world experience teaching the youngsters. Who better to knock those James Bond fantasies out of their heads and show them how to survive than someone who has been there.'

'I am *not* a school teacher,' Tao protested. 'I am a field agent.'

'You *were* a field agent, Ms Tao. One of our finest.'

'Then why won't you put me back where I belong?'

'Because it would be a fatal mistake.'

'You don't know that.'

'You were an illegal in China for over six years. Surviving in deep cover that long is an astonishing achievement, but you can never go back there.'

'All I need is new papers, a new identity.'

Barnett shook his head. 'We were lucky to get you out alive. The MSS played one of your operatives against you. Your cover was blown completely. They have your old identity papers, photographs of you, your fingerprints. You are a fugitive and an enemy of state. That kind of interest by the opposition makes it impossible to recycle you.'

'What about the rest of my network?' Tao asked. 'Chun knew only the one cell.'

'We are cautiously trying to reestablish contact, but it's dangerous for them and for us,' Barnett admitted. 'It will take years to replace your operation, but sending you back will make things worse. Miss Tao, your career in the People's Republic of China is over.'

Tao stifled a mix of rage and sorrow as she listened to Barnett's pronouncement. She'd left too many behind, not just agents but regular people whom she had encountered over the years – friends and even a lover. People who had no part in her work but were now seen as suspect by their government, as somehow contaminated by their innocent contact with her.

'I have given your situation some thought,' Barnett continued, 'and I have a proposition for you. A new assignment.'

'Let me guess,' Tao said sarcastically. 'Analysis: West Africa desk.'

As soon as she said it, Tao knew she'd crossed the line with Barnett.

'If that's what you'd like, I can arrange it.'

'No, sir,' Tao replied, her tone more respectful. 'What do you have in mind?'

'A job in the private sector.'

'You're firing me?'

'Reassigning you,' Barnett corrected her. 'The agency doesn't have the best track record predicting changes in technology. Commercial research and development is so liquid that we, as outsiders, have no way of keeping abreast of sudden developments. To address this short-coming, we created a small company in Silicon Valley. Its a private entity that invests in high-tech firms, works with universities, and forms joint ventures to help the agency keep up with new ideas.'

'I'm not an investment banker.'

'This is real intelligence work, and I think you are ideally suited for it. The difference here is that you'll operate in the open.' Barnett could sense Tao's resistance. 'If you want to stay with the agency, it's either this or the Farm. The choice is yours.'

'Some choice,' Tao said resignedly. 'When do you want me in California?'

'The job I have in mind for you isn't in California, it's in Michigan.'

'*Michigan?* What's in Michigan?'

Barnett ignored the question. 'I want you to open a branch office of this company in Ann Arbor. Initially, it will just be you. There's a man there I want you to meet. He has no formal ties to the agency, but he's worked with us a couple of times, and I think you'll find him to be a valuable resource.'

24

FEBRUARY 24

Christchurch, New Zealand

'You Kilkenny?' an air force captain in a black bomber jacket asked as Kilkenny stepped off *Skier-92*.

'Yeah.'

'Sir, I'm Captain Parker. The general asked me to pick you up as soon as you landed. Did you turn off the lights in McMurdo before you left?'

'They rolled the runway up right after we took off.'

Kilkenny and the crash investigation team were among the last people to leave Antarctica at the end of the summer season – continuing their work at LV Station until the falling temperatures that accompanied the approaching change of seasons forced them to abandon the crash site. They recovered enough of the wreckage to identify the plane as a C-130, but that was all they knew. The ID plate, which would have answered many of their questions, remained hidden in the ice. Saunders's team brought back what they could and photographed everything else in hopes that lab analysis would yet yield some crucial bit of information.

'Sir, there's been a change in your flight plan back to the States.'

'Why?' Kilkenny asked.

'I wasn't given that information, sir. All I know is that I'm to collect you and your gear and put you on a plane to Moscow.'

Upon his arrival at Sheremetyevo 2 International Airport the following morning, Kilkenny was met at the gate by a representative of the FSB, the Russian Federal Security Service. With a wave of his badge, the man walked Kilkenny through customs and out into a waiting car. Forty minutes later, Kilkenny arrived at Lubyanka and was ushered to the office of FSB Director Igor Sergeevich Fydorov.

'Welcome back to Moscow, Nolan Seanovich,' Fydorov said warmly.

'Thank you. This office looks a little bigger than the one you had last summer.'

Fydorov nodded; the new office was befitting of his position. 'In the aftermath of our dealings with that pig Orlov, I was recognized by higher powers and promoted. I guess I have you to thank, or blame, depending on how much paperwork is heaped on my new desk.'

'A small price to pay for bagging that parasite.'

'Agreed. And for that, you still have my thanks. Have you been told why you're here?'

'No.'

'We have uncovered some information regarding the

missile launcher you found in Antarctica. Jackson Barnett and I thought it best that someone from your country be present at this meeting.'

'I may be a bit underdressed for the part,' Kilkenny said. In a heavy Irish wool sweater, jeans, and hiking boots, he looked more like an Aran Island fisherman than an employee of the U.S. State Department.

'For what I have in mind, you are perfect,' Fydorov assured him.

'Who are we meeting with?'

'A general. It should be quite interesting. Because of this individual's high rank, I will be conducting the interrogation.'

From a course in Russian history he'd taken in college, Kilkenny knew that before the revolution, Lubyanka had been the home of an insurance company. The building then became the headquarters of the secret police and, in its bowels, a prison for enemies of the state. Kilkenny wasn't sure if anyone still languished in the subterranean levels of the building, but he was relieved when the elevator he was on stopped at the second floor.

Fydorov led him into a well-appointed conference room. There were four men in the room, three in civilian clothes. The fourth wore the dress uniform of a Russian general.

'Your embassy has loaned us a translator so you can follow this proceeding,' Fydorov said, indicating a man in his mid-twenties standing alone. 'You will sit here, beside me.'

'Who are the guys with the general?'

'Security.'

Fydorov called the room to order. The general sat alone on one side of the conference table; Fydorov, Kilkenny, and the translator on the other. The two security men stepped outside.

'Please state your name,' Fydorov said.

'Lieutenant General Anatoly Dubinsky.' The general's shoulder boards held two stars.

'What is your current posting, General?'

'Currently, I am on administrative leave pending the outcome of this investigation,' Dubinsky said smugly.

'Your previous posting, then.'

'Command of the Northwestern Zone.'

Fydorov glanced at his notes. 'Based in St Petersburg. A prestigious posting, wouldn't you say, General?'

'Yes, it is,' Dubinsky replied. The man's voice betrayed no emotion.

'As I understand it, zone command is an essential stepping stone to a posting in the Ministry of Defense, is it not?'

'I believe so.'

'What were some of the units under your command?'

'The Sixth Combined Arms Army, the Thirtieth Army Corps, Fifty-sixth District Training, and several smaller units. Do you wish me to go on?'

'That won't be necessary,' Fydorov conceded. 'Did any of your forces utilize surface-to-air missile defense systems?'

'Of course. The Northwestern Zone borders on Finland, Estonia, and the Baltic. We are well within range of NATO.'

'In maintaining readiness to defend the motherland, troops under your command train regularly, no?'

Dubinsky shrugged. 'We train as much as our funding permits.'

'Would such training include firing of surface-to-air missiles?'

'Yes, but given the cost of missiles, we don't fire them all that often.'

Fydorov opened a folder and pulled out a typed sheet of paper, which he slid across the table to Dubinsky. 'Can you tell me what this is?'

Dubinsky scanned the sheet. 'It is a report to the Ministry regarding the destruction of a *Ural* launcher during training late last summer.'

'Do you recall the specifics of this loss?'

'One of the missiles exploded while still attached to the vehicle, detonating the other three. The crew was lost along with the vehicle.'

'A tragedy. What became of the wreckage?'

'I don't know. I assume it was scrapped.'

Fydorov scrawled a few notes, then pulled out several color prints and laid them on the table in front of Dubinsky. At a glance, Kilkenny recognized them.

'General, do you know what this is?'

Dubinsky studied the images of a vehicle with caterpillar tracks locked in ice. He paled, but quickly recovered. 'I am not certain. It is difficult to tell what I am looking at.'

'Don't trouble yourself. My colleague has already gone through a great difficulty identifying this piece of equipment. Nolan, would you enlighten the general as to what it is and where you found it?'

'It's one of your *Ural* launchers. We recovered it in Antarctica shortly after it was used to shoot down a U.S. military transport.'

'General, are you aware that the presence of this weapon in Antarctica is a violation of international treaty?' Fydorov asked. 'Also, that its use in a purely offensive manner to destroy another country's aircraft may well be considered an act of war?'

'I know nothing of this.'

'Really?' Fydorov asked. 'I was hoping you could answer a question my colleague uncovered. You see, General, the serial numbers inside this vehicle match those of the one you reported destroyed last summer.'

'What are you accusing me of?' Dubinsky demanded.

'The exact charges to be brought against you will depend greatly on how well you answer my questions. Whether you live long enough to face charges is another matter entirely.'

'Comrade Director, are you threatening me?'

'No. But at some point during this interview, I may need to leave for a moment. My colleague would, of course, remain to keep you company.'

Fydorov paused to let the translator catch up. Kilkenny quickly realized that his host was setting the general up for a round of good cop-bad cop. He nodded for Fydorov to continue.

'In the event this occurs, I feel I should warn you about two things. First, this man represents a powerful nation that is understandably upset and looking for someone to blame. Second, if you haven't already guessed from the way he is dressed, this man is not a diplomat.'

The translator's eyes widened as he repeated Fydorov's last statement in English. 'Excuse me,' he interjected nervously, 'but I can't be a party to human rights violations.'

'No one asked you to be,' Kilkenny shot back. 'Any *conversation* I might have with the general about this launcher and the eight Americans it was used to kill won't require a translator.'

Fydorov translated the exchange for the general in both tone and content. 'And just so you see the situation clearly,' Fydorov continued, 'I have been authorized by our president to employ whatever means necessary to get to the truth of this matter. This includes allowing this man to question you privately.'

'You are bluffing!' Dubinsky scoffed.

'Am I?' Fydorov pushed his chair away from the table and stood up. 'You are not taking this matter as seriously as I am, Comrade General.'

'That's your cue to leave,' Kilkenny told the translator.

Without a word, the translator scurried out the door behind Fydorov, leaving Kilkenny alone with the general. They studied each other warily. Kilkenny guessed Dubinsky was in his mid-fifties. He was short and thickly built, outweighing Kilkenny by a good thirty pounds. Dubinsky stood, placed his palms on the table, and looked down at Kilkenny.

'You do not frighten me,' Dubinsky declared in slow, careful English. '*Yop t'voi yo mat.*'

Kilkenny's hands were on Dubinsky's chest as the last

syllable of the Russian profanity left the general's mouth. A second later, Dubinsky was airborne. Kilkenny yanked him off his feet and lifted him over the table. He held the general overhead just long enough to see that the man was sufficiently in fear of his life before slamming him down.

Dubinsky lay stunned and hyperventilating, his eyes wide with panic. Kilkenny pressed two fingers into the general's fleshy throat, just below his Adam's apple. Dubinsky began to choke.

'I don't know much Russian,' Kilkenny said sternly, 'but I know what you just said, and nobody talks that way about my mother. Understand?'

Dubinsky's head moved in short, quivering nods.

'Now, do you want to answer my questions?'

More quivering nods. Kilkenny eased the pressure on Dubinsky's throat.

'You've been selling your equipment, haven't you?'

'Yes,' Dubinsky spat out. 'Black market.'

'Who bought the launcher?'

Kilkenny could see that the general was weighing his options. He pressed his fingers in a little harder.

'If it helps you decide, General, consider this. Right now, I'm your biggest problem. If you give me a name, you live, and I become your buyer's biggest problem.'

'Black market,' Dubinsky gasped. 'Arms dealer ... Stepan Agabashian.'

25

Ann Arbor, Michigan

The county deputies brought Oswald Eames into the small courtroom in the Service Center. Instead of an orange prisoner's jumpsuit, he wore a shirt and tie, black pants, and a blazer. At the defense table, the deputies removed his restraints and left him with his attorney, Tiv Balogh.

'Good afternoon, Oz,' Balogh said politely.

Eames nodded, then glanced at the prosecutor. McPherson sat at his table looking over some notes on a yellow legal pad. On the bench, he saw a different judge than the one who had arraigned him.

Eames leaned close to Balogh. 'What happened to our judge?'

Balogh looked puzzled for a moment, then smiled when he realized what Eames was really asking. 'Nothing happened. Preliminary exams are assigned to judges on a rotating basis. Judge Thacker drew us today. Don't worry about it,' he added reassuringly. 'It's not a problem.'

'The People versus Oswald Eames for the purpose of a preliminary examination,' the bailiff announced.

'Appearances for the record,' Thacker said.

Balogh and McPherson identified themselves, their statements transcribed by the court recorder.

'Mr McPherson, you may call your first witness.'

'Thank you, Your Honor. The state calls Irene Yale.'

Yale entered the courtroom from the hallway and walked up to the witness stand. She was a small woman in her late twenties dressed in a colorful print dress, her hair pulled closely against her head in a pattern of tightly woven black braids. The bailiff swore her in and she sat down.

'Please state your name and address for the record,' McPherson said.

Yale recited her name and address clearly into the microphone.

'Miss Yale, where do you work?' McPherson asked.

'I'm an emergency dispatch operator for the city of Ann Arbor.'

'And how long have you worked there?'

'Four years.'

'You were working on the night of February fifteenth, were you not?'

'Yes, I had the late shift that night.'

'I see. Do you recall receiving a call that night from a woman claiming that she'd been stabbed?'

'Yes.' Yale's voice faltered, the woman's voice still echoing in her memory.

'Did the woman identify her attacker?'

'Yes, she did.'

'Whom did she name?'

'Her ex-husband, a man named Oz.'

'Your Honor, I have a copy of that conversation between Miss Yale and Faye Olson that confirms this testimony,' McPherson said. 'I have no further questions for this witness.'

'Your witness, Mr Balogh.'

'Thank you, Your Honor. Miss Yale, do you know Faye Olson?'

'No.'

'So it would be fair to say that you wouldn't recognize her voice if she called you?'

'I don't understand.'

'If Faye Olson called you at your home, you wouldn't recognize her voice, would you?'

'How could she? She's dead?'

'What I'm trying to get at, Miss Yale, is that prior to February fifteenth, you would have no way of knowing what Faye Olson sounded like, correct?'

'Yes.'

'So when that call came in on the fifteenth, you had no way of knowing if the caller was indeed Faye Olson, because you'd never heard her voice before, correct?'

'I just assumed that – '

'And that's the problem. In a court of law, it's not what you assume but what you know for a fact. For example, you know for a fact that you received a nine-one-one call from 4731 Pineview. Your computer traces a call once it comes in, correct?'

'Yes.'

'And in that call, you heard a woman who said she'd been stabbed?'

'Yes.'

'But you have no way of knowing if that woman was Faye Olson or someone claiming to be her?'

'I guess I . . . no, I can't say for sure who actually made the call.'

'That's all, Your Honor.'

'Redirect?' Thacker asked.

'No, Your Honor.'

'Then the witness may step down. Next witness, Mr McPherson.'

'The state calls Detective J. R. Fink.'

Fink entered the courtroom and walked directly to the stand, where he was sworn in and recited his name and address for the record.

'Detective, could you describe what you found at 4731 Pineview early on the morning of February fifteenth?'

'I arrived at the scene around two-thirty in the morning. The house had been secured by two Ann Arbor police officers. Inside the house, I found the bodies of two victims, a man and a woman whom we've identified as Lloyd Sutton and Faye Olson. Sutton's body was in the kitchen, lying facedown on the floor with a wound to the throat. Olson's body was in the bedroom. Her body was nude and there were several stab wounds to her torso. She also appeared to have been sexually assaulted, which the medical examiner confirmed.'

'Was there a phone in the bedroom?'

'Yes.'

'What kind of phone was it?'

'Cordless.'

'Was the handset in the charging stand?'

'No, it was on the floor.'

'Did it look like someone placed it there?'

'No. It looked like it had been dropped. The phone was on its side and the battery door was broken off.'

'Did it appear that the victim, Miss Olson, had used the phone?'

'Yes. The evidence technicians found bloody fingerprints on the phone that matched the victim. Also, the position of the body was such that it appeared that she pulled herself over to the nightstand to reach the phone. Her hand was near the edge of the bed, just above where the phone was found on the floor.'

McPherson smiled and looked up at the bench. 'That's all for this witness, Your Honor.'

'Mr Balogh.'

'Detective, were any other fingerprints found on the phone in the bedroom?'

'No, just the victim's.'

'Let me be a bit more explicit. Were there several of the victim's fingerprints on the phone – after all, it was her phone – or just the bloodstained ones from the night of the murders?'

'I believe only the one set of prints was found.'

'The one set being those left by the victim after she'd been stabbed?'

'Yes.'

'Don't you find that a bit odd? Unless the victim wiped her phone clean earlier that day, I would think the evidence technicians would have found multiple prints layered over the phone.'

'Your Honor,' McPherson said. 'Where's defense counsel going with this?'

'I was wondering the same thing, Mr Balogh.'

'I'll get to the point, Your Honor,' Balogh replied. 'Detective, do you know for a fact that Faye Olson and not some other individual placed the call to nine-one-one?'

'No.'

'That's all, Your Honor.'

McPherson declined an opportunity to ask further questions of the detective and Fink was excused.

'Do you have anything else, Mr McPherson?' Thacker asked.

'Just one more thing, Your Honor,' McPherson replied. 'A report from the Michigan State Police Crime Lab in Northville shows the blood drawn from Oswald Eames and the semen found at the crime scene are a perfect DNA match.'

McPherson handed a copy of the report to Thacker and Balogh. Eames opened the report and studied the four sheets of graphs that described the thirteen loci analyzed by the crime lab. Each spike was identical in location and magnitude. Eames became light-headed and felt like vomiting.

'This can't be right,' Eames said softly. 'It just can't be right.'

Thacker looked up from his copy of the lab report. 'Based on the evidence presented, I believe the state has cause to proceed. I'm ordering the defendant bound over for trial in the Washtenaw County Circuit Court.'

26

The door on the prisoner's side of the visitation room opened and a deputy ushered in Oswald Eames. He was dressed in an orange jumpsuit that was at least one size too small. Eames nodded to the deputy politely and walked over to the Plexiglas window.

'Nolan, this is quite a surprise,' Eames said as he sat down. 'I was expecting my lawyer. When did you get back?'

'Late last night. I . . .' Kilkenny stopped, struck by the irrelevant direction of this conversation. 'Look, I was in the back of the courtroom today.'

Eames sighed. 'Didn't go so good in there, did it?'

'No, it didn't.'

'I swear to God I didn't kill Faye and Lloyd,' Eames said passionately.

'After what I heard in court, I'm having a *real* hard time believing that. If you didn't do it, how the hell did they get a DNA match on you?'

'Lab error,' Eames shot back. 'It's the only way.'

'Didn't you and Lloyd just help the state police make their lab procedures damn near perfect?'

'Yeah,' Eames replied defensively.

'So you're either a murderer or a lousy consultant. Either way your reputation is toast. At least you're not claiming this is all a police frame job.'

'Fuck-ups are lot easier than conspiracies to pull off.'

Through the window, Eames looked angry and frightened. 'You think I did it.'

'You know I have to consider that a possibility. At this point, I'm honestly not sure what the hell I think.'

'Are you going to pull the plug on UGene?'

'No, the company's too big for that now. I'll run things until this is all sorted out, then we'll decide what to do from there. I have to take care of the shareholders.'

'What few there are left.'

'The sellers were mostly speculators – they would've bailed as soon as the next big thing showed up. The real investors, the ones who understand our business, are in for the long haul. Admittedly, losing both Lloyd and you would be a terrible hit, but we'd find some way to recover from it.'

A deputy opened the door behind Kilkenny and Eames's lawyer entered the room.

'You must be Nolan Kilkenny,' Balogh said as he approached. 'I saw a picture of you in your father's office. I'm Tiv Balogh.'

Kilkenny shook Balogh's hand. 'I've been a bit out of the loop. What's the situation?'

Balogh pulled up a chair and sat beside Kilkenny in front of the Plexiglas window. 'Mr Eames was arraigned on two counts of first-degree murder and one count of criminal sexual conduct involving penetration.'

'Where are we in the case?' Kilkenny asked. 'Does it go to trial next?'

'No. We're in the discovery phase right now, going through everything the prosecution has and looking for ways to build a defense. The next formal proceeding is the final examination. If I can find any holes in the prosecution's case – improper handling of evidence or violations of my client's rights – I'll file motions with the court. If I can't stop things there, then we go to trial.'

'What about the DNA test?' Kilkenny asked. 'Doesn't that pretty much trump everything else?'

'It's true that the courts view DNA testing as highly reliable,' Balogh replied, 'but there's always the possibility of lab error or contamination of the samples.'

'There has to be something wrong with the lab work,' Eames said.

'If there is, I assure you I'll find it. Actually, I was quite surprised that the prosecution brought up the DNA tests so early in the game.'

'Why?' Kilkenny asked.

'Trial law is all about strategy. As you said, DNA evidence is a trump card, one the prosecution normally holds back until the trial. By presenting it now, the prosecution has told me they don't have much else to support their case. It won't be easy to get the DNA test thrown out, but I'll do what I can to raise a reasonable doubt.'

27

MARCH 4

'Good morning, Nolan,' Loretta Quinn said as Kilkenny entered the MARC executive suite. 'You can go right in, they're expecting you.'

'Thanks.'

Kilkenny walked into the main conference room. He didn't recognize the woman his father was talking with. On the wall monitor he saw Jackson Barnett seated at a conference table at the CIA's campus in Langley. 'Good to see you again, though it's a bit of a surprise.'

'Oh, really?' Barnett said.

'According to the memo I got, my father and I are supposed to be meeting with a new business partner.'

'That's right,' Barnett confirmed.

'Nolan's been thrust into a hands-on management situation at one of our companies,' Sean Kilkenny explained. 'It's keeping him pretty busy, so he's been out of the loop on our previous discussions.'

'Nolan,' Barnett said, 'I'd like to introduce my associate, Roxanne Tao.'

Tao offered her hand. 'A pleasure to meet you,' she said with cool formality.

Nolan guessed Tao to be in her late twenties or early thirties. She was dressed in a stylish blue suit and little makeup. A mane of glossy black hair ran straight down, six inches past her shoulders, framing an oval face whose most striking feature was a pair of intense black almond-shaped eyes.

'Let's have a seat,' Sean said.

Tao sat opposite of Nolan and though she faced him, he got the impression that she was looking beyond at the winter landscape outside. Her body language signaled her displeasure at being here.

'Nolan,' Barnett began, 'I'm sure you recall that after that business with your physicist, we had a brief discussion about developing a working relationship between the CIA and yourself – an arrangement that would provide the agency with a means of acquiring an understanding of rapidly evolving technologies without compromising your position here at MARC.'

'I remember that conversation,' Nolan said.

'A few years ago, the CIA financed a venture capital firm in Silicon Valley for purposes similar to what we discussed. That firm has done quite well and is currently self-sufficient. After a few exploratory conversations with the partners of that firm, we decided the best course would be to open a one-person branch office. Of course, the key to success here would be finding the right person for the job. Roxanne, if you please.'

Tao pulled a thin titanium wallet from her blazer and extracted two business cards, which she handed to Nolan and his father. The glossy red cards were oriented vertically, with Tao's name and contact information listed in crisp black type. The upper half of the card contained two large black letters – *Qi*.

'Is this pronounced *cue-eye* or *key*?' Kilkenny asked, admiring the card's graphic design.

'*Key*. It's Chinese. Are you familiar with the term?' Tao asked condescendingly.

'It's the body's inner energy.'

Tao nodded.

'The name is also something of a double entendre,' Barnett admitted with a smile. 'The letter *i* stands for intelligence, which is what Roxanne is to gather. *Q* is in honor of Ian Fleming's master gadget maker.'

'So, how's this going to work?' Kilkenny asked.

'Qi is going to partner with us on some of our investments,' Sean explained. 'Their small stake will provide them with the ability to independently assess evolving technologies and the players in various fields of research and development.'

'These assessments will be the product Roxanne provides to the CIA,' Barnett added.

'And this can be done without violating any of our confidentiality agreements?' Nolan asked.

'I've run this past the Attorney General and, as long as Roxanne's assessments stay within certain guidelines, there's no legal problem.'

'Nolan,' Sean said, 'given your preexisting relationship with the CIA, you're obviously going to be our interface with Qi. I've already made lease arrangements for Ms Tao – she'll be moving into the office next to yours.'

'I believe that about wraps things up,' Barnett said. 'Sean, it has been a pleasure doing business with you. Nolan, I'll leave Roxanne in your capable hands. I'm certain you will find her to be an intelligent and resourceful collaborator.'

After Barnett signed off, Tao turned to Kilkenny. 'Why don't you show me my office.'

'All right,' Kilkenny agreed. 'I'll even throw in the nickel tour of our building.'

'The price sounds about right.'

Kilkenny eyed Tao for a second, looking for a hint that her somewhat snide comment was actually a joke. All he found were a pair of angry black eyes and tightly drawn lips. He motioned down the main corridor and she walked beside him. In heels, Tao stood about half a head shorter than Kilkenny. She nodded politely when he pointed out a feature of interest, but hardly slowed as if hastening the tour to its end.

'This is our computer center,' Kilkenny said as he swiped his key card through the reader and opened the door. 'In addition to our internal network of various types of machines, we have a pair of super computers that we lease time on to various researchers.'

Bill Grinelli stepped out of his office with a thick computer manual in one hand and a cup of coffee in the other. He was dressed in jeans, hiking boots, a black T-shirt, and an embroidered satin tour jacket from his brief stint as a roadie for The Pretenders. The jacket sleeves were rolled back to his elbows. His graying brown hair was pulled back in a ponytail and his goatee trimmed to a neat point beneath his chin.

'I thought I heard voices,' Grinelli said warmly.

'You mean other than the usual ones?' Kilkenny asked. 'Roxanne Tao, this is Bill Grinelli – he's the guy who keeps all our computers running. I think you'll find him to be one of MARC's most valuable resources.'

Grinelli walked up to Tao and smiled. 'Just call me Grin.'

'A pleasure, Mr Grinelli,' Tao replied, deliberately avoiding the informality.

'Roxanne's leasing that office next to mine,' Kilkenny said. 'When do you think you can get her hooked up?'

'The phones and data are already done,' Grin replied. 'Are we supplying the computer hardware?'

'No, but I'll let you know when my equipment arrives.'

Grin caught Tao's eyes dropping to the tattoo that he sported on his left forearm of a mythological Pan seated on a crescent moon scattering pixie dust.

'Do you like my art?' Grin asked, turning his arm to give Tao a clean view.

'I'm not really a fan of that sort of decoration. Is there any significance to it, or is it the result of a drunken bet?'

'This was a gift from my lady, and it has great significance to me,' Grin replied, his voice cool and steady. 'It's a reminder that there's still some magic left in the world, despite the efforts of those who try to take the fun out of life.'

Taken slightly aback, Tao locked eyes with the MARC computer guru, but offered no further provocation. Kilkenny wondered what kind of person would go out of her way to antagonize someone as warm and congenial as Grin.

'I think we've taken enough of Grin's time, Roxanne,' Kilkenny interjected. 'Shall we move on?'

'Yes,' Tao replied icily.

As Tao turned toward the door, Grin gave Kilkenny a puzzled look that asked 'What's her problem?' Kilkenny shrugged his shoulders – he honestly didn't have a clue. Grin pivoted on his heel and retreated to the semicircular console in the center of the room.

'Good luck,' Grin said as Kilkenny followed Tao out the door.

'What did he mean when he wished you good luck?' Tao asked as they walked down the corridor. 'I hope it wasn't some remnant of adolescent bravado.'

'I'm sure he was just wishing you well in your work here,' Kilkenny lied. 'Your office is the next door on the right.'

The sign beside the door bore the *Qi* logo. Kilkenny opened the door and let Tao enter first. The room was empty except for a phone that sat on the floor. Tao walked up to the window and stared out at the gently falling snow.

'If you like, I can arrange to get some furniture in here on loan until you get things sorted out,' Kilkenny offered.

'Thank you,' Tao replied, her gaze still fixed through the window.

Kilkenny closed the door and walked over to the window. 'When Barnett and I spoke last week, he mentioned that he was sending you. Care to discuss the ground rules?'

Tao faced Kilkenny. 'The structure of our working relationship is very simple – I'm your control. I run the show.'

'No.'

Tao's eyes narrowed. 'No?'

'That's right, Roxanne, I said no. With regards to me, you aren't running a damn thing. I'm not an agent. I don't work for you or the CIA. Whenever I come across something of interest to the agency, I pass it on to you. That's why you're here.'

'You seem to have an overinflated opinion of your worth to the CIA.'

'I'd say my opinion reflects fair market value, but if you want another, just ask Barnett.'

Tao glared with icy silence and Kilkenny realized he'd struck a nerve. Her problem wasn't with him, but with her new job as his liaison with the agency.

'You didn't volunteer for this, did you?' Kilkenny asked.

'No, I did not,' Tao replied bitterly. 'Who in their right mind would *want* to come here? I was in the field for nearly seven years and now I've been sent to a midwestern college town to write reports.'

'Barnett picked you for this job because of your field experience, not your typing skills.'

'Excuse me?'

'You spent the past week in California learning how to be a venture capitalist, right?'

'Yes.'

'Good, because that's ninety percent of what you'll be doing around here.'

'What's the other ten percent, filing and dictation?'

'Barnett asked me to tell you about that when we had some time alone.'

Kilkenny then briefed Tao on the attack at LV Station, the effort to recover evidence from the ice-locked wreckage, and his journey back home by way of Moscow.

'Do you have anything on this arms dealer who bought the Russian launcher yet?' Tao asked.

'Barnett's heard of Agabashian,' Kilkenny replied, 'and he's got some people trying to get a fix on his whereabouts.'

'So, we're in a hold on that.'

'The other lead I want to check out is the planes. The major running the crash investigation was pretty sure it was a Hercules, but without the plane's ID plate he couldn't verify it. Did you know over sixty countries fly C-130s in one form or another, and that most of these planes are still in service?'

'Which means it's going to be difficult, if not impossible, to know just where the two used in Antarctica came from?'

'Maybe. The version we're interested in is the LC-130. According to the guys currently flying these planes, it's not the easiest thing in the world to land something that big on the ice. Also, Lockheed only built a few LC-130s, and the U.S. is the only country to fly them. Since there aren't that many of these planes, there can't be that many experienced flight crews.'

'What are you getting at?' Tao asked.

'Simplicity. The people behind the attack could have modified a C-130 and trained a crew, but both of these jobs would have taken a lot of time.'

'What's the alternative?'

'Hire two experienced crews and acquire a pair of real

LC-130s. The navy used to have a squadron that flew these planes in Antarctica. It was disbanded a few years back, but those pilots are still out there somewhere.'

'And the planes?'

'I got a line on those,' Kilkenny answered, 'but it'll require a trip to Waco and Tucson to check it out. This kind of thing is the real reason Barnett sent you here. It may not be as glamorous as whatever you were doing before, but it's damn important.'

'My previous posting was a lot of things, but only in rare instances would I have ever used the word glamorous.'

28

Waco, Texas

Kilkenny and Tao took a nonstop flight from Detroit to Dallas, then caught an American Eagle commuter flight for the last leg of their journey to Waco. Only two businessmen boarded the twin-engine turboprop for the short flight. Both seated themselves near the front, several rows ahead of Kilkenny and Tao.

En route to Waco, Tao opened a package she'd been given by a courier upon their arrival at the Dallas-Fort Worth International Airport and pulled out two ID wallets and a page of contact information.

'Here,' Tao said, handing Kilkenny one of the wallets.

Kilkenny flipped open the wallet and found an FBI identification card with his name and face on it. He leaned closer to Tao.

'Won't the folks at the FBI take exception to our imper-sonating a pair of agents?' Kilkenny said, his voice barely audible under the drone of the plane's engines.

'What they don't know won't hurt them,' Tao replied nonchalantly as she checked her false credentials. 'This will do.' She flipped the wallet closed and turned toward Kilkenny. 'The agency has an arrangement for this sort of thing, just so long as we don't abuse the privilege.'

'Or cause the FBI any bad publicity.'

'You catch on quick. Our cover story doesn't stray far from the truth. You and I *are* investigating the report that two planes are missing from the government's inventory.'

'Since you seem to have some experience in role play, I'll follow your lead.'

'You and I are going to get along just fine,' Tao said.

The turboprop dropped out of a cloudless sky and touched down at Waco Regional Airport late in the afternoon. After collecting their carry-on bags, Kilkenny and Tao picked up a rental car and drove around to the opposite side of the airport. In a large, fenced-in compound stood the immense white hangars of Raytheon's Aircraft Integration Systems facility.

Kilkenny brought the Taurus to a stop at the main gate and a blue-uniformed security guard slipped open the side window and leaned out slightly.

'Can I help you?' she drawled sweetly.

'Miss, we're with the FBI,' Kilkenny said, offering his fake credentials.

The sweetness quickly turned to wary suspicion. 'What's the purpose of your visit?'

Tao skimmed through the page that had accompanied the ID wallets. 'We're here to see an AIS manager named

David Boyer regarding some planes that are undergoing a retrofit, and no, we don't have an appointment.'

'One moment,' the security guard said before quickly sliding her window shut.

The guard rang her supervisor to explain the situation, her eyes taking nervous glances at Kilkenny and Tao. A moment later, a small white car pulled up on the opposite side of the main gate, then did a U-turn and parked. An overweight man in tan pants and a blue blazer stepped out and walked around the gate to the Taurus.

'Good afternoon,' he said politely. 'May I see your credentials?'

Kilkenny and Tao handed over their ID wallets. The man scrutinized both carefully, then pulled out a cell phone. He stepped away from the Taurus as he waited for his call to be answered, then read off the information from their IDs. A bead of sweat trickled down Kilkenny's neck as he waited. Tao appeared unaffected.

The man thanked the person on the other end, rang off, and walked back to the Taurus.

'Sorry about the delay, folks,' he said as he handed back their IDs. 'We gotta check, you understand.'

'Of course,' Kilkenny replied, dismissing the wait as a minor inconvenience.

'If you'll follow me, I'll take you over to the modification hangar.'

The security chief motioned for the guard to open the gate, then led them into the compound. He pulled beside one of the buildings, and Kilkenny parked in the adjacent space.

'This way,' the security chief said as he swiped his ID card through a reader and opened the door.

The modification hangar contained over eighty-four thousand square feet of area, nearly all of which was the open floor beneath a volume of undisturbed space large enough to hold several aircraft.

'This is what we came to see,' Kilkenny said to Tao, pointing out a wide ski mounted beneath the nose of a military transport.

The security chief led Kilkenny and Tao to a small office on the hangar's far wall. The man inside waved as they approached.

'Sir,' the security chief said as he opened the office door, 'I have some people here who'd like to have a word with you.'

'Send 'em on in,' Boyer replied.

The security chief stepped aside, allowing Kilkenny and Tao to enter Boyer's office. The rumpled senior engineer was ensconced in a disheveled collection of blueprints, technical manuals, computer equipment, and other miscellany.

'Mr Boyer, I'm Special Agent Tao and this is my partner, Special Agent Kilkenny. We're here to investigate the whereabouts of three Lockheed LC-130s that were reportedly flown here from the ASRF facility in Arizona. Are you familiar with these planes?'

'Familiar?' Boyer replied with a snort. 'Ma'am, I have done nothing but eat, sleep, and breathe those three planes for the last couple of months, and I don't expect to have the last of 'em out of my gray hair until summer.' Boyer pointed out his office window. 'There they are.'

'When did the planes first arrive?' Kilkenny asked.

'They were flown in during the first week of January. My people got to work on 'em right away.'

'So none of these planes has been flyable since you received them?'

'That's right. All three of 'em were LC-130Rs. We're upgrading them into 130Hs with new avionics, navigation, and communication systems and displays, so the first thing we did was yank out all the old stuff. We're also doing a lot of maintenance on 'em, too, and installing the latest enhanced traffic collision avoidance system.'

'If you don't mind,' Tao said, 'we'd like to see the identification plates on each of the planes.'

'That's not a problem,' Boyer replied. 'Follow me.'

The three transports were in various stages of disassembly; in several places their protective skins were opened to reveal the inner mechanisms. Boyer led them to the cockpit of each plane where Kilkenny pulled out his Palm Pilot and checked the numbers against the list provided by the Pentagon.

'That's three down,' Kilkenny said as he slipped the Palm Pilot back into his coat pocket.

'Mr Boyer, we're done here. Thank you for your time.'

'Glad I could help. If you don't mind my asking, what are you after?'

'The government has received reports that a South American drug cartel is using a pair of LC-130s to transport their product. The Pentagon's inventory database shows all aircraft of this type are accounted for, and we're making a visual inspection of each plane to verify that none are missing.'

'Don't you think it'd be a little hard to steal one of these from a military base?'

'One would think,' Kilkenny replied. 'But this isn't the first time a big piece of hardware has mysteriously disappeared.'

29

Tucson, Arizona

After spending the night in Waco, Kilkenny and Tao caught an early morning flight to Tucson.

'Just pull up next to that blue Jeep,' the guard at ASRF's main gate instructed Kilkenny as he handed back their IDs. 'Someone will be right out.'

As Kilkenny parked, a woman in jeans and a denim shirt stepped out of the office. 'You the FBI?'

'Yes.' Tao replied, flashing her ID.

'I'm Anne Newburg. If you'll hop into the Jeep, I'll run you out to see the planes.'

Newburg drove them past the neatly parked rows of aircraft that filled the Boneyard. The planes were arranged by type, and as they drove around a cluster of cargo transports, Kilkenny saw the tip of a broad flat ski beneath the rounded black nose of an LC-130. A second sat immediately behind the first, and beside the two planes was a large empty space.

'There they are,' Newburg said as she parked the Jeep.

'We were told you had four of these aircraft in inventory,' Tao said. 'I only see two.'

'Until recently, we had seven. A few months ago, the Pentagon had us prep five for flight to Raytheon-Waco for upgrade.'

'When was the last time these two planes were flown?' Kilkenny asked.

'It's been years, ever since the navy brought 'em in for storage.'

Kilkenny checked the tail numbers against his list. He'd accounted for all but two of the LC-130s that had ever been made. 'We'd like to see the paperwork on the transfer of those five planes.'

'Sure thing.' Newburg put the Jeep in gear. 'It's all back at the office.'

Newburg pulled the files for the five aircraft and set them on her desk in front of Tao and Kilkenny. Kilkenny checked the ID numbers and made two piles.

'We saw these three planes at Waco yesterday,' Kilkenny said, 'and according to the Pentagon's records, that's all they were supposed to get.'

'That can't be right.' Newburg brought up the report on her computer. 'Here. At the Pentagon's request, we prepped five planes for flight. That means we stripped off the protective coating, checked all the electronics, refilled the hydraulic lines, and did about a hundred other things. For an LC-130, all that work takes about sixty days and costs several thousand dollars. This is a civilian facility and the owners won't touch a plane unless the work is paid for, and we got paid to prep *five* planes.'

'The Pentagon says they only paid for three,' Tao said. 'I wonder who paid for the other two.'

'Do your personnel deliver the planes?' Kilkenny asked.

'No, flight crews are provided by the owner. We have two pilots on staff, but they're not rated for every type of aircraft we have in storage, and certainly not the LC-130s.' Newburg leafed through the file. 'Here's the paperwork formally transferring the aircraft over to the owner's representative, in this case the pilot.'

Tao studied the five signed forms. 'Two of the planes were received by a pair of pilots on January third. A day later, a different pilot took possession of the third plane. This pilot then returned on the following two days to fly out the remaining planes.'

Kilkenny compared the numbers listed on the form with those in his Palm Pilot. 'The serial numbers on the planes flown out on January four, five, and six match those on the planes we saw in Waco. As yet, we don't have a fix on the other two.'

'Our release of these planes was by-the-book,' Newburg said, puzzled. 'I don't understand how two could just disappear.'

'Can we get a copy of everything you have on these five planes?' Kilkenny asked. 'I'd like to see every scrap of paperwork from the time they arrived until these pilots flew them out of here.'

'Certainly. Most of what you want is right here, but

I can have my assistant pull the logs on everything else. I've only been the manager for a month; all this happened before I was promoted.'

'What happened to your predecessor?' Tao asked.

'Oh, it was terrible, the poor man. He was bit by a rattlesnake.'

'Sheriff, my partner and I appreciate your seeing us,' Kilkenny said as they entered the man's office.

'You said over the phone that this had to do with the snakebite death out in the park. It looked like an accident, but we still have a few questions before we close the case up for good. Why are you folks interested in it?'

'There appear to be some irregularities at the victim's place of work prior to his death,' Tao replied. 'We're looking to see if there's any connection between the two.'

'Hmmm. What kind of irregularities? Embezzling?'

'No, the theft of two cargo planes.'

'Planes? Probably drug dealers,' the sheriff said, 'which makes me even more interested in this death.'

'You mentioned you had some unanswered questions about this incident. What are you looking into?' Kilkenny asked.

'Evers's body was found up in the hills in the national park; he was trail riding. It looks like he stopped to take a leak, tripped, and fell on a rattlesnake.' The sheriff pointed to a spot on his right arm. 'Bit him right about here. It takes a little while for a snakebite to kill you, so he must have fainted, because he never got up. When the park closed, the rangers saw a car in the lot and went looking for the owner. By the time they found him, he was dead. That's when they called us in. What bugged me about this death was a footprint.'

'A footprint?' Kilkenny asked.

'Yeah. You see, Evers was wearing this backpack thing with a big bag of water inside. When we got to him, there was a print right square in the center of this backpack and, inside, the water bag had burst. We found a few partial prints on the ground, some of which matched the one on the backpack. Now, we checked Evers and the Rangers, and none of their shoes matched this print. I wouldn't have thought much of it, except for the water bag. It was still wet, so we know it held water, which means somewhere along the way it broke open.'

'Could it have happened when Evers tripped?' Tao asked.

'I don't think so. Evers fell forward on the snake, and when we found him he was lying on his stomach.'

'What's your theory?' Kilkenny asked.

'I got two. Somebody found the body first, stomped on it, and rode off. It's morbid, but it's the kind of thing a teenage boy might do on a darc. The plastic on that water bag is pretty thick, so it took a hell of a whack to pop it. That kind of hit, on someone laying on the ground, should have broken a rib or two. The coroner looked into this, but he didn't find any postmortem injuries on Evers's back or chest. Now, if Evers didn't get that print when he was on the ground, he must have gotten it while he was standing up. That means somebody kicked him in the back so hard it ruptured the water bag and pushed Evers on top of the snake.'

'Which would be murder,' Tao said.

The sheriff nodded. 'Manslaughter at the very least.'

30

Ann Arbor, Michigan

After passing the information about the two planes missing from ASRF's inventory and the suspicious death of Jim Evers on to Langley, Kilkenny returned to his duties as UGene's acting CEO. According to the monthly reports charting the health of the young biotech company, except for the share price, all of the numbers still looked good.

UGene's stock took a beating after news broke about the murders and Eames's arrest. So much of the company was built around the work of its two founders that Wall Street had difficulty imagining how it would survive without them. Fortunately, the company had enough work contracted for the rest of the year to cover all their operating expenses and still turn a modest profit.

Kilkenny bought into UGene at the initial public offering and still held all of his shares despite the plunge. It wasn't as though he had much choice. By the time he learned what had happened, the damage to the stock had already been done. At the current price, he was just below breakeven, but the drop from the stock's previous high had erased a paper profit of several million dollars.

Curious, Kilkenny logged onto his brokerage's Web site to check the UGene stock. The share price was still down in the low teens, fluctuating by no more than a few cents. The volume of stock trading was also low, a sign that all the fainthearted investors had already abandoned the stock. Thinking about the volume, he wondered about the movement of people's money in and out of the company. The brokerage site provided a chart of the stock's daily price range over the past few months, but the volume was just a snapshot of today's activity.

He logged out of the brokerage site and accessed the Enth site to do some datamining. Unlike Internet search engines that only provide links to Web pages, Enth is tied to databases of information around the world. When he first encountered the site, Kilkenny tested it by requesting a list of all the American League players who hit over 250 against left-handed pitchers in the past ten years. Enth mined several baseball statistical databases and generated the list.

A few seconds later, Enth returned a spreadsheet of the daily trading volume for UGene stock. Kilkenny converted the data display into a graph. Starting at the IPO, the line shot upward as a large number of investors jumped on the company's bandwagon. Once the initial shares were sold, the volume dropped as most of the investors sat back and waited for the stock to increase in value over time. The trend of low-volume trading continued for several months until mid-February.

'What the hell is that?' Kilkenny asked as he studied the mid-month spikes.

He enlarged that graph to show a two-week period in February. Each day was now easily discernible.

'Sutton was murdered on the fourteenth, and Eames was arrested on the morning of the fifteenth,' Kilkenny said to himself, reviewing the chronology of events in comparison to the chart, 'which explains this spike. But what's going on here?'

In the days preceding the murders, Kilkenny saw a steady increase in trading volume – enough to depress the stock a bit. He was in Antarctica at the time and didn't recall hearing any news that might have affected the stock. After months of low volume, the sudden jump intrigued him enough that he put a call into an old college friend who now watched the biotech sector for a mutual fund company.

'Mike, got a question for you.'

'I'm listening.'

'Back in mid-February, was there anything going on that spooked investors in your sector?'

'You mean other than what happened at your company?'

'Yeah, before that.'

'There was the usual mixed bag of quarterly projections, nothing too far off the mark. I recall the first few weeks of the year being pretty quiet. Why?'

'I was poking around with some data on our stock and I came across an increase in volume just before everything went to hell.'

'Good or bad volume?'

'Bad, I guess,' Kilkenny replied. 'The stock price went down.'

'It happens.'

'Maybe, but I just found the timing odd. What suddenly caused someone who'd been holding our stock for months to up and decide to sell?'

'Investors jockeying for tax time usually drop shares before January first to offset gains and losses. The low-volume trading you see is the little guys who got bored when the stock reached a comfortable level and jumped to something more exciting. I can't see a big holder dumping a position that's doing well.'

'So what do you think this is?' Kilkenny asked.

'Looks to me like a short.'

'A short?'

'Yeah, sell high and buy low. Here's how the play works. Somebody thinks your stock price is too high, so he sells a bunch of shares that he doesn't own. If the price drops, he buys shares to cover his short and pockets the difference.'

'And if the price goes up, he's screwed.'

'Exactly. It's a gutsy play, especially with your stock.'

'Why do you say that?'

'Based on our projections, your stock was priced reasonably. You guys have good cash flow, better than decent market advantage, very little downside. For me to make a short, I want some bad news. I want to see labor trouble or a competitor on the horizon who's going to steal the company's lunch money. If somebody did short UGene, they must have been fucking psychic. Until

Eames killed Sutton, UGene had nothing but blue sky ahead.'

'Eames hasn't been convicted yet,' Kilkenny said.

'You think he's innocent?'

'I'm not sure.'

'If he's not, now's the time to buy. Of course, this short idea is all hypothetical. I don't have a clue why your volume jumped.'

'Is there any way to find out if someone shorted our stock?'

'Not directly, but a short trade has to come through a brokerage house.'

'Why?'

'Since this player is selling something he doesn't own, he has to borrow it from someone else. Brokerages have access to lots of client shares, so they loan him shares with the understanding that eventually he's going to buy shares to cover the short.'

'Can you find out which brokerage houses were behind all those shares?'

'No, only the SEC can do that. This is the kind of thing they look for when they suspect someone of insider trading or stock manipulation. Why?'

'I'm just wondering who thought UGene was due for a fall.'

Roxanne Tao rapped on Kilkenny's door.

'Mike, I gotta go. Thanks for your help.'

'Who was that, your broker?' Tao asked snidely.

'No. What can I do for you?'

Tao placed a thick file on Kilkenny's desk. The label read *Agabashian, Stepan*. 'Your arms dealer has been located in Rio de Janeiro. This is the background on him. Interesting reading. Barnett suggests we pay a visit while he's there. They're working on arrangements. We're booked to leave tonight.'

'I'll pack a bag. Question, on an unrelated matter. Does the agency have any pull in the SEC?'

'There is a point of contact that both the FBI and the CIA use when we need information about certain transactions. Anything in particular you want to know about?'

'UGene. There was an unusual surge in the amount of stock traded in the days just before the murders.' Kilkenny told her about the hypothetical short sale. 'It may be nothing, but if it is a short, it's either a hell of a coincidence or the short-seller knew something bad was going to happen.'

'How could anyone know Eames was going to kill those two people?'

'That's my point. Assuming Eames is the killer, there's no way anyone else could have known what was going on inside his head unless he talked about it several days beforehand. I'm pretty sure most people who think someone's planning a murder would call the police and not their stockbroker. That's why I want to know what's going on behind this short.'

31

Rio de Janeiro

Kilkenny adjusted the binoculars and tightened in on the sleek white form in the middle of the inner harbor. The *Sirvat* – a 187-foot floating palace – dwarfed everything in the water except for two destroyers and a supertanker moored out in the deep anchorages. Kilkenny spotted a man of immense girth seated in the rear of the yacht's upper deck, sipping from a tall glass. The man had thinning dark hair and thick black eyebrows that ran uninterrupted from one side of his fleshy face to the other. Two young women in the barest of Brazilian bikinis lay sunning themselves nearby. Kilkenny estimated their combined body fat at something less than the man's nested chins.

'So that's Stepan Agabashian,' Kilkenny said.

Kilkenny and Tao were in the hotel suite with their local CIA contact, a man whom they knew only as Raul.

'*Si*,' Raul replied. 'It is rumored he is here brokering deals with some of his South American clients.'

According to the file, Agabashian had been born in Turkey to Armenian parents. The details of his early career in gunrunning were sketchy, but by the 1980s Agabashian had definitely hit the big time. Sources pegged his sales to Iraq during its eight-year war with Iran at well over a billion dollars. He sold guns to Christian forces in Lebanon, explosives to splinter factions of the Irish Republican Army, missiles to the Argentineans during the Falklands War, and AK-47s to regional hot spots around the globe. In the realm of black-market arms, Agabashian was known as the Merchant of Death.

'And you've been keeping tabs on his movements?' Tao asked.

'As soon as his yacht pulled into the harbor. So far, he's done most of his entertaining on board, bringing his guests out on the launch. He went into town last night for dinner; the young ladies on the deck accompanied him on the way back. Sources say he's been invited to a private black-tie party in Ipanema tonight.'

'Do you have the layout of the ship?' Tao asked.

Raul nodded and placed a set of floor plans on the table. 'We've acquired these from the builder.'

Kilkenny saw two motorboats tied alongside the yacht; they looked small and fast. Studying the decks of the *Sirvat*, he picked out two men patrolling the main deck, both armed with machine pistols. Sweeping his eyes over the upper decks, he noticed the radar antenna spinning atop the mast, keeping track of the ships around the great vessel.

'I don't think storming that yacht would be too bright an idea,' Kilkenny said. 'A squad of SEALs could pull it off, but we're a little shorthanded.'

'What do you suggest?' Tao asked. 'That we dress up, and crash the party he's attending tonight?'

Kilkenny lowered the binoculars and looked at Tao. 'That kind of thing only works for James Bond, and besides, I left my tux back home.'

'You couldn't get into the party anyway. The guest list is a close circle of Agabashian's peers,' Raul said.

'Which means the protection will probably be more than just rent-a-cops. The place to get Agabashian is not at either end, but when he's moving in between.'

Raul shook his head. 'He travels in an armored Hummer. Nothing short of a rocket attack could stop it.'

'We want to talk with him, Nolan,' Tao said, 'not kill him.'

'That leaves the launch.'

Kilkenny picked up the encrypted cell phone Raul had left them before the second ring. 'Go.'

'The party's over and Agabashian is heading back,' Raul reported.

'Any guests?' Kilkenny asked.

'No, just Agabashian and the driver. ETA twenty minutes.'

'Good. We're moving into position.' Kilkenny ended the call and slipped the phone into his coat pocket. 'Time to go.'

It was just past one in the morning when Kilkenny and Tao reached the Rio de Janeiro Yacht Club. They had scouted out the marina after the *Sirvat*'s launch arrived earlier that evening, blending in with the crowd, but now the docks were all but deserted. The pilot of the launch was seated in the cabin, listening to music as he kept watch. Tao clasped Kilkenny's hand and walked close beside him. Kilkenny checked the time: ETA five minutes.

The launch was tied up alongside the seawall, illuminated by one of the lamps that cast a soft glow on the promenade. Walking toward the launch, Kilkenny placed his arm around Tao's back and drew her close. She wore a red silk dress that stopped just above her knees and made an enticing display of her breasts. Tao pressed her head against his chest, her hair drawn back in a braid to keep the ocean breeze from whipping it about. She felt good beside him, even if her display of affection was strictly for show.

From the parking lot, they heard the unmistakable throaty growl of a Hummer. The driver pulled up into a space reserved for Agabashian's use and opened the door for his employer.

Kilkenny and Tao ignored Agabashian's arrival, acting as a couple enthralled with each other. Close to the launch, Tao became more amorous, nuzzling Kilkenny's cheek and neck. He responded, cradling the back of her head with his hand as he kissed her. They murmured softly, like lovers sharing secret thoughts, and Kilkenny guided her into a shadowed spot against the yacht club wall. Tao's arms slid beneath his jacket, one hand gliding down to grasp his buttocks.

Suddenly relieved of his boredom, the launch pilot grinned as he watched, especially when Tao wrapped a leg around Kilkenny's hip. Kilkenny slipped a hand to his waist, as if to unzip his pants, then moved it up and cupped it over a breast. From the muffled groans, the pilot believed Kilkenny and Tao were having sex.

Oblivious to the lovers, Agabashian shuffled up to the side of the launch and prepared to board. The pilot offered his employer a supportive arm, then threw the driver a sly grin and nodded for him to check out the show.

'Go,' Tao whispered in Kilkenny's ear.

Kilkenny slipped his hand off her breast and grabbed the Taser holstered in his armpit. Tao's hand, which had covered a second Taser holstered against the small of Kilkenny's back, curled around the grip and pulled the weapon free. As Kilkenny spun to the side and cleared her line of sight, Tao fired at the driver. Two electrified projectiles struck the man in the chest, their barbed tips punching through his clothing and into the skin beneath. Instantly, the Taser delivered a 50,000 volt shock to the driver's central nervous system. The man dropped onto the promenade, his muscles spasming uncontrollably.

The pilot's grin vanished when he saw Kilkenny spin away from Tao and take aim. A dot of red laser light appeared on his chest, immediately followed by the stinging barbs. The pilot's legs buckled and he collapsed.

Tao quickly untied the lines as Kilkenny hauled the immobilized driver into the launch. Agabashian looked up as Tao leapt aboard.

'Don't move and you'll get out of this alive,' she said icily.

Kilkenny took the helm and steered a course out into the harbor. A waning crescent moon hung low in the clear sky, providing more than enough light to see by. Tao frisked Agabashian and his men, recovering two Glock pistols.

'You can take a seat in the back,' Tao said, less threateningly.

The arms dealer carefully rose onto his hands and knees, then crawled over to the stern bench. He sat with a great sigh and silently studied his captors. Tao traded the guns for a handful of zip ties from Kilkenny's coat pocket and bound the wrists and ankles of Agabashian's men. When they reached an isolated stretch of water, Kilkenny cut the engines. He sat down beside Tao, opposite Agabashian.

'What do you want?' Agabashian asked.

'Information about one of your clients,' Tao replied.

'I never discuss clients.'

'How well do you swim?' Kilkenny asked.

'What?'

Kilkenny took a tall clear glass from the launch's mini-bar and scooped some water from the bay. Even in the moonlight, the water looked murky and foul.

'This harbor is so polluted that you would no doubt float on top of the oil and raw sewage. If you're a good swimmer, you could probably make it to your yacht or back to shore, but I'd recommend getting a tetanus shot and a strong course of antibiotics once you got there. Of course, if you can't swim, it won't much matter.'

'You would put me overboard?'

'If you don't tell us what we want to know, I'd toss you in without a second thought.'

A voice came over the radio, hailing the launch.

'They've noticed we stopped,' Tao said.

Several crewmen were on the main deck of the yacht, looking in their direction.

'A repair crew should be on its way shortly, with a guard or two,' Kilkenny said, then he turned back to Agabashian. 'This is really quite simple: You can answer my questions and live, or you can die with your secrets. If it helps you decide, I was almost killed by the weapon you sold, so this is personal for me. You have about five minutes before you go swimming.'

Agabashian looked at the water and saw a sheen of oil reflecting in the moonlight. 'What do you want to know?'

'You bought an SA-17 missile launcher from a Russian general named Dubinsky. You remember it?'

'Yes.'

'Who did you sell it to?'

'A Frenchman named Sumner Duroc.'

'Who does he work for?'

'I don't know. All I was told was that he wanted this specific weapon by mid-January and he was willing to pay well for it. The deal was brokered through intermediaries, all very clean. We only met once, at the time of delivery.'

'When and where?'

'In Argentina, Rio Gallegos. I delivered the launcher in mid-January.'

'What did Duroc look like?' Tao asked.

'Tall and thin, like your associate. Black hair and black beard.'

Tao glanced at Kilkenny and he nodded; the description

fit. A searchlight illuminated the launch and they heard the sound of a distant motor.

'Time to get moving,' Kilkenny said.

He started the engines and turned the launch back toward the marina. The pilot of the second boat pushed his throttles forward, chasing after them. They had a good head start, but the other boat was faster and closing the distance. The spotlight widened to illuminate the launch.

'Roxanne, do something about that – '

Tao crouched at the stern and fired twice at the approaching boat, then pointed the pistol at Agabashian's head. The pilot of the second boat eased back on the throttle, allowing them to pull away.

'Message received,' Tao said as she lowered the pistol.

Kilkenny brought the launch back to the same spot at the dock and cut the engines. The second boat held back at a distance, still watching.

'As promised, you have avoided a swim in the harbor tonight,' Kilkenny said. 'Oh, two more things before we go. If it turns out you lied to us about Duroc, we'll be back and not to talk. Also, if the thought of warning Duroc enters your head, just remember that we're here tonight because of something he did with that launcher.'

Kilkenny and Tao stepped out of the launch and ran down the promenade to the marina parking lot where Raul was waiting for them.

'Agabashian's been holed up in his yacht since his men picked him up last night,' Raul announced as he stepped out onto the patio of the safe house where he'd hidden

Kilkenny and Tao after their encounter with the arms dealer. 'We haven't picked up any ship-to-shore traffic either. I think he's scurried back into his hole and has no intention of looking for you.'

'That's fine with me,' Kilkenny said.

Raul sat down at the table and handed Tao an envelope. 'This came in for you from Langley.'

Tao quietly read the contents of the message. 'Nolan, I think you'll find this interesting.'

Kilkenny slid his chair close as she laid down the first sheet. 'What am I looking at?'

'This is an answer to that stock trading question you asked about. Several trades selling shares of UGene stock were executed by different brokerage houses that week.'

Kilkenny studied the pages carefully. 'A lot of little trades.'

'Yes, but their collected increase in the trading volume made the SEC curious enough to dig a little further.' Tao placed the next sheet on the table. 'All those little trades were placed by a small private bank in the Cayman Islands. After the stock fell, the same bank incrementally bought stock to cover the short.'

Kilkenny stared at the pages, stunned. 'I don't believe it.'

'Doesn't this prove that someone other than Eames knew the murders were going to happen?'

'No, this could be nothing more than a coincidence, but I think it's worth a trip to the Cayman Islands to find out.'

32

MARCH 11

George Town, Grand Cayman

They were met at the airport by a courier from the U.S. Embassy in Jamaica. Tao signed for the package, then they picked up a Mustang convertible and drove into George Town. The quaint seaside village had evolved from British trading outpost in the Caribbean into major tourist destination.

'It's hard to believe this is one of the biggest banking centers in the world,' Kilkenny mused as they drove around, getting a feel for the town.

'Two words, Nolan: *no taxes*. Most of the top world banks are headquartered here, as well as several hundred smaller ones.' Tao opened the package and examined the IDs.

'Who are we with today?'

'The SEC.'

'Which leads me to my next question – what about jurisdiction? This isn't the U.S.'

'True, but the government of the Cayman Islands prides itself on the integrity of its financial sector. Part of that reputation comes from their willingness to work with the U.S. and Britain to police that sector. I expect that the Sterling Private Bank will be very willing to assist us just to avoid problems with their government.'

They located the headquarters of the Sterling Private Bank in the second-floor walk-up atop a pirate-themed souvenir shop in a commercial block. The building was narrow, wedged in between two larger brick buildings, with a pair of tall arched windows on the second floor.

'Looks like a one-man accounting firm,' Kilkenny commented as they parked across the street.

'You were expecting a marble foyer with a dozen tellers behind brass screens?' Tao asked.

'No, just something that looked a little more like a bank.'

They climbed up to the second floor and found a panneled wood door with a frosted glass panel that bore the name of the bank in stenciled gold letters. Beside the door was an intercom and a small sign that read RING FOR SERVICE. Kilkenny pressed the button and heard a dull buzzing sound on the other side of the door.

'May I help you?' a half-distracted voice answered through the speaker.

'Yes,' Kilkenny answered. 'We are with the U.S. Securities and Exchange Commission and would like to speak to someone about some stock transactions that were placed by this bank.'

'Do you have an appointment?'

'No, but if you prefer we could check in with the Finance Secretary's office first.'

'No need for that bother. Do come in.'

They entered a room that occupied most of the building's upper floor. The high ceiling was covered with panels of embossed tin, and a ceiling fan of brass and wood revolved slowly. A U-shaped workstation dominated the center of the room and every inch of the desktop was covered with paper or electronic equipment.

A portly man with a thick white beard that ran over the top of his ears and around the back of his bald head removed a telephone headset and turned to greet them. Kilkenny looked around and saw no one else in the office.

'I'm Hugh Harley,' the man said with a crisp British accent. 'May I see your identification, please?'

'Certainly,' Tao replied.

They handed Harley the ID wallets that listed them as investigators with the SEC. Harley inspected the photo IDs carefully, then handed them back.

'What can I do for you?' Harley asked.

'We're looking into a series of stock trades executed through your bank between the twelfth and fifteenth of February, and again on the twentieth. We believe the timing of these transactions indicate insider trading.'

'What stock are we talking about?'

'UGene, a biotech company.'

Harley leaned back in his chair, his hands folded across his stomach. 'I don't recall making any trades on that stock, but don't be alarmed by that. I execute dozens of trades every day. Before I act on your request, I have to check with my lawyer and the Finance Secretary's office about the legality of such a disclosure. The laws here are fairly rigid and I wouldn't want to break one out of ignorance.'

'How long will that take?' Tao asked.

'I expect the rest of the day, if I'm lucky. My lawyer is in court all afternoon, and getting through to the Secretary's staff rarely is as simple a thing as it sounds. Had you checked with the Secretary prior to your arrival here, it would have saved a little time. Are you staying here in town?'

'No, everything was booked up. We've borrowed a condo in West Bay.' Kilkenny pulled a business card out of the ID wallet Tao had provided him and wrote a phone number on the back. 'Hopefully we can tie this up quickly. The owner will be returning later this week.'

Harley took the card from Kilkenny, glanced at the number, then slipped it into the breast pocket of his white linen shirt. 'I'll see what I can do to get you the answers you're looking for. Now, if you don't mind, I have some calls to make, and there are still a few hours left before the American markets close.'

From the arched windows of his office, Harley watched as Kilkenny and Tao walked across the street, got into the Mustang, and drove off. When they were gone, he slipped the headset back on, scrolled through the contact book in his computer, and selected a New Jersey number.

'Duroc,' a stern, familiar voice answered.

'Hugh Harley down in George Town. I have a bit of a problem.'

'What kind of problem?'

'Just a moment ago, I received a visit from a pair of

investigators from the American SEC. It seems your transactions last month have attracted some interest.'

'I thought you took precautions against that.'

'I did, but apparently it wasn't enough for such a small stock. They suspect insider trading and are seeking information about the individuals behind the transactions. A fishing expedition, really. Of course, I stalled for time. They're expecting to hear from me tomorrow. The whole thing is rather odd, though.'

'How so?'

'Requests like this are normally handled through the Finance Secretary,' Harley explained. 'No real need to send someone down here if all they're looking for is a tid-bit of information.'

'What are the names of the two investigators?'

'Roxanne Tao and Nolan Kilkenny.'

Duroc jotted down the names. 'I'm going to check these investigators out. Until you hear from me, tell them nothing.'

33

As Kilkenny and Tao were getting ready to leave for dinner at a restaurant up the beach, the condo phone rang.

'Hello?' Kilkenny answered.

'Oh, good, you haven't stepped out for the evening. Mr Kilkenny, it's Hugh Harley, I spoke with you and your associate earlier today.'

'What can I do for you?'

'Well, I received word a short while ago from my lawyer and I am permitted to speak with you regarding those stock trades. I know you're interested in discerning whether any improprieties have taken place with regard to insider trading, and I've spoken with my client about the matter. He lives here and has agreed to meet with you to put your suspicions to rest. Unfortunately, the rest of his week is a bit of a mess. Are you and your associate available to meet with him tonight?'

'Yes,' Kilkenny replied. 'At your office?'

'No, my home. We're playing cards tonight, usual group, and it's more convenient for everyone. Shall we say around nine?'

'That's fine.' Kilkenny wrote down the directions to Harley's beach house.

Kilkenny and Tao had some difficulty finding Harley's home as the dense foliage between the street and the building proved to be a near perfect camouflage. Were it not for a gray, weather-worn sign with Harley's name carved into it, Kilkenny doubted he would have found the place at all.

He parked beside two other cars in the gravel driveway. The beach house was a modest structure built on pilings with broad eaves for protection from the sun. Noticing headlights in the driveway, Harley stepped out onto the front porch.

'No trouble finding the place, I hope?'

'Only passed it twice,' Kilkenny admitted.

'Well, I do like my privacy. Please come in.'

He led Kilkenny and Tao into a large room that enjoyed an expansive view of the Caribbean and was furnished with comfortable informality. On one side of the room, three men sat around a card table drinking. A fourth stood at the bar mixing a drink.

'Here we are,' Harley said, guiding them toward the bar.

Kilkenny stopped abruptly when Summer Duroc turned to face him. Duroc caught Kilkenny's reaction of surprise and recognition. Harley fled the room and behind them, the three card players were on their feet and rushing toward them.

'Nolan!' Tao shouted.

As he spun around, Kilkenny grabbed a floor lamp and swung it like a baseball bat. The weighted base connected with the nearest man's midsection, doubling him over onto the floor. Tao pushed a chair at one of the men moving at her, then kicked high into the jaw of the other.

Duroc closed in and attacked Kilkenny from behind, throwing tight quick punches into his lower back. Reacting to the pain, Kilkenny swung the bony point of his elbow back and struck Duroc's head just above the ear. Duroc staggered back, dazed by the blow.

Kilkenny's first opponent regained his breath and lunged forward. Like a matador, Kilkenny sidestepped the charge and drove his foot into the side of his attacker's knee. The leg buckled and the man skidded onto the floor. Duroc grabbed a fifth of Bombay Sapphire off the bar and swung it into the back of Kilkenny's head. The bottle made a dull thud when it struck and snapped at the neck. Kilkenny immediately dropped to the floor.

Duroc dropped the bottle's neck and joined the attack on Tao. He dodged a wide arcing kick aimed at his head, grabbed her ankle, and twisted her off her footing. The last of Duroc's men still standing tackled her as she fell onto the floor.

'Harley, tie her up,' Duroc ordered as he held Tao's arms behind her back.

The banker cautiously returned carrying several short lengths of nylon fishing line. He quickly bound Tao's wrists and ankles, avoiding contact with her as if her touch alone might be dangerous. With Tao restrained, Duroc stood up and studied the wreckage. Kilkenny lay in a heap, unmoving.

'Him too?' Harley asked.

Duroc nodded. Harley was still obviously shaken by the

sudden violence and regarded Kilkenny like a dangerous animal that might abruptly spring up at him. He finished binding Kilkenny and backed away from Duroc's two prisoners. The two beaten men slowly regrouped themselves.

'Sit her up,' Duroc ordered.

The man who'd been kicked in the face grabbed Tao roughly and sat her on the floor.

'Why are you here?'

Tao returned his question with silence and a stare of indifference that barely masked her inner hostility. Experience told Duroc he would get nothing from her.

'Search them,' he commanded.

The men pawed Tao, despite the fact that her long-sleeved top and Capri pants left little room for concealment. Her small clutch yielded two slim wallets, one of which contained Tao's SEC identification. The search of Kilkenny's unconscious form produced the keys to the rental car and the condo and Kilkenny's wallet.

'You both travel light,' Duroc commented, finding only their driver's licenses and a few credit cards between them.

He studied the driver's licenses and noted that both were issued by the state of Michigan. Kilkenny's was somewhat worn while Tab's appeared freshly minted.

'I checked, and you are not from the SEC,' Duroc said to Tao. 'I don't know what game you and your friend here are playing, but it has come to an end. Gag her and take them both to the boat.'

Duroc and his men carried Kilkenny and Tao down to the deserted beach. A Zodiac boat sat on the sand just above the high-tide mark. They placed them in the Zodiac, then dragged it out into the lapping waves.

'Dump them in deep water, understand?' Duroc said as he tossed the wallets and the condo keys to one of the men. 'I don't want their bodies washing ashore.'

The two men nodded then pulled themselves into the boat. The outboard motor turned over on the first pull, and the Zodiac motored out across the calm surface of the Caribbean.

As he walked to Harley's house, Duroc handed his remaining man the keys to Kilkenny's rental car. 'Drop it off at the rental agency tomorrow around noon, when they are the busiest.'

The man nodded and left, and Duroc returned to the beach house. Harley was already pouring himself another stiff drink.

'Monsieur Harley, I thank you for your assistance in making the arrangements for tonight.'

'You can thank me after you get my bill,' Harley replied. 'The men I hired were not inexpensive, but they'll do as you've instructed. I've taken the liberty of deducting their fee from your account prior to transferring the balance to Switzerland.'

Duroc nodded his assent and picked up a canvas bag he'd brought with him. 'And what of the stock trades?'

'I've altered the records on my computer, running the trades through dummy accounts so there's no direct link back to your holding company.'

Duroc pulled a silenced Glock pistol from the bag and fired four shots. The first two rounds disappeared into Harley's chest, the frangible projectiles exploding into tiny shards of twisted metal. Duroc's second pair punched through Harley's forehead and shredded his brain.

34

Tao watched as the beach receded in the darkness. Behind her back, she worked against the nylon line that bound her wrists. The flesh at the base of her thumbs was raw and bleeding from repeated attempts to pull free.

A layer of cool salt water sloshed across the bottom of the Zodiac, soaking both her and Kilkenny. Tao worked her legs beneath his head to keep his face from being submerged. From the shallow rise and fall of his chest, Tao knew he was still breathing.

Thirty minutes out from the beach, she saw the lights of a deep-sea fishing boat. The man in the bow of the Zodiac signaled the boat with a flashlight and was greeted with a reply. Another small wave rolled beneath the tiny boat and the layer of water rushed from bow to stern. The surge splashed over Tao's legs and washed over Kilkenny's face. As the water rolled back Kilkenny briefly opened an eye.

The pilot of the Zodiac cut the engine as it reached the stern of a Hatteras, and the man in the bow tossed up the lines. Once the boat was secured, one of the men grabbed Kilkenny by the armpits and started to lift. As the man pulled him to his feet, Kilkenny shifted his weight. The man lost both his balance and his grip and Kilkenny tumbled overboard.

'Shit, I dropped the bugger.'

'Fish him out, man. Duroc wanted them dropped further out.'

'I don't see him. I think he sunk.'

Kilkenny took a deep breath before hitting the water. Beneath the surface, he whipped his bound legs up and down in a dolphin kick and propelled himself under the fishing boat. BUD/S, the Navy's basic training program for SEALs, included an exercise called 'drown proofing,' where trainees were dumped into a deep pool with their hands and feet bound. The purpose of the exercise was to remove the fear of drowning so the trainee could calmly focus on the situation.

Once under the boat, Kilkenny placed his back against the slime-covered keel and worked his way toward the stern. He started to sink and gave a sharp kick to push himself back in place. Near the stern, he bumped into one of the twin propellers with the top of his head, and a few tiny bubbles escaped from his nose. Moving by feel, he worked his hands around the blades and started rubbing the nylon line against the curved brass edge, hoping that the engines wouldn't start.

The fishing line cut into his wrists as he tried to keep it taut against the blade. Weakened by tension and friction, the nylon line snapped and Kilkenny's hands sped away from the propeller. His hands tingled as the blood rushed back into them.

He braced himself against the rudder and repeated the same maneuver with the ties around his ankles. From inside the ship a puttering sound throbbed into the water.

Cooling pumps, Kilkenny realized. *They're getting ready to start the engines.*

As Kilkenny rubbed the line faster against the blade, his pulse raced and his lungs threatened to explode from his chest. On the other side of the fiberglass hull, the boat's twin diesels rumbled to life. Kilkenny pulled hard on his bonds just as the pilot shifted the engines out of neutral. As the propeller engaged, Kilkenny felt the loops of nylon tear into his ankles, scraping off the layers of skin. Salt water burned his wounds and blood seeped through the torn flesh. Suddenly the constriction on his ankles disappeared and his legs flew apart, away from the propeller.

Kilkenny wondered if he'd lost his feet, then the numbness gave way to pain and the warm sensation of reawakened flesh. Pulling with his arms, he dove deep, away from the turning blades, and surfaced in the roiling froth behind the boat. He grabbed hold of the jump deck and caught his breath as the boat picked up speed and headed out to sea.

'Is it okay if I fuck the bitch before we dump her?' one of the men asked the captain of the boat as he leered at Tao from the bridge doorway.

'What do I care?' the captain answered. 'Just don't untie her.'

'No way,' the man replied. 'I took a couple thumps from her already. I like her wrapped up just the way she is.'

The man closed the bridge door, stepped out onto the

stern deck, and crouched over Tao. He pulled her shirt up to her armpits and yanked the cups of her bra away from her breasts. Tao struggled, trying to kick at him, but the man just laughed and sat on her knees. Moving down, he unfastened the top button of her pants and went to work on her zipper. Tao reared up and struck him squarely in the face with her forehead, crushing the fragile bones in his nose.

'You fucking bitch!' the man cursed, his eyes welling up with tears and blood gushing from his nostrils.

Kilkenny pulled himself up onto the jump deck and looked over the stern rail. The boat's engine's were deafening. From behind, he saw one of Duroc's men sitting on Tao's legs. He was cursing violently, his hand wrapped around Tao's throat. Kilkenny vaulted over the rail, grabbed the man's scalp with one hand, pulled back and twisted with the other. The sudden torque snapped the bones at the base of his skull, killing the man instantly. Kilkenny lifted the man off Tao and heaved him over the rail.

'Bloody hell!' the captain shouted.

Kilkenny turned as a man charged toward him from the bridge. He grabbed a pike pole off the rail and jabbed the blunt end into the man's stomach. With a sharp, circular movement, Kilkenny then swept the end up and struck him on the side of his head. The man staggered sideways, colliding with the captain who'd emerged from the bridge with a pistol. Kilkenny spun the pike pole, hooked the captain's ankle, and dropped him on the deck. With the blunt end, he struck the captain's forearm hard enough to break bone. The gun clattered harmlessly to the deck.

Kilkenny picked up the pistol and fired a warning shot next to the captain's head. 'Don't move.'

'You okay?' he asked Tao as he removed her gag.

'Doesn't matter,' she replied, still furious, 'just cut me loose.'

Kilkenny found a knife in the tackle box and cut her bonds. As she fixed her clothing, Kilkenny bound the two men.

'We should toss them overboard,' Tao said.

Kilkenny shook his head. 'No.'

'Why not? You dumped that would-be rapist.'

'He was already dead.' Kilkenny stepped onto the bridge and switched off the engines. 'Anyway, I have a better idea.'

Kilkenny pulled the handset out of the ship's radio and tossed it into the sea. He checked their current position against the charts and programmed a northerly course into the boat's autopilot. He switched on the engines and set the speed at ten knots. The boat turned in a slow arc to the right, straightening out when the compass read zero degrees.

'Time to shove off,' Kilkenny said as he left the bridge.

He stepped down into the Zodiac and grabbed hold of the rail as Tao undid the lines and leapt aboard. The inflatable boat bobbed in the wake of the sport fisher as it pulled away.

'So, where are they going?' Tao asked.

'North,' Kilkenny replied as he started the outboard motor. 'I figure by morning they should be in the territorial waters of Cuba.'

35

Kilkenny guided the Zodiac on a south-southwest course toward Grand Cayman. To his left, the lights of Seven Mile Beach illuminated the shoreline southward to George Town. He was thankful for the calm night, which made the transit easy and gave him a chance to mull over everything that had happened.

Tao reclined in the bow of the Zodiac, partly for comfort and partly to balance their weight. After they'd abandoned the other boat, she sensed that Kilkenny wasn't in the mood for talking and let him be. She watched him in the dim moonlight, his eyes fixed on the horizon but his mind furiously laboring somewhere else. Glancing over the side, she saw the lights onshore.

'Where are we going, back to Harley's house?' she asked.

'No, I couldn't find it from the beach during the day, much less now. I'm heading to George Town. If any evidence of the stock trades still exists, it'll be at Harley's bank.'

'What are you thinking about?'

'The man Harley introduced as his client.'

'I noticed we didn't get a name.'

'Sumner Duroc.'

Tao looked at him, surprised, but Kilkenny didn't notice. His eyes remained on the lights dotting the shore. 'What makes you think that man is Duroc?'

'Because he's the one who led the attack on LV Station. I knew it as soon as I saw him.'

'But what would Duroc be doing here with Harley?'

'I don't know, it just doesn't fit. If Agabashian put him onto us, then we had to have been followed from Rio. I haven't picked up any sign of a tail.'

Tao thought back on the moments after the ambush at Harley's house. 'While you were unconscious, he spoke to me. He asked why we were here. I told him nothing. Then he said he'd checked and he knew we weren't with the SEC.'

'Only Harley saw those IDs.'

'Until you said this man was Duroc, I thought he was just Harley's client.'

'If he is the client, then how did he know UGene's stock was going to crash?'

Using Harley's keys, Duroc entered the offices of the Sterling Private Bank. From the canvas bag, he pulled out a two-liter plastic soft drink bottle filled with gasoline, a package of model rocket engines, a roll of electrical tape, a battery, and a digital timer. He inserted an igniter into the base of the rocket engine, connected wires to both igniter leads, then wedged the cylindrical engine into the throat of the soft drink bottle. Once the bomb was assembled, Duroc placed it on the floor beside Harley's computer tower and started the timer.

Kilkenny cut the engine and rowed the final quarter-mile into George Town Harbor. Lights and the sounds of revelry emanated from a handful of the vessels moored at the docks; the rest were quiet. Kilkenny silently guided the Zodiac into an empty slip between two darkened sail-boats. He leapt up onto the dock, tied a line off on a cleat, and helped Tao out of the boat.

As they walked into town, they felt a bit self-conscious about their appearance – both were wet and disheveled and the bandages around Kilkenny's ankles were soaked through with blood. Fortunately, most of the island's nightlife was north of the town along Seven Mile Beach. They worked their way up the narrow streets while trying to avoid other passersby.

'The bank's just up ahead,' Kilkenny said as they turned a corner.

The street instantly filled with an intense flash of light when Duroc's bomb exploded, and glass from the bank's second-story windows rained down in fractured bits. Hugh Harley's one-man private bank was totally engulfed in flames.

36

MARCH 12

Langley, Virginia

Kilkenny and Tao holed up in an airport hotel for the remainder of the night. In the morning, an agency representative arrived to handle their discreet departure from the island. Higher-level contacts between the U.S. and Cayman governments provided Kilkenny and Tao with a set of encrypted data disks retrieved from a fire safe hidden in Harley's home. It was understood that any criminal evidence recovered from the disks would be shared. By late afternoon, Kilkenny and Tao were brought to Jackson Barnett's office.

'Please take a seat,' Barnett said as he picked up a legal pad and a file from his desk. 'You two have been working together for barely two weeks and already someone has tried to kill you? I never expected such a productive start to this collaboration.'

'It wasn't what we set out to do,' Tao replied.

'No, but it shows you're onto something. Operationally,

I'm turning this investigation over to you, Roxanne. So far, you and Nolan have provided the only real leads, and I'm inclined to play a hot hand when I have one.' Barnett pulled a photograph out of the file and handed it to Kilkenny. 'Is this the man you saw in Antarctica?'

Kilkenny studied the photo carefully, comparing details to those recorded in his memory. 'Yes.'

'This is Sumner Duroc,' Barnett announced. 'At the time that was taken, he was a senior officer in the Operations Division of the DGSE.'

'French Special Forces?' Kilkenny asked.

Barnett nodded. 'DGSE is the French counterpart of the CIA. Their Operations Division includes a special forces-counterterrorism unit. Duroc was a major when he left the service in 'ninety-seven. He received numerous awards and citations during his years of service and even trained with our Rangers and Delta Force.'

'Nice résumé. What's he up to now?' Kilkenny asked.

'He started a company based in Paris called Cerberus Sécurité.'

'Cerberus?' Tao repeated. 'As in the three-headed dog that guards the gates of Hell?'

'I believe that's the image Duroc is trying to project,' Barnett said. 'His company consults on security matters and trains bodyguards for CEOs and other VIPs.'

'Based on what I saw at LV Station, he's doing more than playing secret service to the rich and powerful,' Kilkenny offered. 'He's playing mercenary on the side.'

'But for whom?' Tao asked.

'We ran some checks on Cerberus and found that they have an American subsidiary. Based on their tax filings in both Europe and the U.S., we've pieced together their client list, and it's a short one. Their primary source of revenue comes from a large French pharmaceutical firm, Vielogic. Cerberus handles corporate security for the company as well as personal security for its founder and CEO, Charles Lafitte.'

'Why would a drug company want the Ice Pick probe?' Tao asked.

'I was just thinking the same thing,' Kilkenny said, 'but if a drug company is behind the attack, then I was wrong about what the raiders were after.'

'If not the probe, then what?' Tao asked.

'The samples from Lake Vostok.'

'Didn't you tell me the value of those samples is unknown?' Tao asked.

'It is,' Kilkenny replied. 'The DNA in those samples might be similar to microbial life found elsewhere in the world, or they might be wildly different. If Lake Vostok turns out to be a kettle of new and unique DNA, then biotech companies looking for the next Epogen or Viagra would pay millions to get in on it.'

'But that raid must've cost millions,' Tao said. 'Isn't that a lot of money to spend on a crapshoot?'

'That depends on how you define the risks. They might get nothing for their trouble, or they might find a billion-dollar-a-year wonder drug that cures cancer or stops aging.'

'The pharmaceutical industry spends billions on R&D every year, and a lot of that research never becomes a marketable product,' Barnett added. 'For a company like Vielogic, the cost of stealing those samples is less than what they spend each year on Washington lobbyists. Now, I'd like to hear about this Cayman trip. How does it fit in with your investigation?'

'We're still not sure that it does,' Tao replied, 'but we have strong reason to believe that Duroc tried to kill us because of a stock transaction and not our investigation into the attack in Antarctica.'

'A stock transaction?' Barnett asked.

'It has to do with a small biotech company I'm involved with,' Kilkenny said, before explaining the curious short on UGene stock that he'd discovered. 'We brought back a set of disks that we hope contain evidence linking Duroc to the trades.'

'And what will that tell you?' Barnett asked.

'Either Duroc is psychic when it comes to playing the market, or he had something to do with a couple of murders in Ann Arbor.'

Barnett scrawled a few notes on his pad. 'Based on the evidence you've uncovered so far, I think Vielogic warrants a further investigation.'

37

New York City

Duroc sat in his Midtown Manhattan office reading through two reports prepared by his research staff. The first described the arson fire that had consumed the offices of the Sterling Private Bank and the murder of Cayman banker Hugh Harley. According to the *Cayman Compass*, Harley's murder had become the crime of the year, with rumors about the banker's illicit activities with drug lords running rampant over the islands. Officially, no suspects had been identified and no evidence of motive for the crime found.

Next were routine background checks on Roxanne Tao and Nolan Kilkenny. The report on Tao's personal history was short – she had none. Duroc's investigators failed to find anything on Tao that predated her appearance in Ann Arbor as the head of a new field office for a Silicon Valley venture-capital firm.

The report on Nolan Kilkenny was far more substantial. He was a resident of Michigan, living near the village of Dexter. Living with him at his family's farm were his father and paternal grandparents. Duroc paused when he read the section regarding Kilkenny's employment as a project director for the Michigan Applied Research Consortium and acting CEO of UGene.

So that's why he's nosing around my trades, Duroc thought.

Highlighted in the report was a notation of Kilkenny's graduation from the United States Naval Academy and service as an officer in the SEALs. Like his own DGSE, the SEALs were considered one of the world's premier fighting forces.

The final page tracked Kilkenny and Tao's movements over the past few weeks, starting with the most recent and working back in time. Duroc noted, with some satisfaction, that they had missed the return leg of their Cayman trip. Then he saw recent flights to Rio de Janeiro, Tucson, and Waco.

Tao's trail went no farther back than a flight from Washington to Detroit in early March, when she apparently sprang into existence. For Kilkenny, Duroc's researchers identified a series of commercial and military flights that described a journey to and from Antarctica. That list ended with a note indicating no record could be found for Kilkenny's trip from New Zealand back to Michigan.

He was there on the day of the raid, Duroc realized from the dates.

He rechecked Kilkenny's background and found the

note on MARC. Flipping through the research file on NASA's LV Station project, he found MARC and UGene listed on the project team.

Kilkenny must have been the one who attacked us.

38

Ann Arbor, Michigan

'What do you have for me?' Kilkenny asked.

Inside the MARC computer center, Tao was seated beside Grin at a long worktable covered with printouts. Kilkenny pulled up a chair and sat down.

'Couple of things,' Grin replied. 'I did as you asked and poked around inside Vielogic's network for shipping and receiving records. Did you know they move a lot of stuff around?'

'It's a big company. Anything else?'

'Yeah. Looking at just the receiving side of things, I found that they just recently took delivery on a bunch of equipment in New Jersey. I checked their latest press releases and that's where they put their first U.S. research facility. Most of the stuff going there is from vendors in North America or Europe. All of them look like legitimate scientific supply companies, the kind I can pull a Dunn and Bradstreet on, except this one.'

Grin handed Kilkenny a printout. A single shipment

of security equipment was sent to the New Jersey lab by Cerberus Sécurité, NA.

'That's Duroc's company,' Kilkenny said.

'Actually,' Tao offered, 'it's the American subsidiary of Duroc's company.'

'Knowing what we now know about Duroc,' Grin continued, 'I thought anything touched by his hands was worth a look. This place Vielogic built in New Jersey is pretty wild – lots of sharp angles and rippling walls like that rock 'n' roll museum in Seattle. Well, I remember when we put this place together, and all the security equipment came through the general contractor. Sure, we told him what we wanted where, but the contractor bought the gear and put it in. I figure the same is probably true for this Taj Ma-Lab, and sure enough, it is. All their security was roughed in last summer and finished off in November.'

'So if the contractor put in the security system, what's Duroc shipping there in February?' Kilkenny asked.

'It gets better,' Tao replied.

'I don't know what's in the box,' Grin admitted, 'but I do know where it came from. Going backward from Vielogic's new lab, this shipment came by truck from the Port Authority of New York and New Jersey, where it was off-loaded from a cargo ship; the *Angelina*. According to the ship's records filed with the port authority, the *Angelina* was docked in Rio Gallegos on February first. She took on cargo from Cerberus that day and set sail the following morning.'

'We know that Agabashian shipped the launcher to Rio Gallegos,' Tao said. 'So I think it's safe to assume that Duroc used this as his jump point to and from Antarctica.'

'It'd keep the logistics simple,' Kilkenny agreed, 'and this certainly fits the timeline. Grin, get whatever you can on this lab in New Jersey – layouts, security, anything that'll help Roxanne and me get in and out.'

'I think I can pull something together.'

'Don't forget about the other thing,' Tao said.

'What other thing?' Kilkenny asked.

'Those disks you brought back from the Caymans,' Grin replied. 'Methinks I found your smoking gun.'

'All right, walk me through it.'

'The stack of Zip disks you brought back were encrypted, but with an older, low-level commercial program. Nothing that a little brute force couldn't crack. As you hoped, it's bank data and not the guy's personal stash of Web porn. When I got through decrypting all the disks, I thought what I had were two identical sets of backups.'

'Did you check them both anyway?' Kilkenny asked.

Grin smiled. 'You know me too well, man. Yeah, I checked and on the bottom line, they matched up. It's in the details where things get interesting.'

Grin laid out side-by-side reports of the Sterling Private Bank's stock transactions during the first two months of the year. In the first report, the short trades on UGene stock were placed by dozens of Cayman Island holding companies. The UGene trades in the second were all made by just one holding company: Pont Neuf.

'So, Harley was keeping two sets of books,' Kilkenny said.

'Pont Neuf wasn't the only company Harley's bank was shielding.' Tao pointed to a report with highlighted entries. 'The churn of money through these accounts looks like a laundering operation to me.'

'Let's pass that piece back to Barnett; he can route it to any interested parties. Anything more on this Pont Neuf?'

'It's a Cayman Island holding company that was formed by Sumner Duroc,' Tao replied. 'Now I'm certain that he tried to kill us because of this stock deal.'

'It sure looks that way,' Kilkenny agreed. 'But how the hell did he know UGene was going to crash?'

'Doesn't this show a motive?' Tao asked. 'We're looking at a lot of money here.'

'This shows a *possible* motive, but there is no evidence Duroc had anything to do with the murders,' Kilkenny replied, frustrated. 'The police found Eames's semen in his ex-wife's body. Unless Duroc took semen from Eames or has some other way to make it, only Eames could have committed the murders.'

'Well, what if he *does* have another way to make it?' Grin asked.

'What?' Kilkenny said.

'Just suppose for a minute this guy Duroc has a way to make semen in a lab? I mean, he's hooked up with one of the biggest biotech firms in the world,' Grin explained. 'I've been working with Eames and Sutton for little over a year now, and the way I see it, DNA is just a long string of data. Instead of bits, you've got four molecules, repeated over and over. Maybe someone at Vielogic has figured out a way to make DNA.'

39

'The next matter before this court,' Judge William Zigler announced, 'is the People versus Oswald Eames. The deputies will please escort the defendant into the courtroom.'

Washtenaw County deputies led Oswald Eames in from the court's holding cell. This time, he was dressed in a dark blue suit with a crisp white shirt and a conservative tie. Tiv Balogh stood waiting as one of the deputies removed Eames's handcuffs.

'Good morning, Mr Eames,' Balogh said once the deputies had stepped away from the defense table.

Eames shook Balogh's hand and nodded with a weak smile. His hands trembled slightly and he hoped Balogh couldn't sense his nervousness. Nolan Kilkenny sat in the gallery behind the defense table.

Zigler cupped his hand over his microphone and turned to the clerk. 'Let's get started.'

'The People versus Oswald Eames for the purpose of final conference,' the clerk announced to the courtroom.

'Appearances for the record,' Zigler requested.

'Kurt McPherson, representing the Washtenaw County Prosecutor's office, Your Honor.'

'Tiv Balogh, representing Mr Eames, Your Honor.'

'Very well,' Zigler began. 'Mr Balogh, I have your motion to quash the bind over on your client.'

'Yes, Your Honor. The prosecution does not have sufficient evidence to make its case.'

'Mr McPherson, any comments?' Zigler asked.

'Only that we wholeheartedly disagree with the defense's motion, Your Honor.'

'I thought as much. The motion to quash the bind over is denied. Moving on to the motion to suppress evidence acquired as the result of illegal search.' Zigler looked up from his file. 'Mr Balogh?'

'Your Honor, the search of my client was illegal under the Fourth Amendment. There was no probable cause to justify it. The blood sample taken from my client is the fruit of an illegal search, and the subsequent DNA test must be ruled inadmissible.'

'Mr McPherson?'

'Your Honor, there was a great deal of blood at the crime scene. There was also evidence that Miss Olson had been sexually assaulted. Those two facts led police to reasonably assume that DNA evidence from the assailant would also be found at the scene. The nine-one-one call placed by Miss Olson – '

'Objection, Your Honor,' Balogh interjected. 'There is no proof that Faye Olson made that call.'

McPherson rolled his eyes. 'Let me rephrase that, Your Honor. A nine-one-one call was placed from 4731 Pineview that implicated the defendant in these crimes. Based on this call, the detectives had cause to suspect Oswald Eames of these crimes and certainly had cause to believe they would find DNA evidence linking him to the crimes in a blood sample.'

'I find nothing improper with the warrant. It is specific as to the item sought – the suspect's blood sample – and the location where such a sample would most likely be found. I also find that there was probable cause for the search and that Mr Eames's Fourth Amendment rights were not violated as a result of the search. The motion is denied, and the blood sample and subsequent DNA analysis are deemed admissible,' Zigler announced. 'Moving forward, Mr Balogh, I assume you would prefer a jury trial?'

'Yes, Your Honor.'

'Very well,' Zigler said as he checked his calendar. 'The trial will start on Tuesday, the eleventh of June, at ten o'clock.'

40

Kilkenny sat in the narrow booth adjacent to the court-house holding cell. On the other side of the Plexiglas window, Eames paced the floor of the large gray concrete room. He was the only person in the cell. When Kilkenny rapped his knuckles on the window, Eames looked up and walked over.

'That certainly didn't go well,' Eames said as he sat down opposite Kilkenny.

'Balogh didn't expect it to, but he had to file the motions anyway.'

'So, what did you want to talk to me about?'

'I'm working on something. I don't know if it means anything yet, but it just might. What do you know about a company called Vielogic?'

'They're French and one of the biggest of the new biotech pharmaceutical companies. About a week before the murders, Lloyd and I had dinner with Charles Lafitte, the CEO of Vielogic.'

'You're kidding. Where?'

'At his home in Manhattan. Lloyd and I were there attending a conference, as was Lafitte. It was a social thing, but Lloyd and I did have a brief business conversation with Lafitte. He wanted to buy UGene.'

'Did he make an offer?' Kilkenny asked.

'No, just put out a feeler. I turned him down because I really don't want to work for the guy.'

'What do you know about Lafitte?'

'Not much, really,' Eames replied. 'The guy is very bright and worth a ton of money. If that dinner's any indication, he's got great taste in food and wine. Lafitte understands science as well as business, and he is very aggressive in both arenas.'

'You ever hear of a guy named Sumner Duroc? He runs all the security for Vielogic.'

Eames thought carefully for a moment, then looked at Kilkenny. 'No, not that I remember.'

'How about a little company in the Cayman Islands called Pont Neuf?'

'Again, no. Why do you ask?'

'Duroc owns Pont Neuf,' Kilkenny replied. 'It's just a holding company. He's using it to make stock trades. So far, the only trades he's made were for shares of UGene.'

'Then he got screwed like all the rest of my shareholders.'

Kilkenny shook his head. 'Duroc made a bundle. He shorted your stock, and when it fell he cashed out and netted about twenty-six million dollars.'

Eames let out a long whistle.

'Yeah. Either Duroc is the luckiest man alive or he *knew* your stock was going to take a hit. And the only way he could have known was if he had something to do with the murders.'

'Jesus!' Eames was on his feet. 'Jesus! We gotta tell Tiv!'

'Oz, listen! We got nothing hard on this, nothing that's going to get you out of here, but I'm working on it.'

41

MARCH 16

New York

Following Grin's directions, Kilkenny and Tao arrived at a turn-of-the-century factory in Greenwich Village that had been reclaimed as residential lofts. As soon as they were inside, Grin closed and locked the door. Stripped to bare steel and brick, the old building was transformed into a shell in which sleek contemporary planes and curves described a hypermodern living environment.

'Interesting place,' Kilkenny said as his eyes followed the line of a warped partition.

'It belongs to a buddy of mine and his wife,' Grin explained. 'Both of 'em are into CGI, doing graphics for the movies. They're in Europe working on a film right now, but they let me crash here whenever I'm in town. This place is wired with *all* the best toys, which is just what we're gonna need tonight. If I wasn't running the shop at MARC, I'd probably be working here. After I arrived, I went to work collecting information about

Vielogic's facility in New Jersey. It's relatively new and, thankfully, equipped with the very latest in computer-ized building management and security systems.'

'And why are we thankful for that?' Tao asked.

'Because it made my job a lot easier. I have a detailed computer model of the entire building that I can transmit into Nolan's heads-up display.' Grin smiled at Kilkenny. 'Once inside, you'll be able to see around walls. I also found a dedicated phone line used by the security contractor to maintain the system. It's already mine.'

'Great,' Kilkenny replied. 'Let's see what we're getting ourselves into.'

Grin led Kilkenny and Tao into the studio. The dull hum of cooling fans filled the space with white noise. In addition to four graphics workstations, one wall of the studio was covered with a large high-definition flat screen surrounded by several smaller video displays. Grin typed a command into one of the workstations and the large wall monitor filled with a model of the Vielogic facility and surrounding property.

'You weren't kidding when you said this building was different,' Kilkenny said, then turned his attention to the grounds. 'Flat lot, large parking areas, minimal landscaping on a few islands around the perimeter. On the plus side, we don't have to deal with any fences or razor wire. There's a drainage creek running across the back property line and large parcels on either side.'

'Both are occupied by large pharmaceutical companies,' Grin said. 'This stretch of road is affectionately known as Research Row.'

'How is the security?' Tao asked.

'The guards are all Cerberus Sécurité. The electronics are top of the line – good cameras, motion sensors, mag locks – and all of it is integrated into a computerized operations center.' Grin changed the image to show the plan of the building's main floor highlighting the security suite. 'Vielogic runs a pretty standard five-day work week with hardly anyone working on the weekends.'

Kilkenny nodded. 'A nice quiet Saturday night, just the way I like it.'

'The newest piece of the research wing was completed in January. It contains Vielogic's first Level Four bio-containment lab – essentially a building within a building – accessible only through an internal secure corridor.'

'Isn't Level Four for the real nasty stuff?' Tao asked. 'Like deadly viruses and biological weapons?'

'That, and stuff nobody has ever seen before, like what you might find in a twenty-million-year-old lake buried under a couple of miles of ice.'

42

Bridgewater, New Jersey

Shortly after midnight, Kilkenny parked the rental car in a residential neighborhood that abutted the drainage creek about a mile downstream from Vielogic's U.S. headquarters. Icy drizzle fell continuously from the dark, overcast sky, making hard surfaces slick and the ground soft and spongy. The cul-de-sac was dark except for the bluish flicker of television sets that leaked through the blinds and drapes of a few nearby homes.

Kilkenny donned his dark gray SEALskin just as he had in Antarctica, and he wore a throat mike connected to a secure digital transmitter and a pair of wrap-around glasses that could project holographic images. Tao was dressed in a form-fitting black Lycra cat suit with flat rubber-soled boots.

Kilkenny led the way into the drainage ditch. As they moved quietly along the banks of the creek, the noise of wind and trucks on the nearby highway overwhelmed the faint sounds of their progress.

'We're on the move. Do you copy?' Kilkenny mouthed.

'Loud and clear,' Grin replied. 'I show you just under a mile from the target.'

Kilkenny glanced at the way point readout on his heads-up display. The numbers appeared to float ten feet in front of him. 'That's a good read. I'll keep you posted. Out.'

The combat electronics Kilkenny wore transmitted a secondary signal across the digital connection to Grin, providing a link between the small computer on his body and the more powerful machines in the Greenwich Village loft.

The facilities along Research Row appeared as hazy islands of light shrouded in the darkness. Kilkenny got used to staring through the droplets on his glasses, each glistening with a distorted image of the distant lights. They emerged from the creek at the rear of Vielogic's property and ran across a large meadow toward one of the strangest buildings they'd ever seen. Kilkenny reached the sharp edge of the nearest wing, followed by Tao. The cold stone surface glistened with reflections in the tiny droplets of rain.

'About thirty feet ahead you'll find an entry,' Grin said, his disembodied voice quietly speaking in Kilkenny's ear. 'It's got card-reader access, mag lock, and an alarm. There's also a camera on the roof and another inside trained on the door. Hold your position while I deal with all this stuff.'

Grin studied the images on the display wall. All the smaller monitors showed live video pulled directly from the building's security cameras. He was seeing everything the guard in the command center saw.

From the three-dimensional image of the building on the large screen, Grin selected the exterior camera aimed at the door Kilkenny and Tao planned to pass through. He recorded thirty seconds of video showing the door and the dark, rain-soaked side of the building. Grin created an alternate video feed for the monitor in the building command center. Instead of a live view from the camera, the security guard now saw a seamless loop of recorded video. Grin repeated the same trick on the camera that watched the same door from the inside.

'I got you covered. You can move in.'

Kilkenny took the point and motioned with his hand to move toward the door. As he and Tao approached, they heard an audible click as the mag locks released. Kilkenny opened the door and led his team in.

'Just close the door behind you,' Grin said into Kilkenny's earpiece.

'We're in,' Kilkenny mouthed.

'Go left,' Grin instructed, 'then hold about ten feet from the end of the hall while I deal with the next camera.'

The corridor was dark except for strategically placed light fixtures that were always kept on in case of an emergency. They moved silently, the soft rubber soles of their boots muffling their careful footsteps.

Grin guided them down secondary corridors, avoiding the brightly lit main atrium that was the circulation back-bone of the complex. The pattern of their incursion consisted of cautious moves forward, interrupted by tense moments of waiting while Grin cleared the next leg.

'There's a security man headed toward you. Duck into the suite two doors ahead on your right,' Grin instructed. 'I'll pop the lock.'

As Kilkenny neared the door, the mag lock buzzed loudly and released the door.

Shit! Kilkenny thought.

The noise from the mag lock echoed like a cannon shot on the hard surfaces of the walls and floor. Kilkenny pushed the door open wide and waved Tao inside quickly, then he eased the door closed.

'Grin,' Kilkenny mouthed, though shouting in his mind, 'don't reset that mag lock until the security guard is gone. It makes way too much noise.'

'Okay, I'll wait.'

Down an intersecting corridor, the security guard heard the metallic sound of a mag lock releasing a door. He reached over to his shoulder and switched on the mike clipped to his epaulette.

'Danny, it's Carl. I'm down near the intersection of corridors one-five and one-six. Do you show any mag locks being opened?'

'Negative. All doors in your area show secure.'

'We may have another fault. I'd swear I heard one of 'em release. I'll check it out.'

As the guard turned the corner, he caught the reflected image of a closing door in the glass protecting a signed lithograph. He studied the reflection for a moment, then moved toward the door. The light on the door's card reader glowed green – the door was unlocked.

The guard drew out his Beretta, then turned the handle and cautiously pushed the door open.

Kilkenny yanked the door, pulling the guard toward him. As the guard stumbled forward, Kilkenny struck his extended forearm just below the wrist, and the pistol fell onto the carpeted floor. Kilkenny swung upward with his hand flat, fingers extended. He chopped the side of his hand sharply against the guard's neck and knocked the man unconscious. Kilkenny caught the guard before he hit the floor and pulled him into the suite.

Tao picked up the Beretta and closed the door while Kilkenny pulled some zip ties from his belt pouch and bound the man's hands and feet. He then removed the guard's dark blue tie and gagged him with it.

'Get his card key,' Tao said.

Kilkenny unclipped the badge from the man's breast pocket. 'Grin, how's it look out there?'

'While you were holed up, I hit the rest of the cameras. You're clear to the research labs. I'll keep an eye out for any other patrols.'

'Good, because somebody will eventually miss this guy and go looking for him.'

They moved with silent efficiency through the final stretches of corridor. As promised by Grin, the surveillance cameras had all turned a blind eye, and they encountered no other security guards along the way.

Once inside the single-story laboratory wing, Kilkenny pulled a small wireless computer from his thigh pocket and switched it on. The device – a modified Palm X – began emitting a short-range transmission tuned to the specific frequency used by the Ice Pick probe. Even though the probe was hardwired to the computer system at LV Station, wireless communications had been built in to allow the researchers to test the probe's ability to remotely receive instructions. Unfortunately, the combination of Ice Pick's short reception range and interference caused by the shielding around Vielogic's labs meant that Kilkenny had to be fairly close to communicate with the probe.

Beyond the entry doors, the wide corridor ended abruptly in an alcove. Doors to gendered locker rooms faced each other from opposite walls, and directly ahead a pair of automated stainless steel and Plexiglas doors formed the first barrier to an air lock through which large pieces of equipment could be brought into the laboratories.

Grin unlocked the locker room doors as they approached.

'This way,' Kilkenny said.

They moved through the men's locker room into another alcove, this one leading to a Level 2 decontamination space.

'Yo, man,' Grin said, his voice clipped by static, 'we got a couple of problems.'

'Talk to me,' Kilkenny replied.

'Your signal is getting a little sloppy.'

'I'm surrounded by a lot of metal. What else?'

'The building data I acquired is a little out of date. I don't have control over the systems inside the Level

Four suite. I can open the Level Three staging area, but you're on your own after that.'

'Understood.'

Kilkenny stripped off his glasses and throat mike and handed them to Tao. 'Here, you keep in touch with Grin and hold the corridor.'

'I'll bang on the door if anything comes up,' Tao said. 'Be careful in there.'

Grin bypassed the security on the next air lock and Kilkenny stepped inside. Once the door closed, he was bathed in ultraviolet light. After several minutes, the normal lights came back on, and the next doorway slid open with a pneumatic hiss.

The walls of the eight-foot-wide corridor were modular panels of stainless steel and glass, with black gaskets at the seams. There were four Level 3 labs in this section, two on each side of the corridor. The corridor was rated Biohazard Level 2 and kept separate from the labs by means of positive air pressure in the corridor and negative in the labs.

Kilkenny held out the Palm X. The handheld computer reported no contact with the probe. He jogged down to the end of the corridor. The door to the Level 3 staging area was already open. Like the labs, the staging area had negative air pressure relative to the Level 2 corridor. Kilkenny stepped into the staging area and the door slid closed behind him.

He walked past the decontamination shower and bathroom and entered the gowning area. Along the wall he saw alcoves containing Chemturion biological space suits. Each suit bore the name of the researcher who used it, and Kilkenny quickly selected one he thought would fit. He slipped on the bulky, multilayered outfit and gained an immediate appreciation for the discomfort endured by spacewalking astronauts.

He carefully picked up the Palm X – his sense of touch greatly diminished by the rubber gloves – and stepped into the final air lock. The air inside the suit was already getting warm and his faceplate was fogging up because of his body heat and respiration.

Kilkenny passed through the air lock into the Level 4 lab. He located an umbilical line dangling from the ceiling and connected it to his suit. Immediately, Kilkenny felt a rush of air. His faceplate cleared, but he was still sweating heavily and his hands felt slick inside the rubber gloves. He checked the Palm X:

CONTACT WITH ICE PICK PROBE ESTABLISHED.

Where? Kilkenny thought, looking around the large, equipment-laden space.

43

'Carl, you there?' the senior security guard stationed in the Operations Center called out over the radio.

No answer.

'Hey, Jon, you read me?'

'Loud and clear, Danny. Whassup?'

'Carl's gone off the air. He said he was gonna check out a mag lock that was actin' up near the intersection of one-five and one-six. Can you head down there and see what that jerk-off is doin'?'

'Sure, Danny.'

The guard leaned back in his chair and resumed watching the security monitors. Other than the occasional flicker, the picture never seemed to change. He watched as a bank of four monitors switched over to the laboratory wing.

'Lab one, two, three, and four,' he recited as the images appeared on the screen.

Thirty seconds later, the next series appeared.

'Level F – ' The word choked in his throat. 'What the hell!'

The guard bolted upright and grabbed the microphone.

'Heads up, guys. We got an intruder in the Level Four corridor. Mark, Jon, Jeff, get your asses over there and seal it off.'

'The guy's in Level Four? Ain't that the hot zone?'

'Yeah, but I'll make sure that he gets hosed off real good on the way out. Now move it!'

'What about Carl?' Jon asked.

'Fuck Carl! If we don't nail this intruder Duroc's gonna hang us all by our balls from the flagpole.'

Kilkenny found the Ice Pick probe in a far corner of the lab. Thick orange cables ran from wall outlets into jacks on the probe's exterior, providing power. The spherical cryobot had been removed from the probe and placed in a support frame on the lab bench.

Kilkenny scrolled through a list of commands on the Palm X and selected *Cryobot Access*. The upper hemisphere of the cryobot spun 180 degrees, then separated from the lower half. A hydraulic lift in the center of the cryobot telescoped upward, opening a twelve-inch gap between the halves.

Inside the lower hemisphere, Kilkenny found the hexagonal storage drawers where the sample capsules were stored. Most of the spaces were empty. Kilkenny reached in and tried to grip one of the capsules with his gloved hands but found it difficult to extract the tiny objects.

The people working on this must have the same problem. Kilkenny thought. *How'd they solve it?*

Kilkenny searched the countertop and found a pair of blunt-nosed tongs. He placed the looped ends of the tongs over his thumb and forefinger, then carefully extracted one of the metallic capsules.

I got what I came for. Time to go.

'Roxanne!' Grin called out. 'There's two – no, three – guards heading your way. They must have spotted Nolan in the lab.'

'Understood,' Tao replied.

She glanced back at the door that led to the Level 4 lab, mentally urging Kilkenny to walk through it.

Kilkenny disconnected his umbilical line, reentered the air lock, and closed the door behind him. Immediately, shower heads mounted in the ceiling and walls of the air lock began spraying his suit with chemicals designed to kill any pathogen that might try to hitch a ride out of the lab.

The chemicals had no effect on the metallic capsule he'd recovered from the probe, but they quickly destroyed the Palm X. The screen flickered, then went blank, and the plastic shell began to disintegrate in Kilkenny's gloved hand.

'Grin, how close are the guards?' Tao asked.

'Two of them are closing fast. You and Nolan better get out of there now.'

'He's not back yet.'

Tao looked around the locker room for some defensive cover, but found nothing. The room was lined with metal lockers. Once the guards reached the entry door, they would have a clear shot at her.

Tao looked up at the two-by-two acoustic tile ceiling. 'Grin, how much room is there above the suspended ceiling?'

Grin sliced a sectional view through the computer model of the locker room. 'About four feet.'

Tao set the guard's card key and the Beretta on the floor. She was loathe to give up the weapon, but reasoned that leaving these things where the guards would find them increased the odds that they would think Kilkenny was acting alone.

She then stood atop one of the long steel benches, pushed up on the ceiling tile above her head, and slid it off to the side. Grabbing hold of the steel studs that supported the drywall soffit over the lockers, Tao pulled herself through the opening into the ceiling. Sealed metal ducts, cable trays, and dozens of pipes and conduits filled the darkened space. Once she found her footing, she pushed the ceiling tile back into place.

The decontamination cycle ended with a clear water rinse and a blast of high pressure air to blow off the excess water. Finally, the door to the staging area unlocked, and Kilkenny quickly exited the claustrophobic confines of the air lock. Inside the staging area, he set the capsule down on a stainless-steel bench, tossed the wrecked Palm X into one of the lockers, and began stripping off the cumbersome space suit.

'I'll take a wet suit over this thing any day,' he muttered.

He left the space suit in a heap on the floor, grabbed the capsule, and headed for the door. He stepped into the next air lock and was run through an ultraviolet-light

258

decontamination cycle. Once the cycle completed, the door began to slowly slide open.

'Freeze!'

At the far end of the corridor Kilkenny saw a guard with a surgical mask over his face pointing a pistol at him. He ducked behind the open door, popped the sealed metal capsule into his mouth, and swallowed.

'I said freeze, goddammit! You deaf, motherfucker?'

Kilkenny stood in the fully open doorway, hands raised.

'If you so much as move a goddammed inch, I'll shoot you! Face the wall and put your hands behind your head.'

Kilkenny complied and the guard trained his pistol on the back of Kilkenny's head. A second guard stepped out into the Level 2 corridor.

'You got him, Mark?'

'Yeah,' Kilkenny's captor replied.

'He clean?'

'How the fuck should I know?'

'He was in the hot zone, man!'

Kilkenny's captor recalled what he'd been told about Level 4 as part of his training for this facility. 'The air locks wouldn't have opened unless he ran a decontamination cycle, so don't worry about it. Cuff him.'

The second guard holstered his pistol as he walked down the corridor and bound Kilkenny's hands behind his back.

'Danny,' Kilkenny's captor called into his radio, 'we got him.'

'I was beginning to wonder. Bring him in while I call the boss.'

The two guards marched Kilkenny through the Level 2 air lock, where all three men were exposed to ultraviolet light. They moved through the alcove and back into the men's locker room.

'These must be Carl's,' the guard said, picking up the Beretta and card key. 'Duroc ain't gonna be happy with him.'

'Shut up,' Kilkenny's captor ordered. 'If any of us still has a job after this, we should consider ourselves lucky.' He smacked his hand against the back of Kilkenny's head. 'How the fuck did you get in here?'

44

A third man, winded from a long run, met up with Kilkenny and the other security guards in the main corridor outside the lab wing.

'Hey, Jeff, you and Jon check the locker rooms for anybody else. I'll stay here with the prisoner.'

The two guards went into the women's locker room with pistols drawn. Kilkenny's captor looked him over with contempt.

'So, tough guy, you got any friends here with you, or are you flying solo tonight? Bet you're some kind of liberal, tree-hugging, no-nuke, Greenpeace, animal fuckin' rights advocate. Am I right?'

Kilkenny remained silent.

'You got the wrong place, asshole. No cute little bunny rabbits getting perfume sprayed in their eyes here. We cure diseases 'n' shit. We help people. Too bad we can't find a cure for dickheads like you.'

The two guards returned through the men's locker room.

'We swept 'em both and found nothing.'

'You check all the lockers and the stalls?'

'Yeah, they're empty.'

'Okay. Jon, you help me escort this turd back to Ops. Jeff, go see if you can find where this guy left Carl. He disappeared near corridors five and six, this level.'

'Got it,' Jeff said as he holstered his pistol and walked off.

'They're leaving with Nolan,' Grin's voice spoke into Tao's ear. 'The corridor is clear.'

'I read you,' Tao replied in a whisper.

Tao carefully pulled a two-by-two ceiling tile out of the grid and slid it off to the side. Through the square opening she peered into the locker room below. It was dark and empty. Silently she lowered herself through the opening and dropped onto the floor.

'Where's Nolan?' Tao asked.

'They're moving into the administration wing. Best bet, they're taking him to the Security Operations Center. You better think of something before they call in the cops.'

'Can you cut off the phone lines?'

'Nope. Right now, I can only tweak building security. I could hack some of the other systems, but that would take time that Nolan doesn't have.'

'All right, Grin,' Tao said. 'I need you to guide me to the Ops Center, and I need to know the location and numbers of security personnel.'

'I'm already on it,' Grin replied. 'Do you see the map?'

An overhead view of the first-floor plan around her position appeared in front of Tao – a holographic projection from Kilkenny's glasses. A thin yellow line extended from the point where Tao stood down the corridor.

'Yes, I see it.'

'Good. I plotted out the quickest route to the Ops Center; just follow the yellow line. I'll mark hold points if I need you to stop for some reason, and I'll holler if any of the guards get too close.'

Tao began following Grin's illuminated path, moving swiftly through the partially darkened corridors.

'Good work, boys,' the senior security guard said as Kilkenny was brought into the Operations Center. 'Straddle his ass in that chair and tie his feet.'

The man watched as the two guards bound their prisoner to the chair. Kilkenny was drenched with sweat, like he'd been in a sauna.

'I'll take it from here,' the senior man said. 'Do a perimeter sweep and see if you can find out how this guy got in.'

'You got it,' one of the guards replied, and the two men left.

'So, Harry-fucking-Houdini, how the hell did you get in here?'

Kilkenny looked straight into the man's eyes, but said nothing.

'You are in a world of hurt, my friend. Deep shit, and nobody's gonna throw you a line. You tell me why you're here and my employers might cut you a little slack. We just need to know what you're doin' here. You some drug company's spy or just a troublemaker?'

Kilkenny still remained silent. He looked past the

guard at the bank of video monitors, looking for flickers in the images.

'Fine, play the hero. I could give a shit. You're the one goin' to jail.'

'Hold up, Roxanne,' Grin said. 'There's a guard in the next corridor to your right, heading toward you.'

Tao slowed down and began moving with deliberate steps toward the intersecting hallway. She could hear the security guard approaching, the slapping sound growing louder with each footfall on the terrazzo floor.

Near the intersection, Tao pressed her back against the wall and waited. Her eyes were fixed on an imaginary line her mind drew across the end of the corridor. After several seconds, a foot appeared and, moving forward in stride, it crossed her line. Turning like a hinge, Tao pivoted on her right foot and shot the ball of her left into the guard's groin.

The guard staggered back, doubling over, as Tao's knee struck his face. The man's head whipped back, blood and teeth sprayed from his mouth. As he fell, Tao grabbed his head and slammed it against the floor. The guard lay limp and motionless. Tao crouched over him, disconnected his radio, and pulled the Beretta from his holster.

'Your route is clear all the way to the Operations Center,' Grin said.

'I'm moving.'

The guard grabbed the phone and hit the speed dial. Duroc picked up the line before the first ring faded.

'What's happening?' he asked brusquely.

'Sir, I have the intruder here in the office. It appears he was acting alone, but I have the men running a full sweep of the building in case there are others.'

Kilkenny saw a flicker on one screen. A moment later, it flickered again.

'Good. Have you gotten any information out of him?' Duroc asked.

'Not a thing, sir.'

'Describe him.'

'He's a white guy, about six foot, lean and muscular, clean shaven, red hair cut short. Looks almost military issue.'

'Red hair? Send me his picture,' Duroc demanded.

'Hold on, sir.'

The guard pressed the hold button, set the phone down, and picked up a digital camera. Behind the guard, another monitor flickered.

'Smile, asshole,' he said as he snapped a picture.

The guard connected the camera to a computer and e-mailed the photo to Duroc. Then he picked up the phone and took Duroc off hold.

'The picture is on the way, sir.'

'I am opening the file now.'

Duroc's stomach tightened when Kilkenny's face appeared on his monitor.

'*Merde!* Hold him there. I'm on my way.'

'Do you want me to bring in the police?'

'No, I will handle this myself. Stay with him until I arrive.'

'Yes, sir.'

The guard looked at the phone in his hand in wonder for a second before placing the handset back in the cradle.

The monitor showing the corridor outside the Operations Center flickered.

'Well, buddy, your life just took a serious turn for the worse. The guy on the other end of that phone has taken a personal interest in you. He's on his way for a little chat, and I don't think you're gonna find him to be as nice as me.'

'Then we'll just have to leave before he gets here,' Tao said as she aimed the Beretta at the guard's forehead. 'Cut him loose.'

Startled, the guard slowly took a pair of scissors from the desk and cut the plastic ties around Kilkenny's wrists and ankles.

'How are we doing on time?' Kilkenny asked.

'About three minutes before another guard swings back this way,' Tao replied. 'Less if somebody calls in and doesn't get an answer from your friend here.'

Kilkenny sat the guard down in the chair and restrained him.

'This even things up between us?' Tao asked as she handed him the combat electronics pack and the glasses.

'It does in my book,' Kilkenny said with a smile. 'Grin, plot us a clear path out of here.'

'Good to hear your voice again, Nolan. I've killed the exterior lights around the building. Just follow the route on your display.'

True to his word, Grin led them quickly out of the building. They sprinted across the darkened lawn with only the distant illumination of the adjacent buildings to light their way. They slowed as they reached the rear corner of Vielogic's property near the drainage ditch.

Kilkenny stepped down into the ditch first and quickly led the way back toward their car. They soon heard the sound of rotors beating the air. Kilkenny held his hand up, halting their progress.

Looking just over the tree line, north of where they stood, Kilkenny saw a blinking red light appear in the sky. As it moved closer to the Vielogic building, the thumping of the helicopter blades grew louder. It touched down briefly on the helipad, just long enough to drop off a passenger, before returning to the air.

As the helicopter rose, its floodlight cast a powerful beam of cool white illumination. It swept around the building perimeter first, then moved on to the grounds.

'Let's get moving,' Kilkenny said. 'If that chopper gets anywhere near us, find some cover quick.'

Kilkenny and Tao moved as quickly as they could in the slippery, uneven terrain of the ditch. Tree roots and thick brush grabbed at their feet. The sound of the helicopter grew louder, and Kilkenny saw the bright beam moving in their direction. They quickly scrambled up the muddy sides of the ditch and ducked beneath the boughs of an overgrown pine.

Slowly, the helicopter moved toward them, the pilot searching for any sign of the two intruders. Tiny slivers of white moved over Kilkenny and Tao as the pine needles filtered the light. The helicopter stopped, hovering with its light aimed at the pine tree.

'Shit,' Kilkenny hissed angrily. 'He must have caught a reflection off my glasses.'

Kilkenny turned his head facedown and cupped his hands over his temples. The helicopter hovered for several seconds and Kilkenny could see fragments of the intense light probing through the tree. Then all was dark and the helicopter moved on.

'Do you think they spotted us?' Tao asked.

'I don't know, but I don't think we should wait here to find out.'

They ran along the edge of the drainage ditch until they reached the cul-de-sac, where they had parked the car. Kilkenny and Tao waited in the shadows but found no sign of Vielogic security.

'You drive,' Kilkenny said, handing Tao the keys. 'I'll navigate. Grin, you still there?'

'Ready and waiting.'

'Great. We need a good route out of here.'

45

New York City

'Hello, New York,' Tao said warmly, breaking the silence that had accompanied their departure from the Vielogic facility and the circuitous drive back to Manhattan.

'If you see an all-night pharmacy, pull over,' Kilkenny requested.

Tao turned around to look at Kilkenny. 'Are you all right?'

'Fine. I just need something.'

'There's one at the end of this block,' Tao said, pulling the car alongside the curb.

Kilkenny started to move for his door.

'Stay here,' Tao said. 'In that outfit, you look like an extra from a *Mad Max* movie. I'll go.'

Kilkenny arched an eyebrow. 'And you think you'll just blend right in?'

'A woman in a skintight black cat suit in New York at

this time of night on a weekend?' Tao asked sarcastically. 'I won't even get a second glance. What do you need?'

'An emetic.'

Tao looked at Kilkenny and he appeared to be fine. 'I'll be back in a minute.'

After Tao completed the errand, they parked the car in a nearby garage and returned to the loft. Inside, Kilkenny stripped off the top of his suit and walked directly to the kitchen sink.

'What are you doing?' Grin asked. Tao stood beside him looking concerned.

'Retrieving evidence.'

Kilkenny peeled the safety wrapper off the syrup of ipecac, read the directions, and took a swallow from the bottle. He leaned over the sink, waiting for the emetic to take hold. He didn't wait long. Grin and Tao turned away as Kilkenny vomited, heaving the contents of his stomach into the sink. Slowly, the spasms subsided and Kilkenny's bout was over.

Tao moved beside Kilkenny and reached for the faucet. The stench was overwhelming.

'Don't,' Kilkenny said, panting heavily. 'There's a metal capsule in here. We need to find it.'

'Sit,' Tao ordered, moving Kilkenny next to a window she'd opened.

The cool night air refreshed him and lessened the intensity of the foul smell from the sink. Using the hose sprayer, Tao diluted the thick vomit and quickly found the metal capsule.

'This it?' Tao asked, her hands dripping with water.

'Yeah,' Kilkenny replied hoarsely.

'Good.' Tao opened the drain and rinsed out the sink. 'Are you all right?'

'Yeah. I haven't puked my guts out like that since I left the navy. At least this time I won't have the hangover.'

'What is that?' Grin asked.

'A sample container from the Ice Pick probe. I found the probe in the Level Four lab. Most of the samples had already been removed, but one's enough to tie Vielogic to the raid.'

Grin pulled a can of ginger ale from the refrigerator and handed it to Kilkenny. 'Here, this will settle your stomach.'

'Thanks,' Kilkenny said, accepting the drink. 'Until I actually stood in front of the probe, I had my doubts that a company would launch a military raid, but there's the proof. And if Vielogic sent Duroc to raid LV Station, then I think it's quite possible they had him attack UGene as well.'

'But how'd they do it?' Grin asked. 'The cops have a DNA match on Eames. This whole thing just sounds so unreal.'

Kilkenny looked at the metal capsule in his hand. 'It only takes a bit of hard evidence to prove that something unreal is true.'

46

Bridgewater, New Jersey

Dominique Martineau stripped off her Chemturion space suit and returned to the outer corridor, where Lafitte and Duroc stood waiting.

'One of the sample capsules is gone,' she announced.

'Damn it, Summer!' Lafitte cursed. 'How could your men have let this happen?'

'The man was captured as he left the Level Four suite,' Duroc replied calmly. 'He had no contact with his accomplice. He was searched and my men found nothing. He must have hidden the capsule inside his body.'

'But how could he know the probe was here?' Lafitte demanded.

'I believe this is the same man I encountered in Antarctica. His name is Nolan Kilkenny.'

'Kilkenny,' Lafitte repeated. 'I know this name. There is a Kilkenny who is now in charge of UGene.'

'He also works for MARC, which was a partner with

272

NASA on LV Station. Kilkenny is a veteran of navy special forces, and I have information that places him in Antarctica during our raid.'

'How could he have known?'

'He couldn't have,' Duroc said confidently. 'In missions, things rarely ever go as planned; there are simply too many variables. Kilkenny was in the right place at the wrong time. What I don't know is how he managed to track the probe here. There may be some kind of transmitter on board.'

'Now he *knows* we have the probe,' Lafitte said bitterly. 'Dominique, process the remaining capsules and prepare everything from the probe for disposal. Sumner, I want you to retrieve that capsule from Kilkenny immediately.'

'Do you want me to kill him?' Duroc asked.

'No, his death now would attract even more attention. For the moment, we only need to relieve him of the capsule. Also, do not report the intrusion into the building to the police. We will act as if nothing has happened, which will weaken Kilkenny's credibility.'

'I understand. The men will be informed that this was a security test.'

Martineau wiped the perspiration off her face with her sleeve, then looked at the damp green cloth. 'Has anyone other than me been in the staging area or Level Four since the break-in?'

'No,' Duroc replied. 'Kilkenny was taken in the Level Two corridor. My men did not go any further than that.'

'Gentlemen, Kilkenny may have taken something valuable from us, but I believe he's left something equally valuable behind.'

47

Ann Arbor, Michigan

Kilkenny took three cold beers from his refrigerator as Grin set a box containing a deep-dish pizza on the dining table.

'Quite a place,' Tao said as she accepted a bottle from Kilkenny.

'It's just an old barn, but I call it home.'

'I received word from Barnett,' Tao said. 'He sends his congratulations at proving Vielogic was behind the raid in Antarctica.'

'I'm sure they're quite relieved this wasn't an act of war against the U.S.'

'So, where do we go from here?' Grin asked. 'Are they going to send in the cops?'

'I don't think so,' Tao replied. 'The capsule we stole is the fruit of a highly illegal search. Even if the police were sent in, they wouldn't find anything – the probe is gone by now. This has turned into a delicate investigation

274

against a major international corporation. The justice department will need a lot more evidence before they take Vielogic to court.'

Kilkenny pulled a slice of pizza out of the box. 'Tomorrow, I'm going to show Eames the capsule, then I'll take it over to UGene so his people can take a look at what's inside. If the life we found in Lake Vostok is genetically unique, we've got a tool we can use against Vielogic.'

'What do you mean?' Grin asked.

'If the samples collected by the probe contain DNA that could only have come from Lake Vostok, and we know what to look for, we can prevent Vielogic from patenting any of the valuable sequences.'

'Or we could blackmail them,' Tao added.

'By *we*, I assume you're speaking of the U.S. government,' Kilkenny said, 'and not us personally.'

'Of course,' Tao replied in a way that left Kilkenny wondering.

'I can see the value of the Vostok samples,' Grin said, 'but what does Vielogic get out of framing Eames for murder?'

'They're after UGene,' Kilkenny replied. 'The CEO of Vielogic put out a feeler just before the murders, and Oz turned him down.'

'With what we know already, can't we get Eames out of jail?' Grin asked.

'No,' Kilkenny said matter-of-factly. 'Duroc's short trade and his ties to Vielogic aren't enough to prove a conspiracy. All the evidence still points to Oz as the murderer. That's the thing about both of these incidents – they were laid out to be perfectly explainable. An accidental plane crash and a jealousy-induced double homicide. Now that we've proven Vielogic was behind one, I'm even more convinced they're responsible for the other. Trouble is, I don't have a clue what to look for in order to prove that Eames is innocent. Hopefully, he can help me out with that.'

Duroc sat in the passenger seat of the gray Chevy Blazer carefully listening to the conversation taking place inside Kilkenny's home. The truck was parked in the new subdivision across the road from the Kilkenny family farm, with a clear line of sight to Kilkenny's home.

One of three men he'd brought with him stood in the open attic of a rough-framed house firing a low-intensity laser beam at the picture window in the barn's loft. The coherent beam of light struck the smooth glass and absorbed the minute vibrations caused by the sounds created inside the barn before being reflected back across the road to the receiver.

The driver pulled his headset off and turned to Duroc. 'Kilkenny and Tao are both there and they have the capsule. Do we move in to take it?'

'It's foolish to move against this man in his own home. Kilkenny has given us the information we need to retrieve the capsule with a minimum of force.'

48

Kilkenny and Balogh sat by the window in the visitation room as a deputy brought in Eames. The deputy removed Eames's handcuffs, then stepped outside and closed the door. Eames slowly walked over to the window; the days of imprisonment had clearly eroded his confidence.

'How are you holding up?' Kilkenny asked.

'Okay, I guess,' Eames lied.

Kilkenny turned to Balogh. 'If he's convicted, what kind of time is he facing?'

'The prosecution is going for double life on the murder charges, plus additional time for the rape. With those kind of numbers, the first shot at parole is about thirty years away.'

Eames's head dipped lower as Balogh spoke, as if the years were piled on his shoulders like a great weight.

'I'll be well over seventy then, not that it matters. The men in my family rarely get past sixty-five.' Eames let out a halfhearted laugh. 'Bad genes, I guess.'

'Then we'd better make damn sure we prove you're

innocent. To do that,' Kilkenny said, 'I need your help in figuring something out.'

'Shoot.'

'I don't know how else to put this, but how is it possible that the police found your DNA inside your ex-wife's body?'

Eames stared at Kilkenny for a moment before he realized the question wasn't an accusation. 'I can't explain it. Tiv and I reviewed the lab report, and the only suspect DNA sample recovered from the crime scene was semen. Now I haven't ever donated semen and I haven't had sex with anyone since separating from Faye. I also haven't undergone any surgical procedures that required a general anesthetic, so there's never been an opportunity for someone to take a sample from me while I was out. Since I don't have an identical twin brother, the only explanation I have for the DNA match is lab error. Unfortunately, I haven't found anything wrong with their procedures, and I'm an expert.'

'There might be another way,' Kilkenny said. 'What if someone acquired a sample of your DNA, and from that sample manufactured the evidence being used against you?'

Eames stared incredulously into Kilkenny's eyes. 'Nolan, that is one humongous giant *if.*'

'I know,' Kilkenny admitted, 'but is it *possible*?'

'In theory, but it sure wouldn't be easy. You'd need some good clean copies of DNA to work with and some-place to implant it – host cells of some kind. Once that was done, you'd have to find a way to dedifferentiate these cells.'

'Dedifferentiate?' Kilkenny asked.

'In the first few weeks after conception, all the cells present are undifferentiated – that is, all the cells are identical, and each has the potential to become any part of the body. The offspring of some of these cells will become muscle, others nerves and organs, but at this stage they are all the same. By the time you are born, your cells have become differentiated, specialized, and a skin cell can no longer produce a bone cell. Something happens to the DNA in the differentiated cells that makes it ignore any information that is irrelevant to that cell's specific task.'

'So the DNA in a nerve cell will only use the instructions dealing with the operation of nerve cells and ignore everything else?'

'Exactly. Now, it's possible to dedifferentiate DNA, which is how one group of researchers cloned some cows, but it's *not* easy. Of course the real trick would be to insert the DNA into the nucleus of some stem cells and train the cells to grow specific tissues, say skin, blood, and hair, in a petri dish.'

'If they can clone a cow, why not just make a copy of you and harvest the cells they need to plant the evidence?' Balogh asked.

'Maturity,' Eames replied. 'Human males don't get pubic hair or produce semen until puberty, which means they would have to have started making this clone ten, twelve years ago. This is all just bull anyway. The stuff we're kicking around isn't possible now, and certainly wasn't possible back in the nineties. Just to do the blood, you'd have to make not only the blood cells, but also the plasma and everything else that's in a normal blood-stream. Sperm cells and semen would be even trickier. I'd be surprised if anything like this got pulled off before the end of the century.'

'I believe it may be possible now,' Kilkenny said.

'Can you prove it?' Balogh asked skeptically.

'No, but let me show you something.'

Kilkenny pulled out the sample capsule and held it in front of the window. Eames studied the capsule for a moment, then his eyes widened.

'Oh my God. Is that . . .'

Kilkenny nodded.

'I thought the probe was destroyed in the crash. Where did you get it?' Eames asked excitedly.

'It was in a Vielogic lab in New Jersey, along with the rest of the undamaged Ice Pick probe.'

'How did it get there?'

'I can't say, and for the time being neither of you saw this, understand?' Kilkenny asked as he pocketed the capsule.

Eames and Balogh both nodded.

'Hypothetical question,' Kilkenny said, looking through the glass at Eames. 'If Vielogic manufactured the DNA evidence used to incriminate you, where would I find proof that they could do it?'

'There's only a handful of people in the world who could even attempt this,' Eames replied, 'and only one of them works for Vielogic – Dominique Martineau. I met her last month in New York at that dinner with Lafitte; it looked like they were very close. Martineau's brilliant. She's done a lot of pioneering work in cellular mechanics and genetics – mostly to do with how cells reproduce and what tells them to stop. From the papers I've read, she's interested in cancer, aging, and fertility. She's got a private lab near Paris and carte blanche from Vielogic to pursue her own lines of research.'

'An artist with a wealthy patron,' Balogh opined.

'You think Martineau and Lafitte are responsible for killing Faye and Lloyd?' Eames asked.

'I don't know for sure, Oz,' Kilkenny replied, 'but it sure looks that way to me.'

'A case like this boils down to three things,' Balogh said, 'means, motive, and opportunity. Nolan, can you prove any of this?'

'I'm making progress on motive, and someone like Lafitte makes his own opportunities. Unfortunately, the means used here are so unbelievable that I *have* to find the smoking gun, or in this case a test tube with your DNA in it, to prove these people set you up.'

49

'He's left the jail. Heading south on Carpenter,' the man tailing Kilkenny reported.

'Understood.'

Duroc signaled to his men to get into position. The two men stepped out of the Blazer and looked around the parking lot. It was full of vehicles belonging to employees of the firms that leased space in the research park. Duroc's men expertly popped the locks on two older vehicles – a pickup truck and a Cadillac Sedan de Ville – and began hot-wiring the ignitions.

'On Ellsworth,' the tail reported. 'Approaching the turn. He's signaling.'

Kilkenny turned his Mercedes ML-320 onto the research park's private drive and followed the curve around back to UGene's building. He spotted a few empty spaces in the far corner and headed down the aisle toward them.

The driver of the Cadillac watched as the black SUV cruised toward him. He estimated Kilkenny's speed at fifteen miles per hour. Counting down the spaces, he waited until the SUV was only ten feet away, then shifted into gear and hit the accelerator. Powered by an ancient 472-cubic-inch V-8, the Cadillac shot out into the aisle.

'Oh, shit!' Kilkenny cursed.

He stomped down on the brake, but there wasn't enough room between the two vehicles to stop. The Mercedes plowed into the passenger side of the Cadillac. Instantly, the plastic cover on the steering wheel flew off as the SUV's front air bags deployed. Kilkenny's forward motion was immediately halted by the nylon bag inflating at two hundred miles per hour in the opposite direction.

The driver of the pickup shifted into reverse and rammed the black SUV. Both passenger-side doors buckled inward and the side air bags deployed. Kilkenny was jerked sideways into the door, his head impacting on the glass.

Duroc's two drivers abandoned their vehicles and ran over to the SUV. They yanked open Kilkenny's door, cut off his safety belt, and threw him to the ground. He was stunned from the blow to his head. The driver of the Cadillac punched Kilkenny twice in the stomach, then both men quickly frisked him.

The pickup driver said, 'Got it,' when he located the capsule.

Duroc pulled the Blazer around and the two men climbed inside. They pulled away just as the first people emerged from the surrounding buildings to investigate the crash.

'How are you?' Tao asked as she entered Kilkenny's private room at University Hospital.

'I took another whack on the head, but I'll live.

They got the capsule back. We didn't even have a chance to get the damn thing open.'

'I'm surprised they didn't kill you.'

'I'm not complaining, but we're running out of time on this.'

Tao shook her head. 'The probe is scrap by now. There's no way we'll find anything that can be identified as part of it. The government will just have to go after them in other ways to make them pay for the raid.'

'With what, fines and sanctions? Big fucking deal!'

'You have to be realistic about this.'

'My sense of what's realistic disappeared when Duroc blasted my plane out of the sky. Vielogic murdered eight people in Antarctica for business purposes, and, right now, I'd bet the house that they framed Eames for murder in order to take over UGene.'

'But can you prove it?'

'At this point, I don't care if I can prove it in a court of law. We shook them up by breaking into their lab in Jersey. It's time to take things up a few notches.'

Tao recognized in Kilkenny the same drive that made her want to return to China. She'd left good people behind, people who deserved to be protected. For Kilkenny, Eames was such a person.

'What's your plan?' Tao asked.

'We're going to Paris,' Kilkenny replied, 'or at least you are, while I'm stuck in here under observation.'

50

MARCH 19

Paris

Tao's eight-hour Northwest flight from Detroit arrived at Charles De Gaulle Airport shortly before eleven in the morning. After clearing customs, she rolled her bag out to the taxi stand. A swarthy driver flicked his cigarette butt on the sidewalk and ground it out with his heel as she approached his car.

'*Deux Avenue Gabriel,*' Tao said as she handed him her suitcase.

'The U.S. Embassy, *non?*' he asked.

'*Oui*, the embassy,' she replied, pleased she wouldn't have to push her rudimentary language skills very far this morning.

At the edge of the city, the driver peeled off the highway onto the Boulevard Périphérique, a beltway that encircled the city like a concrete necklace. The driver hugged the turns like he was racing at Le Mans, with Tao swaying slightly as she watched out the window. Five kilometers later, they exited onto Avenue de la Grande-Armée and entered the city. Rounding the L'Arc de Triomphe, they continued down the Champs-Elysées toward Embassy Row.

When the Champs-Elysées came to an end at Place de la Concorde, the driver turned into the cyclone of traffic swirling inside the square.

'You can drop me here,' Tao said.

The taxi pulled up along the Rue de Rivoli side of the square. Directly ahead Tao saw the imposing edifice of the American Embassy flanked by two large bald eagles in stone. The driver pulled her suitcase from the trunk, and after paying him, she crossed the street and presented her credentials at the embassy gate.

Once inside Tao was led to a small, windowless conference room and offered a cup of coffee. A tall, thin man with dark brown hair wearing a navy pinstripe suit entered the room a few minutes later.

'Ms Tao,' he said in a cowboy drawl, 'I'm Udall Walker, the CIA station chief here in Paris.' He pronounced it Pair-ee, exaggerating the vowel sounds.

'I'll bet that's something you don't often admit to publicly,' Tao said, offering her hand.

Walker smiled. 'No, ma'am. Officially I'm just a midlevel bureaucrat from the IRS, so folks generally try to avoid me. Our whole operation here is listed as an audit team.'

'Did you have any luck locating the information I requested?'

'It's a beautiful spring day outside,' Walker said. 'Let's take a walk.'

Tao left her suitcase in the conference room and accompanied Walker out onto Rue Boissey-d'Anglas. They crossed the street and began walking down Rue de Rivoli, passing the spot where the taxi driver had let her off. Hundreds of people filled the sidewalk ahead as the street ran alongside the Tuilleries toward the Louvre, bustling around restaurants and shops.

'Do you see that obelisk over there, in the center of that traffic island?' Walker asked.

'Yes,' Tao replied.

'It came from the Temple of Luxor in Egypt, a gift from the Egyptian viceroy to the king of France.' Walker came to a stop at the corner where Rue Royale inter-sected with Rue de Rivoli. 'Right now we're standing next to the Hôtel Crillon – expensive, but worth it. The building across the street – the one that looks just like the hotel – is Vielogic's world headquarters. Lafitte's office is up on the third floor, beneath the pediment. He's probably up there right now. Both he and Martineau got in on the Concorde yesterday.'

Tao glanced up at the windows, then across the Place de la Concorde at the Seine and Rive Gauche beyond. 'He has a nice view.'

'For a hundred million francs he ought to. Lafitte's purchase of that building from the French navy still has tongues wagging around here. There's an apartment next to Lafitte's office that he uses when he's working late. Otherwise, he stays at his château near Verneuil-sur-Arve, a little over a hundred kilometers west of Paris. That place is over three hundred years old – a lot of land, horses, and what appears to be fairly capable security.'

'Cerberus Sécurité?'

'Yeah.'

'What about Martineau?'

'She has an apartment in town and a lab down in Evry. All the particulars you asked for are back in my office. I just thought you'd like to take a quick peek at Vielogic's home office, seein' as they're our neighbors and all. I'm assuming you'll come back later to scout it out once you've settled in.'

Tao nodded. 'And my arrangements?'

'All set,' Walker replied. 'We've got an apartment for you to work out of, a car – all under your cover name – and the equipment you requested. Per the director's orders, we'll provide whatever logistical support you require.'

'Thank you,' Tao replied, returning her gaze back to the obelisk, her mind searching for a scrap of an old memory, something she'd read years ago. 'Place de la Révolution.'

'Excuse me?' Walker asked, barely catching her words above the rumble of traffic.

'The name of this place, or at least what it was called for a brief time a couple hundred years ago. Right over there,' Tao said, pointing at the obelisk, 'was where the revolutionaries set up their guillotine and dispensed justice. They executed about twenty-eight hundred people; the area was so soaked with blood that cattle refused to cross it.'

'Grizzly business.'

'Revolutions in which one form of tyranny supplants another are never peaceful. And I can assure you, from personal experience, that sustaining a tyrannical revolutionary government requires frequent blood sacrifice.

In a way, it's ironic that Lafitte would place his headquarters here.'

'Why's that?'

'Vielogic is on the front lines of a scientific revolution, one completely bound in matters of life and death, and Lafitte is showing all the signs of a tyrant.'

51

MARCH 20

Evry, France

Dominique Martineau parked her BMW behind a non-descript two-story brick building and entered through an unmarked door in the rear. The building, constructed in the 1850s, had originally been a bakery. Vielogic had acquired it six years earlier and transformed the lower floor into retail shops and the upper into Martineau's private research facility.

Off the second-floor landing, Martineau entered an empty room that served as a vestibule for her lab and walked up to a flush stainless-steel door. She placed her hand on a glass plate mounted on the wall beside the door. The device scanned her palm and compared the unique configuration of her hand to data it already had on file. It found a match and unlocked the door.

Inside the outer gowning room she removed her clothing, stepped into the air lock, and closed the door. The air lock was dark for a few seconds, then her body was bathed in ultraviolet light to kill any microbes present on her skin and hair.

Martineau's heart always beat faster as she stood nude waiting in the air lock, though not for any sense of nervous modesty. She often thought this was how the shamans and high priests of old felt as they performed their purification rituals before entering their sacred places – the anticipation of an encounter with the magical and mysterious. Like those ancient seekers, Martineau cleansed herself of impurities, though her ritual was more a matter of pragmatism than piety.

When the decontamination cycle ended, the inner door released and Martineau entered and walked past a shower stall and lavatory. She ripped open a hermetic-ally sealed bag and pulled out the disposable surgical scrubs and booties. She completed her wardrobe with a hair net, surgical mask, and a pair of latex gloves.

Through the final door, Martineau entered her sanctum sanctorum. The lab was a mix of whites and cool blues – calm, thoughtful colors – and the only sounds heard within its walls were the dull humming of the refrigerators and cryogenic freezers and the white noise of air being stripped of microscopic contaminants as it flowed through high-efficiency particulate filters.

Martineau stepped over to a lab bench and, using a pipette, extracted a small amount of fluid from a glass beaken. She placed a droplet on the slide tray and peered though the eyepiece of the microscope at her work in progress. The sample teemed with newly formed stem cells, each completely identical, each capable of developing into any specific type of cell in the body.

Martineau extracted a larger sample from the beaker and inserted the fluid into an SG machine. SG stood for spermatogenesis, the process by which the male of a species creates spermatozoa. The SG machine was designed to artificially reproduce mammal sperm and seminal fluid from a sampling of genetic material. Its counterpart, the OV machine, created viable ova for in vitro fertilization.

Both machines evolved from Martineau's research in cellular mechanics and were initially designed to extend profitable bloodlines in horses and other livestock and to reestablish endangered and recently extinct species. The technology also held the promise of helping infertile couples produce biological offspring.

In an extrapolation of the SG machine's potential, Martineau once submitted a proposal to Lafitte to produce a biological daughter of a lesbian couple, fabricating sperm with one of the women's DNA. She even toyed with the idea of building an ovum from a man's genetic material. The fertilized egg would require a donor womb, but for the first time a man would be the biological mother of the child. The more Martineau grew to understand the intricate inner workings of cells, the more godlike power she felt over the mechanics of life.

In other avenues of her research, Martineau pushed the limits in coaxing undifferentiated cells into becoming different parts of the body. She grew skin, muscle, and nerve cells in dishes, and was making progress with internal organs and bone marrow.

All of Martineau's machines were in the early testing phase, still years away from government approval for commercial use. The one critical element she still lacked was speed. The time it took to read the entire length of the human genome had dropped from a decade, to three years, to now just under a year – but for Martineau this was still far too long.

Vielogic's eventual acquisition of UGene promised to cut the time it took to read a person's genome down to a matter of days. Such speed would allow Vielogic to custom-tailor pharmaceuticals to individual needs – an innovation that would shake the rest of the drug industry like a violent earthquake.

Martineau opened the door of her lab freezer and retrieved a test tube. Inside, the clear Tris-EDTA solution remained liquid, preserving the delicate strands of DNA she'd painstakingly extracted the previous day. Since her return from the U.S., she had begun retrieving DNA samples from the sweat left by Nolan Kilkenny during his visit to the Level 4 lab in New Jersey. Her work was nearly complete.

52

Paris

Checking the online financial news, Charles Lafitte found UGene's stock still trading at around ten dollars per share – an all-time low for the promising biotech company. After the stock's initial collapse, the market settled down and traders took a wait-and-see stance on the company. The future of UGene rested on the outcome of Eames's upcoming trial.

The drop in share price had transformed UGene from an expensive acquisition into a bargain, and Lafitte's rumored interest in the company was one of the factors that kept the price from falling further. The other was the intellectual property developed by Eames and Sutton. For his part, Lafitte had done nothing to substantiate the rumors of an impending takeover and, through Vielogic public relations, released a statement dismissing such speculation as gossip. Still, the market took note that he hadn't sold any of his shares either.

The time isn't ripe yet, Lafitte thought as he read another analyst's view on a possible takeover, *but soon it will be.*

Lafitte brought up the charts for UGene since its initial public offering. He'd bought early, and his 5 percent stake had helped double the share price on the opening day. From a pure investment standpoint, UGene had performed well for him right up to the crash, which erased all of his paper gains and some of his principal.

Switching from share price to trading volume, Lafitte saw the initial spike when UGene first appeared on the public market. The volume then leveled out until February, when it spiked again. Lafitte zeroed in on the volume surge that described the frenzied sale of UGene shares and discovered that the increase in volume started in the days just before the murders. Checking the share price for that week, he noted it was down a bit. Taken on its own, the small drop in the stock price was well within normal market fluctuations, but combined with the increased daily volume, it told Lafitte that someone was selling.

'What are you furrowing your brow over, Charles?' Martineau asked as she entered his office.

'A coincidence, I think, but a very puzzling one.'

Martineau sat on the edge of the inlaid desk, kicked off one of her shoes, and placed her foot in Lafitte's lap seductively. 'Oh, what is it?'

'UGene. A lot of shares changed hands in the days before the murders,' Lafitte said as he massaged her foot. 'People were selling.'

'Is that unusual?'

'I'm not sure. It is either a fluke, or someone who knew what was going to happen took advantage of the situation. Ah, but that's impossible, isn't it, my love?'

Martineau felt Lafitte's hands move up her calf and tighten around the shapely muscle. 'Of course. How could anyone have known about the murders before they happened?'

'My point exactly.'

53

MARCH 21

Paris

After parking her BMW in the closed lot, Martineau entered the Pierre de Taille building in the Eighth Arrondissement, collected her mail, and scaled the winding stairway to her fourth-floor apartment. Her building was located on Avenue Montaigne, one of the most expensive addresses in Paris and just a short walk to Vielogic's headquarters.

Over her arm, Martineau carried a woven bag that held a few items she had picked up for dinner. Her keys jangled in her hand as she approached the tall door of her apartment. She slipped a key into the dead bolt and turned it – but the dead bolt was already unlocked.

Odd, she thought. *I swear I locked the door this morning.*

Cautiously, she opened the door to her apartment. Inside, the lights in the main room were on and music was playing softly.

'Charles?' Martineau called out.

'I'm afraid not, Dominique,' Duroc answered, stepping in from the terrace.

'What are you doing here? Where is Charles?'

'At his château.'

'Shouldn't you be overseeing security?'

'My men don't need me to hold their hands,' Duroc said confidently. He closed the distance between Martineau and himself, casually draping his black leather coat over the back of her couch. 'I have the night off.'

'And you thought you would spend it here,' Martineau said disdainfully, 'with *me*?'

Duroc walked up to Martineau and stood just inches from her. She held her ground, refusing to be intimidated by the large, muscular man. He reached around her and palmed her derrière, kneading her flesh with his steely hands as he pulled her body into his. Martineau's bag slipped off her arm and dropped onto the marble floor.

'That is exactly what I thought I would do.'

Martineau stared into Duroc's inky black eyes, then reached up and pulled his mouth against hers. Martineau's tongue darted feverishly about his lips, probing excitedly. Her pelvis rocked against him, moving in rhythm with the contractions of his hands on her buttocks.

Her hands slid from his head, down the front of the collarless cotton shirt that clung to his chest like a second skin. Deftly, she unfastened his belt, peeled open his pants, and slid her hand down.

Martineau pulled her mouth away from his, kissing and licking his cheek as she moved toward his ear. 'As always,' she said in a low whisper, 'you are overdressed.'

Martineau and Duroc stripped each other where they stood. She embraced him around his shoulders, pressing her flesh against his. He once again grabbed her derrière and, as he lifted her up, Martineau curled her legs around his torso and locked her feet behind him.

Duroc stood with his legs slightly bent at the knees, shoulder-length apart, as Martineau's inner thighs pressed against his hips, drawing him inside her body. Duroc struggled to maintain his balance, his muscles tensing as he approached ecstasy.

Both their bodies wet with perspiration from the effort, Martineau felt his body lock. Slowly, she arched her back, trusting that he would not drop her while simultaneously excited by the danger that he might. She moaned and ground her pelvis into his, as he responded with a tight squeeze of her buttocks. He held his breath, then exhaled with a sharp burst.

She pulled herself against him, Duroc's strength ebbing with his release. Slowly, she unwound her legs and he gently lowered her to the floor.

'Shower?' she said softly.

'*Oui,*' he replied, his breathing returning to normal.

They bathed each other in the shower, then made love again before rinsing off.

'I'm impressed,' Martineau said as she handed Duroc a thick terrycloth robe.

'It's been longer for me than it has for you. Did you miss me?'

'Every time I made love to him, I missed you.'

'Then why do you do it?' Duroc asked.

Martineau laughed as she cinched her robe. 'Business,

299

of course. He knows it, too. You, *mon chéri*, are for pleasure.'

Duroc embraced her and kissed her still-damp neck. 'Perhaps, but he is not the only one with money.'

'What are you talking about?'

'The future. I know all about the doctors he sees. Charles won't live forever, and I'm certain that you and I are not mentioned in his will.'

Martineau pulled away, clutching her robe tightly. 'Sumner, what have you done?'

'I made a modest fortune in the stock market recently. Nothing compared to Charles's vast wealth, but enough for the two of us to live comfortably for the rest of our lives.'

'UGene?'

'Yes.'

'You idiot! I was with Charles yesterday. He has discovered that many shares of UGene were sold before the murders. He is very curious about this.'

'He will find nothing that connects me to the trades,' Duroc said confidently.

'How can you be so sure? If he finds out, Charles will view this as a betrayal.'

'Trust me, Dominique. Soon, only you and I will know, and neither of us is going to tell him.'

54

MARCH 22

Paris

After his release from the hospital, Kilkenny caught the first flight to Paris. He'd been in regular contact with Tao as she collected the reconnaissance information needed for their next move. His plane touched down at Charles de Gaulle Airport late in the afternoon. All he brought with him was a carry-on bag and his briefcase, so he reached customs well ahead of his fellow travelers. The passport Tao had arranged for him looked as if he had used it for years, and the customs official gave it a cursory glance before adding another stamp and handing it back to him.

Once he cleared the security checkpoint and entered the main terminal, Kilkenny walked about casually as he looked for any sign of surveillance. He browsed in a few shops, went to the rest room, and bought a newspaper. After twenty minutes and no indication that he was being followed, Kilkenny began moving toward the ground transportation exit.

As the automatic doors swung open and Kilkenny walked outside, he heard the distinctive wail of a European police siren. The sound grew louder and Kilkenny looked around for the source. He spotted a black police van racing up the access road toward the terminal, closely followed by a gray sedan. The van pulled up to the curb, its doors flew open, and five men dressed in black assault uniforms stormed out. Kilkenny stepped out of the direct line between the men and the terminal doors. The men broke into two groups – three to one side of Kilkenny and two on the other. Then Duroc stepped out of the sedan.

'I want him alive, if possible,' Duroc announced.

Kilkenny swung his carry-on bag and hurtled it into the pair to his left. It struck one of the men in the head and sent him stumbling back to regain his balance. He dropped his briefcase and took up a defensive posture. Another man moved in and Kilkenny thrust his open hand like a spear into his throat. The strike hit so hard, Kilkenny's fingertips felt the vertebrae. The man's eyes bulged out and he began choking. Kilkenny pushed him into his comrades, then turned to deal with the two men behind him.

Focusing on one of the men, Kilkenny threw a pair of kicks in rapid succession – one to the groin, one to the head – and sent the man sprawling back onto the sidewalk. The other man held his ground and Kilkenny closed the distance, quickly trying to find an angle of attack while escaping the pincher he was in. The man countered his move, then Kilkenny caught him taking a brief look beyond him.

Kilkenny spun around just as a third man bore down with a nightstick. Kilkenny deflected the blow with a sweep of his left arm, grabbed the wooden stick just above his attacker's hands, and twisted it backward. The tip smashed into the man's nose, turning it into a bloody pulp and knocking several of his teeth onto the sidewalk.

A stream of pungent liquid struck Kilkenny in the face. Almost immediately, the sidewalk spun out from beneath his feet. Kilkenny's head pounded and everything was turning wildly, like he was inside a barrel rolling down a steep mountainside. He dropped onto the pavement, unconscious. Duroc's two remaining men bound Kilkenny, then loaded him into the van.

'Take him to the garage,' Duroc ordered. He looked disapprovingly at the three men Kilkenny had beaten, only one of whom was still conscious. 'And drop them off at our doctor.'

55

Evry, France

Evening had settled over the small city on the banks of the Seine and there were few people on the streets. Tao scouted the area around the building first by car, then on foot, searching for any sign that Martineau's lab was being watched; she found none.

Martineau set her own hours, working an erratic schedule. This posed a problem for Tao in planning when to break into her lab. Udall Walker solved that problem for her when he learned that Martineau and Lafitte would be attending a dinner at the British Embassy that evening.

Prior to Kilkenny's departure from the States, they'd agreed to meet outside Evry around seven o'clock. When he missed that rendezvous, Tao moved on to the fallback point closer to the lab. She checked her watch – Kilkenny was overdue and their window of opportunity was closing.

It's either go, or no go, she thought, then decided to proceed alone.

Tao slipped on a pair of surgical gloves as she approached from the alley. At the back door, she punched in the access code she'd acquired by spying on Martineau. Inside, she carefully ascended the stair, the thin rubber soles of her boots silent on the treads. When she reached the landing, Tao saw a wide black metal door and frame set into the masonry wall. The locks were purely mechanical and she picked through them in less than thirty seconds.

Tao entered an empty room. On the opposite wall, she saw a flat metal door. Beside the door was a square glass plate set flush into the wall – the palm reader. Another of Udall Walker's contributions was a schematic of the security for Martineau's lab, which allowed her to prepare for the device.

Tao moved her face close to the reader and exhaled. The moisture in her breath fogged the glass, revealing the oily impression of a woman's palm print. Tao slipped off her backpack and pulled out a black object about ten inches square and three inches thick. She pressed a button on the side of the device and four hydraulic legs rose out of the corners of the top face of the device. Centered among the legs was a dark glass plate. Tao carefully placed the device against the wall such that the legs straddled the palm reader.

She pressed a second button on the device and the legs slowly retracted, pulling the face of the device close to the reader. When the two glass plates were separated by less than the thickness of a human hair, a bright light flashed from her device as it scanned the image of the woman's handprint from the reader plate.

Tao heard a muffled clink as the legs on her device retracted further and the two glass plates came into contact. Immediately, the palm reader flashed out its bright white light, searching for the features of a human hand. Using the information it gathered from the handprint on the glass, Tao's device projected a holographic image of Martineau's hand onto the palm reader's sensors and unlocked the door.

The lights came on as Tao entered a changing room. Upon reaching the next door, Tao found no security devices of any kind. A black rectangular panel was placed about eye level next to the door. Close inspection revealed it to be an illuminated display of the word OCCUPÉ. She pulled open the door and saw a magnetic lock mounted in the door frame.

Tao stepped through the door into a room a bit larger than a phone booth – an air lock. On the opposite wall was another door. As soon as she shut the door, she heard the magnetic lock activate. The dark space was filled with bluish ultraviolet light. Tao closed her eyes and listened to the low electronic buzz of the chamber. After a few minutes, a white light came on and the magnetic lock on the next door released.

She opened the door and entered the gowning room. A rack of metal shelves held sealed bags of surgical scrubs, booties, hats, masks, and latex gloves. Adjacent to the room was a shower, toilet, and sink.

All the comforts of home, Tao thought.

Tao donned a mask and passed through the final door into Martineau's lab. The modern, antiseptic research space was the polar opposite of the building that contained it. Except for a phone on the wall and what Tao assumed was a networked computer, Martineau's lab was isolated from the world outside. Tao stood still for a moment; all she could hear was the faint sound of air whooshing through filters.

She walked over to the computer; the screen saver was painting fractal landscapes. She tapped the space bar and a spreadsheet appeared, showing an experiment Martineau was working on. Tao scrolled up on the screen and found a header of information for the experiment. On the donor source line, Tao saw KILKENNY, NOLAN. She studied the header closely, trying to find anything that would tell her what Martineau was doing with Kilkenny's cells or how she had acquired them. Tao became so focused that she didn't notice that the white noise of the air-handling system had disappeared.

A strobe light began flashing wildly, accompanied by a beeping alarm. Small nozzle heads popped out of the ceiling and the loud hiss of pressurized gas blasting through them filled the lab. Tao looked around the room, but found no sign of fire anywhere. In the corner, she saw a cluster of red pressure tanks chained to the wall. Each tank bore the characters CO_2.

Carbon dioxide!

The colorless, odorless gas rapidly displaced the oxygen in the room as it sought to smother the non-existent fire. Tao held her breath and ran back the way she came. She pulled on the door, but it was locked. She ran to the tank farm and began turning valves, but the gas continued to flow.

The air inside Tao's lungs was growing hot and stale,

expanding. Finally, it burst from her mouth in a spasm. She reflexively inhaled, breathing in air that was almost 70 percent carbon dioxide. She coughed as if choking on a mouthful of water.

Her vision clouded and grew narrow, and she became increasingly dizzy. She dropped onto the floor, coughing and gasping, until she succumbed.

Beside the air lock door, the black rectangular panel displayed the illuminated word OCCUPÉ. A moment later, a man entered Martineau's lab, his face obscured by an oxygen mask. He walked over to Tao and placed two fingers on her bluish neck. He pulled a two-way radio out of his pocket and checked his watch.

'She's out,' he announced into the radio. 'Switch off the gas.'

The high-pressure hissing ceased and was soon replaced by the white noise of the air filtration system. Almost immediately, the warm color returned to Tao's face. The man bound her hands and feet with tape, then covered her mouth with another strip. The man looked at the air lock door just as Duroc stepped through. Duroc walked over and glanced down at Tao's unconscious body.

'Nicely done,' Duroc said.

Udall Walker stripped off his oxygen mask. 'When can I expect the rest of my money?'

'As soon as you drop her off at the estate. A cashier's check is waiting for you there.'

'You're not coming?' Walker asked.

'I'll meet you there later. I have another appointment in Paris. Let's get her down to the car.'

56

'Wake up,' a distant voice commanded.

The acrid scent of ammonia filled Kilkenny's nostrils, attacking his olfactory nerves and sending an overload of stimuli into his brain. The smell cut through the chemically induced fog that smothered his consciousness like damp gauze. Slowly, he opened his eyes.

Everything was dark at first, then he saw spots of light. As his eyes regained focus, details became clear. He was lying on the floor of a van, his wrists and ankles bound. The rear doors were open and someone was leaning over him, holding a packet of smelling salts under his nose.

'He's coming around.'

'Wake up,' the voice demanded again.

Kilkenny recognized the man rousing him as one of his attackers at the airport. The man backed away and a man dressed in a tuxedo accompanied by a woman in a black dress with a shatoosh shawl stepped up to the doorway.

'Welcome to Paris, Mr Kilkenny. I am Charles Lafitte and this is Dr Dominique Martineau.'

'You'll both excuse me if I don't get up.'

'Of course,' Lafitte replied. 'I just wanted to thank you for coming here. You see, you've saved me a great deal of trouble.'

'How's that?' Kilkenny asked.

'I want UGene, and you're going to sell it to me.'

'Like hell I am.'

'Ah, forgive me, I must be using the incorrect tense. We have already agreed to the terms of the sale, which are most generous considering the company's recent devaluation.'

'You're nuts.'

'Earlier today you signed a letter of intent outlining the sale of UGene to Vielogic. The deal will, of course, become final after Oswald Eames is found guilty of murder and sentenced to prison. This was the purpose of your trip to Paris.'

'Funny, I don't recall signing anything today.'

'I'm not surprised,' Lafitte said smugly. 'My public relations staff will issue a press release to the wire services tomorrow announcing the buyout.'

'Along with my obituary, I suppose.'

'Quite correct.'

'Why did you steal Ice Pick? You had no way of knowing if we'd found anything of value in Lake Vostok.'

'It was a calculated risk.'

'Were the murders of Lloyd Sutton and Faye Olson calculated risks as well?'

'No,' Lafitte replied. 'Sutton was open to negotiation, but Eames refused. He left me with no choice.'

'You could have walked away.'

'But then I would not have gotten what I wanted.

Thanks to your timely arrival, I am now closer to acquiring UGene.'

'But why? What are you after?' Kilkenny asked.

'Immortality.'

'You're kidding.'

'I'm afraid he's not,' Martineau replied, 'though in the short term we will settle for good health and longevity.'

'You've lost me,' Kilkenny admitted. 'How does Ice Pick and UGene fit with your desire to live forever?'

'I assume you are familiar with the theory of evolution?' Lafitte asked.

'Yes.'

'Survival of the fittest. Organisms that survive in extreme environments do so because they are more fit than their weaker counterparts. The life that exists in Lake Vostok has done so in complete isolation for millions of years. Their environment consists of extremes in temperature ranging from freezing to scalding, tremendous pressure, and extremely low levels of oxygen.'

'I understand the uniqueness of Lake Vostok,' Kilkenny said, 'but what makes you think that microbes from there will teach you the secret of eternal life?'

'It can teach me how they survived,' Lafitte replied.

'DNA is at the core of every living thing on this planet,' Martineau explained, 'and each species has its strengths and weaknesses. There's a one percent difference between the DNA of a mouse and that of a man. Encoded within the mouse's genome is a phenomenal recuperative ability – they heal far more quickly from injuries than humans do. They pay for this with a higher metabolism and a far shorter life span. What do you know about cancer?'

'I know that I don't want it,' Kilkenny replied.

'As an illness, I would agree, but as an organism cancer has much to teach us. Our bodies age because our cells only reproduce for so many generations, then they stop. Not so with cancer. Each generation is the same as the one that preceded it. If the rest of the cells in the human body could learn that trait, you would never grow old.'

'So you intend to cut and paste DNA, picking off the best bits you can find?'

'Crudely put,' Lafitte said, 'but essentially correct. The biggest problem is the time it takes to decode a genome.'

'Which is where UGene comes in,' Kilkenny said.

'Yes. UGene's technology will allow Dominique and the rest of my research staff to parse through genomes in a fraction of the time it takes now. I could have made Eames a wealthy man, but he turned me down. *C'est la vie*.'

'You have to realize that killing me isn't going to solve anything. The U.S. government knows what happened in Antarctica, and that Vielogic is responsible.'

'Let them take me to court. They have no evidence. Publicly, your government still claims the plane crash was an accident. To say otherwise now, with no proof, would be a great embarrassment. As for Eames, there is more than enough evidence to convict him.'

'Almost perfect,' Kilkenny offered.

'Close enough, I think.'

'In fact, we probably wouldn't be having this conversation right now if Duroc hadn't gotten greedy and shorted the stock.'

Lafitte stared angrily at Kilkenny. 'Explain.'

'Duroc owns a holding company in the Cayman

Islands called Pont Neuf. Through it, he shorted UGene stock just before the murders and netted over twenty million dollars. That's what led me to Vielogic.'

Lafitte reddened as Kilkenny spoke, his rage becoming visible.

'Idiot,' Lafitte hissed.

'I guess your dog got off his leash,' Kilkenny said.

'It is no concern of yours,' Lafitte shot back. 'I have the samples from Lake Vostok, Eames will be convicted, and UGene will be mine. *Adieu*, Monsieur Kilkenny.'

As Lafitte and Martineau stepped back, the man who'd roused him reappeared and sprayed Kilkenny in the face. Once again, Kilkenny's world faded to black.

57

'Gloves on, everyone,' Duroc commanded.

The men donned latex gloves and then pulled Kilkenny out of the van. They followed Duroc and Martineau into the lower level of an ancient brick apartment building in a seedier block of the Montmartre section of Paris. Low-wattage lightbulbs barely illuminated the battered hallway. A mangy cat hissed and scampered away as they moved farther into the building. The place smelled of rotting food, sweat, and urine.

'Place him on the bed,' Duroc ordered as he unlocked the door to a studio apartment.

A layer of grimy filth coated the surfaces of the windowless single-room apartment. Rooms such as this were illegal since they were a health hazard, but then so was the occupation of the people who rented them for business purposes. Flakes of paint that had peeled from the walls and ceiling like festering scabs littered the floor with other bits of trash and debris.

A double bed dominated the tiny room, a simple wooden frame now battered and scarred with cigarette burns and carved initials. Soiled sheets covered a decaying mattress whose center had long ago collapsed into an oblong crater. The men carrying Kilkenny dumped his body into the bowl and the mattress sank a little farther. Several cockroaches scampered into the shadows.

In a corner near the bed, a woman sat lifelessly on the floor, her head leaned back against the wall, her vacant eyes aimed up at the disintegrating plaster ceiling. A mop of matted stringy hair hung like a liquid film from her head and garish makeup accented her face in a way so as to overcompensate for the pallor of her skin. What little clothing she wore – a gold tube top and a black elastic miniskirt – was wadded and rolled onto her abdomen, exposing her breasts and genitalia. Needle tracks scarred her limbs, and a small trickle of blood oozed from a hole in her arm – the site of her final dose. A syringe lay on the floor nearby.

'Strip him and bind his hands and feet to the frame,' Martineau ordered.

As the men removed Kilkenny's clothes, Duroc pulled out his pistol and switched off the safety.

'Nervous?' Martineau asked.

'Cautious,' Duroc corrected her. 'Several of my men are dead or injured because of him. He is not to be underestimated.'

'He told Lafitte about your stock transaction,' Martineau said softly.

'*Merde*. How did he take it?' Duroc asked.

'He was not pleased.'

Martineau and Duroc watched as the two men removed Kilkenny's clothing. Martineau enjoyed the unveiling of each new section of skin while Duroc looked for any sign of consciousness. She draped Kilkenny's clothing over a wooden chair as if he had carefully disrobed there himself, then placed a wallet containing cash, credit cards, and Kilkenny's driver's license into the prostitute's handbag.

The two men handcuffed Kilkenny's wrists around the center spindle of the headboard, then tied ropes around his ankles and lashed the ends to the footboard. Duroc checked the restraints and, satisfied, holstered his pistol.

'I think I can handle the rest,' Martineau said, eyeing Kilkenny's chiseled body.

'Are you certain?' Duroc asked.

'You're jealous, aren't you?' Martineau laughed. 'Sumner, my dear, you have nothing to fear from a dead man. Go on back to the estate and leave me to my work. Just as I did in Ann Arbor, there are things I need to do to make this scene believable for the police. Anyway, don't you have to deal with that Asian woman?'

'Yes, though in her case the body will never be found.'

'Then go. I'll meet you at the château in a few hours. I'll be fine.'

58

After Duroc and his men left, Martineau locked the apartment door and slowly walked over to the bed, her eyes roaming over Kilkenny's lean, muscular form. She sat down on the bed beside him and ran her fingers through the tufts of red hair on his chest. Lafitte's body was bare like a little boy's, while Duroc was covered with thick black coils. Like Duroc's, Kilkenny's body bore many scars, which she traced with her fingers.

Kilkenny's heart beat slowly beneath her hand, his body artificially at rest. She reached into her purse and pulled out a wooden-handled knife and a packet of smelling salts. She cracked open the paper-wrapped caplet and held the salts under Kilkenny's nose. He jerked as if hit with an electric shock.

'What the – ' Kilkenny tried to sit up but found he couldn't lift his torso more than a few inches off the warped bed.

'*Bon soir, chéri*,' Martineau said, smiling sweetly at him. 'Don't bother trying to get up.'

Kilkenny felt her hand gliding over the skin on his

chest. He looked down and saw that he was nude. 'I'm really not into S&M.'

'Too bad, it's a wonderful way to add excitement. Let me show you.'

Martineau stood up, stepped out of her shoes, and slowly removed her dress. She wore nothing beneath and her body was smooth and devoid of hair. Catlike, she climbed over him, her breasts brushing up against his chest. She licked his neck and chin before aggressively kissing him on the mouth. Kilkenny felt her teeth chipping into his, her tongue probing his clenched mouth. Martineau bit his lip hard and warm salty blood flowed from the wound.

'Why are you doing this?' Kilkenny demanded.

Martineau sat up, stretching her arms toward the ceiling, towering over her victim.

'Because I can, and because I want this to be as real as possible. In this room, the police will find everything they need to explain the unfortunate circumstances of your death.'

'What do you mean?'

'After your meeting with Charles, you decided to celebrate with a visit to Montmartre – a very touristy thing to do. While there, you met a young woman – Zara, I believe – who brought you back here for a little Parisian entertainment.' Martineau waggled her finger at him. 'You naughty boy.'

'There isn't a person who knows me who'd believe I picked up a prostitute.'

Martineau laughed. 'You are a healthy young man, in Paris alone, celebrating a big business deal. The temptations here can be irresistible.'

'I've resisted that kind of temptation in ports all around the world. What could make me change now?'

'Your personal character is irrelevant when compared to the facts: Your body will be found here with that of a dead prostitute. You made the unfortunate choice of picking a girl who also happens to be an intravenous drug user, and there is a very dangerous form of heroin circulating in Europe these days. In a drug-induced psychosis, she stabbed you to death, then injected a lethal dose into her body. A tragedy, really.'

'Like Faye Olson and Lloyd Sutton?'

Martineau pouted at Kilkenny, then smiled. 'Exactly, but enough of this talk. I have work to do. In order for this scene to be truly convincing, you have to have sex before you die. Since poor Zara isn't up to the task, I'll have to do it myself.'

'I guess you really throw yourself into your work, body and soul. Just like Zara.'

Martineau struck Kilkenny across the face.

'My mistake,' Kilkenny apologized. 'You don't have a soul.'

Martineau picked up the knife and laid it on Kilkenny's chest with the tip pointing at his chin. 'Please me and I promise your death will be very quick.'

'Sorry, you're just not my type.'

'What? You don't like women?' Martineau rubbed her groin against Kilkenny, trying to arouse him.

'I prefer women who are warm-blooded.'

Frustrated, she grabbed the knife, raised her arm up, and plunged down. The blade sliced a shallow groove in the side of Kilkenny's chest as it tore into the mattress.

Martineau pulled herself off Kilkenny, stood up, and put on her dress. Kilkenny adjusted his legs and found a little slack in the ropes tied to his ankles.

'Despite your lack of interest, I've done enough to make it appear that you have been with a woman. There's no need for me to take you inside my body, though you have denied yourself a great final pleasure.'

Kilkenny gripped his hands tightly around the spindle and twisted. The spindle slowly turned.

'Doesn't look so great from where I'm sitting.'

Martineau smiled smugly at Kilkenny, then picked up her purse and pulled out a test tube and what looked like a small turkey baster. She held the test tube close to Kilkenny's face.

'Do you know what this is?' she asked.

'No clue.'

'It's your seed, or at least my very close approximation of it. When the police do their DNA test, this will prove that you had sex with Zara.'

'How did you make that?'

'You provided me with the raw material when you broke into the lab in New Jersey. I made it from the DNA I found in your sweat.'

Kilkenny tilted his head back and yanked himself toward the headboard. The sharp impact of his forehead broke the wooden spindle. He yanked the upper half of the spindle from the headboard. Its jagged edge gouged a bloody groove from his hairline down to the bridge of his nose.

Kilkenny threw the broken spindle across the room as he swung his arms over his head and around Martineau.

The cold steel of the handcuffs dug into her neck as he pulled her head against his chest. The test tube fell from Martineau's hands and shattered on the floor. Martineau dug her nails into his sides. Kilkenny grimaced and clamped his hands to her head.

'It doesn't take much to break a neck, then you'll be the one they find with poor Zara. Let me know when you're ready to deal.'

Martineau released her grip on Kilkenny's sides and pulled her hands away from his body.

'Don't even think about that knife, Dominique. You'd be dead before you had the chance to use it. *Comprenez-vous?*'

Martineau nodded.

'Good. Now I want you to turn around, so you're facing toward my feet.'

Kilkenny slipped his hands around her throat and pushed her head off his chest. Martineau turned so that her back faced him.

'Untie my ankles,' Kilkenny commanded.

Martineau unfastened the ropes around his ankles and Kilkenny wrapped his legs around her waist.

'What to do, what to do? Eh, Dominique?' Kilkenny sighed. 'Handcuffs. I assume you have the key somewhere.'

Kilkenny squeezed his legs together, crushing Martineau's abdomen.

'The purse,' she gasped. 'The key is in Zara's purse.'

'Let's find it, shall we?'

Kilkenny pushed Martineau over to the side of the bed. He then guided her over to where Zara's purse lay on the floor.

'We are going to slowly crouch down. I want you to pick up the purse and empty it on the floor.'

Martineau dumped the contents of the purse on the floor and raised her hands where Kilkenny could see them.

'Very good, Dominique. Do you see the key down there?'

Martineau looked down. 'Yes.'

'Pick it up very slowly.'

With one hand, Martineau reached down and picked up the key.

'Now unlock the handcuffs.'

Martineau felt for the keyhole in the bracelet around Kilkenny's right wrist. She slipped the key in and turned, and it sprang open. She unlocked the one on his other wrist.

'Keep the key in your right hand and put the handcuffs in your left.'

Martineau did as he instructed.

'Now we're going to stand up. Ready?'

'Yes.'

Kilkenny rose and Martineau followed. When they were both standing, Kilkenny grabbed Martineau's left arm and twisted it around her back, then pulled the handcuffs out of her hand and clasped one of the bracelets tightly around her wrist.

'I seem to recall your saying you liked it rough,' Kilkenny said. 'Put your other hand between your legs.'

From behind, Kilkenny reached between Martineau's legs, grabbed Martineau's right hand and pulled it through, bending her over awkwardly. He then brought her left arm down her back and closed the other bracelet around her right wrist. Martineau stood up as best she could, her dress bunched up with the handcuffs at her groin.

'There, now the only thing you can play with is yourself, though be careful of all that metal. Which reminds me.' Kilkenny reached between her thighs and pulled the key from her right hand. 'Sorry about that. I bet you really wished you put some underwear on today.'

Kilkenny picked up his clothes and put on everything but his jacket and tie. He picked up Martineau's shawl; the fabric felt soft and light.

'Is this shatoosh?' Kilkenny asked.

Martineau nodded.

'Expensive?'

'Very.'

'If I remember right,' Kilkenny said, appraising the fabric, 'this comes from some kind of endangered antelope – endangered because people like you make shawls out of them.' He wiped the blood off his forehead with it. 'That ought to get me a life membership in PETA.'

Kilkenny placed the shawl at the foot of the bed, pulled the knife out of the mattress, and tossed it on the floor. He lifted up Zara's body and reverently laid her down on the bed. Kilkenny adjusted her clothing for modesty and covered her body with Martineau's prized shawl.

'I'm sorry you got brought into this,' Kilkenny said to the corpse. 'God speed.'

'What are you doing? She's dead.'

'True,' Kilkenny replied, 'but she didn't deserve what you did to her. I hope you have a car around here?

Otherwise, you're going to look very silly walking through the streets of Paris trussed up like that.'

'It's in the garage up the street. The keys are in my purse?'

Kilkenny rummaged through Martineau's purse and found her keys, a digital phone, and a black cylindrical spray bottle. He held it up to Martineau's face.

'This what they used to knock me out?'

Martineau nodded, wincing.

'What is it and what exactly does it do?'

'A neural inhibitor. It interferes with neuro-electrical activity in the brain.'

'I've still got a headache from it.'

'It will pass with no permanent damage.'

'How does it work?'

'It must be absorbed into the bloodstream. The mouth, eyes, and nose are good targets.'

'Good to know,' Kilkenny said, pocketing the canister.

'What about the key to the handcuffs?' Martineau asked.

'We don't need it. Let's go.'

59

'It's over there, under the light,' Martineau said.

They passed a few battered Renaults and a VW Passat before reaching Martineau's BMW.

'Z8,' Kilkenny said when he recognized the car's sleek curves. 'You have taste.'

He punched the trunk release on the remote fob and the lid sprang open. Inside the small trunk, Kilkenny found a black leather briefcase containing Martineau's laptop.

'What's on your computer?'

'What do you mean?' Martineau asked, surprised by the question.

Kilkenny tossed his jacket in the trunk and held up the black briefcase. 'This laptop computer – what the fuck is on it? Is this where you keep your experiment logs?'

Martineau's eyes grew wide. 'Yes.'

'Is there information on Eames?'

'Yes, and you, too,' Martineau replied.

'Show me,' Kilkenny demanded.

He set the laptop on the Z8's removable hardtop and

switched it on. The Mac booted up quickly and asked for a password.

'What's the password?' Kilkenny asked sternly.

'GATCCATCGA'

'A DNA sequence, cute.' Kilkenny typed in Martineau's password. 'Where's the information about Eames?'

Martineau talked Kilkenny through her file directory. He skimmed through her notes and found that she'd harvested Eames's DNA from cells she recovered from a water glass that he'd used while dining at Lafitte's New York home. From that sample, Martineau fabricated sperm cells that were genetically indistinguishable from the real thing.

'I don't know whether to be impressed or horrified. I guess I'm a little of both. What a waste of ability. It's time to go talk to the police.'

'Aren't you forgetting about Roxanne Tao?'

'What?' Kilkenny demanded.

'She broke into my lab while we were having dinner. Duroc captured her. She's at Lafitte's estate right now, and I am certain Duroc's men are enjoying her immensely,' Martineau taunted. 'I'm told she's quite attractive.'

'You know where she's being held?'

'Yes, but if you take me to the police, they will want to get warrants and permission from the government before they search the house of a man as powerful as Charles Lafitte. No one is going to rush out to save your associate, and by the time they do get there, she will be dead and her body gone. Then it will be your word against Lafitte's. But there is an alternative.'

'What?'

'A trade, me for your associate.'

'I've got a better idea. You show me where Roxanne is, and I'll tell the authorities you were cooperative. It may make the difference between life in prison and the death penalty. *Comprenez-vous?*'

'*Oui,*' Martineau replied nervously.

'How far to Lafitte's château?'

'It's a little more than a hundred kilometers, about an hour away.'

'Not the way I'll be driving.'

Kilkenny opened the passenger door for Martineau, then helped her into the low bucket seat. Because of the handcuffs, she had to sit with her legs folded beneath her. Kilkenny pulled Martineau's phone out of his pocket and dialed a long string of numbers.

'MARC Computer Center,' the familiar voice answered, 'Grin here.'

'Grin, it's Nolan. I've acquired a laptop containing evidence on it that should clear Eames. You think you can hook something up real quick to download this puppy? I have a digital phone that can patch into the laptop's modem. Problem is, I have to do this from a car and we've got less than an hour to do it.'

'Gimme a sec while I open up a window for remote access.'

Kilkenny waited, listening to Grin humming as he typed.

'All right, Nolan, I'm ready for you. Call my machine's direct line and I'll do the rest. If we get a good satellite connection, I can pull twenty gigs out of that laptop in under thirty minutes.'

'Thanks. Talk to you later.'

Kilkenny ended the call, patched the digital phone into Martineau's laptop, and keyed in the number for Grin's computer. Once Grin had control of the laptop, Kilkenny set it in the leg space in front of Martineau's seat.

'Dominique, I wouldn't kick that computer if I were you. It would upset me.'

Martineau guided Kilkenny out of Paris and onto N12, the national highway that ran west from Paris into the Normandy countryside and all the way to Brest. Once on the highway, Kilkenny quickly ran through the Z8's six-speed gearbox, at times pushing the car past 150 kilometers per hour.

Near Dreux, a musical flourish sounded from Martineau's laptop.

'What's it say?' Kilkenny asked, keeping his eyes on the winding road.

Martineau glanced down at the laptop. 'Your friend says he got everything.'

Kilkenny downshifted, pulled off the road, and parked; there were no other cars in sight. He picked up the laptop and saw that Martineau had told him the truth. After typing a quick reply to Grin, he shut the laptop down and placed it back on the floor.

'How far from here?' Kilkenny asked as he slipped the Z8 into gear and punched the accelerator.

'About thirty-five kilometers.'

'Tell me about Lafitte's château and the layout of the property.'

'The grounds around the château are very large, many hectares of property – rolling woods, pasture, gardens, and the riverbank. Along the roads, there is a very tall, thick privet hedge.'

'Any fencing or gates?'

'The only fences are around the pastures, for the horses. Lafitte has a large stable. There are two guarded gates – the main gate and the service entry.'

'What kind of security?'

'There are four guards on duty at all times, more during large functions. There are cameras and motion-detection equipment around the property and alarms on the buildings.'

'Describe the buildings.'

'Entering from the main gate, you'll pass a small gate-house. There is usually one man there. As you drive up the road, you will see a long, low stone building on your right – that is the stables. On the left are some cottages and service buildings. The security staff occupies one of the cottages. The rest are for groundskeepers, equipment, and Lafitte's automobiles. The road ends at the château.'

'Tell me about the main house.'

'The château dates back to pre-Revolutionary times. It's shaped like a wide H. The center contains the public spaces, while the wings hold bedrooms, the kitchen, and servant quarters.'

Fifteen minutes later Kilkenny slowed and pulled off the highway into the countryside near Verneuil-sur-Arve, a small historic town situated on the Arve River. A few kilometers outside the village, a fifteen-foot-high wall of dense foliage appeared alongside the road.

'This is the border of the estate,' Martineau announced.

Kilkenny slowed the BMW and studied the hedge. 'No getting through that without a chainsaw. How far from the hedge to the guardhouse?'

'Over a kilometer, I think.'

'Motion detectors would nail me before I even got close. Where's the main gate?'

'Just up ahead.'

They rounded a curve in the road and saw an illuminated opening in the privet hedge. Kilkenny pulled into the driveway and stopped short so that their faces stayed out of the light. The BMW's high beams poured light at the gatehouse and through the baroque ironwork into the manicured grounds beyond.

'What are you doing?' Martineau asked.

'Just making it up as I go along,' Kilkenny replied, lowering the window.

Kilkenny beeped the horn just as the guard stepped out of the gatehouse near the gate. A uniformed man held his hand up to shield his eyes from the glare of the high beams.

'Dr Martineau?' he asked as he stepped around to the side of the BMW. He recognized Martineau's car, but could not see who was inside.

Kilkenny lifted his arm through the open window and squeezed down on the spray can he'd taken from Martineau's purse. The guard clutched his face, passed out, and fell to the ground.

He dragged the unconscious man back into the gatehouse. The man reeked of Martineau's chemical spray.

Kilkenny held his breath to avoid another assault on his senses as he stripped the guard of his pistol – a Glock 9mm – and checked the clip. The weapon had a full load. Kilkenny slammed the clip back in place, chambered a round, and checked the safety. Armed, he punched the button that opened the gate and returned to the BMW.

'Did you miss me?' Kilkenny asked as he put the car into gear and drove through the open gate.

Martineau scowled at him uncomfortably. Her knees were stiff and she'd lost all feeling in her calves and feet. She cursed each time Kilkenny drove over a bump in the road, causing the handcuffs to rub against her like a steel thong. 'It looks pretty much the way I pictured it,' Kilkenny said as he followed the main drive into the estate.

A white wooden fence surrounded the paddock and on the far side stood a long stone building with a gabled roof. A series of small square windows punctured the thick walls and the eave bowed into eyebrows over the large barn doors. Ahead, he saw the long masonry facade of Lafitte's château softly illuminated.

'Is that the guardhouse, up on the left?'

'Yes.'

Kilkenny switched off all the car's lights and turned onto the side road that led to the guardhouse. He pulled the car off the road behind a large trimmed shrub and parked.

'Don't go anywhere,' he said while taking the keys from the ignition and opening the door.

'I hope they catch you, Kilkenny,' she said, her voice low and seething with anger. 'Then I'll cut off your testicles and feed them to you before you die.'

'I'll miss you, too.'

60

As Kilkenny stepped away from the BMW, Martineau heard the door locks pop closed. Her eyes never left him as he disappeared into the darkness.

When she was sure he was gone, Martineau shifted position in her seat. She balanced all her weight on her left knee, leaning her torso against the inclined leather seat. She felt the rush of blood into her legs, and a sharp stinging of a thousand needles replaced the numbness.

Martineau took several deep breaths, then lifted her bent right leg up and extended it over the center console and the driver's seat. Slowly, the stinging ebbed. She flexed the sculpted muscles of her thigh and calf, then slowly folded her leg as she pulled it toward her. Her thigh rose up against her chest, her knee just below her chin.

A shudder rippled through her left leg as she struggled to maintain her balance. She pulled her calf tight against the back of her thigh while keeping her foot square with her leg and her heel pressed up against her right buttock. Martineau took a deep breath and slowly eased her cuffed wrists around her foot. When the handcuffs slipped past her toes, she released her breath in a single burst.

She turned forward and slipped back down into her seat, both legs burning from her contortions. When she regained feeling in her legs, Martineau opened the door. Awkwardly, she retrieved her laptop from the floor of the car and, clutching it against her chest, began to run toward the château.

The grounds of Lafitte's estate were covered with large shrubs and ancient trees, some over four feet in diameter and towering upward of a hundred feet. Kilkenny made the most of this natural cover, moving quickly from position to position.

In the darkness he approached the tidy cluster of service buildings. Light poured out of the windows of one, which Kilkenny surmised was the guardhouse. A carriage lantern by the door cast a grazing light across the cottage's ivy-covered walls and gravel drive.

Kilkenny kept his eyes away from the light-filled windows, attempting to preserve his night vision until he was ready to attack. As he neared the guardhouse, he began to hear music. At first it was all bass, then he heard notes in higher frequencies until a melody of sorts became apparent – electronic dance music.

In the corner of his eye, Kilkenny saw something move. He lost it, then caught it again. Martineau had somehow managed to free her arms and was now running toward the château. Kilkenny knew there was no way he could catch her before she reached the château, leaving him precious little time to work before the alarm was sounded.

As he moved around the tree trunk, a guard ran out of the door toward the Jeep. Seeing Kilkenny, the guard reached for his pistol. Kilkenny fired and two rounds struck the guard just above his right eye.

'Charles! Sumner! It's Dominique, let me in!' she screamed. 'Hurry!'

She pounded on the heavy wooden door for nearly a minute before a security guard finally opened it. Martineau burst through the opening and limped straight to Lafitte, trembling uncontrollably. She stumbled and lost her grip on the laptop computer cradled in her arms. It fell to the marble floor and its black plastic case cracked.

'Dominique, what has happened?' Lafitte asked.

'Kilkenny is here!' she announced, out of breath.

'What?' Duroc shouted. 'You were supposed to kill him!'

'He escaped and took me prisoner.'

'How? When I left, he was unconscious.'

'I revived him,' Martineau admitted. 'After all the trouble he has caused, I wanted to see the look in his eyes when he died. He broke free.'

'*Maudite vache!*' Duroc cursed.

'Calm down, Sumner,' Lafitte commanded. 'And you, remove her handcuffs at once.'

After the guard unlocked the manacles, Lafitte led Martineau and the others back into his study. Udall Walker was seated there with a glass of bourbon. Lafitte poured Martineau a glass of cognac and handed it to her.

'Now, Dominique,' Lafitte began, 'where is Kilkenny?'

'Heading for the guardhouse. He's come for the woman.'

Kilkenny ran up to the guardhouse door, kicked it in, and entered a large room with a kitchenette. He held his pistol chest high, the barrel pointed in the same direction as his eyes, both sweeping the room for a target. He found nothing.

The music still pounded on. Kilkenny moved to the next room and found communications equipment and a bank of video monitors. One of the monitors showed Martineau at the château's front door. Down the hall, he cleared the bathroom and guards' armory. Unfortunately, a keypad controlled the magnetic locks on the steel mesh door securing the weapons and ammunition.

Kilkenny braced himself against the wall beside the last door. He could feel the beat pulsing through the plaster. He spun around, raised his leg, and kicked the door. Splinters flew from the jamb and the door sprang inward, crashing into the plaster wall with Kilkenny right behind it searching for a target.

'Nolan, look out!' Tao screamed, her hoarse voice almost inaudible with the blaring music.

He caught a blur of motion out of the corner of his eye and turned just as a wooden chair crashed down on his forearms and wrists. Kilkenny's arms dropped with the forceful blow and one of the chair's wooden legs caught the back of the Glock and stripped it from his hands. The pistol slid across the floor and disappeared beneath the bed where Tao lay bound and nude.

To his right he saw a naked man holding the chair.

Kilkenny snapped a side kick into the man's face, then pulled his leg back and delivered a second kick to the same spot, trying to drive his heel through the man's head. The guard reeled back, his nose flattened against his cheek. Several broken teeth protruded through his bloody lips.

Gripping the chair legs like a plow, Kilkenny rammed the naked guard into the wall behind him. The backrest shattered, as did several of the guard's lower ribs, and the tips of the broken spindles skewered into the man. Blood poured out of his mouth. The guard growled, reached out, and grabbed Kilkenny around the throat. Kilkenny pressed his body forward against the chair's bottom supports, driving the broken spindles farther into the guard's body, and bent his legs into a deep wide stance. With the broken chair braced between them, Kilkenny drove his hands upward like a wedge between his attacker's elbows, broke the man's hold on his neck, and speared his fingertips into the guard's eyes.

The soft orbs ruptured and gelatinous blobs of vitreous humor oozed out around Kilkenny's fingers. Instinctively, the guard recoiled, but there was nowhere for him to go. His head impacted the wall with a dull thud as Kilkenny's fingertips broached the eggshell-thin sockets of his eyes. The last thing he consciously felt was Kilkenny's fingers sliding through his face into the gooey mass of his brain.

Survival instincts took over and the guard thrashed wildly for a minute, emitting guttural noises until his body finally went slack. Kilkenny pulled his fingers from the man's skull and let him fall. On the floor near the guard's body, a boom box continued to thud out a monotonous dance beat. Kilkenny yanked the plug from the wall socket, bringing a welcome silence.

'Thank you,' Tao said with relief.

'I got here as soon as I could,' Kilkenny said as he covered Tao's torso with a sheet. He sat on the edge of the bed beside her, wiped his hands clean on the end of the sheet, and began untying Tao's wrists. 'Are you okay?'

'They were rough, but I'm still alive.' Tao massaged the ligature marks on her wrists to get the blood moving in her hands. 'What about you? You look terrible.'

Kilkenny showed her the marks on his wrists. 'Let's just say they had a similar idea for me.'

He untied her ankles and massaged both joints tenderly. 'How's that?'

'Much better.'

'Good.' Kilkenny scooped up Tao's clothes and back-pack from the floor. 'Get dressed. Martineau is up at the château right now warning them about me. How many guards?'

'I only saw four.'

Kilkenny knelt down beside the bed and searched for the Glock. 'That jibes with what Martineau told me. I killed two and left a third unconscious and unarmed. That leaves one more, along with Duroc, Lafitte, and Martineau. Look, I've uploaded some information out of Martineau's laptop to Grin back in Ann Arbor – it ties Vielogic to everything. It's not perfect evidence, but it's a start. We've both had enough for today. I say we get the hell out of here.'

'We can't, Nolan.'

'Why not?'

'Udall Walker, the CIA's Paris station chief. He sold us out to Lafitte. He and Duroc captured me inside Martineau's lab. Walker is here now, and if we leave, he'll send teams out to hunt us down. We might get word to Barnett, but Walker can jam up the official channels long enough to make sure we disappear. Then it's a matter of spin control.'

Kilkenny stood up and checked the pistol; it was undamaged. 'In that case, we finish this now.'

61

The phone in the guardhouse rang and Kilkenny looked at Tao. It rang several more times, demanding an answer, then it stopped.

'Well, they know I'm here,' Kilkenny said, 'and since nobody answered, they've probably figured out something has happened to their men. If you were in their position, what would your next move be?'

Tao thought for a moment. 'They only have two options: sit tight or send somebody out. I'm guessing they'll stay put and wait for us to come to them.'

'And if we just leave, Walker makes a few calls and sends the wolves after us. I assume Duroc and the last guard are armed, but Lafitte doesn't seem the type to carry. What about Walker?'

'He's an Operations man. Treat him as armed.'

'Inside the château, they have the home field advantage. We've got to neutralize that. Grab that bedsheet while I look for matches and some bottles.'

Tao hastily folded up a sheet. 'Molotov cocktails?'

'Something like that. A billionaire like Lafitte really hates it when the power goes out and his sorbet melts,

340

so he has to have an electrical backup. We have a generator out at the farm, but for a place this size, there's probably a small building full of generators. We take that out, the château is back to using candles.'

They killed the lights in the guardhouse and, once their night vision had returned, Tao followed Kilkenny outside. Their footsteps were carefully placed and silent. Tao glanced down at the body of another of the men who'd raped her and saw a wide bloody hole in his forehead.

Karma, she thought, with a hint of a smile.

Kilkenny moved up to the nearest building, his pistol held in front of him in a modified Weaver grip, the barrel tracking in line with his eyes. Looking through a window, he saw several very expensive automobiles. He hand-signaled Tao that he was proceeding to the next building. Pivoting around the corner of the garage, Kilkenny scanned the area for threats and found none.

Adrenaline coursed through Kilkenny's bloodstream, punching his normally low heart rate up. He breathed in through his nose, feeling the air push down to his center, then released his breath slowly through his mouth. As he'd been taught by his karate master, he used the cycle of his breathing to focus his thoughts and harness his energy.

Kilkenny moved into position and scanned the area ahead for targets. No threats, move on. He methodically cleared the gardeners's tool and equipment building, a storage building, and a potting shed. No sign of threats and no sign of generators.

He swept the alleyway between the potting shed and

the last building. It was smaller than the garage, but similar in that it had carriage doors facing the gravel roadway. He looked through a window and, in the dim glow of lights on a bank of electrical service panels, he saw six large metal boxes on the floor in three rows of two. Kilkenny signaled to Tao that he found what they were looking for.

Just beyond the building, the roadway ended in a cul-de-sac at the edge of which Kilkenny saw a small building about the size of an outhouse. As he closed on the small structure, details became clearer. A coiled hose hung from a hook on the building's side and two thick rubber hoses emerged from the front, just under the soffit – a fuel pump.

The filling station was set in the middle of a rectangular concrete slab. Kilkenny studied the surface of the slab until he found two metal circles – one marked diesel, the other petrol. He returned to where Tao waited near the generator building. He tested the side door, found it locked, and kicked it in.

'I don't think there's anybody out here, but stay sharp,' Kilkenny said, flipping on the Glock's safety and sliding the weapon into his belt. 'Rip that sheet into two long strips and a couple short ones while I look for some tools.'

A tool bench ran along the length of a wall inside the generator building. Kilkenny quickly found a pair of tin snips and a large wrench used to unscrew the lids on the underground fuel tanks.

One by one, Kilkenny opened the covers on the generators to expose the engines, then cut the fuel lines with the tin snips. Gas leaked from the severed lines onto the floor.

'Done,' Tao announced, after she had finished tearing the sheets.

'Good, follow me.'

Kilkenny led Tao outside to the filling station, where he opened the lid on the first tank.

'Tie a couple of tight knots on the ends of the long strips and lower them into the tank.'

'A fuse?'

'Yep. We're making two regular Molotov cocktails and two jumbos.'

Kilkenny unscrewed the second lid, then filled the wine bottles with gasoline.

'I'm set with the tanks,' Tao said.

'Stand back.'

Kilkenny pulled the fuel hose out from the station, aimed the nozzle at the long strips of cloth, and doused them with gasoline. The gray concrete turned dark and wet. When the strips were soaked, he dropped the hose and picked up the wine bottles.

'Light 'em up.'

Tao struck a match and ignited the rags dangling wet from the necks of the bottles. Yellow-orange flames licked at the edges of the sheet, then spread quickly upward engulfing the cloth. Kilkenny ran toward the open door and tossed the bottles inside. The first landed in the middle of the generators, shattering against the concrete floor. Kilkenny threw the second against the wall, just beneath the electrical service panels. Flames raced up the wall, consuming the spray of fuel.

One by one, the puddles of fuel inside the generators began to ignite. The fire was spreading quickly. Kilkenny jogged over to Tao.

'Light it and run,' Kilkenny said.

Tao struck another match, watched the flame curl and expand, then tossed it into the puddle of fuel. The long strips of cloth gave direction to the flame, channeling it down into the fuel tanks. Both tanks were more than half full and the upper section of each was thick with explosive vapor.

Kilkenny and Tao felt the blast behind them as a fireball erupted from the pump, destroying the filling station. Flames illuminated the generator building like a jack-o-lantern.

62

The windows of the château rattled from the sound of the distant explosion. Then the lights went out. Inside Lafitte's study, an eerie yellow-red glow from the windows provided the only illumination.

'Everyone, get down!' Duroc shouted as he crouched and moved toward the windows.

'What is happening?' Lafitte demanded.

Pressing his body against the wall beside one of the tall windows, Duroc glanced out onto the grounds. He saw the skeletal outline of a building, charred and black, enveloped within a raging fire. A second explosion ripped open a section of the roof and showered sparks and embers in every direction. Fire consumed the ivy that covered the outbuilding, blackening the fieldstone underneath.

'They've destroyed the generator building!' Duroc announced. 'We've lost power, communications, and security systems.'

'What should we do?' Lafitte asked.

'You and Dominique go upstairs and find someplace

to hide. Walker and I will remain down here with the guard.'

'Can't you get more of your men here?' Lafitte asked.

'There's no time. We'll kill him once he enters the château, then deal with the rest of this mess afterward.'

63

Kilkenny and Tao circled around the château and approached from the south side. They kept to the shadows to avoid being silhouetted by the fire, Kilkenny leading with Tao covering their rear. The burning generator house created an artificial dawn and the large house cast a wide, exaggerated shadow across the sloping landscape that Kilkenny and Tao used to conceal their closing advance.

They ran up behind a gazebo placed in line with the château's symmetrical rear façade. The circular wooden structure straddled the outer edge of a brick-paved terrace surrounded by a low stone balustrade. Glock and eyes tracking as one, Kilkenny scanned the terrace from side to side looking for threats in the shadows behind the windows.

Kilkenny scooped up a pair of potato-sized stones from a landscaped bed and handed them to Tao. She looked at him quizzically, but followed as he dashed through the gazebo and across the terrace. They pressed up against the masonry walls of the château near a French door on the west wing. Kilkenny pointed at the stones in Tao's hands, then at two windows about fifty feet away. He held up his fingers for a three-count and Tao nodded.

On three, Tao hurled the stones at the windows. As the stones struck, Kilkenny shattered a pane in the glass door beside him with the Glock. Kilkenny reached through and popped the lock.

Inside, Kilkenny scanned the room, eyes and Glock probing the darkness in search of a target. He glided sideways along the near wall with Tao behind him, still searching the shadows for any sign of movement. Outside the room, they heard two distinct sets of footsteps – one set upstairs and the other rushing toward the rooms with the broken windows.

Kilkenny signaled that he was moving to the next room. He passed through a wide archway into a large space that spanned the width of the main section of the house. Two windows on the north wall danced with fire-light. The room had four entry points, two archways on each end of the long walls facing opposite each other. Kilkenny swept left to right, then back again slowly, their footsteps silent as they edged along the wall.

We've got time, Kilkenny reminded himself. *No need to rush.*

He stepped past a large fireplace in the center of the wall and detected movement. He turned toward the archway on the opposite wall and locked on a target. As he squeezed off a double tap, his target fired and Kilkenny felt a bullet tear through his left shoulder.

'Jeezus!' Kilkenny hissed under his breath.

Both of Kilkenny's shots landed in the kill zone and the guard fell backward onto the marble floor of the foyer.

'Here,' Kilkenny said, handing Tao the pistol.

'How bad?'

Kilkenny gingerly felt his upper arm and found the entry and exit wounds. 'Hurts like a sonuvagun, but it passed through. You take the lead.'

Tao cleared the next room ahead. When they reached the foyer, they found the body of the guard who had exchanged bullets with Kilkenny. Kilkenny picked up the man's pistol. They continued their methodical sweep of the main level, finding only dark and empty rooms. In the servant's wing, Tao carefully opened a door to a narrow staircase.

'What do you think?' Tao asked quietly.

'The rest are upstairs and it looks like there's only two ways to get there. It's stupid for us to split up. I say we block this door and take the main stair.'

'Agreed.'

Tao wedged a chair in front of the door. They moved back through the dining room and into the two-story foyer. The main stair swept up in a wide gentle curve. Glocks and eyes scanning the upper landing, Kilkenny and Tao began their ascent.

As they neared the top, Kilkenny's visual sweeps focused on the two doorways that faced each other on opposite ends of the upper floor landing. Both doors were ajar, and the light from the fire that illuminated the foyer only served to make the rooms beyond the doors seem that much darker.

Which one? Kilkenny pondered, studying the narrow view he had into the rooms.

Just as his eyes cleared the edge of the upper floor landing for a better look, a muzzle flash illuminated the dark opening to his right. Kilkenny and Tao dropped back, three rounds splintering the woodwork, just missing his head. Kilkenny reached his right arm up over the top step and returned fire. Rounds slammed into the wall and door with little hope of finding a target. Kilkenny and the unseen attacker continued to trade rounds in an apparent stalemate.

'What's the plan?' Tao asked.

'Move up behind me. On three, drill a few shots into the right side of that doorway. I'll run up along the left side, bolt through the door, and pop him. As soon as I hit the door, you follow me in.'

'Shouldn't I be taking the run?'

'You ever done this before?'

'No.'

'I have. You cover my tail in case this plan goes sideways on us. Ready?'

Tao moved into position and recited a slow count. On three, she fired into the dark opening to cover Kilkenny's charge, then held her fire. The door on the opposite side of the landing flew open. Tao rolled across the top tread, caught sight of Udall Walker raising his pistol, and fired. She emptied the Glock into Walker's chest, driving him back through the doorway.

Kilkenny kicked the door wide open and lunged into the darkened room, his back pressed against the door, the Glock held at eye level. Starting a quick right-to-left sweep, his outstretched hands struck something, then a muzzle flashed directly in front of him and a bullet slammed into the door beside his head. Kilkenny's left cheek stung with burning fragments of spent powder, his ear echoing painfully with a high-pitched ringing.

The residual image of the muzzle flare robbed Kilkenny of his night vision, but he didn't need it – the shooter was standing right in front of him. As he squeezed off his final shots, something struck his right arm, pushing his aim off target. Two pistols flared in the darkness in front of him. To his left, a window exploded into tiny shards of glass.

Kilkenny dropped his empty pistol and grabbed hold of the arms in front of him. One of them felt warm and moist. He snapped a short kick, waist high, and connected with something solid. The shooter doubled over and leaned into the dim light by the doorway. Duroc.

Duroc lunged, ramming his shoulder into the left side of Kilkenny's chest. He pinned Kilkenny against the door and pulled his arms free. Kilkenny felt two of his floating ribs break against the door's decorative brass knob. Duroc shifted to the side, placing Kilkenny between himself and the doorway. Both men were gasping for air. Duroc straightened up, his height just shy of Kilkenny's, and leveled his pistol at Kilkenny's chest.

Kilkenny reached out and grabbed Duroc by the wrists and drove a knee into his groin. Duroc folded over. Pivoting left, Kilkenny turned and Duroc followed, locked in orbit. Picking up momentum halfway through the spin, Kilkenny released his hold on Duroc's wrists and let him fly. The tall multipaned window shattered into pieces of broken glass and splintered wood as Duroc sailed through it. His body made a soft thud when it impacted on the terrace below.

Kilkenny glanced out the window. Duroc's body lay still on the patterned brick surface, his neck bent at an impossible angle.

64

From behind the locked door of the master bedroom, Lafitte heard an exchange of gunfire, then silence.

'Duroc?' Lafitte called apprehensively.

'I'm afraid not,' Kilkenny replied.

Martineau sat on the side of the king-sized four-poster bed sobbing, her arms wrapped tightly around her torso. Lafitte stared at her – his most brilliant scientist, his lover and trusted confidante – and felt nothing but hatred and betrayal.

'This is your doing, Dominique! You and Duroc are responsible for this!'

'No, Charles,' Martineau pleaded tearfully.

Lafitte walked toward the bed. In his right hand he held a broad knife of Damascus steel. It glowed orange-red in the reflected light of the burning generator building. He normally kept the blade in the safe in his closet, but he had pulled it out tonight after Duroc ordered him and Martineau upstairs. The fear in Duroc's eyes was unmistakable. Lafitte had seen it. Now Duroc was dead.

'How could you both have been so stupid!' Lafitte raged. 'You and your lover have ruined everything!'

'Charles, I swear I didn't know what Sumner had done.'

Lafitte stood with his face inches from hers, glowering at her. Martineau looked down to avoid his eyes.

'You stupid whore. I gave you the chance to create the future.'

Lafitte grabbed her by the throat with his left hand and pushed her back onto the bed. Martineau's eyes grew wide as Lafitte lifted the dagger over his head. Terrified, she wrapped her legs around his and kicked the backs of his knees with her heels. Lafitte's legs buckled. Martineau pushed his chest as hard as she could, forcing him back. He tried to regain his faltering balance, but Martineau tightened her grip around his legs and lunged at him.

The momentum of her body carried them both away from the bed. Lafitte flinched reflexively as he fell back, Martineau riding him down, then his head struck the wooden parquet floor. Martineau grabbed the knife from Lafitte's hand and screamed wildly as she plunged it into his chest.

The ancient blade slipped easily into Lafitte's body, stopping only when it passed through the other side and struck the floor. She pulled the knife out and thrust it back in again and again.

'Got any ammo left?' Kilkenny asked softly.

Tao shook her head. 'All out.'

Kilkenny checked the pistol he'd taken from Duroc.

The last round had struck the door just inches from Kilkenny's head. 'Maybe we can bluff him.'

From inside the master bedroom, they heard Lafitte shouting. Then his diatribe was suddenly replaced by a banshee-like scream.

'What the hell?' Kilkenny whispered.

Kilkenny reached for the doorknob and found it locked. He took a half-step back and kicked the paneled door just above the knob. The oak stile split straight up the grain and the door flew open.

Splattered with Lafitte's blood, Martineau looked up as Kilkenny entered the bedroom. She flipped the knife around in her hand, holding the blade to slash instead of stab, and lunged at him. He backed away, holding his bent arms shoulder-high, trying to keep from being sliced. Martineau closed, sweeping the blade back and forth wildly.

Martineau angled closer to the door, trying to keep Kilkenny from escaping. She was breathing hard, almost panting. Kilkenny slid along the wall, inching away from her – Martineau was herding him into the corner. She lunged again, and Kilkenny sucked in his stomach, making his body concave. The tip of Martineau's blade drew a razor-thin line just above his navel. Blood seeped in droplets from the long cut.

As Martineau slashed again, Tao stepped through the doorway and hurled an empty pistol at her. The two-pound weapon struck the scientist squarely in the back of the head. Kilkenny grabbed her wrist and twisted. The knife fell to the floor and Kilkenny kicked it out of reach. Dazed, Martineau's knees gave out. Kilkenny guided her fall and laid her facedown on the floor.

'See if there's anything in the closet we can use to restrain her,' Kilkenny said as he held Martineau's arms behind her back.

Tao looked over the contents of Lafitte's neatly arranged closet. 'There's some Hermès silk ties.'

'Perfect.'

Kilkenny bound Martineau's hands and feet, checking his knots carefully before getting up. Tao picked up Lafitte's knife, intrigued by the wavy damask pattern on the blade. In addition to the wet red smears of blood, she saw dried spots as well.

'Nolan, this was used before. There's old blood on it.'

Kilkenny took a closer look at the blade. 'The Ann Arbor police didn't find the knife used to murder Olson and Sutton – maybe this is it. Wrap it up in a towel.'

Outside, Kilkenny and Tao heard sirens approaching the château.

65

Paris

Kilkenny walked with Tao along the riverbank of the Rive Droite. The Seine glittered with the lights of Paris, a glow with which only the brightest of the night stars could compete.

'Are you going back tomorrow?' Tao asked.

'Yes. I want to see Eames as soon as possible. His attorney is working on getting him out on bail until all the new evidence can be processed and the charges dropped. It's still a mess, but at least there's a positive end in sight.'

'What about Martineau?'

'Eventually, she'll be extradited to stand trial for the murders of Sutton and Olson. French and American authorities are also going over Cerberus to identify which of Duroc's men were involved in the raid on LV Station.'

'Are they going after Vielogic as well?'

'I don't think so. The Vielogic board has been very

cooperative, and the evidence so far suggests Lafitte did all this on his own. The rest of Vielogic's board will get immunity in exchange for full disclosure of all Lafitte's activities and the return of everything stolen from LV Station. The SEC is also going after the money Duroc made on his short sale – something to do with illegal stock manipulation. Speaking of stock, I forgot to mention something I did before I came to Paris.'

'What?' Tao asked

'Just a little trade,' Kilkenny said smugly. 'Actually Duroc gave me the idea.'

'You didn't?'

'Yes, I did. And so did you, or at least your company. I put together my own little holding company – composed of Qi, UGene, MARC, Grin, and myself – and we shorted Vielogic. I checked CNN just before we went to dinner. Vielogic has taken a terrible hit. Collectively, we're up about twenty-two million.'

'Aren't you concerned the SEC will frown on what you've done?'

'No, my trade was based on exposing the truth, not the commission of a felony.'

When they reached the point where the river widened and split around the Ile de la Cité, Tao led him onto the long span of Pont Neuf. At the center, Tao stopped and gazed at the island that was the heart of Paris. Beyond the elegant mansions and regal government buildings loomed the towers of Sainte-Chapelle and Notre Dame.

'Well, Nolan, this is the real Pont Neuf,' Tao said, not taking her eyes from the view. 'The name means New

Bridge, but it's the oldest one in Paris. What do you think?'

'It's spectacular. Definitely a place to take a stroll with a beautiful woman,' Kilkenny said wistfully.

'I'll take that as a compliment, even though you sound a bit disappointed.'

'Sorry, Roxanne,' Kilkenny said, realizing his faux pas. 'My mind was elsewhere.'

Tao reached over and clasped Kilkenny's hand. 'I want to apologize for my less than congenial attitude during these past few weeks. Accepting this assignment was difficult for me, and I took some of my anger out on you. In the future, I will try to be more amiable.'

Kilkenny looked at Tao as she spoke and could see this was hard for her. She hadn't volunteered for this job and accepting it meant that the alternative was, in her mind, even worse.

'This has all the appearances of an olive branch, Roxanne. I accept.'

'I think you and I are alike in that there aren't many people in this world we consider true friends. I know it is a term that I don't use lightly.'

'Friendship is something that's earned, like respect and loyalty.'

Tao slipped her arms around Kilkenny's neck and drew him close; the suddenness of the move caught him off guard.

'You've earned that,' she said, 'and more.'

Read on for an extract from Tom Grace's previous novel, *Quantum*

Prologue

DECEMBER 10, 1948

Ann Arbor, Michigan

In the shadows of a small white building near the center of the University of Michigan campus, a young man stood motionless as he watched and waited. He was tall and wiry with harshly chiseled features, as if he'd been carved rather than born.

From his concealed vantage point near the eastern end of the L-shaped Economics Building, the man-made canyon formed by the four-story masonry bulk of the Randall Physics Laboratory and the equally massive West Engineering building lay open before him. The two buildings defined one corner of a large campus quadrangle. A pair of diagonal walkways crisscrossed the formal lawn from opposite corners of the square, intersecting at a large concrete plaza in front of the Graduate Library. The plaza and campus green surrounding it were known as the Diag.

A wide flat hole surrounded by mounds of earth and

debris lay to his right, just beyond the concrete walkway that extended out from an alley toward the center of the campus. A few days earlier a demolition crew had brought the aging boiler house and its attendant smokestack to the ground. The scene around him vaguely resembled many towns and villages of Europe he'd prowled as the Allied forces fought their way into Germany.

He put aside those thoughts and, instead, focused on the two men who stood in the illumination of a street-lamp not one hundred feet away. From this distance, he struggled to hear the men speak as a steady wind out of the north swallowed the sound of their conversation. Snow swirled into vortices around them as they shuffled and stamped their feet, trying to stay warm.

A few minutes later the older of the pair, a wood-worker who built large model ships in a shop in West Engineering, shook his friend's hand and walked off at a brisk pace. The snow barked under his boots, echoing off the surrounding buildings. The woodworker quickly rounded the far side of the Economics Building and disappeared from view as the other man then climbed up the stone steps that led to the rear entrance of the Physics Lab.

A light flickered and then illuminated a small third-floor office, and from the shadows the hunter watched as Johann Wolff hung up his hat and coat and sat down at his desk.

Might as well settle in, the hunter thought as he crouched down atop his duffel, behind the thick ever-green shrub.

He shrugged off the cold and discomfort – conditions

he'd been hardened against long ago – and instead focused on his mission. If Wolff followed his usual routine, like a typical German, then he could expect the young physicist to work late into the night before returning to his rented room a few blocks away.

Johann Wolff pulled six notebooks out of his battered leather briefcase and set them carefully on the desk. He'd started the oldest of the slim volumes in Germany after the war, and each marked his painstaking progress in the pursuit of a scientific vision.

He opened the newest of the notebooks and carefully ran through the calculations again, following the flow of numbers through his complex mathematics. This was new territory. The methods he'd developed to describe what he saw as the next logical step after Einstein and Heisenberg were as radical as the calculus created by Isaac Newton to describe gravity.

Wolff's formulas allowed him to move fluidly back and forth in time. The nearly musical cadence of the variables described an evolving universe of heretofore unimagined elegance and sophistication. The notion that the universe was static and unchanging had died nineteen years earlier when Edwin Hubble discovered that the cosmos was indeed expanding, as was predicted by Einstein's theories.

'*Mein Gott!*' Wolff cried out as an image of the delicate, multidimensional structures that define both matter and energy clearly formed in his mind.

Wolff flipped to a blank page in his notebook and quickly began to sketch the mental picture before it faded.

His skilled hand produced the image of a coiled loop that twisted and wound into itself like a knotted ball – an image that attempted to represent a subatomic-sized chunk of the universe possessing seven additional dimensions beyond the readily apparent three dimensions of space and one of time.

Smiling with childlike wonder, Wolff stared at the drawing and realized that, at twenty-nine years of age, he now stood ready to overthrow everything in the realm of theoretical physics that had preceded him.

'I've got to let Raphaele know about this,' he said excitedly as he rummaged through his briefcase.

Wolff extracted the pages of a letter he'd started earlier that day while riding the train back from Chicago. The words and formulas flowed rapidly from his pen as he briefly laid out the framework of a theory that would describe the structure of everything from the tiniest bits of matter to the entirety of the universe. The letter quickly grew from a few pages of personal news to a thick sheaf filled with concise fragments of his blossoming theory. The six notebooks on his desk were the seeds of a larger work he knew lay ahead of him, one whose publication would shake the world.

Shortly before midnight Wolff shut off the light in his office. Bundled against the evening chill, he exited through the building's side door and began walking toward the center of campus.

'Excuse me,' a voice called out.

'Ja?' Wolff answered cautiously, still unable to see whom the voice belonged to.

'I'm down here.' A hand waved furiously at him from the excavation behind West Engineering.

Wolff stepped over the barricade and peered into the void left by the demolition of the boiler house. He saw a dark-haired young man in a soiled gray coat standing in the pit below.

'Be careful near the edge, it might give out on you. That's how I ended up down here. Think you could give me a hand getting out?'

'Sure,' Wolff replied. Judging by the smears of dirt on the man, it looked as though he had already made a few unsuccessful attempts to climb out on his own.

Wolff set his briefcase on the ground and knelt in the snow close to the edge of the pit. The young man moved toward him, and Wolff reached down to grasp his hand.

'I'll start climbing on three. Ready?'

Wolff nodded.

'One, two . . .'

Before the count of three came, the young man yanked hard and pulled Wolff headfirst into the pit. Wolff felt his shoulder burn, his arm rotating behind him as he fell. Deftly, the man bent Wolff's forearm upward, pressing the physicist's hand between his shoulder blades as he drove his face into the ground. Wolff's forehead plowed through two inches of freezing mud before slamming into the hardened earth. A crack of bone resonated inside his head, followed by a sudden rush of warm fluid into his sinus cavity – the bridge of Wolff's nose crumbled as it impacted a large stone.

The man crouched over Wolff, pinning him to the

ground. The weight of the attacker's body bore down on the point where the man's knee met Wolff's spine.

'Why? Why are you doing this?' Wolff shouted with globs of dirty snow and mud spraying from his lips. 'Let me go!'

Wolff struggled to pull free, but the young man had the advantage of strength and leverage.

'You are Johann Wolff. From 1939 until 1945 you were a research scientist with the Reichsforschungsrat. Your job was to devise more efficient ways of killing people.' The man spoke deliberately, each word carrying the weight of a pronouncement. 'Under your supervision, over two thousand men, women, and children lost their lives as test subjects and slave laborers. The Nokmim, the avengers of your victims, have found you guilty of crimes against humanity and have sentenced you to death.'

'Lies! I did not help the Nazis! I am a scientist. I killed no one!' Wolff countered, vainly trying to face his accuser.

The man shifted his weight and drove Wolff deeper into the mire. With his free hand, the man pulled a long serrated knife from the sheath strapped to his thigh and plunged it into the side of Wolff's neck. The stainless-steel blade sliced Wolff's carotid artery, several muscles, and the jugular vein. Wolff blacked out as the blood pressure in his brain, temporarily heightened by adrenaline, abruptly dropped. The sharpened edge passed effortlessly through Wolff's throat, nearly decapitating the physicist. The breath in Wolff's lungs escaped with a gurgling hiss, the warm moist air mixing with the steam already rising from the expanding pool of blood.

The tension in Wolff's body waned as he slowly descended from unconsciousness into death.

The assassin quickly dragged Wolff's body to the far end of the excavation and placed it in a partially buried maintenance tunnel at the base of the demolished smoke-stack. He then retrieved the physicist's briefcase and placed it with the body.

As the winter storm increased, he opened his duffel bag and took out a folding shovel. Without a glance, he expertly flipped the folding shovel head open and tightened the neck to lock it in place. Quickly and quietly, as the cold wind howled above him, the assassin entombed Wolff in the tunnel and removed any evidence of the murder. Within a week, according to what the workmen had told him, the entire site would be filled and leveled with the surrounding lawn.

'Vengeance has been served,' the young man said softly as snow began to blanket the final resting place of the war criminal Johann Wolff. 'May God have mercy on your soul – and mine.'

1

JUNE 5, PRESENT DAY

Ann Arbor, Michigan

Nolan Kilkenny punched the accelerator of the Mercedes ML 320 and piloted the black SUV into a sharp right turn onto the Huron Parkway. The yellow signal switched to red as he passed beneath.

In the passenger seat, Kelsey Newton stripped the towel from her head and began brushing out her shoulder-length mane of blond hair. The still-damp strands clumped together, and beads of water sprang off Kelsey's brush with each flick of her wrist.

'Hey, watch it,' Nolan said as a few errant drops struck his face.

'You want me beautiful, don't you?' Kelsey replied, her face hidden behind a veil of hair.

'You always are.'

'Well, thank you, but it doesn't just happen, you know.'

Kelsey set the brush down on her lap and quickly wove her hair into a French braid. She then put the brush back in her purse and pulled out her mobile phone and began dialing.

The SUV's speedometer edged over fifty as they passed the large blue-and-white sign that announced their entry onto the grounds of the University of Michigan's North Campus. A smaller road sign set the speed limit at twenty-five miles per hour.

'We'll be there in a few minutes,' Kelsey said reassuringly as Nolan sped down the winding road that led to the Michigan Applied Research Consortium.

Kelsey set her phone back in her purse. Ahead, nestled deep within a wooded site, stood a glistening ribbon of glass and stainless steel that defined the curvilinear form of the MARC building. The ultramodern structure was the physical embodiment of a vision that Nolan's father had nurtured throughout his career in international finance: the idea that a bridge needed to be built between cutting-edge academic research and the businesses that fueled the nation's economy. In operation for less than three years, Sean Kilkenny's bridge carried a steadily growing flow of valuable technology from the university's research labs into the world, and an equally impressive flow of money back into the university's coffers.

Nolan parked in the first spot he found. Kelsey was already out her door and moving at a near run toward the building's main entry by the time he pulled his briefcase out of the backseat and locked the SUV. After a short sprint, he caught up with her just as she passed through the door. In the lobby, Sean Kilkenny stood waiting for them.

'Glad you two could make it.'

'Sorry we cut it so close, Dad. Traffic on US Twenty-three was a bear.'

Kelsey gave Sean a peck on the cheek. 'Thanks again for letting me borrow Nolan. I really doubt I could have replaced the entire tube array in only two days.'

'You're welcome, Kelsey. Anything to advance the cause of science.'

'Dad, you should see this proton detector experiment. Imagine a sixty-foot cube of water hidden in a salt mine under Lake Erie. It's pitch black down there, and the walls are lined with a couple of thousand jumbo-sized flood lamps.'

'Photomultiplier tubes,' Kelsey corrected.

'Whatever. Strangest underwater job I've ever been on.'

'I'm just glad I had an experienced diver down there with me,' Kelsey said as she squeezed Nolan's hand. 'The PDE tank can be a little disorienting.'

'I wouldn't let anyone dive alone in that thing, especially you,' Nolan said lovingly.

'I assume that this project has been put to bed?' Sean questioned.

Kelsey shot a furtive glance at Nolan, who reddened slightly. 'We finished our part. The physics department can now handle the rest of the upgrade.'

'Good, because after Sandstrom makes his pitch to the board, I have a feeling that MARC's newest project director is going to have his hands full.'

Kelsey brushed a fleck off Nolan's tweed jacket, causing Sean's mood to relax slightly as he watched her evaluate his son's appearance. It reminded him of how his late

11

wife used to fuss over him before an important meeting, and it pleased him to know that his son had someone who cared for him in that same way.

Kelsey and Nolan had known each other since the earliest days of their childhood, when her family moved in to a home just a few doors up the street. They had attended school together, and both had distinguished themselves academically and athletically. They'd been best friends for years, sharing the strong bond of kindred spirits.

At eighteen, their ambitions took them on separate journeys. Kelsey attended the University of Michigan, where she pursued her passion for physics through to a doctorate and a faculty position. Nolan embraced the challenges of the United States Naval Academy, deferred his entry into the navy two years for a graduate degree from MIT, and then surprised his family and friends by joining the Navy SEALs.

Their friendship survived the twelve years of separation through a steady stream of phone calls, letters, and holiday visits. Eighteen months ago, when Nolan left the navy and returned to Ann Arbor, they resumed the comfortable pattern of their platonic relationship.

Both were ready for something more, but neither was willing to risk the security of what they had for the unknown – until they were nearly killed by a group of industrial spies. In the year following that brutal attempt on their lives, the two began enjoying an increasingly amorous relationship.

'Okay?' Nolan asked as she straightened his tie.

'Handsome as ever, dear.'

'You both look fine,' Sean said impatiently, checking his watch. 'The break's about over. Let's get inside. Nolan, Sandstrom and Paramo are waiting for you.'

Nolan followed his father and Kelsey into the conference room.

'Excuse me while I go make sure everything's ready for Sandstrom's dog and pony show,' Sean said before making a beeline for the podium.

From the doorway Nolan and Kelsey surveyed the crowd. The attendees had broken into several small groups, enjoying both the refreshments and the conversation.

'I see them, Kelsey. Look by the windows. The blond guy with the red beard is Sandstrom. Next to him – the older man, about a foot shorter with white hair and tortoiseshell glasses – that's Paramo.'

Beside the curved wall of glass that bowed outward into the woods, Kelsey spotted Ted Sandstrom and his mentor, Raphaele Paramo.'

'Nolan,' Sandstrom called out as they approached, relief visible on his face. 'I was afraid you weren't going to show.'

'Wouldn't miss it, Ted,' he replied, then introduced Kelsey to the two physicists.

'Professor Newton,' Paramo said, shaking her hand enthusiastically, 'this is indeed a pleasure. I've read your paper on optical electronics. Very interesting work.'

'Thank you,' Kelsey replied, enjoying the admiration of a respected peer.

Sandstrom then clasped her hand warmly. 'I understand we have you to thank for our being here today.'

'That may be overstating things a bit,' she demurred. 'All I did was look over the report that Notre Dame sent to MARC regarding your research. After I read it a few times – I admit it took more than one pass to really comprehend what you and Professor Paramo have accomplished – I told Nolan's father that he'd be a fool not to take a closer look.'

'Well, thank you for your vote of confidence.'

Across the room, Sean Kilkenny began to address those assembled. 'Ladies and gentlemen,' his amplified voice resonated above the murmuring conversations, 'if you'll kindly take your seats, we can move on to the next item on our agenda.'

The MARC board of directors, a mix of business executives and university regents, took their places at the conference table. Around the periphery of the room, members of the still-forming Notre Dame Applied Research Consortium (ND-ARC) and important guests of both universities returned to their seats. Sean Kilkenny waited until everyone was ready before proceeding.

'Last fall I had the pleasure of meeting our guest presenter while in South Bend for the Michigan–Notre Dame football game. While I am sure that some of us were pleased with the outcome of that game' – MARC's founder paused as a ripple of laughter followed his remark – 'I am doubly sure that others here are looking forward to the rematch this fall.' Another pause for partisan laughter. 'Be that as it may, my encounter with Ted Sandstrom, a professor of physics at Notre Dame, left a far greater impression on me than the game. Fellow board members and honored guests, I would like to introduce Professor Ted Sandstrom.'

The MARC director stood aside as Sandstrom approached the podium carrying a large Halliburton case.

'They're all yours, Ted,' Sean said quietly as he clipped a wireless microphone to Sandstrom's lapel.

Sandstrom looked over his audience. He recognized among the guests several wealthy Notre Dame alumni and a few of the regents. The presidents of both universities were seated together along the left wall. A sudden wave of nausea hit him, but it quickly subsided as he realized that this was no different from any classroom he'd ever been in. He was there to teach these people something about physics, and that was something he did very well.

'Good afternoon. As Mr Kilkenny said, I am a physicist. More precisely, I am an experimental physicist, which means I like to test ideas to see whether or not they work.'

Sandstrom pressed a button on the podium; the lights dimmed and the Asian symbol for yin and yang appeared on the large, flat wall display.

'In declaring that E equals mc squared, Einstein linked energy and matter together in such a way that the two are inseparable and, in some ways, indistinguishable. Matter is a manifestation of energy. If you label the left side of this symbol as matter' – Sandstrom pointed to the black yang – 'and the right as energy, then the region that I'm interested in is here.'

Sandstrom traced the S line that defined the border between yin and yang.

'Here, in the boundary between matter and energy,

resides the realm of quantum physics. This is where the classical physics of Newton and Galileo fall apart. The mathematical precision that we use to describe the motion of the planets is dethroned by an uncertainty principle that replaces absolutes with probabilities. In this thin edge, the distinction between matter and energy blurs.'

Sandstrom touched the podium keyboard again, and the image transformed into a horizontal grid, tilted slightly upward to show perspective. At random intervals two sections of the plane would distort, one spike warping upward while another went in the opposite direction. The warped areas would break free like water droplets and form gridded spheres that moved about briefly before being reabsorbed by the plane.

'The plane you see in this illustration represents a negative-energy state. This condition exists only in a vacuum in which all matter has been removed. In this state, quantum theory predicts that fluctuations in this energy allow for the spontaneous creation of both matter and antimatter.' Sandstrom pointed at the gridded spheres. 'Theory also states that these particles disappear rather quickly, and being a balanced system, the net energy is essentially zero. This just shows, even at a quantum level, that you can't get something for nothing.'

The gridded plane expanded and curled around on itself, forming a sphere.

'One theory about the origin of our universe puts it in a negative-energy state at the start of the Big Bang.'

Sandstrom zoomed in on the gridded sphere just as thousands of tiny blue and red particles appeared inside it.

'Now if matter and antimatter are created in equal amounts, then all these new particles should have collided with their opposites and annihilated each other in a burst of energy – leaving the universe a net zero.'

The red and blue particles quickly disappeared, and the gridded sphere collapsed into nothingness.

'This outcome is true only for a perfectly symmetrical universe. Suppose that our universe was asymmetrical, and at the moment of the Big Bang, there was more matter than antimatter.'

The new animation showed thousands of red and blue particles racing around, each collision giving off a brief white flash. After a few seconds the gridded sphere held only blue particles. The view panned out as the sphere expanded until it evolved into a spiraling galaxy and then gradually changed back into the yin-yang symbol.

'If this theory is valid, the question becomes: What caused the universe to be asymmetrical, allowing unequal amounts of matter and antimatter particles to be produced?' Sandstrom paused briefly and looked over his audience. 'At this point, I suspect that more than a few of you are wondering where I'm going with this presentation. So let me backtrack a bit for you. Eleven years ago Professor Raphaele Paramo and I began to investigate the effect of strong electrical fields on totally evacuated spaces. Our experiments had some very interesting results.'

Sandstrom tapped the keyboard, and a photograph of a laboratory, scorched and in shambles, filled the screen.

'This one got away from us.' A brief laugh rose from

the audience. 'Based on the theoretical calculations, the energies involved in this experiment should have been very low. As you can see, theory and reality were not in agreement. When we activated our test apparatus, an energy surge built up inside the evacuated chamber. The chamber quickly ruptured and a ball of lightning emerged. This coherent sphere of electricity floated around the lab for a few seconds before landing on an electrical panel. The explosion and resulting fire did significant damage to our lab. Fortunately, no one was hurt.'

The President of Notre Dame nodded, recalling the incident clearly.

'We rebuilt our laboratory and began to probe further into the discrepancy between theory and experiment. Here is the result of that work.'

Sandstrom switched off the projector, and the lights came back up. He then picked up the Halliburton case, set it on the conference table, and extracted what looked like a twelve-inch hexagonal nut made of matte black metal. Centered in the top face, in place of a threaded bolt, sat a six-inch-diameter hemisphere of clear Lexan. Sandstrom set the device down on one side so those in the room could see into the transparent dome. Clearly visible beneath the Lexan cover were three nested rings of a gold-tinted metal. A bluish, semitransparent sphere sat in the center of the rings like a gemstone in a jeweler's setting.

'The blue sphere, the heart of this device, contains nothing – it has been evacuated as completely as current technology allows. Surrounding it are three rings of a room-temperature superconducting material recently developed at Stanford University. The rings provide the strong electrical field I mentioned a moment ago.'

Sandstrom then pulled two small, freestanding digital devices from the case and plugged them together in series.

'These are standard watt meters that we use to measure the electric power on the input and output sides of the device. The calibration on both meters' – Sandstrom paused as he plugged a cord from the first meter into a wall receptacle – 'should be identical – which I am pleased to see is the case.'

Both meters registered identical 2200 watts. Satisfied the audience understood that both meters were operating properly, Sandstrom unplugged the cord, disconnected the meters, and reconnected them to jacks on opposite sides of the device. He then stood beside the table, holding the cord to the first meter in one hand.

'According to the first law of thermodynamics, the total amount of energy coming out of a system must be equal to the total amount of energy going in. This phenomenon is known as conservation of energy, or the "no free lunch" law. It's a good law that has proved itself time and again – until now.'

Sandstrom plugged the cord into the wall socket. The first meter jumped to life, registering the voltage that coursed through it like before; the second meter registered zero. Inside the device, the centermost golden ring began to spin. As it accelerated, the next ring began rotating, and finally the outermost ring joined in the orbital dance. The spinning rings created the illusion that the bluish globe was floating in a golden haze; then sparks appeared within the orb. The sparks increased in number and intensity until the vacuum within the sphere held a ball of brightly glowing energy. The audience shielded their eyes from the intense glare emanating from the device until Sandstrom took an opaque black cover from the Halliburton case and placed it over the Lexan dome.

'It does get a bit bright,' Sandstrom said sympathetically as several members of the audience blinked their eyes. 'If you'll please take a look at the meter measuring the energy output.'

Several members of the MARC board stood and moved closer to get a better look at the meter.

'Is that thing registering correctly?' asked an electrical engineer who'd made his fortune in the computer industry.

'This isn't possible,' said another, straining to believe what her eyes were showing her.

'That's exactly what I said when I first saw the numbers. The energy output from this device is approximately two thousand times what we're putting in. Now, since I firmly believe that energy can be neither created nor destroyed, the only conclusion I can draw is that this device is a faucet and the energy I'm using to create a strong asymmetrical energy field has opened the faucet, and that energy from some other source is pouring through it.'

The room buzzed with dozens of conversations as several people tried to shout questions at Sandstrom. A tidal wave of sound erupted from the normally diplomatic attendees as each tried to comprehend the impact of this discovery. Overwhelmed by the chaos that was overtaking the room, Sandstrom looked to Sean Kilkenny for help in subduing the crowd. Kilkenny, a boardroom veteran, quickly grabbed a microphone.

'And when Professor Sandstrom finally does determine exactly how his invention works,' the MARC founder said loudly, demanding the attention of the audience, 'he will likely win the Nobel Prize. In the meantime, this discovery quite literally changes everything. Quantum technology will irrevocably alter the global economic landscape. The small size and weight of quantum power cells – relative to the energy they deliver – finally give electric motors a huge power-to-weight advantage over internal-combustion motors. This advantage will cause a stampede in the transportation industry as manufacturers rush to exploit it, and a panic in the fossil-fuel industry as they look for ways to cope with this advancement. The last time a technological shift of this magnitude occurred was almost a hundred years ago when small, efficient, fuel-burning engines supplanted the horse and carriage.'

Audience members with ties to the Big Three automakers and the petroleum industry nervously nodded agreement.

'These industries are mature and established, and possess very deep pockets. While it might be possible for a maverick inventor with a better mousetrap to play David and Goliath with the likes of General Motors, the battle would be bloody and fierce. As much as I enjoy rooting for the underdog in an impossible fight, I also recognize that a young firm, one in control of a technology that promises to change how so many things in our world are done, could instigate a global economic war. The failures of the Asian and Russian financial markets in the late 1990s would pale in comparison to the sudden collapse of the industrial pillars that support our modern world.'

Sean Kilkenny let that thought hang over the now silent audience for a moment as he scanned the faces of so many people that he knew and respected.

'To his credit, Professor Sandstrom is not an ivory-tower scientist. He cares about the effect his work will have on the livelihood of millions of people, and his concern is legitimate. The manner in which this quantum technology is unleashed on the world poses a very real dilemma.' Sean Kilkenny then paused dramatically, and smiled. 'It has also presented us with a unique opportunity. Those of you who know me well know that I believe in the concept of MARC, of the absolute necessity in building bridges between the worlds of academic research and industrial production. This is what I have chosen to do in my retirement, and I promote this cause with the fervor of an evangelical preacher on a crusade.'

'Amen, Brother Kilkenny,' one of the board members shouted out.

'Amen, indeed. My introduction to Professor Sandstrom was no accident.' Sean motioned to the Catholic priest seated beside the University of Michigan's President, 'Father Joseph Blake, the President of Notre Dame, is familiar with what we've accomplished with MARC and is very interested in transplanting the concept. I, of course, agreed to help in any way I could. The fruit of that initial discussion is twofold. First, the Notre Dame Applied Research Consortium officially opened for business this morning.'

Polite applause from the MARC board to their colleagues on the ND-ARC board filled the room.

'Second, as chairman of the MARC board, I have received a formal offer from Suzanne Tynan, my distinguished counterpart at ND-ARC, to enter into a joint venture, the purpose of which is to patent any technological application for Sandstrom's quantum power cell that we can think of, and to license these applications to any and all parties who believe that they can make use of them. In short, we have been asked by our colleagues from South Bend to work with them in managing an intellectual property that may well be to this new century what the electric light, the internal-combustion engine, and the microchip were to the last.'

The momentary silence that followed the announcement evaporated, along with any semblance of parliamentary procedure, as the MARC board erupted with questions.

'How's this thing going to work?'

'Sean, what kind of commitment are we looking at?'

'Do we have any projections?'

Sean turned to where Sandstrom stood with Paramo, Kelsey, and Nolan and smiled. He lived for moments such as this.

'Mrs Quinn,' he said loud enough to be heard over the din of questions being called out at him, 'would you please distribute the prospectus for this venture.'

Loretta Quinn, Kilkenny's trusted assistant for more than thirty years, nodded and made a quick circuit around the conference table, handing each of the board members a sealed and numbered packet of documents.

'Due to the nature of the information contained in these packets, I feel it is my duty to remind you that this is a confidential matter, and the premature disclosure of any of this material would invite legal action equivalent in severity to the wrath of God. To answer a few of your questions, I have signed a letter of intent with ND-ARC. We have thirty days to review our proposed arrange-ment and iron out any wrinkles. While we debate percentages and punctuation, I have authorized the use of some of our resources by ND-ARC. If, at the end of thirty days, we decide not to pursue this venture, all materials will be returned and we will be compensated by ND-ARC for any resources used during this period. Most of your remaining questions should be answered in the prospectus, which I request you read thoroughly. In short, this discovery' – he motioned with his hand toward Sandstrom's quietly running device – 'is the future. At this time I move that we adjourn and further discussion of this matter be added to the agenda for the closed board meeting next week.'

'I second the motion,' called out board member Diana LaPointe, a respected attorney specializing in patent law and intellectual property.

'All those in favor?' Sean asked.

'Aye,' the board unanimously responded.

'The motion is carried, and this meeting is adjourned. Thank you all for coming.'

As the meeting broke up, board members carefully placed the sealed packages they had been given into brief-cases, treating the documents with the same reverence one would give an original draft of the Constitution. Nolan, Kelsey, and Paramo moved to the front of the room, where Sandstrom was carefully placing his equipment back in the Halliburton case under Sean's watchful eye.

'So, Sean,' Sandstrom asked as he flipped the latches on the case closed, 'what happens now?'

'You go back to work. Over the next week the board will digest what we've just given them. I suspect the meeting next week will be a doozy. In the end, I doubt we'll take the entire thirty days to decide. This deal is just too interesting to pass up. By the way, Nolan,' Sean said, turning to his son, 'now it's official: You're our co-ordinator for the quantum project. Your first assignment will be to relocate Ted's lab off campus.'

'Something a little bigger, I hope,' Sandstrom said.

'A bit,' Nolan replied. 'But some of the space we need is for business activities related to your work. Now that you've discovered a new way to print money, you'll need some room to stack, count, and store it.'

'How's lunch next Tuesday look?' LaPointe asked as she eyed her planner.

'I'm open,' Conrad Evans replied. 'Noon at the Gandy Dancer?'

'Works for me.'

Evans and LaPointe penciled the lunch meeting into their calendars.

'See you on Tuesday, Conrad,' LaPointe said with a smile as she zipped her leatherbound planner closed and walked away.

Evans slipped a thin booklet into the interior pocket of his double-breasted blazer and picked up his briefcase. He then scanned the room for a moment, and located the attractive brunette in the tailored linen suit. For Evans – a long-divorced, slightly overweight middle-aged work-aholic – Dr Oksanna Zoshchenko was a breath of fresh air.

A chemist by training, Zoshchenko discovered early in her career that her true gifts lay in administration. Her native intelligence coupled with a skillful sense of diplomacy was cited as the primary reason for her rapid ascent to the highest levels of the Russian Academy of Sciences. Among those whose position in the academy she eclipsed, rumors imputed Zoshchenko's meteoric rise to her considerable physical assets and her willingness to use them to further her career.

'So, Oksanna, what did you think?' Evans asked as he approached the sultry brunette.

'It was quite illuminating.' Zoshchenko's Ukrainian accent was soft, a hint of something both foreign and exotic.

'Very diplomatic of you. Normally, these board meetings are fairly dull. At least that surprise show-and-tell we had at the end livened things up a bit. Oh, and regarding that, I'm afraid I must ask you not to mention the Sandstrom presentation to anyone, at least until after they've published their research. It's all covered in the nondisclosure agreement you signed.'

'I was a scientist long before I became a bureaucrat, so I understand discretion with regard to research. I promise I won't discuss what I've seen here.'

'Thank you, and again, I apologize. This was one meeting I couldn't bow out of, and I didn't want to abandon you in the lobby for two hours. Thank you for your patience.'

'Your apology is unnecessary, Conrad. I truly found this meeting quite educational. Our economy, our way of thinking is so different from yours. We have many brilliant scientists, like this Sandstrom, but no mechanism to transfer technology to our industries. No way to capitalize on innovation. This consortium is a very good idea, one of many that I will take back to Moscow with me.'

'Well, then, as a regent of this university, I am pleased that your visit here has been a productive one.' Evans glanced at his watch. 'If you like, we still have time for a decent meal before you leave.'

'I'd like that,' Zoshchenko replied appreciatively. 'It's a long flight back to Moscow, and the food served on airplanes is not so good.'